W9-BOL-503

DEADLY ILLUSIONS

BRENDA JOYCE

THORNDIKE PRESS

A part of Gale, Cengage Learning

GALE
CENGAGE Learning·

Detroit • New York • San Francisco • New Haven, Conn • Waterville, Maine • London

GALE
CENGAGE Learning™

Copyright © 2005 by Brenda Joyce Dreams Unlimited, Inc.
Thorndike Press, a part of Gale, Cengage Learning.

Thorndike Press® Large Print Romance.
The text of this Large Print edition is unabridged.
Other aspects of the book may vary from the original edition.
Set in 16 pt. Plantin.

LIBRARY OF CONGRESS CATALOGING-IN-PUBLICATION DATA

Joyce, Brenda.
  Deadly illusions / by Brenda Joyce.
    p. cm. — (Thorndike Press large print romance)
  ISBN-13: 978-1-4104-3654-2
  ISBN-10: 1-4104-3654-3
  1. Manhattan (New York, N.Y.)—Fiction. 2. Irish Americans—Fiction 3. Large type books. I. Title.
PS3560.O864D43 2011
813'.54—dc22   2010053990

Published in 2011 by arrangement with Harlequin Books S.A.

Printed in the United States of America
1 2 3 4 5 6 7 15 14 13 12 11

This one's for the ladies on the boards:
Thank you for your unwavering
support!

CHAPTER ONE

New York City Tuesday, April 22, 1902 5:00 p.m.

The crime scene was a gruesome one, indeed.

Chilled, Francesca Cahill stared at the woman. The victim was clad only in her corset, chemise and drawers, lying in a pool of blood the same dark red-brown color as her hair. Shivers swept up and down Francesca's spine, shivers that had nothing to do with the temperature of the day, as it was warm and sunny outside, a perfect spring day.

Not that one would ever guess that fact from this tenement flat. The railroad apartment that Francesca had so boldly entered was long and narrow, consisting of a single room. A window at each end let in some light, but not much, as the brick building just a few feet behind this one blocked out much of the daylight. At the flat's far end was the victim's bed, where she lay in her underclothes. Francesca stood in the doorway, the dark, dank corridor behind her. Between her and the victim were so many signs of a vital if impoverished life — a small sofa, the muddy-hued fabric torn and ripped, a faded and torn throw rug upon which sat a pail of water, as if the victim had been soaking her feet before bed. Beyond the small salon area, there was a rickety square table and two equally despairing chairs, one with a leg tied together. In the kitchen's area, there was a wood counter covered with some stacked plates and utensils, a wood-burning stove and a sink containing a pot and some other items. In the other direction, behind Francesca, there was a police sawhorse in the doorway of the flat. An officer had placed a Do Not Cross sign upon it.

A man carefully viewed the body. Portly, of medium height, his suit shabby and tweed, Francesca recognized him instantly. She coughed to make her presence known and started forward, her navy blue skirts sweeping around her, tendrils of blond hair escaping her chignon and smart little navy blue hat. In her gloved hands, she clutched a purse.

He whirled. "Miz Cahill!" he cried, clearly

surprised to find her there in the apartment.

She smiled warmly, determined not to be ousted from the crime scene although this was not her case, as she had no client requiring her to investigate this murder. "Inspector Newman, good day. Although from the look of things, this has not been a good day for the victim." She cast another glance at the dead woman, who appeared, at this closer range, to be in her early twenties. She had been a pretty woman. Newman had closed her eyes.

He met her halfway. Flushing, a sheen of perspiration on his forehead, he said, "Are you on this case, Miz Cahill? Is the c'mish with you?"

Her heart did a little flip. She hadn't seen the police commissioner in weeks, not really. Passing him in the hall of Bellevue Hospital the times she had planned to visit his wife did not count. "I'm afraid I am alone. Does this appear to be the work of the Slasher?" she asked, her gaze drawn to the victim as a moth is drawn to candlelight.

Newman blinked. "Her throat was cut, Miz Cahill, like them first two. But this one, well, she's dead. To my eye, it looks similar to the first two victims. Of course, until the coroner has examined the body, we cannot be sure."

Francesca nodded gravely, her gaze briefly on Newman. If the newspapers were to be believed — and Francesca knew very well one could not always believe what the dailies reported — there was a pattern here. According to the *Tribune,* the first two victims had been young, pretty and Irish. The victims, however, had not been murdered, but merely had their throats slashed and were understandably traumatized. But the second slashing was sensational enough to warrant a headline. Of course, this third woman was dead, so maybe there was no connection. But Francesca did not believe that for a moment.

She had learned since embarking on her profession of criminal investigation that she had very accurate instincts. They shrieked at her now. The Slasher was at work here — and the stakes had suddenly changed.

Murder was now the name of the game.

And that most definitely made the case her affair — as people she cared about lived two doors down. "Do we know her name?" she asked softly, noting the way the woman lay. Her arms were flung out, her head turned to the side. There had been a struggle. She felt certain that the dead woman was also Irish.

"Yes. Her name is Margaret Cooper." He

also turned to stare at the victim.

Francesca started at the name, which was no more Irish than her own. She was surprised she had been wrong, but there was still a pattern. She went grimly forward but Newman suddenly detained her. "Miz Cahill? Should you be here? I mean —" and he blushed crimson "— this is a police matter and if the c'mish is not here, I am not quite certain you should be."

Francesca didn't hesitate. "I am officially on this case, Inspector, and we both know the commissioner will be supportive of that." She smiled, at once friendly and firm. But she no longer knew just how supportive of her investigative work Rick Bragg would be. So much had changed — and so quickly.

"Well, I guess I won't have to decide!" Newman cried in relief as footsteps sounded behind them from the hallway.

Francesca didn't have to turn to know who it was. She tensed as the police commissioner strode past the sawhorse and into the room.

He was a handsome, charismatic man. Once, she had thought him the most handsome man on the planet, but that had been before she had learned of his estranged wife and his on-again, off-again marriage. Rick Bragg stood a bit over six feet tall, his stride

11

long and purposeful, his shoulders broad, the brown duster he wore for motoring swinging about him. His complexion was dark, his hair golden, and no one looking at him could mistake his air of authority and purpose. In fact, the night they had met at a ball held by her family, in spite of the crowd she had seen him the moment he entered the room. But that felt like a different lifetime, and she had been a different woman, oh yes.

Their gazes met and held.

She realized she had bit her lip and that her fists were balled up. Her pulse had also accelerated. "Hello," she said, trying not to be nervous. But it was hard. Once, they had been in love. Now she was engaged to his most bitter rival — his half brother, the wealthy and notorious Calder Hart.

If he was surprised to see her, he did not evince it. "Francesca," he said, pausing before her. His gaze did not move, not even once, from her to the victim or the crime scene. "This is a surprise."

She stared into his amber eyes and instantly saw how tired he was, both emotionally and physically. She ached for him. She knew he had agonized over the condition of his wife. And suddenly she did not want to talk about Margaret Cooper — she wanted to talk about him, his wife and the two children fostering with them. She wanted to take his hand, she wanted to help.

Instead, briskly, she said, "I ran into Isaacson from the *Tribune*." She tried to smile but it felt like a grimace and he simply stared, saying nothing. Her anxiety increased and she clutched her purse with both hands. "He must have been at headquarters when the call came in. When he told me that it might be the Slasher, and that the victim lived on Tenth Street and Avenue A, I had to come directly over. Maggie and her children live two doors away, Bragg," she said earnestly.

"I know," he said. His expression softened. "I was concerned myself." He hesitated, studying her with some intensity, his gaze dipping to the way she held her purse.

She smiled a little at him. He did not smile back. It was simply awkward now, being with him. What should she say, what should she do? Were they still friends? Did he hate her? Had he forgiven her for becoming engaged to the man he bitterly despised? Had he accepted the fact that one day she would marry Hart? For she had finally, with great difficulty, accepted the fact that Bragg belonged with his wife.

Francesca wanted to reach out to him and

demand answers to all those questions, but she did not dare. How selfish it would be. But God, there was no one she admired more, no one more noble, more determined, more honorable than Rick Bragg. He had been appointed police commissioner with the charge of reforming the city's infamously corrupt police department, but it was like spitting into the wind. He had fired some officers, hired new ones, reassigned entire units, but every small step forward was gained at a painful cost. The press hounded his every move. The clergy and the reform movement demanded he do more; politics demanded he do far less. Tammany Hall had lost the last election, but still ruled most of the city. He was up against Platt's political organization, and the mayor, elected on a reform platform, did not always back him up, afraid of losing the working man's vote. An election loomed, one Mayor Low did not want to lose. Bragg fought it all, alone.

She knew he would never give up.

And all this with his wife lying in the hospital, the victim of a tragic carriage accident. "I heard that Leigh Anne will be going home soon," she suddenly said, reaching for his hand without thinking about it. He started as her fingers closed over his, and realizing what she had done, she quickly released him.

"Yes. In fact, they will release her tomorrow." He looked away.

Francesca knew him so well — or once she had. Now she could not tell whether it was grief or guilt that made him flinch and turn away. "Thank God she regained consciousness within days," Francesca whispered, a small hurt inside her heart. Why couldn't she simply hug him and hold him close? He needed to be comforted, that much she knew. She might be engaged to another man, but she would always love Rick, too.

He was grim and he did not speak.

"Is the prognosis the same?" she asked. She had gone to the hospital several times, but in the end had only visited with the rest of the Braggs, who had been coming and going to see Leigh Anne, and not with Leigh Anne herself. She had been afraid of her reception; she had not wanted to upset the other woman, either.

"She will never walk again." His tone was flat, final. He glanced past her at the victim. "If this is the work of the so-called 'Slasher,' then we have a serial killer on the loose." He walked over to the bed.

Francesca followed until they both stood

within feet of the victim. "But the first two victims survived, if the reports I have read were correct."

He grimly surveyed the body in the bed. The sheets were a cheap coarse cotton, and except for the bloodstains, freshly laundered. The woman's hair was undone and some of it lay across her neck. "They did survive. Both attacks were one week apart, exactly, each on subsequent Mondays."

"Oh dear," Francesca said, intrigued in spite of the terrible tragedy she was witness to. The reporters had failed to note that. "Was this woman killed yesterday?"

"She was found at noon today. But I am going to hazard a guess that she was killed last night, Francesca." He gave her a significant look.

If the woman had been in her underclothes, then she had been murdered either first thing in the morning, or in the evening before bed. "Rick, I had read that the first two victims were Irishwomen in their twenties. Is that true?"

He leaned over the woman and moved her long, tangled dark red hair away from her neck. Her throat was brutally slit. Francesca wanted to gag; instead, she closed her eyes and breathed hard. No matter how many cases she had, she was certain she would

16

never grow accustomed to violence and death. Of course, there had only been six investigations thus far. Her career as a sleuth had begun last January when her neighbor's son had been abducted. She had tried to help, never imagining how it would change her life.

Bragg straightened. "Both victims were Irishwomen in their twenties, yes. Both were estranged from their spouses. From the look of this cut, I would say the Slasher has been at work again, but this time with deadly results."

Francesca stared, forgetting all about her fiancé. She fought her queasiness. "This woman is not Irish. The name Cooper is as American as apple pie."

"A pattern remains. Three attractive young women, each without means, assaulted on subsequent Mondays."

Francesca agreed. "Do you think she was killed accidentally? Or is murder now the Slasher's intent?"

"I have no idea. But if she was murdered Monday, and if the Slasher holds true to the course he has set, there will be another victim in six days exactly." He faced her and their gazes met.

"We will find this killer, Bragg. And I do mean it."

He started and, finally, began to smile at her. "If anyone can find him, you can."

She was thrilled at the gesture of intimacy and she smiled back. "I also assume the Slasher is a man, but we cannot rule out a woman. Remember, the Cross Killer turned out to be Lizzie O'Brien," she said, referring to a previous case.

"Of course I remember," he said, and then his expression changed and she thought he was remembering everything that had once been between them. He cleared his throat. "The two previous victims were Kate Sullivan and Francis O'Leary. Neither woman saw the Slasher, as he assaulted them from behind. But it was a man."

She nodded. "Who alerted the police?"

"A Mrs. O'Neil found her. Apparently, she has the flat next door."

Francesca stiffened. "Bragg! Not Gwen O'Neil?" An image of the striking redhead assailed her mind.

His tawny eyebrows lifted. "Yes, that is her name. And she is at headquarters. She is very upset," he added. "Do you know her?"

She seized his arm. "Not only do I know her, you know her, too!"

After spending an hour or more with Bragg

at the crime scene, Francesca went two buildings down to visit the seamstress who had become her dear friend, Maggie Kennedy. As she went up the narrow staircase to the flat Maggie let, she was thoughtful. A killer was on the loose, unless the last victim had been accidentally murdered. All three victims had several characteristics in common: they were young, pretty, working class and they all resided within two square blocks. The first two victims, Francis O'Leary and Kate Sullivan, also lived alone. Apparently Francis O'Leary's husband had vanished two years or so ago, while Kate Sullivan had left her spouse. Margaret Cooper had not worn a wedding band and there had been no sign of a male occupant in her flat — apparently, she had been single, too, although that they would have to confirm. All the victims had been assaulted on a Monday, each a week apart. There was almost no doubt that there would be another assault next Monday and the likelihood was high that it would be somewhere in the ward and that the victim would be pretty, young, working class, single and female.

Fortunately, the first two victims were alive, which meant she could interview them, perhaps even that afternoon. Although the police had spoken with them, she had not a doubt they had missed crucial clues. Bragg had not been personally involved in the case at that time. Then she remembered her mother's dinner party and sighed. She would have to attend or there would be a vast price to pay — Julia Van Wyck Cahill was not to be crossed lightly. The interviews would have to wait, as it was well past six already. And then there was Gwen O'Neil. Francesca intended to interview her, too. She wasn't thrilled that Gwen and her daughter, Bridget, lived right next door to the last victim, just as she wished Maggie did not reside so close by with her children, either. However, the neighborhood was filled with impoverished young women.

As she paused before Maggie's flat, she thought about the distance now separating her and Bragg. Perhaps she had been a fool to think that he could reconcile with his wife and she could marry another man and somehow they would remain friends. She could not help but be saddened. On the other hand, it was clear to her that he loved his wife, and she was certainly infatuated with Hart. In fact, he had gone to Chicago on business almost two weeks ago and it had been very hard not to think about him constantly.

At least Leigh Anne would be leaving the hospital and going home tomorrow. She wondered if she dared to call on her at home. Then she heard childish shrieks and laughter. Francesca began to smile as she knocked upon the door. Maggie was a widow and was raising four children by herself.

Eleven-year-old Joel Kennedy, once a pickpocket and now Francesca's invaluable sidekick, promptly answered her knock. He had pitch-black hair and fair skin and his sleeves were rolled up to his elbows. He knew the city like the back of his hand and had helped her out of danger too many times to count. His face was flushed and he looked extremely annoyed. When he saw Francesca, though, he brightened. "Miz Cahill!"

She glanced past him into the one-bedroom flat, which was usually tidy. Now, goose feathers floated about the family room. Joel's two young brothers, Matt and Paddy, had clearly been in a pillow fight. The boys were on the floor, holding the mostly empty pillows, howling with laughter. They had clearly eaten, as she saw plates with bread crumbs on the kitchen table. Joel followed her gaze and scowled. "Idi'ts," he said. "Mum will be fierce unhappy when she sees them down feathers all wasted like that."

"I see there has been no homework to-day?" Francesca asked. She knew that Maggie had Matt in school, unlike many other working-class families. Too many of the city's impoverished classes needed the extra income their children could generate. There was also a question of extreme overcrowding and underfunding for the city's public schools. It was a shame.

Joel, who could read and no longer attended school, shrugged. "He got some letters to do. But he don't want to do homework now. I didn't want to fight about it. Got better things to do."

Francesca closed the door behind her as Joel's little three-year-old sister came stumbling out of the bedroom, clearly having been napping. "Joel, if they have eaten, Matt should sit down and do his letters. You know how to read — don't you want your brother to have the same skills and advantages as you? Hello, Lizzie!" She tousled the sleepy child's silky black hair.

Joel scowled at her. "Are you here on business, Miz Cahill? It's been awful quiet for way too long."

Francesca set her purse down on the sofa. "Yes, I am. And I agree with you — it has been a quiet spell for us. Shouldn't your mother be home at any moment?"

"She should be home real soon. So what case are we on?" he asked with an impish grin. His dark eyes sparkled.

She patted his shoulder. "We are of a similar nature, you and I," she said fondly. Then, her smile fading, she said, "A woman was murdered two doors down, Joel. She was Gwen O'Neil's neighbor."

He paled. "Miz O'Neil an' Bridget?"

"They're fine," she assured him. "Can you start asking questions in the neighborhood? Did anyone notice a suspicious sort lurking about Margaret Cooper or her apartment or building? Was she afraid? Did she know she was in danger? Who were her friends? Did she have any visitors recently? We suspect the killer to be a man. And it might be the Slasher," she added.

His eyes were wide and he nodded eagerly. "I can get started the minute Mum comes home," he said.

"Get started on what?" Maggie Kennedy asked, letting herself into the flat. A paper sack filled with groceries was in her arms. "Francesca!" She smiled brightly. "How nice to see you!"

"We got another case," Joel told his mother in a rush as she gave him a hug.

23

"Been a murder, right on this block!"

Maggie paled.

"Joel, please, let me explain," Francesca said.

Maggie moved to hug the rest of her children in turn, but Francesca could see her distress. "What is this mess?" she asked the two younger boys. "You know I can't afford more down! Now start picking up the feathers, every single one. Shame on you both," she added, a tremor in her tone.

Francesca knew that Joel had worried her. She laid her palm on Maggie's back as the other woman straightened and smiled reassuringly at her. "Shall we sit?"

"Of course, where are my manners!" Maggie cried, flushing. She rushed to the small dining table not far from the stove and sink and pulled out one chair. "Let me boil some water for tea."

Francesca went to her and took her arm. "Please, Maggie, do not stand on ceremony. I really wish to discuss the case with you." She gave her a significant look.

Maggie met her gaze and slowly nodded. As they sat down, Joel slammed out of the apartment. Maggie started, clearly unhappy. "It's a miracle, really, for you to be giving him a salary, but . . . I worry so!"

Francesca had quickly realized just how

invaluable Joel was, so she had offered him employment as her assistant. He, of course, had been thrilled. "You know I would never knowingly put him in the path of danger," Francesca said, meaning it.

"I know. You have saved my life — and you have really saved Joel's life, by taking him away from a world of thievery." Briefly, she cupped her face in her hands, her eyes closed. Then she sighed. "I am glad that Joel works for you, truly I am . . ."

Francesca knew that Maggie was very tired from the long hours she put in sewing at the Moe Levy Factory. She touched her hand. "If you do not want him to work for me any longer, I will change it."

Maggie shook her head. "He adores you. And he no longer is out on the streets, stealing purses behind my back. I'm just distraught today."

Francesca could sense that and she wondered why. "Gwen O'Neil found her neighbor's body," she said after a pause.

Maggie made a choking sound. "Is she all right?"

Francesca took her hand. "I don't know. Bragg said she was upset. I imagine she will be home shortly, but she was at police headquarters this afternoon. We suspect it is the Slasher at work again, Maggie. But unlike the others, Margaret Cooper did not survive his latest attack."

Maggie made a sound. "I knew them all! They live — lived — nearby."

Francesca leaned forward eagerly. "So you are acquainted with all of the victims?"

"In one way or another," Maggie cried. "Francis and I seem to shop for our groceries at the same time — she is so kind and so sweet — I often bump into her at Schmidt's Grocery Store. She was so happy," she added in a whisper. "She recently told me she was seeing someone she thought very special."

Francesca sat up straight. "Isn't she the one whose husband disappeared some time ago?" If so, then she was still wed.

"I know she was once married. I had thought she was a widow, actually," Maggie said with some surprise.

Bragg had reviewed the file with her, and Francis O'Leary was no widow. "Do you know the name of the man she is seeing?" Francesca asked.

"No. She didn't say. But she lives two blocks from here."

"Yes, on Twelfth Street." Francesca decided she must interview Francis O'Leary immediately on the morrow. "Where does she work?"

"She is a shopgirl at the Lord and Taylor store," Maggie said. "But when I saw her at church yesterday, she looked terrible. I think she wore a bandage under the collar of her gown and she had a black eye. Perhaps she is not back at work yet."

Francesca absorbed all of that. If she called early enough, Francis O'Leary would be at home. "And you also knew Kate Sullivan and Margaret Cooper?"

"I don't really know Kate, but we nod to one another at church on Sundays. She seems very sweet, but a bit shy. You know I'm friends with Gwen, and I met Margaret at her flat one evening when I had to borrow some sugar. She was so nice as well!" Maggie cried.

A circle of friends, Francesca thought grimly, then revised her assessment of the situation. It was a circle of acquaintances, all hardworking women who lived very close to one another and would bump into one another in the course of the day or the week. "I want you to be careful," she finally said.

Maggie stared, pale, and then glanced anxiously at her children. "Margaret Cooper lived two doors down, Francesca, and Kate Sullivan lives right around the corner. Not even a block away." She inhaled harshly. "Am I in danger?"

"None of the three victims had children," Francesca said truthfully, although she felt that Maggie could very well be in danger. "Just keep your wits about you," Francesca advised. "And I feel certain the children are not in danger. I believe the odds are that you are not, either. Still, we will exercise caution. Next Monday, I want you and the children to stay with me."

Maggie started. "You mean in the mansion?"

Francesca nodded. This would not be the first time she had put up Maggie and her children in her father's Fifth Avenue home. "The Slasher seems to be striking on Mondays, Maggie. It is just a silly precaution." She smiled but it felt grim instead of reassuring.

Maggie hesitated, clearly torn. "I don't want to impose," she finally said.

Francesca took her hand. "We are friends! It is not an imposition."

"I'll think about it," Maggie returned slowly. "Maybe the Slasher will be caught by then."

"I do hope so!" Francesca cried fervently.

Maggie smiled a little, perhaps at Francesca's passionate outburst. Carefully she gazed at the table. Not looking up, she asked softly, "Has Evan returned home?"

Francesca did not answer at first. She sat back in her chair, recalling how solicitous her brother had been toward Maggie and her children when she had been living briefly with them — and ever since. Not for the first time, she wondered if she had witnessed a romantic spark between them. But it was an impossible match — a seamstress from the Lower East Side and the son of a millionaire. Of course, Evan had recently been disowned by their father. "No, he continues to reside at the Fifth Avenue Hotel. I am so very proud of him for standing up to our father."

"I heard he took employment," Maggie said, her eyes still lowered.

"Yes, as a law clerk." Society thought it unbelievable — Francesca had heard the gossip — that he would walk away from his family and his fortune.

Maggie paused. "We haven't seen him since he came to take the children to the park last month."

Francesca did not know what to say. "I haven't seen him very much since he moved out. This has to be hard for him, working as a clerk and living in a hotel."

"I suppose he is still seeing the beautiful countess Benevente?" Maggie murmured.

Francesca did not know what to say or

do. Then she decided the truth was the best course. "Yes, they are often seen together. Evan has always gravitated toward bold women like Bartolla Benevente."

Maggie finally looked up. "She is so beautiful. They make an astonishing couple. If he marries her, it will be a good match. Don't you agree?" And she smiled, but it did not reach her blue eyes.

Francesca could not mistake what she was witnessing. Maggie Kennedy was fond of her brother in spite of the huge social gap between them. Francesca was at a loss. Even if Evan shared her feelings, it would be extremely difficult for them to make a match. But Evan did not return her feelings, clearly, as he was so thoroughly preoccupied with the beautiful countess. "Yes, it would be a socially acceptable match." She hesitated. "But I am not sure Evan is ready to marry anyone, Maggie. Not only is he a bit of a rake, you know, but after leaving the family the way that he did, I think he needs a bit of time to reorganize his life."

Maggie stood abruptly. "I am sure he will come home one day. I think I'll make that tea."

"That's a good idea," Francesca agreed, relieved to end the subject of her brother.

■ ■ ■ ■

Night had fallen, the day's spring temperature suddenly gone. Francesca shivered as she stepped out onto the sidewalk, wishing she had her coat with her. Now that the workday was over, the neighborhood had come alive with the sights and sounds of its residents. Men and women were coming and going on the streets, a gang of adolescent boys was playing stickball, ignoring a heavily laden passing dray. There was tremendous activity in a corner saloon, and many windows were open, candles burning inside. The aroma of roasting meats wafted onto the gas-lit street.

Francesca had not taken the Cahill coach downtown, and now, glancing around, she regretted it. Obviously there were no cabs in this area. If she walked four blocks, she could catch a horse-drawn omnibus crossing town and then hail a cab from Union Square. But it was dark now, and many of the passersby on the street were a rough, rowdy lot. In fact, she mused as one of a pair of brawny men passing her turned to look at her in her fine skirt and jacket, anyone could be the Slasher.

But he would not strike again until next

Monday — *if* he chose to follow the pattern he had set.

She wished that she was not alone. Of course, she did have a small pistol in her purse. She had learned from experience to carry protection. Francesca started forward, clutching her simple black bag. Hart would murder her for being out in such a neighborhood after dark, alone and without transport.

Someone hurrying her way, a child with him, bumped into her as he passed. Francesca tensed, continuing on, when she was seized from behind. Her heart slammed with fear.

"Miss Cahill!" a woman cried, her brogue as thick as an Irish bog.

Francesca turned, relief swamping her, and met not the gaze of a man, but that of a frightened, distressed woman. An instant later she realized that Gwen O'Neil had grabbed her and that Bridget stood closely by her mother. "Mrs. O'Neil! You startled me."

Gwen released her. Her eyes were wide in her blanched face. "I cannot believe it's you! A friendly face — a sight for sore eyes," she cried.

Francesca was now calm and attuned to the fact that Gwen was far more than relieved to see her. The woman looked ready to leap out of her skin from fear. She smiled at Bridget and instantly realized that the eleven year old knew all about her neighbor's murder. She stood stiff and frozen beside her mother, her eyes huge in her small face. "Mrs. O'Neil," she began, smiling and hoping to calm them both. But this was an opportunity not to be missed. Never mind that she was terribly late for her mother's dinner party — she would see these two safely home and catch a brief interview. Or perhaps even a substantial one, at that.

But Gwen jumped as if she had caught on fire, glancing wildly around her, her eyes huge with fear. Francesca took her arm. "Mrs. O'Neil? What is it? What's wrong?"

Gwen's dark eyes met hers. She opened her mouth but no sound came out.

Bridget was the one who spoke. Tears thickened her voice. "We're bein' followed," she cried.

CHAPTER TWO

Tuesday, April 22, 1902 7:00 p.m.

Francesca glanced around but saw nothing amiss. Men and women continued to pass on their way home after a long day's work and the boys continued to slam the ball around in the cobbled street with their sticks. She faced Gwen grimly. "Let me take you up to your flat," she said.

"Would you?" Gwen cried in obvious relief.

Francesca took her arm. "Let's go," she said kindly. As Bridget preceded them, she glanced over her shoulder one more time. She half expected to see the Slasher standing against the tall iron street lamp, watching them. But nothing on the street had changed.

There was no light in the small entry hall, and the stairs were also dark with shadow, but that was not unusual in these terrible tenements. "I assume there are no gas-lights?"

"No," Gwen breathed, fumbling in her shopping bag. "But I have a candle and matches."

Francesca carried a candle and matches as well, but she waited for the other woman to light the wick. Gwen's hands were shaking so badly, though, that Francesca took the candle and match from her, struck a spark and lit it. Instantly the small, grim entry was illuminated. Someone had hung a cracked mirror on one peeling wall in a futile attempt at decoration. "Let's go, Bridget," she said with false cheer, shivering.

They hurried upstairs in single file, the steps creaking beneath their feet. Gwen and her daughter lived on the second floor, as had Margaret Cooper. When they passed Margaret's flat, Francesca saw that the door was padlocked, meaning that the police had left. The sign Police Line had been nailed to the door. When she and Bragg had left the flat together, a photographer had just arrived. Bragg had conceived of the singular notion of photographing the victim and the crime scene for reference during the investigation. It was a brilliant idea.

Gwen unlocked the door, her hands continuing to tremble. The moment they were all inside, she said tersely, "Bridget, light another candle," as she quickly bolted the door behind them.

Francesca wondered how she was going to live in such a state of fear. She studied her from behind as the other woman turned, managing a smile and unpinning her straw hat. Instantly, her hair tumbled down.

Francesca stiffened. She already knew that Gwen had dark red hair, but now she was struck by the fact that it was almost waist length, rather curly, and very much like the hair of Margaret Cooper. And while Gwen and Margaret did not look at all alike — Margaret had been pretty but in a soft way, and Gwen was striking — the similarity between them now was unmistakable. And Gwen lived next door to Margaret. . . .

"You're staring," Gwen breathed.

"I'm sorry. I know you found your neighbor, Mrs. O'Neil. I am so sorry. It must have been terrible." Behind her, another candle flamed to life, illuminating the long, single room more drastically.

Gwen nodded. "It was terrible," she whispered. She put her hat on a peg and her wool shawl followed. She wore a simple print blouse and dark skirt. As she leaned over, Francesca realized she was taking off

36

her shoes. Once in her stocking feet, she turned with a small smile. "My feet hurt," she whispered.

Francesca guessed that her shoes were not store-bought and were either too small or had holes in the soles. Then, as she heard water running at the kitchen sink, she thought about the bucket of water she had seen in front of the sofa in Margaret's apartment. Had she had sore feet, too? Had she been soaking her feet before her murder? Was that how the killer had caught her?

She smiled at Gwen. "Please, do not mind me. Are you certain that you were being followed?"

Gwen hesitated and then moved to the small square table covered with a bright yellow tablecloth. A chipped glass was in its center, a single daisy there. She gripped the back of one chair. Bridget was lighting the stove and setting a pot of water to boil. "No. I mean, I'm not certain — but I am sure of it!"

That made no sense. Francesca took off her gloves, laying them on the cheerful tablecloth. Bridget put a carrot, a potato and an onion into the pot. A pinch of salt followed. "Tell me why you think you were being followed," Francesca said softly.

Tears filled Gwen's eyes. "I don't know! I

didn't see anyone when I left police head-quarters. But I had this feeling, a real strong feeling, that I was being watched! Haven't you ever had that feeling?" she cried.

Francesca touched her arm. "Of course."

"Oh Lord, where are my manners tonight? Miss Cahill, you have been nothing but kind to my daughter, saving her from those terrible men last month! Please, sit down. Bridget! Put on water to boil. We have tea," she said brightly, the tears shining on her cheeks. "English tea. It's special — I brought it with me," she added, clearly referring to her recent move from Ireland to New York.

"Thank you," Francesca said, taking a seat. Gwen continued to stand. "So you did not see anyone?"

"No. I didn't. But I couldn't shake the feeling, not the whole way from the police station."

Francesca nodded. "Why don't you sit, too? You have had an exceedingly difficult day."

But Gwen had gone to the stove to stir the soup pot. "You probably think me mad," she said over her shoulder.

"No, I do not."

"Bridget, wash your face and hands."

Bridget had been standing quietly in the corner of the room where the counter next to the stove met the sink. "I want to go home!" she suddenly cried. "I hate it here! But mostly, I hate Lord Randolph!"

Francesca stood, the urge to take the child in her arms overwhelming. She wondered who Lord Randolph was. Instead, Gwen rushed to her daughter, enfolding her against her bosom, holding her tightly. "I know, darling, I know. But we can't go home. You know we can never go back."

Bridget burst into tears and ran behind the curtain that clearly partitioned off a sleeping area. Gwen stood staring at the mustard-colored drape, clearly torn and anguished. Francesca could not fathom Gwen's last words. Why couldn't she and her daughter return home?

Francesca went to her and laid her palm on her shoulder. "How hard this must be for you and your daughter, making a home for yourselves in a new land."

"It's hard," Gwen whispered. "I tried to find good work, but all I could find was work in a factory. We make candles all day long. At home, I was a ladies' maid in a mansion on a hill. We were never hungry," she added.

Francesca had recently hired a new maid for her own home, when the staff was already full. Ellie had been a vagrant but had witnessed a murder. Now she was the most dedicated maid at the Cahill home. She knew her mother, Julia, would not allow another addition to the household.

Francesca wondered if her sister needed another servant. How perfect that would be! "Do you have references?" she asked.

Gwen looked away. "I'm afraid not."

Francesca was startled. She wondered what the lack meant, but knew that now was not the time to pursue it. And she did not doubt that Gwen had been a fine ladies' maid. She was a fair judge of character, and trusted Gwen's sincerity. Then a brilliant idea occurred to her. Calder Hart. She brightened. He wouldn't care if she hired another maid for that huge mausoleum he called a home. She made a mental note to place Gwen in his domestic employ immediately. "May I ask you some questions, Mrs. O'Neil? I am taking on the case of Margaret's murder."

Gwen nodded, moving to sit down. She let out a sigh of exhaustion as she did so.

Francesca sat beside her. "Did you know Margaret Cooper?"

Gwen nodded. "She was already living here when we moved in. She was very pleasant, very friendly, offering to show me and Bridget around. She helped me get my first

40

employment, but the work was so far downtown that I quit when I found the opening at the candle makers. We had supper together once or twice. She was a good person, Miss Cahill. She did not deserve to die!"

"So she was not married?"

"No, she was entirely alone in this world," Gwen said.

"Did she have a gentleman friend?" Francesca asked, thinking about the fact that there had been no sign of a male visitor in her flat.

"No. In fact, I found it odd, as she was so pretty and kind."

Francesca took a notepad and pencil from her purse and made some notes. "Margaret must have had some kind of personal life."

"She went to work six days a week and to church every Sunday. You do know," Gwen added, "that I have already told all of this to the police."

"I would love to hear your answers for myself, if you do not mind. I care very much about this case and about bringing Margaret's killer to justice," Francesca said earnestly. "The police have a great many investigations to handle. I have just one."

"Of course." Gwen smiled a little for the first time that evening, apparently beginning to relax. The water began to boil and she got up to make the tea.

"What faith was Margaret?"

"She was Baptist," Gwen said over her shoulder. Then she smiled again, her eyes softening. "I took her to my church once. She was very religious, Miss Cahill. Her mother was Irish. Did you know that?"

Francesca sat up straighter. Here was another link, she thought eagerly. Kate Sullivan and Francis O'Leary were Irish — and now, Margaret had turned out to be of Irish descent. "No, I hadn't known. Where did Margaret work?"

"She was a shopgirl. She worked in some fancy sweet shop uptown. I don't recall the store's name but she referred to the fact that it was next door to A.T. Stewart's."

A.T. Stewart's was a popular department store. The sweet-shop shouldn't be that hard to locate. Gwen brought her a cup of tea carefully, as there was no saucer to catch any spills. Francesca smiled her thanks and inhaled. "It does smell delicious," she said, meaning it. The tea was strong and spicy, exotic, and obviously expensive. It seemed like quite an indulgence for Gwen O'Neil.

"It is wonderful," Gwen said almost proudly. "I put a spoon of sugar in it. I hope you do not mind."

"Thank you so much," Francesca said, knowing that sugar was another expense Gwen could not afford. She took a sip and found the tea as rich to the palate as it was aromatic. She set the cup down. "How did you find the body and when did you find it?"

Gwen's smile vanished. "This morning. I was leaving to go to work. I was late because Bridget has a cough and I made her an elixir before I left. I let her stay home from school yesterday and today." She began to cry. "As I went down the hall, I saw that Margaret's door was open. That was odd, so I glanced inside . . . and saw her lying there on her bed, as dead as could be." She began to shake.

Francesca stood and hurried to her. "There, there, it's all right. It's fortunate that you found her. Was her door ajar Monday night when you returned home from your employment?"

"I don't know. I don't recall. If it was open last night when I came home, I didn't notice. Miss Cahill, was he killing her, right next door, while me and my baby slept?"

Francesca hesitated and clasped her shoulder. "We do not yet know when she was murdered, Mrs. O'Neil."

Gwen sobbed. "Dear God, it could have

been me or my little girl!"

It took forty-five minutes to get uptown, and by the time the doorman let Francesca into the Cahill mansion, situated on Fifth Avenue across from Central Park, the gilded clock on the marble mantel in the salon adjacent to the receiving room indicated that it was half past eight. As Francesca handed off her hat and gloves, she did not need to know the exact time in order to know just how late she was. The dining room was several doors down, but she could hear the robust conversation of her mother's dinner party. As it was accompanied by the tinkle of crystal glassware and the tapping of silver upon china, she knew that supper was already in progress.

Her head throbbed and her new, white kidskin shoes were too tight. Like Gwen O'Neil — and perhaps Margaret Cooper — her feet were sore. She knew there would be some huge cost to pay, but she'd already decided to sneak up to her room, avoiding the party altogether. Besides, how would she explain that she was late? Her parents frowned upon her sleuthing, as she was only twenty years old and still a part of their household. Of course, she had no doubt she could be thirty and married with children and Julia would still despair over her reputation should she continue investigative work. Many times she had half promised Julia that her days as a sleuth were over. But the half truths were merely that. As much as she disliked lying to her mother, she had found her calling in life. She was an excellent investigator, and she had the record to prove it.

Attending supper was out of the question. Francesca smiled at the doorman and began to cross the long receiving room. The press had dubbed the Cahill home the "Marble Mansion" upon its completion some eight years ago. Her father, raised on a farm in Illinois, had become a butcher and eventually expanded into the country's largest meatpacking business. Francesca had been born in Chicago, but the family had moved to New York City when she was a child. The press had had a field day with her home — and even as a six-year-old, she had read the dailies. At the time, Andrew and Julia Cahill had outdone the Astors and the Melons. Almost the entire room she now sought to cross was marble — the black-and-white floors, the pale Corinthian columns, the carved panels on the walls.

The mahogany dining-room doors were open. Francesca touched her hair, trying to tuck some loose blond tendrils behind her ears. By now, the bit of rouge she had started wearing on her cheeks and lips had long since vanished, the hem of her skirts was dirty and she was quite an untidy mess. She hoped no one would note her passing.

As Francesca started past the open double doors, she stole one sidelong peek into the room, where twenty-two guests sat at the linen-clad table. The table sat ten on each long side, one at both heads, hence twenty-two guests, unless a place remained vacant for her. Then Julia's entourage would number twenty-one. She glimpsed a room filled with fine crystal and gilded china, the ladies in evening gowns, the men in tuxedos, and she grimaced, ducking and increasing her pace.

But there was no escaping Julia. "Francesca!" Julia Van Wyck Cahill cried. Her tone was stern and it halted her daughter in her tracks.

Her cheeks warmed with guilt. Francesca felt like a thief caught with her hand in someone else's safe, not for the first time. Well, there was no escaping now. Slowly, she returned to the threshold of the room, attempting a pleasant smile for the large audience.

All conversation stopped. Mild stares were

46

turned her way.

Julia stood. There was no mistaking the resemblance between Francesca and her mother. Julia was blond, blue-eyed and still of a fine figure. She had been a reigning beauty in her day. As always, she was resplendently dressed in a blue evening gown of silk and lace with three-quarter sleeves, with sapphires at her ears and neck to match. She seemed rigidly displeased, but Francesca did not notice. Instead, in shock, her gaze whipped past her mother to the dark man sitting so indolently at the table in its center.

There was no vacant place, because Calder Hart had taken it.

But he was supposed to be in Chicago, *wasn't he?*

Her heart slammed and raced. *Calder was home.* "You're back," she whispered, stunned, and their gazes locked.

He slowly got to his feet, a very slight smile on his dark face, and he bowed.

Francesca had missed him and there was no denying it. Maybe her attraction to Hart was purely physical, but she dearly hoped not. And if it was, then she was not the first to be so foolishly smitten.

Francesca had always assumed she would one day marry a man like her father, someone respectable, admirable, honorable, a reformer and an activist — someone like Rick Bragg. Instead, she was engaged to the city's wealthiest businessman and most notorious womanizer. She still remained uncertain as to how this had happened, and so quickly. One moment she was friends with the enigmatic and oh-so-charismatic Hart and he was under suspicion for murder. The next, they were secretly engaged — until he had taken matters in his own hands, tired of her procrastination, making a public announcement. How had she fallen in love with Calder Hart? And was it even love?

Whenever she was with Hart, she felt as if she had boarded a locomotive that had lost all its brakes and was speeding downhill on an endless track. But as frightening as it was, she would not jump off, oh no.

She had made up her mind.

Francesca could hardly breathe as Julia said, "Are you going to join us, Francesca? You are a bit late, of course, but I am sure the traffic must have been terrible. And as you can see, your fiancé called. Of course, I invited Calder to stay and dine with us."

Francesca had the utmost difficulty tearing her gaze from Hart. But there was an odd note in Julia's tone, anxiety, perhaps, or tension. And then she gave up, simply staring at the man who had somehow, inexplicably, offered marriage, mumbling, "I had better go upstairs and change."

Calder stepped away from the dining table. With some alarm, he said, "Francesca, are you about to faint?"

Francesca had no clue as to what he was speaking about. Before she could react he was at her side, his arm around her waist as if holding her up. "I'm afraid my fiancée needs some air," he said firmly, and before either Andrew or Julia could speak, he was propelling her from the room.

Hart was a tall, broad-shouldered man. He was clad in a dark suit. The pitch-black wool might have been dour on another man, but on him it only heightened a sense of danger and made him more alluring. Hart's gaze moved over her face and Francesca knew she blushed, her heart continuing to race wildly. His dark eyes — midnight blue flecked with gold — slipped down her jacket and skirts.

She began to smile, leaning against him. They crossed the hall and entered a salon, Hart's strong arm an anchor about her waist. He stopped just inside the salon, one with a dozen opulent seating areas. Smiling back at her, he pushed the door closed with his foot.

She choked down her rising laughter. "That was painfully transparent."

He took her in both arms. "I have been away for two very long weeks, Francesca," he murmured, "and we both know I don't care what the present company says or thinks."

She knew she should protest as his hands slipped to her shoulders. Not because she did not want his kisses, but because her father was very opposed to Hart and was testing him in every way to see if he was worthy of her. Julia, on the other hand, wanted the match and openly gloated about it. She grasped his shoulders, too. "I think you missed me, Hart." She felt certain that he had and she grinned, never mind the heat slamming through her body.

"How clever a deduction," he said. "And it's Calder, darling — or am I making you nervous?" A dimple winked in his cheek.

He *was* making her nervous, damn him for knowing! They had only shared a few hours of intimacy together, and she had forgotten how devastating it was being in his arms, his hard, strong body pressed up against hers. Clearly he was aroused, and she decided to ignore the question. "Are you going to kiss me or not?"

"Bold wench," he said, and she heard

laughter in his tone. "You did not answer me, darling. Why am I making you nervous?" And he stared intently into her eyes, no longer smiling at all.

She stared back, her breath suspended. "I don't know," she finally said. "These past few weeks have felt so odd. I have been drifting about in a fog. It's almost as if it has all been a dream. I expect to wake up and find you a figment of my imagination!"

Surprise was there in his eyes, which were turning the color of ash. But his grip tightened on her. "I'm flattered, Francesca, but I am not a dream. In fact, some women find me a nightmare."

She wet her lips, well aware of all the broken hearts he had left in his wake. "I don't," she began. "Calder —"

He cut her off, pulling her close and covering her mouth with his.

Francesca lost all coherent thought. He knew how to kiss a woman, as he had seduced so many, but this time he wasn't interested in seduction. As his mouth instantly opened hers, as he penetrated deeply with his tongue, she sensed his need to possess. She melted as he kissed her again and again, some how standing, her legs useless, desire pooling between her thighs, a flood. Hart had come to hold her face in his hands

51

as he continued to kiss her as deeply as he could. Somehow, she managed to realize that he had really missed her. His desire felt explosive. She was beyond thrilled.

She tore her mouth from his. It was hard to speak as she clung to him. "Why don't you take me home tonight," she finally gasped.

His eyes widened. "I won't pretend I am not tempted and highly so, but nothing has changed. We wait until our wedding night, Francesca."

Her hands fisted and she pounded him once on the chest. "Damn it! I hate your nobility!"

He smiled at her. "I'm the least noble man you know. But I won't treat you like the others."

"You've never offered marriage to anyone else, so even if we share a bed before the wedding, you are not treating me like the others!" she cried. But this was a useless battle and she knew it. They'd had it several times before.

He stepped away from her, murmuring, "I'll take care of you, but this is not the time or the place."

She finally began to breathe, trembling now. She knew what he meant. She had been in his bed, once, for a few hours. He had touched and kissed her everywhere, giving her more pleasure than she had ever dreamed possible. It had been sheer ecstasy. She blushed just thinking about it. "When?"

He laughed and turned away, raking his hand through his coarse, dark hair. "As soon as the opportunity presents itself," he said, amusement in his tone.

"What is so entertaining about this?" she demanded, hands on her hips.

He stood at the fireplace, both hands on the marble mantle, and he gave her a look over his shoulder. His eyes were hot; his tone was not. "This is far harder for me than you, darling. Trust me."

"Let's move up the wedding," she demanded.

"You know it is your father who insists upon a year."

"I am going to change his mind," Francesca vowed grimly.

He turned and faced her, making no effort to come close. "There is blood on your jacket," he remarked.

Surprised, she glanced down at herself. When she saw a large, obvious smear of dried blood on the bottom of her blue wool jacket, she gasped. Then the comprehension dawned and horrified, she looked up.

His smile was grim. "Only you would walk

into a dinner party covered in blood. Another case . . . darling?"

She found her voice. "No wonder Mama sounded so strange! Oh, dear! And I am not covered in blood — it is one smear!"

"There's a patch on your skirt, too." His tone was flat and surprisingly calm.

Which meant nothing. With Hart, it could be the lull before the storm. Francesca carefully noted a spot near her left knee. "I must have brushed the sheets," she remarked, more to herself than to him.

"The sheets? Care to elaborate?" How casual he sounded.

She wrung her hands and met his gaze. "Did everyone see?"

"Undoubtedly." He softened, approaching and taking her small hands in his large ones. "We will be the talk of the town, will we not, darling? I can see it now. My indiscretions, my past, my penchant for depravity, my shocking art — all will become passé. You shall meet me at an affair covered in blood, or with the smell of gunpowder on your clothes and in your hair. Now, instead of gossiping about me behind my back, they will gossip about you. They shall whisper that we are the oddest match, but that we deserve one another." He actually smiled, clearly enjoying the notion.

"This isn't funny," she said, her heart sinking. "I know you don't care about your reputation, but I do care about mine, or at least, Mama cares, desperately, and —"

He suddenly reached out and reeled her back into her arms. "I know it hurts you to be called an eccentric, but with me at your side, they can call you far worse and it simply will not matter. As my wife, you will be able to do as you want. Surely you know that, Francesca? Our marriage will give you more freedom to be what you truly are than you have ever dreamed of."

She stared, stunned. Of course, she knew Hart liked to shock society, as he so disdained its conventions, and he had the wealth and power to do whatever he pleased, whenever he pleased. But she frankly hadn't considered the power she would gain as his wife. He was right. They might gossip about her behind her back, but as Mrs. Calder Hart, no door would ever be closed to her. As Mrs. Calder Hart, she could do whatever *she* pleased, whenever she pleased to do it.

The concept was stunning.

He chuckled softly. "You are usually a step ahead of the game, Francesca. I see how surprised you are, and how pleased." He added, "I am glad that is not the reason you are marrying me. It isn't my wealth you are after and it isn't position and power. Hmm. It must be my kisses. Now, tell me about this latest case."

She became aware of his powerful body and snuggled closer. "It is definitely your kisses, Hart, that have so ensnared me." She laughed softly as the notion of marrying any man merely from desire was so absurd, but then her smile faded. Hadn't she been worrying about that very possibility just that afternoon? The notion was far too frightening. She quickly changed the subject. "Did you read about the Slasher in Chicago?"

His gaze as intent but far different, he shook his head. "No."

Francesca quickly told him about the first two victims. "Do you remember little Bridget O'Neil?" she asked.

He nodded. "Yes, I do. Of course. We rescued her from that child-prostitution ring."

"Her mother found a woman murdered next door to their flat. And from the look of it, it was also the work of the Slasher. At least, that is what we think." She thought about the trip she must make to police headquarters that next morning. It was her first order of business, actually. She needed to know if the police had surmised that the Slasher had indeed been the murderer.

Afterward she would call on Francis O'Leary.

Then Francesca realized that Hart had tensed, and she knew what was coming. She wished she had chosen her words with more care.

"We?" he asked, his gaze direct, his tone sharp.

She winced to herself and sighed. "Bragg was at the crime scene. He was as concerned as I was for Maggie Kennedy's safety. We happened to be there at the same time and apparently we are both on the case." She avoided his eyes, wondering if there would be a jealous eruption. With Hart, she never knew what to expect. He was entirely unpredictable, at times arrogant and secure, at others, jealous and enraged.

His jaw flexed. "Of course, your latest investigation involves my dear, so *noble* half brother."

She met his gaze and sensed the storm clouds, but did not see them. "He is the commissioner of police!"

"He has more to do than investigate common crimes — he has a detective force for that." Hart walked away from her. His shoulders seemed rigid now.

She followed. "You have no reason to be jealous," she said, and the moment she spoke she regretted it.

He turned. "I never said I was jealous. The last thing I am is jealous of Rick." His eyes had turned dark.

"If he wishes to pursue an investigation, I can hardly stop him."

"Of course not. But the question is, do you welcome his attention?" And his tone was mocking.

She tensed. "Hart, we are engaged. I have made my choice and a sincere commitment. Good God, a moment ago I was fainting from passion in your arms! I don't want Bragg to be between us, especially not when my profession will constantly bring me into contact with him."

He sighed. "You are right. I am jealous. I have been gone for two weeks, and every day I have been acutely aware of the fact that at any moment, you could change your mind and take him back."

She was stunned. "He is married. Leigh Anne almost died. In fact, she is going home tomorrow. He would never leave her, especially not now."

Hart stared at her, clearly not accepting her every word.

Francesca did not like it. She was being sincere. She wanted to marry Calder Hart, never mind that there would be no white picket fence, never mind his reputation and his ex-lovers. The only thing she could not get past was how much courage was involved in being with such a man.

"And if he did leave her? Then what?" he asked softly.

She felt chilled. "You already know my answer."

"Do I?" He was grim.

Francesca felt real despair. It was on the tip of her tongue to tell him that she loved him, but she knew that everyone whose opinion she held dear would advise her against it. And even a woman of no previous experience knew better than to tell the city's most notorious womanizer that she was in love. Besides, her emotions were so turbulent she wasn't sure it *was* love. "Hart, you do know." She hurried to him and took his hands in hers. "I want to be with you. I think I have been clear."

He just looked at her and she wished that she could read his mind, but at times like this, it was impossible to know what he might be thinking. And then he spoke. "I am your second choice, Francesca, and there are times when it is crystal clear."

And in that moment, she had a terrible premonition that he would never forgive her for wanting Rick Bragg first, for once thinking him her true love. Uneasy, she stood on tiptoe and tried to kiss him. As she feathered his unmoving mouth with hers, she said, "Please believe me. Remember, there have never been any lies between us. I will never lie to you, Calder. Not ever. It is you I want."

He made a disparaging sound, but his arms went around her, tightening. "You want me in bed, darling. And while I do not mind, we both know neither one of us would be here like this if Leigh Anne had stayed in Europe."

Francesca stiffened. For once she was at a loss and could not think of a good reply.

His gaze was fixed on the candle shining in the apartment window across the dully lit street. A single passing carriage, too fine for the ward, could not distract his eyes. He did not blink, not even once, but simply stared and stared.

He waited for a glimpse of her, moving about her flat, and he shivered, but not from the cold. He was used to damp and cold far more bitter than this. No, he shivered from excitement.

He stared unblinking at the hint of shadows moving inside the flat. And suddenly he saw her. The trembling ceased.

He was sick of them all.

Every single one, all of them whores, just like *her.*

Rage filled him — rage and need. *Bloodlust.*

He had made a terrible mistake and he knew it, but soon, very soon, his knife would cut, and this time, it would not be a tragic mistake, oh no. This time, the faithless bitch would die.

He smiled and his fingers twitched and then he found the hilt of the knife and he gripped it with great care. And watching her, he slowly stroked the blade.

CHAPTER THREE

Wednesday, April 23, 1902 9:00 a.m.

He had come to hate the city's most renowned hospital. Now, instead of getting out of his roadster, Rick Bragg stared at the entrance of the pavilion in which his wife was being treated, gripping the Daimler's steering wheel so tightly his fingers ached, dread forming in his chest.

The hospital took up several city blocks, from Twenty-third to Twenty-eighth Streets, from the East River to Second Avenue. The many buildings that comprised it had been erected independently of one another, so that some of the pavilions were narrow and tall, others broad, whitewashed and squat. Just to his left, there was new construction under way for the tuberculosis clinic that would open early next year. A crane was lifting huge blocks of granite, the workers in their flannel shirts shouting encouragement to the operator.

He knew he was a coward. He had been sitting in his motorcar for twenty or thirty minutes, delaying the inevitable moment of alighting from the vehicle, of entering the accident ward, of walking down the sterile corridor, of crossing the threshold of the room that contained his wife.

It was not that he did not want to see her. It was that being with her took every ounce of his strength.

But she was alive, he reminded himself, fiercely relieved. Alive, conscious, with no apparent impairment to her brain. He didn't care that her left leg was useless, that she would never walk again. Not when weeks ago it had seemed as if she might never wake up.

The guilt crushed him.

And for one moment, it was as if one of the granite blocks being carried to the new construction site had landed on him, making it impossible to breathe.

Decisively, Bragg got out of the Daimler. He laid his gloves and goggles on the front seat. Two passing male nurses nodded at him. He tried to recall their names and failed.

His duster over his arm, he strode up the concrete path to the Accident Pavilion and pushed through the wood-and-glass door.

Nurses, both male and female, and doctors stood around the reception desk. Someone saw him and waved him on through.

Her door was open. He paused, his heart beginning to race, and as he looked inside the sterile whitewashed room with several beds, all unoccupied except for hers, he saw that she was sitting up against her pillows, flipping through *Harper's Weekly.* His heart quickened impossibly. She wore one of her own peignoirs, lavender silk and cream lace, and even crippled, she was the most beautiful woman he had ever seen.

She realized he was standing there, staring, and she looked up, slowly putting the magazine aside.

He somehow smiled. He was perspiring now. So many emotions ran riot that he had more trouble breathing, thinking. The most dominant feelings were vast relief and crushing guilt.

"Good morning," he heard himself say.

She carefully returned his smile. "Good morning." Leigh Anne was a petite woman, barely five feet tall, with the face of a china doll. Her perfect features — large green eyes, tiny nose and rosebud mouth — were accentuated by a delicate ivory complexion. Her hair was thick, silken, straight and black. No man could enter a room where she was present and not look twice and then stare.

He noticed several new flower arrangements on the windowsill.

She followed his gaze. "Rourke came last night."

"In the middle of the week?" His half brother was attending medical school in Philadelphia.

"Apparently he has applied for a transfer to the Bellevue Medical College and he has an interview this afternoon."

Rick nodded, unable to focus on his half brother's plans. "How are you today?" he said, pulling up a chair and sitting by her side.

She never looked directly at him anymore, it seemed. Her gaze on Rourke's yellow hothouse roses, she said, "Fine."

He wanted to reach over and take her tiny hands in his. And in spite of all the passion they had once shared, he did not dare touch her. He was afraid that she would reject him — as she should. "You must be so pleased to be going home today."

She seemed to smile but she did not answer, her gaze now wandering to the magazine on the bed. Idly, she pulled it closer to her hip.

Ever since the accident, it had become like

this, an utter failure of communication, utter awkwardness. He was sweating now. He wanted to pull her against his chest and stroke her hair and beg her for forgiveness, but of course he did not. At least, thank God, she was coming home. "I will come by at four or five, if that suits you," he said.

She slowly looked up, her expression very hard to read.

"The girls are terribly excited," he added, trying to smile. But he was a policeman, and before that a lawyer, and he knew when something was wrong.

"You didn't bring them this morning," she said softly, clearly dismayed.

Katie and Dot were two orphans who were fostering with them, and whom he intended to adopt. He had brought them to visit Leigh Anne every day. "You will see them this afternoon," he said, smiling with an effort.

She turned her head away.

Alarm mingled with dread.

Then, not looking at him, she said, "I'm afraid it's far too soon for me to go home."

He started. Then, in an uncharacteristic rush, "The doctors think it would be best. I've hired two nurses to attend you round the clock. The girls are expecting you. *I am expecting you!*" he heard himself cry.

Her jaw hardened visibly and she looked him in the eye and repeated, "I'm afraid it's too soon for me to go home, Rick."

"Are you certain that you don't want to go inside?" Francesca asked, teasing.

She stood with Joel on Mulberry Street just outside of police headquarters. Joel was slouched with his hands in the pockets of his trousers, which had holes at both knees. He had plopped a black felt cap on his head, and he scowled at the two front doors of the station house. Roundsmen in their blue wool uniforms and leather helmets were coming and going, a police wagon was parked not far from where they stood and Bragg's Daimler was being surreptitiously watched by another patrolman. All of this was in the midst of one of the city's worst slums.

Even now, a prostitute in a very revealing robe stood in the basement doorway across the street, taunting both the policemen and the male passersby. A drunk had just urinated on a tree, and several shabbily clad children were playing hooky from school. Francesca looked up at the bright blue, cloudless sky and she smiled, happily.

Hart's image filled her mind.

Even now, she could feel his hard demanding mouth on hers.

He was back, it wasn't a dream — she was engaged to the city's most notorious bachelor and she couldn't be happier.

Never mind his foolish jealousy of the night before. It would pass — it always did.

"I'm not going inside," Joel said flatly. To emphasize his point, he spat on the sidewalk near his boot-clad feet.

He despised the police, having been apprehended, roughed up and incarcerated more times than he would ever admit. He also despised Rick Bragg, refusing to see past the fact that he was the police commissioner. Francesca stopped smiling and tried to be stern, no easy task when her heart was singing. Tonight she and Hart were dining at the Waldorf-Astoria, alone. She could hardly wait.

"Joel, spitting is ungentlemanly and it was uncalled for."

He sighed. "Sorry. I'll wait over there," he said, gesturing with his head in some other direction.

"I won't be long," she said, smiling again. She patted the cap on his head and hurried up the granite steps and into the reception room.

As always, it was filled with civilians lodging one complaint or another, newsmen looking for a scoop, recently apprehended thugs and rowdies waiting their turn to be formally charged and locked up, and the policemen and officers handling it all. Several staff were behind the long reception counter, including Sergeant O'Malley, and she waved at him. He nodded at her and called out, "He's upstairs. Door's open, I think."

She had become a frequent visitor at police headquarters and needed no formal permission to come and go. No one seemed to have noticed, though, that she had not been present at the station in several weeks. Turning to hurry upstairs — she never used the elevator — she bumped into a man.

It was Arthur Kurland from the *Sun,* a snoop whom she thoroughly disliked. She should have expected this, as he was always at headquarters and just as often seeking her out. He smiled at her, steadying her. "I haven't seen you at the station house in a long time, Miss Cahill. What brings you here?" He seemed delighted to see her.

She did not even try to pretend that she didn't dislike him. After all, he was privy to far too many secrets. He had uncovered her brief romantic attachment to Bragg and Francesca sensed he was waiting to reveal the fact of their past liaison when it would be the most harmful for everyone.

"Good morning." She was brisk. "Surely you have heard by now that a woman was found murdered yesterday and that it might be the work of the so-called Slasher?" Trying to be imperious, she raised both pale eyebrows.

"Yes, I have. I take it you are on the case?"

"I am."

He whipped out his notepad. "Any new leads?"

"I'm afraid it is far too soon to be speaking to the press."

"Dear God, an arctic chill has just entered the room!" He laughed and tucked the pad and pen back into the breast pocket of his jacket, then adjusted the felt fedora he always wore. "You were only too eager to spill the beans last month when you were chasing after Tim Murphy and his gang."

She scowled. "I had hoped that leaking information to the press might aid my investigation. This investigation is in the preliminary stages. I refuse to compromise it. Good day." She shoved past him.

He quickly caught up. "Hmm, compromise. An interesting word. So, Miss Cahill, there are some things you will *not* compromise?"

Aghast, she faced him, feeling all the color

drain from her face. She had been compromised more than once when alone with Rick Bragg and this man knew it. "That was unbearably rude. What do you want from me?"

"Does your fiancé know you are here and working with the man he hates more than anyone else?"

She stiffened. How did Kurland know that? "Calder doesn't hate Rick Bragg. Calder and Rick are half brothers. They are close." And, as she lied so baldy, she felt her cheeks turn red.

He laughed. "If you say so! But isn't it difficult, spending the day with one man — and the evening with the other?"

She could barely respond, she was so livid. "You have the social grace of an ape, Mr. Kurland." And she stalked away.

He followed. "It's why I'm such a good reporter. Sure you don't have a lead for me? Anything?"

She halted in her tracks and whirled and he crashed into her. They leaped apart. Panting, she said, "Are you attempting to blackmail me?"

"Moi?" He was incredulous. "Never, Miss Cahill."

"A wise decision." She wondered if she dared tell Hart about how dangerous this

71

man was becoming. But then she would have to reveal the extent of her prior relationship with Bragg to him. And that would be dangerous, indeed. "Good day." Her tone was final and she hurried up the stairs.

He stood at the bottom landing and called up, "And to answer your previous question, Miss Cahill, I haven't decided what it is that I want from you."

She glanced down and met his cool gaze and stumbled. As she righted herself, he tipped his hat in the most disrespectful manner and walked away. Filled with unease, she stared after him.

She knew she must warn Bragg. Quickly she turned and hurried up the hall to his office. His door was ajar but not open, solid wood on the bottom, the glass opaque on the top. She knocked and it swung wide.

His desk faced the door, a window that looked out over Mulberry Street behind him. She expected to find him up to his elbows in work — his desk was always stacked high with files — but instead, she found him sitting there, staring off into space, looking impossibly sad. She froze.

This was not the time, she realized, to burden him with Arthur Kurland. But what was wrong?

He started as he realized that she was

present and jumped to his feet, smiling slightly, but Francesca knew him well enough to know the expression was forced. He was preoccupied and disturbed. And she had not mistaken the sadness in his eyes.

"Good morning," he said, coming forward. There was a fireplace on the other side of his desk with numerous photographs on the mantel, mostly of his vast family, although several were of him with President Roosevelt or with the mayor. But there had never been a picture there of Hart, his half brother, or of Leigh Anne, his wife. Now the first thing she saw was a huge portrait of Leigh Anne in an oval silver frame. It dominated the mantel and every other photograph placed there.

She quickly tore her gaze from the photograph, managing a smile. "Good morning. I hope I am not interrupting."

And suddenly his facade vanished. His smile gone, he took her arm, guiding her to one of the two upholstered chairs in front of his desk. "You could never be an interruption," he said.

She did not sit. "What's wrong, Rick?"

Instantly he turned away. "Nothing."

She didn't move, staring at his back until he sat down behind his desk, facing her once again. He lifted a file. "Heinreich is almost certain that the same knife was used on all three victims."

She did not want to discuss the case now. Something was terribly amiss. "Has something happened? Are the girls all right?"

"The girls are fine. The Slasher is at work, Francesca, and now the question is who will his next target be, and will he strike again on Monday?" Bragg handed the file across the desk. "I am glad you are on this case," he added. "We don't have much time."

She took the file but did not open it; she could only stare. He looked away. Clearly he did not wish to discuss anything personal with her. Yes, everything had changed, because not very long ago he would open his heart to her without a moment's hesitation. The urge to be his friend — a real friend — and to help him now overcame her, but so did guilt. What right did she have to the happiness she had just been feeling when his life was causing him such anguish? Surely, whatever was wrong, it could be fixed. Surely she could help! She *had* to help. Otherwise she was no friend at all.

But now was not the time to push or pry. As hard as it was to back away, she would do just that. She took a deep breath and opened the file. "Margaret Cooper was killed Monday afternoon, between noon and 4:00 p.m.," she read from the file's notes. A chill tickled her nape and she knew she was missing something very important. "So Margaret was not attacked at night like the others."

"No."

She glanced back at the file. "Her neck was cut with a blade no more than three inches long." Surprised, she looked up. "Would that not be a common pocket-knife?"

"Yes."

Diverted now from Bragg's private dilemma, she saw that it had not been an easy task to sever Margaret Cooper's jugular. Some sawing had been involved. And the same dull blade had been used on all three victims, the cutting from right to left. She looked up. "In all likelihood, the Slasher is right-handed."

"Yes." He was intently focused on her now. "Apparently there is a nick on the murder weapon, a small indentation on what Heinreich believes to be the right side of the blade. That nick has caused a slight vee on the track of the slit on Miss Cooper's throat. He said he noticed it on Kate Sullivan's wound as well, but at the time thought nothing of it."

"That is a wonderful clue!" She handed

the file back to him and sat staring at him, wide-eyed. He stared back as thoughtfully. Her mind raced, but not conclusively. Something continued to nag at her, but she could not identify it. She heard herself wonder, "Is he going to sharpen that knife? And if so, will the nick be filed out?"

"Your guess is as good as mine." Bragg rocked in his cane-backed chair. "I hope not," he added.

She continued to think. "I see that there was no forced entry at Margaret Cooper's. Did he pick the lock? Attain a key? Follow her inside?"

"There was no forced entry at Sullivan's or O'Leary's, either. None of the two women have any idea how he got inside their flats," Bragg said. "I take it you will interview both women today?"

"I intend to try," Francesca said grimly. And then she knew what she was missing and she shot to her feet. "Bragg!"

His eyebrows lifted and he stood. "What is it?"

"Bridget O'Neil stayed home from school on Monday! She had a cough. She was at home — *alone* — when Margaret Cooper was murdered."

For one moment, he simply stared back at

her. Then, "I cannot get away for a few hours."

She almost smiled, for she knew exactly what he was thinking. "I did not notice her coughing yesterday. She is probably in school now, anyway."

"Yes. How does 4:00 p.m. sound?"

"I'll meet you at the O'Neils'."

It was noon when she stepped out of a hansom cab in front of the attractive limestone building that housed the Lord and Taylor store on the corner of Nineteenth Street. Paying the driver, she thanked him and hurried up Fifth Avenue to the wide, arched entrance. Once inside, Francesca saw that the ground floor was already crowded with dozens of ladies. Bragg had told her that Francis worked at the perfume and soap counter. She had not been to Lord and Taylor's in some time, having no personal inclination for shopping, so she had no idea where that counter might be amongst the many others.

Facing her was a long counter filled with gloves, surrounding shelves of hats. Francesca glanced aside and saw a counter selling French and Belgian chocolates, and then she froze in disbelief. Had she just seen Hart's former mistress at the glove counter?

Slowly, she looked back toward that glove display and her heart lurched wildly. Standing there, pulling on a delicate pair of beaded evening gloves, was none other than Daisy Jones.

Francesca felt hot. She started to fan herself with her purse. Daisy had yet to see her, and of course, Hart no longer visited her. Not only had he promised Francesca fidelity from the moment she had accepted his proposal, she had been eavesdropping on him when he had bluntly told Daisy of his intention to one day marry Francesca. That had been well before Francesca had had any intention of ever accepting him, and his words to his mistress had been a shock. He had coldly told Daisy that their relationship would be over from the moment Francesca became his fiancée.

Fanning herself did not help and she unbuttoned her gray jacket. She had gotten into a lot of trouble that day, for she had also watched Hart and Daisy indulge themselves in a bout of raw passion. She would never forget what she had seen.

She was at a loss, unsure of whether to approach Daisy or not, as once they had been on friendly terms. Of course, that had changed with her engagement to Hart — and the realization that she really wanted to marry him, that she had very strong feelings for him.

Francesca decided that there was no point in greeting the other woman. Because Daisy and Hart had originally agreed to a six-month liaison, he continued to allow her to live in the house he had bought for her, in spite of their breakup, until that six-month period had lapsed. There were still three full months left on that arrangement and Francesca knew that for a fact. But as she was about to hurry away, Daisy laid the evening gloves down, apparently declining to buy them, and turned and saw Francesca.

Her beautiful blue eyes widened.

Francesca halted and smiled so widely her face seemed to turn to plaster. "Daisy!" she cried as if the other woman were her very best friend. "I haven't seen you in so long! How are you?" She went forward and grasped the slim woman's shoulders while pecking her cheek.

Daisy smiled back. She was one of the most beautiful women Francesca had ever seen, so delicate and fragile in appearance, as pale as an alabaster statue with her platinum hair and fair complexion. Francesca knew exactly why Hart had made her his mistress and as always, when faced with just how lovely Daisy was, she failed to understand how he could refuse her bed now. There was simply no way that Francesca could ever compete in beauty, grace and elegance. The other woman also happened to be from a genteel background, although Francesca had never learned why she had become a fallen woman. When confronted with Daisy in the flesh, Francesca always felt tall, overweight and gauche.

"Francesca, this is such a pleasant surprise," Daisy said softly in her wispy, childish voice. "Are you shopping?" She seemed mildly incredulous.

"Actually, I am on a case. I am here to interview someone." Francesca continued to smile, although it had become painful. Of course, Hart would choose the most beautiful woman in the city to warm his bed, just as he bought the most controversial art, the most handsome and modern carriage, the fastest, most elegant horses. So the real question was, why did he wish to have Francesca in bed?

She could understand his rationale for marriage. They were friends. Hart admired and respected her and had never, not once in his life, had a friend before. But why not marry her and keep women like Daisy for his sensual entertainment? Now Francesca was sweating. She reminded herself that

Hart did want her in bed, and he had proven it to her more than once, including last evening.

"I so admire you." Daisy smiled, touching Francesca's arm very lightly. "You are so clever, so bold. And Hart clearly thinks as I do. He is so proud of you, Francesca."

"I'm not sure of that," Francesca said, finally allowing her smile to vanish. Her cheeks ached anyway.

"Can I see the ring he gave you?" Daisy asked almost eagerly.

Francesca pulled off her kidskin glove. For one moment Daisy was still as she gazed at the huge diamond, which must have cost several fortunes. Then she smiled and looked up with admiration in her gaze. "Calder must be smitten."

"Hart doesn't believe in love," Francesca said, and the moment the words were out, she wished to kick herself. It was true — Hart felt love was for fools and had been clear from the start that he was not about to succumb to the emotion, even if it could exist for him. Still, why not let the other woman think that Hart was in love?

Daisy's very pale eyebrows lifted and her nearly turquoise-blue eyes were wide. "Still, he wishes to marry you. You are the talk of the town, Francesca, and the envy of every lady of marriageable age. Rose and I were just discussing it last night."

Francesca desperately wanted to change the topic. "How is Rose?" she asked quickly. Rose and Daisy were best friends and, Francesca knew, longtime lovers, a relationship that both shocked and fascinated her.

"Wonderful," Daisy said with a happy smile. "Now that Hart no longer visits me, she is allowed to come and go as she pleases." Her smile vanished and she leaned close, confiding, "He was simply so possessive when we first began our affair. He was livid at the thought I should even want to chat with Rose and he refused to allow her even platonic visits. How jealous and controlling he was!"

Francesca hugged herself. That certainly sounded like Calder Hart.

Daisy smiled again. "But you must know that. I mean, you are now the focus of his attention, so surely you are receiving his outbursts of jealous rage."

Francesca felt warning bells go off. She knew she must end this conversation and find Francis O'Leary. "Yes, Hart can certainly be jealous and demanding. Daisy, I must go." But she felt oddly ill. Not too long ago Hart had been jealous over Daisy. Now he was jealous where she was concerned.

But Daisy took her hand, holding it tightly so that she could not leave. "Francesca, I must have a word with you!" she cried, appearing worried now.

Francesca knew that no good could come of any further conversation. "I really must go." She shrugged free and started to flee.

"Rose and I are so worried about you. You are too naive to manage a man like Hart!" Daisy cried to her back.

Francesca halted in her tracks. Slowly, she turned to face the woman she had once sincerely liked and was now desperately afraid of. "I am not naive."

Daisy went to her and gripped both of her hands. "Three months ago, Hart could not stay out of my bed. Night and day, he was there, and any man who looked at me was the target of his jealous rage."

"Just stop," Francesca said, wanting to plug up her ears like a child.

"No, you have to listen before he hurts you terribly! I know he truly wants you, and why not? You are beautiful and clever and he has never met a woman like you before, that much is clear. And you may last longer than all of the others, really — after all, he has become fond enough of you to ask you for marriage. But Francesca, Calder Hart is a very sensual man. You know this. You know his reputation, you know it is not false. Do you really think to keep his attention where it belongs — on you and only you?"

Francesca knew there was not one drop of blood left in her face. She simply could not speak, because every word coming from Daisy's horridly pretty mouth was the truth.

"He is fascinated with you now. Not so long ago he was fascinated with me. And before that, there was someone else and before that, someone else. There will be someone after you, Francesca. Sooner or later, his gaze will wander, his gaze and his interest, and we both know that when that happens, his promises will mean nothing."

Francesca knew that Daisy was right. She had known this all along, and it was why she had not been able to accept his proposal at first. It was why, after accepting, she had fled the city for an entire month, grappling with her emotions, her fear. It was why, in the darkest hours of the night, she would wake up in a sweat, terrified of her engagement, her impending marriage, terrified of Calder Hart. Daisy was right. There was simply no way a man like that was going to stay happily and faithfully married to any woman, much less herself. And the day he wandered was the day the sunshine would leave her life.

But she had to speak. So she drew her shoulders back. "I know."

Daisy started.

Francesca somehow smiled, holding her head high. "You are hardly telling me anything new, Daisy. Remember, when I first met Hart I was in love with Rick Bragg. We became friends first, not lovers, and I know more about him than anyone else." That was a stretch of the truth. She continued calmly. "We remain friends. And we share desire. He admires me, I respect him. It's really very simple — we make a good match. It's hardly a love match." And she continued to smile.

"So you are marrying him because you cannot have the man you really want?" Daisy asked, her gaze intent and unblinking.

The question felt dangerous. For a split second, Francesca hesitated, then prayed her answer would not come back to haunt her. "Yes," she lied. And she thought about what Hart had said last night. "And I am marrying him for wealth and power. As his wife, I can conduct my business affairs as I choose. We both know how independent I am. I will have more freedom than a woman could possibly dream of. Hart has assured me of that."

Daisy stared. Then, with some admiration, she said, "You are clever, Francesca. You had me fooled. I thought you naive enough to have fallen in love and to think Hart your knight in shining armor. I apologize. Rose and I need not worry. This shall be a very good match, indeed."

"We both think so," Francesca said, hoping that Daisy did not see her relief. She began to tremble.

Daisy sighed and kissed her cheek. The most delicate floral scent emanated from her. "Please come and call on us. We would love to receive you," she said.

"I will try," Francesca said, not meaning it.

Daisy took her hands warmly in hers. "I hope you do not mind my speaking out. You are always forthright. I assumed you would appreciate my honesty."

"Of course I do," she lied with another smile.

"Hart is a lucky man," Daisy said. Smiling at Francesca, she gave her an odd look and walked away.

Disturbed by that last remark and the lingering glance Francesca felt her knees give way. She collapsed against the counter, barely able to breathe. Tears rapidly filled her eyes.

She was naive and she was a fool. She had believed, or she'd wanted to, that Hart would be faithful to her forever! But Daisy was right. She was a current fascination, and only that. Marriage or no, one day his interest would wander and when that day came, she would be destroyed.

"Ma'am? Are you all right?"

Francesca faced the shopgirl behind the counter. "I'm fine," she managed. "Thank you." But even as she spoke, she wondered what she should do. These past few weeks she had managed to control her deepest, most secret fears. The recent encounter with Daisy had brought them to light again. Nothing had changed.

Hart did not love her, did not even believe in love, and she was falling head over heels for him. Dear God, what should she do?

If she was smart, she would walk away. That much, at least, was clear.

Either that, or she would have to be very, very brave.

CHAPTER FOUR

Wednesday, April 23, 1902 1:00 p.m.

Having composed herself, Francesca paused before the counter selling soaps and perfumes. A pretty, brunette shopgirl was discussing the merits of a lavender soap with an older, elegant lady. Francesca waited at the counter and stared.

The shopgirl was in her early twenties. Her black dress had a white collar and cuffs and did not quite conceal all of her throat. Today, Francis O'Leary wore no bandage. A pale pink line on her neck indicated that she had been the Slasher's victim.

The lady opened her purse and took out some coins. Francesca noticed Francis's rings. On the fourth finger of her left hand, a tiny red stone winked in a band of silver. Francesca wondered if the ring had any significance.

Her soap wrapped and in a small shopping bag, the buyer left. Francis approached

Francesca with a smile. "May I help you, miss?"

Francesca smiled in return, handing Francis O'Leary her business card. It read:

Francesca Cahill, Crime-Solver Extraordinaire
No. 810 Fifth Avenue, New York City
All Cases Accepted, No Case too Small

Francis read the card, her dark eyes growing wide. With a small gasp, she looked up. "What is this about?" she said on a note of fear.

"Are you Francis O'Leary?" Francesca asked kindly.

Francis tried to hand her back the card. "Yes, I am! This is about the Slasher?" She seemed panicked.

"You may keep my card, please, in case you need to reach me," Francesca said. "Yes, this is about the Slasher. I have taken the case, Mrs. O'Leary."

Francis had paled. "I told the police everything I could," she whispered.

"Would you mind repeating it all to me?"

She hesitated. "No, I don't mind . . . but I am trying to forget it, *him!*"

Francesca clasped one of her hands. "We must prevent him from striking again. Did you hear that there was a third victim this past Monday — and that she died?"

Francis cried out. "But he did not want to kill me! I am certain of it!"

"How can you be certain?" Francesca asked.

"I'm sure of it! He could have killed me if he had wanted to!"

"Please, Mrs. O'Leary, just tell me what happened."

Francis hesitated and nodded. She continued to clutch the glass counter, her knuckles white. "I had no idea someone was in my flat. I had worked all day. I was tired, very tired, and hungry." Tears filled her eyes. "I had bought a loaf of bread on my way home with some dried corned beef. I thought to soak my feet a bit and then eat."

Francesca wondered if every shopgirl in the city had ill-fitting shoes. "Go on."

"I unlocked my door, then closed and locked it. I was about to sit down on the sofa when he grabbed me from behind." Her wide eyes shimmered with the tears that had yet to fall. "He held the knife to my throat, the blade barely touching my skin. He said something in a hoarse whisper, and then he cut me. And then he shoved me away, to the floor. When I looked up, he was gone."

"The police say you cannot recall his words."

Francis simply looked at her. The tears fell now.

"I am so sorry to upset you," Francesca whispered. "But I do not want another woman hurt — or murdered."

"I dreamed about him last night."

Francesca was surprised. "What did you dream?"

"It makes no sense. I dreamed he called me a faithless woman." She looked down at the display beneath the glass countertop. She whispered, not looking up, "I think . . . I am almost certain that he called me a faithless . . . bitch."

Her surprise increased. Francesca leaned forward. "You think that because of your dream or because you can remember his words?"

Francis gazed at her. "It was so real. Like remembering something you should have never forgotten."

If the Slasher had called her faithless, that would imply that he knew Mrs. O'Leary. "Would you recognize his voice again if you heard it?"

"Yes!" She shivered. "Of course I would."

Francesca was thoughtful. Then she held up Francis's left hand. "Is that an engage-

91

ment ring?"

Francis blushed, smiling. "Yes. My friend gave it to me Saturday. The attack made him realize how much he loves me."

"Your friend?"

"Sam Wilson. My . . . husband . . . died two years ago. There's been no one since. It's been so long . . . and then I met Sam." She was smiling and clearly in love. "We met in March. March 3rd, to be exact."

"I am very happy for you," Francesca said, hiding her surprise. Bragg had told her that Francis's husband had disappeared over two years ago, clearly having decided to leave his wife. But she was claiming that he was dead — while preparing to marry another man. Did her fiancé, Sam Wilson, know the truth? Francesca wondered. And she could not help but note that Francis had met Sam Wilson a month before the Slasher's first assault.

"Mrs. O'Leary, the police commissioner told me that your husband abandoned you two years ago. That he simply left one day and never came back." Francesca stared at the woman.

Francis turned crimson. "Oh," she said, sitting down on a stool behind the counter. "Oh," she said again. Tears filled her eyes.

"So he isn't dead?" Francesca asked, this

time gently.

Francis shrugged. "He's dead to me, Miss Cahill. Please, please don't tell my fiancé! Sam has made me so happy!" she cried.

"I won't say a word," Francesca said. She felt sorry for the young woman now. "Why would anyone, much less the Slasher, label you as faithless?"

Her dark eyes widened. "I wouldn't know! I adored my husband, Miss Cahill, until the day he left. Until that day, he was a good, solid, honest and hardworking man — or so I thought! I was never faithless to Thomas."

Until now, Francesca thought silently. She decided to ask Bragg if the police could attempt to locate Francis's errant husband. "And what about your loyalty to Sam?"

"I would never be faithless to the man in my life. I've seen no one but Sam since my husband left me."

Francesca met the other woman's unwavering gaze. She did not look away as most liars did, and there was no change in her coloring. Francesca felt rather strongly that Francis had buried her husband some time ago — that, to her, he was really dead. If Francis had been called a faithless bitch, it had probably meant nothing more than the words of a maddened killer. "Mrs. O'Leary, do you have any idea where your husband is? Have you heard from him at all since he left?"

Francis set her jaw. "I have not had a single letter — not a single word! But I do suspect he went West. He was always talking about the open ranges of Texas and California. And Miss Cahill, if he did go out West, well, then he could be dead, couldn't he? They say that land is a dangerous, lawless place."

Francesca realized that trying to locate Thomas O'Leary could be like looking for a needle in a haystack. "Let's get back to the Slasher. You seem to think he was already in your flat when you came in that night."

"He must have been there, waiting for me." She shivered, blanching again. "I'm sorry. I can't forget that man. He was terrifying — at first I thought he meant to kill me!"

"But how would he get into your flat when you left it locked that day?"

"Perhaps he found an open window," Francis said. "Perhaps I had left a window unlocked. The police said they were all locked, but he could have locked it after entering."

"It is certainly a possibility, considering you live on the ground floor. Could he have followed you inside? You said you unlocked the door, closed and locked it immediately and only then, when you were about to sit down on the sofa, he assaulted you."

"Yes." But she appeared uncertain now.

"But what did you do with your bag of groceries, your purse? And I assume you wore a hat and perhaps a coat or shawl? Wouldn't you put your bags down first and then remove your hat and shawl and after that lock the door?"

Francis stared. After a moment, she said, "You're right. Of course you're right. There were a few moments when the door was unlocked, maybe even ajar, while I did those things." She flushed. "I seem to remember the door being ajar when I went back to lock it. Oh, God! He slipped inside while I was unpinning my hat or some such thing!" she cried.

"Yes, I think the Slasher could have slipped inside after you. I am assuming you did *not* light a candle yet?" Francesca now made some rapid notes.

"I never had a chance to light a candle that night, Miss Cahill. It hadn't become fully dark yet. After I locked the door I went to sit, and that was when he seized me." Her eyes remained wide, but respect filled them now.

Francesca smiled briskly. "You have been

quite helpful, Mrs. O'Leary. Would you mind if I spoke to Mr. Wilson?"

"No, of course not, but why would you think to speak with my fiancé?"

"Perhaps you told him something that you have forgotten to tell me," Francesca said lightly. But that was not the real reason. She could not rule out any man who knew any of the victims as a suspect, including Francis's fiancé — or her errant husband.

Of course, at this point in time, Francesca could not dismiss the possibility that a madman was choosing pretty women as his victim, purely by random.

But oddly, she did not think so. "We will be in touch," she said.

The law offices where Evan Cahill worked were just a few blocks uptown from the Lord and Taylor store. As she was on her way uptown to interview Kate Sullivan and then to meet Bragg to interview little Bridget O'Neil, she had the perfect opportunity to call on her brother. She hadn't seen him in a week; when he had been living at home they had seen one another on a daily basis.

The offices of Garfield and Willis were housed in an older building built at the turn of the previous century. It was still stately, with a brick facade and classical front. After being shown to a small reception room, Francesca was asked to wait for Evan there. She admired the dark wood floors, well worn but gleaming with wax, the wood paneling on the lower half of the walls and the gold fabric above and the large crystal chandelier overhead. She did not sit. Still thinking about her interview with Francis O'Leary, she also recalled her conversation with Maggie Kennedy last night. She wondered what Evan would say when he learned of her new case.

He strode into the room, smiling. "Fran! What a wonderful surprise."

Francesca rushed to embrace him. As always, her brother was smiling and he appeared happy. Evan had a sunny nature. He was also tall, dark and dashing, and until his fall from Cahill grace, he had been a premier catch. Francesca smiled up at him, searching his eyes. "You seem very well."

He laughed and shrugged. Then, "I haven't been at the tables in over a month, Fran."

She cried out in surprised delight. Evan had a passion for gaming and, to her dismay, she had learned that his debts exceeded a hundred thousand dollars. That had been one of the causes of friction between him and their father. Recently, the man to whom he owed the vast sum of money had threatened his life. Francesca had borrowed fifty thousand dollars from Hart to pay him partially back, and Hart had called on the creditor as well, to make it clear that Evan's life would not be forfeit for his debts. Since then, there had been no more threats and no more assaults. But on several occasions in the past Evan had lapsed into his old habit of gambling. Francesca was thrilled that he had managed thus far to stay away from the nightclubs. "That is wonderful," she said. "And there is no temptation?"

He gave her a dark look. "There is always temptation, Fran. I will be tempted until my dying day." Then he lightened. "But the countess is keeping me quite busy and very distracted."

An image of the radiant, auburn-haired widow came to mind. "Has it become serious?" Francesca asked lightly. She happened to like the flamboyant countess, but she did not quite trust her. Bartolla Benevente had once meddled in her private affairs when she had been infatuated with Rick Bragg.

Evan hesitated, running his hand through his dark hair, and paced over to the wall of windows, which looked out onto Madison Avenue. Francesca followed him. Below, the street was filled with carriages and trolleys; the city was doing business in full swing. Pedestrians — mostly darkly clad gentlemen — hurried up and down the street. She suddenly thought about Hart and the evening ahead and she smiled.

Then she thought about Daisy and she frowned, her heart skipping with fear.

"I don't know," Evan finally said, facing Francesca directly. "I am in love, but . . . I have been in love before."

How mature his assessment was. Francesca was impressed. "Yes, you have. And you do gravitate to the Bartolla Beneventes of this world."

He smiled a little at that. "Yes, I do. She would make a good wife."

"I doubt she wishes to wed a law clerk."

"Yes, I agree, and I have thought about that. She urges me frequently to make up with Father."

Francesca met his gaze and touched his arm. "You do what you need to do, Evan. I am very proud of you."

He shook his head, his expression self-deprecating. "And how are you? You seem radiant, Francesca, but then I look into your eyes and I see that you are worried. Is everything all right?"

Now it was Francesca who hesitated. It

crossed her mind to tell Evan about the awful conversation with Daisy, but she had no wish to dwell on the painful subject. "I am on another case," she said, an attempt to distract herself. Then she gave up. "I ran into Daisy a few hours ago."

Evan started. "Daisy? You mean that lovely creature whom Hart . . . you mean —" he coughed "— Hart's, er, Daisy Jones?"

Francesca hugged herself. "I know that he was keeping her as a mistress, Evan. You need not be discreet with me."

Evan stared, his forehead creased. "Fran, it is over?" Doubt filled his tone.

She knew she should not have raised the subject. "He broke it off with her when I accepted his proposal."

Evan spoke with care. "What I love most about you is your loyalty and trust."

"What does that mean?" she asked with dread.

"Fran, I don't know how to say this, but he keeps her still!"

She stiffened. "If you mean she continues to live in his house, the house he bought for her, I know that. He promised her six months and will live up to that agreement. But he stopped seeing her the day I accepted his proposal. I happen to know that for a fact — I was spying on him with Daisy when he told her he would be faithful, Evan. And Daisy even admitted he no longer sees her now that he is engaged."

Evan laughed, visibly relieved. "I am so pleased! I did not know." Then he sobered. "But Fran, everyone thinks she remains his mistress. It is unwise for him to allow her to live in that house."

Francesca stared. "Do you mean that society assumes Calder has a mistress, in spite of his engagement to me?" she cried in dismay.

"Yes, I do."

She gaped, and then she was furious. "But it's not true! Is that really what everyone says?"

He sighed and took her hand. "I'm afraid that it is the obvious conclusion to be drawn. And why is Hart being so honorable with such a woman?"

She pulled free. "He is quite noble, Evan, I have learned that in the few months since we met. He gave his word and he is keeping it." Now she really began to worry. "If Father learns of this, we are through! He dislikes the match enough as it is."

"I agree with you," Evan said. Then, ruefully, he added, "I am sorry to be the one to burst your bubble, Fran."

She walked away, still angry but also

somewhat mortified. "They are all gossips and hypocrites," she huffed.

"Many of them are. Is that why you look so worried? Because Daisy still resides in that house?"

She slowly faced him and did not speak.

He stared for a long moment. "Francesca?"

"I am such a fool," she whispered. And she felt tearful again. "I think I have fallen in love with Hart, Evan. What will I do?"

He quickly came forward, taking her hands. "But that is wonderful. You will marry for love! As you, of all people, should, Fran. And Hart — well —" he smiled "— I think he has finally found his match."

She pursed her lips and it was a moment before she could speak. "Even if I am his match intellectually, I am not half as lovely as Daisy or the other women he has been with."

He was incredulous. "Is that what is bothering you?"

"Yes . . . no. I am in love with a dissolute man, Evan. How will I manage to avoid a broken heart?"

Evan was silent for a moment. Then he put his arm around her and guided her to the sofa, where they both sat. "Well, if anyone can answer this question, I suppose it is me. I certainly qualify, do I not?"

She knew that he referred to his own womanizing ways. She nodded.

"I won't lie to you, Fran. You may be in for heartbreak and sorrow. But on the other hand, there is a saying, and it is said for a reason. Every dog has its day. Hart would not be the first rake to be reformed by a good woman."

For a long moment she stared, terribly desperate for reassurance. "What do you really think?" she finally asked.

He was grim. "I like Hart. I think he is very fond of you. But . . . he is the most jaded man in town. I can't help but worry about the future — the way that Father does."

She nodded, hating what he had said.

He said, "If you break this off, though, you will never know what might have been."

Francesca looked at him. "I don't want to break anything off."

"Then don't. Give him the benefit of the doubt. So far he has treated you with the utmost respect."

That was true. She nodded, feeling a bit better. "And he has never even considered marrying anyone until he met me," she added.

"That is true, and it does speak volumes."

Evan smiled again and stood. "I have to get back to work. Is that why you called?" He became teasing. "To ask your black-sheep older brother for his questionable advice?"

She also rose, relieved to change the subject. "Actually, no. I came to tell you about the case I am on, because I am just a bit worried about Maggie."

His reaction was instantaneous. "Is Maggie in danger? Are the children in danger?" he demanded.

Francesca was so surprised by his vehement tone that she blinked. "I don't know. I hope not. Have you read about the Slasher, Evan?"

His eyes widened impossibly. "Damn it, Francesca, get to the point! Is Maggie in any way involved with the Slasher?"

She touched him. "Calm down. She is not involved with the Slasher. There was a third victim on Monday, and she died. She also lived two doors from Maggie. I merely want Maggie to be cautious. I suggested that she and the children stay with us next Monday, as we suspect the Slasher will adhere to his pattern and strike again then."

Evan was quite pale. Then he said grimly, "I hate the circumstances she lives in! How can she raise those children in such a hovel? Before I walked out on my fortune, I had wanted to get her and the children situated in a better area. But it was not my place and she is so proud, I knew she would refuse. Now I have no funds. Francesca, it is simply intolerable for her to live in that slum." His blue eyes blazed.

His passionate outburst amazed her. "Evan, I know you are fond of the Kennedy children, but is there something more? Are . . . are you more than fond of Maggie herself?" Francesca heard herself boldly ask, in real confusion.

And he was clearly startled. He backed up. "*What?* I mean, of course I am fond of Mrs. Kennedy. How could I not be? She is a wonderful woman, so kind, so compassionate, so caring. And my God, she has raised those children on her own, working herself almost to death to give them a good home. But what, exactly, are you suggesting?" His disbelief grew. "Surely you are not suggesting some kind of romantic attachment on my part?"

"I don't know," Francesca said carefully.

He laughed in disbelief and walked away, then began to pace in consternation.

Francesca watched him carefully. Was it possible that Evan did have a romantic attachment but that he refused to admit it, even to himself?

He turned. "I want her to move uptown, now. I will speak with Mother and make certain there is no issue."

Francesca felt certain that Evan cared far more than he was admitting. But he was also very involved with the countess, so she did not know what to really think. "She is proud, as you have said. She dislikes charity, which we both know. She isn't even certain she will move uptown on Monday, Evan. I doubt she will pack up and go today."

He glared. "Yes she will," he said. "I am taking the afternoon off — to hell with everything. She will not refuse me — you watch and see."

Francesca began to smile. It had become clear which way the wind blew. Carefully she hid her smile and her satisfaction as she watched her brother storm from the room.

Somehow, mostly through tearful pleading, she had gained permission from her supervisor to leave work an hour early. All day, Gwen had thought about little other than her daughter as she poured tallow into mold after mold. She had not wanted Bridget to miss another day of school, so she had dropped her there that morning. Within five minutes of leaving her daughter on the public building's front steps, she had begun to worry.

A killer was on the loose. He was in their neighborhood. Bridget's school was only a few blocks from where the killer had last struck. Would Bridget be safe in school? Gwen thought so. But she did not want her daughter setting one foot out on the street by herself — not after school, not before school, not ever. If anything happened to her daughter, she would die. Bridget was her life.

Standing in the aisle of the horse-drawn omnibus, Gwen clung to the safety strap, surrounded by strangers. Bridget had already walked home from school and she prayed that she was safe. Maybe they shouldn't have left their home in Ireland. With everything that had happened in the month and a half since their arrival in America, Ireland seemed far safer than New York City, which had become cold and lonely, a dark and threatening place.

She bit her lip so she would not cry. There was no going back and she knew it. They were trapped here, in the merciless city, trapped in poverty, hopelessness and, now, real danger.

Briefly she closed her eyes as she swayed in tandem to the rocking omnibus. Briefly, she saw the vast, manicured green lawns that swept up to the imposing, stone-gray palatial residence where she had once been employed. For one moment, it was as if she stood at the foot of the long, winding, graveled driveway, watching the gardeners tend the various blooms. And in that moment, she watched the master of the house appear on the wide, flat front steps, a tall, dark man in a riding coat, breeches and high boots — a handsome man who had never smiled in the entire first year she had worked there.

Her heart still ached with the memories and it was an ache that would never go away.

Gwen inhaled hard, forcing the past far away, and that was when she felt eyes boring into her back.

She straightened, her grip on the safety strap tightening as the bus lurched to a stop to discharge a passenger. The feeling of being watched did not disappear. It became hard to breathe. Very slowly, she turned around.

But the men seated behind her on the crowded bus were reading dailies. She looked down the aisle at the other standing passengers. No one was looking her way, no one at all. The back doors swung closed and the omnibus lurched forward.

Glancing wildly around, she thought, *I*

must be losing my mind.

On the sidewalk, he watched the bus disappearing.

CHAPTER FIVE

Wednesday, April 23, 1902 5:00 p.m.

Francesca smiled as her cab halted in front of the building where Gwen O'Neil lived. Bragg's black roadster was parked on the street, a conspicuous sight amidst the drays and wagons on the block. Bragg stood leaning against the hood, his hands in the pockets of his brown wool suit jacket, appearing thoughtful.

As the bay in the traces lowered his head, the driver turned around and opened the small window behind his back. The front seat was elevated and he smiled down at her. "Twenty cents, miss."

Francesca handed him twenty-five. She reached for the door but Bragg was already opening it. "Am I late?" she asked, unable to help being cheerful. They were working together again. She and Bragg made a fine investigative team — they had the track record to prove it — and now, why, they

110

would solve this case in no time.

He smiled back at her. "I only just arrived." He helped her to the street. Francesca regarded him closely and saw that the dark cloud he had been under that morning had lifted. She was relieved. She felt certain it was because Leigh Anne had gone home from the hospital.

As they entered the building, he asked, "You look pleased. What did you learn today? I take it there must be something new."

"I think my brother has strong feelings for Maggie Kennedy." The words just tumbled out.

He stopped and looked at her.

"I am not playing matchmaker," she said defensively. Then she sighed. "And I know that heirs do not marry seamstresses. Still, I am certain he cares quite a bit for her."

"Try not to get involved," he said mildly. He gestured for her to precede him up the narrow stairs.

"Is that all you have to say?" she cried. "You have seen them together. What do you think?"

"He is not currently an heir," he said, pausing on the second-floor landing.

She met his gaze and their glances held. Well, that was to the point. Then she forced herself to stop thinking about her brother and Maggie. "Shall I brief you before we go inside?"

He nodded. "Please."

She quickly told him all that she had learned from Francis O'Leary, including the dream she had had and her uncertainty over whether or not the Slasher had called her a faithless bitch.

Bragg leaned against the wall, reflective.

"I would tend to believe that it was just a dream, as there does not seem to be anything faithless about her," Francesca said.

"You are supposing that he knew her and deliberately chose her as his victim. He might have a vendetta against all young, pretty women, Francesca, based on some experience he has had with one particular woman. He might only vaguely know his victims and they might not know him at all."

"I have also thought of that. It would be helpful if the killer knew his victims and chose them deliberately." She was grim. "If he randomly attacks women, how will we ever find him?"

"I have assigned extra men to patrol this ward. I have expanded the two square blocks in which all the victims were found to six square blocks."

"That is a good idea, but that will not

change the fact that we need to knock on doors. Someone must have seen someone suspicious lurking about last Monday near here."

"I hope so," he said. "This case will involve a lot of legwork."

That was her cue. She smiled at him. "And what should we do about Francis O'Leary's missing husband?"

He smiled in return. "Find him?"

"I was hoping you would say that!" she cried. "Of course, that will involve even more legwork and we may never locate him. He could be dead, for all we know."

"When you look at the current case file, you will see that Newman began a preliminary search for Thomas O'Leary. He interviewed his friends, co-workers and employer. No one had any idea that he would abruptly walk out on his wife or his life. I should not be surprised if we learned he was dead — or if we never learned where he went and where he is now."

She agreed wholeheartedly. "Rick, why would a man who abandons his wife come back to assault her, and then assault a similar woman before murdering Margaret Cooper? I should love to interview O'Leary, but he is not high on my list of suspects."

With some fond amusement, he said,

"And is there a list of suspects?"

She rolled her eyes. "It is a list of zero."

He laughed. Then, "I am truly pleased to be on another case with you, Francesca."

"So am I," she said with a grin. "Perhaps Joel has discovered something useful. So, is Leigh Anne home? The girls must be ecstatic."

His smile vanished. "She is undoubtedly walking through the front door as we speak." The moment he spoke, he grimaced, clearly displeased with his choice of words. He knocked abruptly on Gwen O'Neil's door.

She was stunned. What was this? Why wasn't Bragg with her? Why wasn't he ecstatic? "Perhaps you should be home as well. I can interview Bridget by myself, Rick, and relay all the pertinent information to you later."

Not turning, he knocked again. "She is aware of my schedule," he said.

There was no mistaking the tense note in his tone or the rigidity in his back. She laid her hand on his shoulder. "Is everything all right?" she asked carefully, almost wishing she had not brought up this obviously painful topic.

He glanced sidelong at her. "Yes."

Francesca did not know what to think, but clearly, Bragg did not wish to discuss his wife. She knew she must respect his wish for privacy, but what had happened? Everything was *not* all right, any fool could discern that. Then she realized there was still no answer to the knock.

"No one is home. We will wait," Bragg said flatly.

Rather relieved to be distracted from Bragg's personal life, Francesca stepped past him and rapped smartly on the door. "Mrs. O'Neil?" she called. "Bridget? It is I, Francesca Cahill."

Bragg smiled a little at her. "You remain the terrier with the bone. No one is home, Francesca."

She started to try again, when the door suddenly opened and Bridget appeared there, white-faced and shaken. There was no mistaking her fear. "My mum's not home yet," she whispered.

"We have scared you!" Francesca cried, putting her arm around the pretty red-haired child. "I am so sorry!"

Bridget's eyes filled with tears. "I thought it might be the Slasher."

"You are right to exercise caution," Bragg said as they stepped inside.

"The Slasher does not knock," Francesca told her, guiding her to the table. Then she realized that they did not know that, not at all, as they did not know how he got into the first two women's flats. Perhaps he *had* knocked on Margaret Cooper's door, only to con his way inside. She glanced at Bragg and clearly, he was reading her mind. "Did you go to school today?" she asked.

Bridget nodded, still trembling. "I'm not coughing today."

"That's wonderful. Bridget, can we ask you some questions?"

The small red-haired child stared anxiously, even suspiciously, at her. "What kind of questions?"

"You know that Mr. Bragg is the police commissioner?"

Bridget nodded, glancing his way.

"We are trying to find the man who murdered Margaret Cooper," Francesca said.

"I know," Bridget returned. And then tears filled her eyes. "Why did we have to come here? I hate America!"

Francesca shared a glance with Bragg and sat down beside her, taking her small hands in hers. "I know how hard this must be for you, leaving your home behind. But one day, this will be your home, too."

"It will never be my home. I hate it here! I wish we could go home, but we can't, I know that." She wiped her eyes with anger.

The reason why the O'Neils could not

return to Ireland was not her concern and had nothing to do with the case. But Francesca was curious, and past investigations had taught her never to leave any stone unturned. Before she could get the words out, Bragg said, "Why can't you return to Ireland, Bridget?"

Bridget looked at him. "Because Papa hates us."

Francesca's eyebrows lifted and bells shrieked alarmingly in her mind. "I'm sure your father doesn't hate you," she said.

Bridget crossed her arms over her chest and pursed her mouth hard together.

"Why would your father hate you?" Bragg asked quietly.

She shrugged, looking away, clearly determined not to respond.

"Where is your father?" Francesca tried.

Bridget glanced sullenly at her. "In jail."

Francesca bit her lip and quickly exchanged a glance with Bragg.

"Is he in a prison in Ireland? Or is he in the city?" Bragg asked quietly.

"He's in Limerick."

Francesca was disappointed. Briefly, she thought they might have had a lead.

Then Bridget started to cry. "He's still supposed to be there. But today, after school, I thought I saw him across the street!"

Francesca stood, staring at Bragg, who stared back. "Darling," she said, clasping Bridget's shoulder, "you think your father is here, in the city?"

"I swear I saw him!" Bridget was in tears. "But if Mama finds out, she will be more afraid than she is now!"

Francesca knelt before the child, clasping both of her hands. "Why do you think your father hates you? Why was he in jail? And why would your mother be afraid if your father were here in the city?"

She bit her lip. Finally she whispered, "Mama says I am not allowed to speak of it."

"This is a police matter," Francesca said gently. "You cannot withhold information from the police. It is against the law."

"I can go to jail?" she gasped.

"No one is sending you to jail," Francesca said firmly. "But surely you wish to obey the law?"

Bridget nodded glumly. Then, in a rush, she spoke. "Papa tried to murder Lord Randolph!"

Francesca stood. She didn't have to ask. Bragg said, "Who is Lord Randolph?"

Bridget covered her face in her hands.

118

"The man Mama loves."

As he took the steps in the narrow stairwell two at a time, Evan Cahill was well aware that his heart was racing. He could not shake the conversation he had just had with Francesca from his mind. But his leaping pulse had nothing to do with romantic matters. He felt sure of it. He was very fond of Maggie and the children, but his adrenaline was the result of fear and determination, nothing more.

Still, he had not visited her and the children in some time and he was eager to see them all. He was equally aware of that.

He paused before her door, noticing that it was freshly painted a cheerful shade of blue. As he finger-combed some pieces of hair back into place, he wondered if she had painted the door herself. He hoped that Joel had done it for her. She worked herself to the bone as it was. The last time he had been there, the brown paint on the door had been flaking and peeling away from the wood.

He straightened his tie and knocked. As he waited for a response, his heart tightened unmistakably, and then he heard Maggie's voice on the other side of the door. He felt himself smile.

"Paddy, stop. You know we do not open doors until we know who is on the other side," she scolded.

Paddy was five and a mischievous handful. He looked just like Maggie, except that his red hair was far brighter. "It's Joel," Paddy cried in protest.

"Probably," she said. "Who is it?" she then called.

He felt his smile increasing. "Evan Cahill." An image of her pretty blue eyes filled his mind and he could imagine Paddy pressed against her skirts.

And he felt her surprise and could almost see her hesitate. A moment later the door opened and she stood there in a simple dove-gray skirt and white shirtwaist, her hair swept back into a bun, her eyes wide with surprise. She appeared breathless.

"Hello," he said. And even as distressed as he was with the circumstance of the Slasher striking two doors down, he held a paper bag filled with cakes and cookies in his arms. He knew Maggie would refuse a sack of groceries.

Her mouth trembled. "Hello, Mr. Cahill. I . . . I'm sorry, we were not expecting company. The flat is a mess!" And as she spoke, Paddy cried out in delight and tackled him about the knees, hugging him there.

"Mrs. Kennedy, please do not stand on formality with me. I was in the neighborhood and I thought to bring the children some treats." He made no move to step inside but he could see from the corner of his eye that the flat was as clean as a whistle and as tidy as always. He did not know how she fed and housed her four children so properly. His admiration for her knew no bounds. "Paddy, my boy, if you do not loosen up I may keel over." He was joking and he winked at Maggie.

But she did not smile now. "Please, come in," she whispered nervously.

As he did, Mathew whooped and barreled over to hug him, too. Evan set the bag down on the kitchen table, draped in a blue-check tablecloth, and he slapped the seven-year-old on the back. "How are you, buddy?" he asked with a grin.

"Great," Mathew grinned. "I got an *A* in arithmetic!"

"That's wonderful," Evan said, meaning it and feeling oddly proud of the child. "And what grades did you receive in reading and writing?"

"*Bs,*" Mathew said earnestly, eyes wide. Like Joel, he had midnight-black hair and the dark eyes to match.

"Good job," Evan said softly, pulling him close for a moment. Then he felt Maggie come to stand behind him and his entire body tensed. Slowly, he released the boy and turned, uncertain now of why he reacted to her so. He felt somewhat breathless.

"I'll put up some tea. Lizzie just went to sleep and Joel is out," Maggie said, her eyes wide and riveted on him.

He gave up. There was something so pretty about her, and why deny it? That meant nothing, of course, as he was very involved with Bartolla, whom he would probably one day marry. And Bartolla was the kind of woman he was insanely attracted to — gorgeous, bold and far from innocent. But Maggie was lovely and he had always had an eye for attractive women, so of course he would notice her. But there was something else about her, something he could not put his finger on. In a way, she was like a ray of the purest light.

However, Maggie and he were from different worlds. They both knew it. The gulf of class and economy that separated them was as wide as the Atlantic Ocean. So even if Francesca was right — which she was not — any feelings on his part, other than the noble ones of admiration, respect and friendship, were entirely inappropriate.

"Thank you," he said very quietly. He was uncharacteristically shaken.

"Joel and your sister are on a case," Maggie said, hovering over the kettle she had just set to boil.

He stared for a moment at her slim back. Most women who had had four children had long since gone to fat. Maggie remained slender. Not for the first time, he thought her a touch too thin. But then, he knew her rather well now and he knew she gave the best of everything, including their meals, to her children. He saw a pot on the stove. Now curious, he wandered over.

She whirled and they were face-to-face, mere inches separating them, her back to the stove.

For one moment, he did not move, impossibly aware of her, realizing that she wore the faintest scent, floral and sweet. Then he stepped aside. "I beg your pardon," he murmured, glancing into the pot. She was making a stew, a few potatoes and onions simmering with some bones. There was no meat to be seen.

Maggie had scurried to the kitchen table and grasped the back of a chair. "Have you had supper?" she said very breathlessly. "I mean, we do not have much, but you are welcome to dine with us."

He knew he had made her nervous and he hated that she was so skittish around him. Maybe she sensed his admiration could have been something more, if the circumstances had been different. Suddenly, he wished that the circumstances *were* different.

Confusion stunned him.

"Mr. Cahill?" she asked.

He leaped away from the stove, smiling. But he remained shaken. "I'd like to take you and the children to supper," he said.

Her eyes widened.

Now that he had spoken, he liked the idea. He'd put a huge meal into them all.

"You want to take us to supper? You mean, to a restaurant?"

"Yes, that is what I mean. We should wait for Joel," he decided.

Maggie hugged herself. "I can't accept."

His smile vanished. "Mag— Mrs. Kennedy, please. I'm hungry, and not in the mood for soup. A nice beef roast would do." He smiled encouragingly now and could almost feel her mouth water.

"Surely you did not come all this way to take my family to dinner?"

He became sober. "Francesca told me

124

about your neighbor." Then he glanced at the children. "I'd like to find a private moment to discuss this with you."

She bit her lip, also glancing at the two boys, who were playing with some toy soldiers, all in Confederate gray. "It is very unsettling," she whispered.

He walked directly to her and took her hand. He also lowered his voice. "Two doors down, Maggie? It's not acceptable. I must insist that you take my sister up on her offer."

A mulish expression appeared on Maggie's face. "I know that Francesca means well, as do you, but we are not a case for charity." Her tone rose with some anger.

And he was as angry. Still, he fought to keep his voice down. "This is not about charity. This is about the safety of your children and your own safety, too."

"I have thought about it. On Monday we will stay with my brother-in-law."

He started, surprised. And while he would prefer her to be safe and sound in the Cahill home uptown, this was better than nothing. "Where does he live?"

"A bit farther uptown, right on the East River at Twentieth Street. He won't mind. Since my husband died, he is the only family we have here in the city. He's a good man and very fond of the children," she added.

"You would be safer uptown," he said, and by that he meant Fifth Avenue and Sixty-first Street where the Cahill mansion and his own home, now abandoned, were.

"I heard that all of the victims lived between Tenth and Twelfth Streets. My brother-in-law's flat is far from this vicinity," she said stubbornly.

He sighed. "I can hardly twist your arm."

"No, you cannot." And then she softened. "Do not misunderstand. I truly appreciate your concern. Really."

"I will surrender — but only if you agree to have supper with me," he said. The moment he realized how flirtatious his tone had become, he tensed. "With the children," he added quickly.

She stared. "I . . . I don't know," she said helplessly.

He had been chasing and seducing women his entire adult life. Taking her hand was sheer instinct. "It's only supper, Mrs. Kennedy. One you and your children shall thoroughly enjoy." The same instinct widened his smile and intensified his persuasive stare.

Her cheeks turning red, she tore her glance away. "While we wait for Joel," she

126

said, low, "I'd like to tidy up the children."

He had won. Grinning, he realized he held her hand and almost lifted it to his lips. Instead, he released it. "I'll go see if I can find Joel," he said, still smiling.

Maggie nodded, slipped past him and called for the two boys.

"Can I give you a lift home?" Bragg asked as they paused before his motorcar. Night had fallen, a pleasant warm evening filled with winking stars and the remnants of last night's full moon.

"Actually, I have to stop at Sarah's." Her friend, the artist Sarah Channing, had sent a note that morning asking Francesca to come by at her earliest convenience.

"I'll drop you there, then," Bragg said with a smile. He walked around the car and held open the passenger door for her.

Francesca got in, picking up the spare pair of goggles. He closed the door, cranked the motor and then got in beside her. Their interview of Bridget had not produced any further clues. The child had not seen or heard anything Monday afternoon, which was frankly a blessing. They did not need Bridget to have any knowledge of the murder that might put her in danger. Gwen had arrived home shortly after their talk with her daughter.

As Bragg turned onto Tenth Street, she turned toward him. "I feel sorry for Gwen O'Neil."

"Why? Because she fell foolishly in love with a man she should have never looked twice at?"

They had spoken with Gwen, as well. "Lord Randolph was her employer! Any attraction on his part was as faulty as any on hers. But now I know why she does not have references," she said. Still, it had been apparent from Gwen's expression and tone that she had fallen in love with the Irish aristocrat and that she loved him still. Francesca felt certain that he was a cad. She had quickly sensed that they had been lovers. No wonder her husband, David Hanrahan, had tried to kill Randolph. Gwen had been using her maiden name since leaving her husband.

But was he still incarcerated in Limerick, or was he now in the city? If he had arrived in New York, then he was on her exceedingly short list of suspects.

"Why are you concerned about her lack of references?"

"I intend to find her better employment, as a lady's maid," she said.

Bragg smiled. "Will you become involved

with each victim or near victim on every single case we work on?"

She faced him fully and his smile faded. Softly, she said, "You are implying that there will be more cases for us, Rick."

He finally glanced at her. "I doubt you will give up your newfound profession. And while I am currently police commissioner, I will not turn my back on you should you ever need my aid."

Francesca stared, touched. But what was he implying? "You sound as if you are not certain of your future."

"I'm not," he said. "You are aware of the politics surrounding my job. I may be out of my position far sooner than I would choose, before I can really make the changes this department needs."

Francesca forgot about their investigation for a moment. The press had begun to note the increase in activity of the city's saloons and so-called hotels on Sundays. One of the hottest debates in the city since Bragg's appointment was whether or not to enforce the blue laws against serving liquor on the Sabbath. That issue was constantly fueled by the clergy and the goo-goos — the good government reform movement. Early in his term Bragg had closed a number of establishments violating those laws; recently, the police department seemed to be looking the other way at those infractions. "Is it true? Have the police begun to ignore the Sunday saloon openings?"

He sighed heavily. "We have been selectively enforcing the law, Francesca, and only closing the worst offenders. Low asked me to ease up."

She gripped his arm. "Why?"

He glanced at her. "The mayor is worried about reelection, as well he should be. Every time we close a saloon on Sunday, he loses votes to Tammany Hall. Which is the greater goal? Reforming the corrupt police or reelecting a great reform mayor?"

"But he appointed you to uphold the law!" she cried, frustrated for the dilemma in which he found himself.

"Yes, he did. But there is so much of an outcry by the working community against the closings that he has asked me to exercise the arm of the law with caution and care." He was grim. "I am torn, Francesca. If I do my job as I wish to do, Low will lose the next election. It has become very clear."

"And you are loyal to Low, instead of to the people who believe in you and the cause of reform?" She felt despair, for she was one of those people who so believed in the law, the cause of reform — and in him.

"I am focusing on the corruption within the department now. I have an internal investigation in progress. When it is concluded, a number of officers will be dishonorably discharged."

She blinked. Then, filled with admiration for him, she touched his arm. "I am proud of you," she said.

He smiled at her then.

Traffic had become heavy as they had turned onto Fourth Avenue, where a huge excavation was in process for the new railroad line that would terminate in the Grand Central Station. A trolley crept slowly forward just ahead of them, while several carriages and a hansom penned them in. Francesca suddenly realized that Bragg's home wasn't far from where they now waited, ensnarled in traffic, and that his wife had come home as scheduled but he was not there to greet her.

She looked at him. "Please, Rick. You should not be driving me all the way across town. You should be at home with Leigh Anne."

His jaw tightened. It was a moment before he spoke. "You will never catch a hansom at this hour. I am happy to drive you to the Channings and I am sure they will send you home in one of their coaches."

His reply was not satisfactory. "I know you well, Rick. Why didn't you take Leigh Anne home from the hospital? I am starting to think that you are avoiding going home." She stared at his handsome profile, which now seemed cast in stone.

He stared at the back of the trolley and finally said, "You are right."

She was stunned. "I am right?"

He sighed and, not looking at her, replied, "I am avoiding going home."

"What?"

He was grim. "Leigh Anne did not want to leave the hospital today."

Francesca blinked. "She did not want to come home?" But everyone wanted to leave the hospital as soon as they could!

"I don't blame her." And finally he glanced at her, his eyes filled with anger.

"What does that mean? And why didn't she want to leave the hospital?"

The trolley moved. Bragg took a moment to shift gears and the Daimler crept forward. "She didn't want to come home because I am there."

"What?" That was nonsense, Francesca was certain.

He faced her, his eyes wide with anger and anguish. "Cease all pretense, Francesca. We both know that this is entirely my fault."

"What are you talking about?" she cried.

"The accident," he spat.

"The accident?" She was thoroughly bewildered. "You mean, Leigh Anne's accident?"

"Yes, of course, her accident, what other accident would I mean?"

She could only stare.

"She would not be in this predicament — a cripple for life — if not for me." He slammed his hands on the wheel.

Francesca jumped in her seat. Then she seized his wrist. "Dear God! You had nothing to do with the accident. It was just that — an accident. You speak as if you were driving that runaway coach that ran her down!"

"I might as well have been the driver," he said savagely.

"Why are you doing this? Why are you blaming yourself?" she gasped, horrified.

"Because I was trying to drive her away, to drive her from the house, to drive her away from me!" He halted the car so abruptly she almost slammed into the dashboard. "A witness saw the entire thing. Apparently she was standing in front of a shop, crying. She was so distraught she never saw or heard the runaway carriage until it was too late. And we both know why she was crying," he added darkly.

A horn blared behind them. Francesca hardly heard. "Even if she was crying, you do not know why. But to say that you made her cry and then to conclude that makes you responsible for the accident, why, that is absurd."

"I wished her dead," he said suddenly, his tone raw. "I did, Francesca, I did, and my wish was almost granted."

The horn blared repeatedly now.

Francesca took his face in her hands and forced him to look at her. "It doesn't matter what you wished. It doesn't matter how angry you were with her. You have every right to your feelings. But your feelings then do not make you responsible for that accident. They do not! You must stop blaming yourself."

"I can't," he whispered. "And do you know what makes matters even worse?"

She swallowed, shaking her head, and felt tears well in her eyes.

He inhaled harshly. "What makes matters even worse is that finally, too late, I realize I still love her."

CHAPTER SIX

Wednesday, April 23, 1902 6:00 p.m.
The Channing home stood alone on a large lot, a huge affair of eclectic design. Three towers jutted out from the roof, and from the oddly placed parapets and balconies, gargoyles frowned viciously down. The mansion was partly gothic, partly neoclassic, and Francesca could never quite decide why it had been so designed. But the entire Channing family was eccentric, which might explain it. Sarah's now-deceased father had studded the interior walls with animal heads and the floors with exotic skins, despite the gilded walls and European furniture, as he had been an avid trophy hunter. Mrs. Channing stood out from society for her very guileless and equally foolish manner, although she always meant well. Sarah, who had once, briefly, been engaged to Francesca's brother, was renowned as a recluse. She was also a brilliant artist.

135

Having thanked Bragg for the ride, she was let inside the Channing home. Sarah materialized almost instantly.

"Francesca!" she cried in delight.

Francesca was as pleased to see the young woman who had become one of her best friends. Sarah was truly remarkable — in a way, she and Francesca were kindred souls. Sarah's passion was her painting, and when she had been engaged to Evan, she had been miserable. Of course, the match, concocted by both families, had been truly ill conceived, as both parties had nothing in common. Sarah was small, plain and considered shy and timid, clearly not the kind of woman to catch Evan Cahill's eye. In fact, Sarah was thoroughly independent and unconventional. Unlike most young women of marriageable age, Sarah had no interest in shopping, dreaded social engagements and gave not one thought to romance or marriage. Her life was her art. Francesca empathized completely.

Now, Sarah had smudges of paint and charcoal on her face, hands and the bodice of her green dress. The moss-hued garment might have been flattering on another woman, but Sarah had olive in her complexion and her hair was chocolate brown, so that the gown washed her out. Francesca

136

had never, not even once, seen Sarah appropriately garbed. Sarah did not care what she wore and her choice of clothing — usually decided by her mother with the best of intentions — made that clear. The styles in her wardrobe, while expensive, overwhelmed her small stature and the colors usually dulled her coloring, her eyes and hair.

"I am so glad you could come by," Sarah cried breathlessly.

Francesca looped her arm in hers. "What has put that sparkle in your eye? I know it is not a man! Let me guess. Something to do with a painting?" she teased.

"Hurry with me," Sarah said with a grin. Her long, curly brown hair was pulled haphazardly back into a loose ponytail, and some paint had gotten into the stray curls around her small, heart-shaped face. Her big brown eyes, long-lashed and round, positively sparkled. The more time Francesca spent with her, the more she changed her initial opinion of Sarah. Sarah no longer seemed plain or timid at all. She was one of the most vibrant and interesting women Francesca had ever met.

"Are we going to your studio?" Francesca guessed as they hurried down a long corridor leading to the back of the house.

"Of course," Sarah said with a grin. The

door was open. The large room was filled with canvases, some finished, others in various stages of execution. Sarah favored portraits of women and children, although two landscapes were also present. She had clearly, at one time, been influenced by the romantics, and later by the impressionists. Her work now was bright and bold — she clearly adored color — but her strokes were far more realistic than one would expect. "I have finished your portrait," Sarah said, pausing before an easel that was draped with cloth.

Francesca's heart leaped with excitement. Hart had commissioned her portrait some time ago, when she had thought herself in love with Bragg. He had only done so because he had wanted to annoy her, and he had done just that. Francesca had no time for any sittings at the beginning, but as their relationship had changed, sitting for a portrait he wished to hang in his private rooms had become thoroughly exciting. A month ago he had asked Sarah to make the portrait a nude. Francesca had agreed, and every sitting had become exhilarating.

Now, on pins and needles, she asked, "How is it?" Shamelessly, she could not wait for Hart to hang her nude likeness in his rooms.

Sarah laughed with happiness. "Why don't you decide for yourself?" And she swept the cloth from the canvas.

Francesca started in surprise.

The naked woman who sat with her back to the viewer, looking over her shoulder, was stunning. Francesca knew she was no beauty, yet the woman in that portrait most definitely had her face. Her features were classic, her lips full, her nose tiny. But there was nothing ordinary about her face. Somehow, Sarah had made her captivating. Francesca simply gaped.

In the portrait, her gleaming, honey-colored hair was carefully coiffed, as if for a ball, and she wore a pearl choker about her throat. The fact that it was all she wore was infinitely seductive as well. Francesca realized her cheeks had grown warm. She finally found the courage to look at the rest of the portrait.

Her body was as alluring as her face. Francesca was amazed. The line of her back was long and elegant, but her buttocks were sensually full. The intriguing profile of one breast escaped her arm, and not far from where she sat, a red ball gown lay in a puddle of opulent fabric, clearly abandoned in haste.

The portrait was suggestive, terribly so.

Francesca tugged at her shirt collar. The humming became a drumming in her ears. Was that really how she looked? Was this what Hart saw when he looked at her? Surely Sarah, being so fond of her, had exaggerated all of her features.

"What do you think?" Sarah whispered.

Francesca bit her lip. She still could not quite speak. The portrait was an amazing feat — to take a sensible, professional woman like herself and put her features together in the manner that Sarah had. It was her face, but the expression did not belong to an innocent woman, or a skilled sleuth — it belonged to a passionate lover, a creature of the bedroom and the night.

"Don't you like it?" Sarah asked tersely now.

Francesca whirled. She thought she might be crimson. "I love it," she cried. "But Sarah, how did you do it? That's not me — yet it is! In that portrait, I am almost as alluring as Daisy."

Sarah smiled in relief. "For a moment, I thought you did not like it," she exclaimed. "And painting your likeness was easy enough. It's what I do," she added. "Do you think Hart will be pleased? Have I gone too far? The theme is frankly sensual. It might be too risqué, considering you will one day be his wife."

Francesca knew Hart would like the painting. But Daisy's image had loomed and her words echoed painfully.

You know his reputation — you know it is not false. Do you really think to keep his attention where it belongs — on you and only you?

"Francesca?" Sarah interrupted her terrible memory of that afternoon.

"It's not too risqué for Hart, I am quite certain."

There will be someone after you, Francesca. Sooner or later, his gaze will wander, his gaze and his interest, and we both know that when that happens, his promises will mean nothing.

"If you like it, and you feel certain that he will like it, why do you look so distressed?" Sarah askcd, plucking her sleeve. Her forehead was creased with worry. "You must be honest with me, Francesca."

She did not really hear Sarah. Instead, she stood at the glove counter in the Lord and Taylor store, facing Daisy, who was every bit as lovely and seductive as the woman in the portrait, but who, unlike the woman in the portrait, actually existed and had already warmed Hart's bed.

How could she compete with such a rival? And to make matters worse, there were hundreds of rivals just like Daisy Jones. The city was filled with lovely women with whom Hart had dallied. Her spirits, briefly so high, sank.

Francesca looked at Sarah. "If I really looked like that, then maybe I would have a chance," she said with some despair.

Sarah searched her gaze. "What are you speaking of? Of course you look like that. It is you that I painted, not some figment of my imagination. What do you mean, maybe you would have a chance?"

Francesca inhaled, the sound harsh, and looked at the portrait. In spite of her fear, she had to admire the painting and the woman in it and she felt that tingle of excitement in her veins. *Hart would like it, oh yes.* "Sarah, I am a sleuth, a woman of common sense, a woman with a business, a woman of intellect. I am hardly that seductive creature."

Sarah squared her shoulders and pursed her lips. "I beg to differ with you," she finally said.

"What?"

"When you sat for me, you were not the city's most infamous amateur sleuth. You were thinking about Hart, not some cold-blooded killer and all kinds of clues. And that was how you looked," she added stubbornly. "I worked very hard to capture your expression as precisely as I could."

"Really?" She so wanted to believe Sarah.

"You do not see yourself clearly, Francesca, perhaps because Hart has awakened a side of you that you are unfamiliar with. I have portrayed that side — that seductive creature you have spoken of — and because it is so new to you, you simply fail to recognize it."

Francesca started. There was no question that Calder Hart had aroused her to a passion she had never before dreamed of. When she was in his arms, she quite frankly lost herself. There was no thinking, no present, no past, no future, there was only Hart's touch, his taste, his kiss and the side of heaven that awaited them both. What if Sarah was right? What if she did appear that passionate when the moment was right?

Francesca touched her throbbing temples. But whom was she fooling? She was an intellectual, not a seductress. She knew that she was the first sexually innocent woman Hart had ever pursued.

"What's wrong?" Sarah asked quickly.

Francesca sighed and walked over to the small table in one corner of the studio, sitting down. "I saw Daisy today."

"Oh." Sarah hurried to her and sat, taking

her hands. "Clearly she upset you."

Francesca nodded. "Very much. Sarah, I'm not sure what to do. Daisy pointed out that eventually Hart will lose interest in me and find someone else. She is right! Isn't she? I mean, he has had so many lovers, all far more intriguing than myself. I am so happy right now and simply could not bear his straying."

Sarah stared at her, wide-eyed. "I am not sure what to say," she began.

"There is nothing to say."

"No, there is plenty to say. First, Daisy has been jilted — and replaced by you. I know you like her, but I do not think an ex-mistress and a bride should speak at all."

Francesca almost smiled. "How conventional you sound."

"No, hear me out. Daisy would be very happy if Hart broke your engagement, as she could then warm his bed and receive more of his gifts. I doubt she wants to leave that house he bought for her. And didn't you tell me once that you thought she was falling in love with him herself? How she must envy you. Perhaps she even hates you."

Francesca was now wide-eyed. "Apparently I cannot see clearly, or think clearly, when it comes to my personal life."

"Who can?" Sarah smiled. "She cannot

wish you well. She might even think to cause trouble. And why else would she be so cruel? I would dismiss all that she has said. And you are more intriguing than Daisy Jones and all her ilk. The city is filled with beautiful women, but you are beautiful *and* clever *and* kind *and* brave! Hart is smitten. I can tell. For a man of his reputation, that speaks volumes."

Sarah is right, Francesca suddenly thought. She might not be quite as pretty as the others, but she had so much more to offer a man like Hart. She felt vastly better. "My brother advised me as you have." Then, "I knew when I agreed to marry him, it would not be easy to be with such a man."

"How is Evan?" Sarah asked with such a pleasant manner that it was clear she had no ill feelings at all for him or second thoughts about their failed engagement.

"He is fine. Apparently he spends most of his free time with Bartolla." The countess Benevente was Sarah's cousin and friend.

"I know. Bartolla speaks of him constantly." Sarah grinned. "I am happy for him. I am happy for them both." Her tone became brisk. "So? When do we unveil the portrait for Calder?"

Francesca hesitated, and perhaps it was her sensual side that Sarah had so skillfully

145

captured on her canvas that won. "Tomorrow?" she heard herself ask, her heart racing. And she recognized the growing heat in her body. It was explosive. *How would Hart react when he saw that incredible portrait?*

"I'll send him a note tonight," Sarah cried in delight.

Francesca leaped to her feet, wringing her hands, her courage suddenly vanishing. "God, what if he doesn't like it?" she cried. "Oh, I do hope I am not fooling myself."

Sarah ran to her. "Francesca, do not let that harlot Daisy interfere with your feelings for Hart. I sense she wishes to cause trouble for you both. Ignore her, please!"

Francesca nodded, but with the hour of the unveiling now approaching, she was too nervous for words.

"He loves you," Sarah said softly, smiling.

"He is fond of me," Francesca corrected, her mouth dry, her temples throbbing.

"Fond enough to want to marry you," Sarah said flatly. "That is very fond, indeed."

Francesca smiled at that. She turned her gaze upon her likeness, thinking about Hart gazing at it, too, and lost her ability to breathe. "I do have one request. You must promise me, Sarah."

"What is that?"

"I want to be here when you unveil it."

Sarah grinned. "Of course."

Francesca changed into an evening gown in record time. She had donned the new one, made by Maggie Kennedy, a turquoise silk. Grabbing her purse, she dashed toward the stairs, amazed that Calder had not yet arrived. She was about to descend when she saw Julia coming up.

She skidded, panting, to a stop.

Her mother frowned at her as she ascended to the landing where Francesca stood.

Francesca grimaced. She was in trouble now.

She had not spoken a single word to Julia since the prior evening when she had arrived late for the supper party — since Hart had used that foolish excuse that she might faint to take her from the party so that they could have a private moment together. When he had decided he should leave, preparing to make his excuses to her mother, Francesca had simply fled upstairs.

Dressed for supper in a dark red evening gown, rubies at her throat, Julia looked her up and down. "Calder just arrived. So has that little hoodlum, Joel Kennedy."

Francesca promptly forgot about the way she had avoided her mother last night. Had

147

Joel found a lead? Why else would he have come all the way uptown to see her? "Joel is here?" she asked, starting past her mother eagerly.

Julia detained her. "You aren't wearing any jewelry, Francesca." Her tone was brisk.

Francesca touched her throat and found it bare. She sighed, knowing full well that her lack of jewels was not the real issue. "I did not want to keep Hart waiting," she began.

"I have wanted to speak to you all day," Julia exclaimed. "But you were gone at the crack of dawn and arrived home just moments ago. You are on another investigation, aren't you?" Julia accused, her blue eyes darkening.

Francesca grimaced. "Mama," she began.

"Do not Mama me!"

"I guess I had better get a necklace and some earrings," Francesca cried, hoping to avoid a battle. There was no winning if she dared to take a direct stand against her mother.

Julia took her wrist. "Are you going to answer me?"

Francesca met her gaze. "Please don't worry. This case won't be dangerous, I assure you."

Julia cried out in dismay, turning pale.

"Mama, please consider that I have successfully solved several cases since the new year and I am in one entire piece," Francesca tried brightly. "And your dearest dream is coming true — soon I shall marry, and the best catch in town at that."

"You are barely in one piece! You have been held prisoner, you have been shot at, a knife has been held to your throat and you have been burned! You will wind up a corpse before a bride!"

Francesca paled. "Mama, that's a terrible thing to say."

Julia realized it, because she clapped her hand over her mouth, her eyes wide and shimmering with tears. "I love you so," she whispered. "And you terrify me with your reckless adventures. Why was there blood on your jacket and skirt last night? Why? And need I add that several of the ladies remarked on your appearance? The gossip at lunch today was simply delightful. Mrs. De Witt suggested that Hart would break off the engagement if you continue your sleuthing ways."

"Is it really my safety you are concerned about or is it my reputation — and yours?" Francesca said before she even thought about it.

Julia stiffened. "I demand an apology," she said.

"I'm sorry!" Francesca cried, meaning it. "That was a thoughtless thing to say. I know you fear for my welfare. But I also know you fear for my reputation."

"Your welfare is my primary concern. What mother is pleased when some murderous thug holds a knife to her daughter's throat?"

Francesca winced. That had happened on her last investigation into a child-prostitution ring. "That was a threat, Mama. He never meant to hurt me."

Julia made a desperate, scoffing sound. "And you think to console me with that interpretation?"

"Oh, Mama," Francesca whispered, wishing she could somehow soothe her mother's fears.

"Of course, when you marry Hart — if you live to do so — your reputation will hardly matter. No one will ever close their salon to you once you are his wife. But, Francesca, I truly fear that your wedding day may never come, not if you continue this frightening new inclination of yours."

Francesca inhaled and debated having it out with her mother. She debated telling her that sleuthing was no mere inclination or hobby, that she had found the profession she wished to practice for the rest of her life. Then she decided to postpone such a terrible confrontation. The time to tell her mother was after she was wed.

But her mind raced. Her father was as disapproving of her sleuthing as Julia was. It had become tiresome, not to mention difficult, working on each and every case while living in their home. And the way things were progressing, it would be a year before she married Hart and had the freedom to come and go as she pleased. She sighed.

Her life would be so much easier if she had her own flat. She was instantly excited at the idea. Her parents would not agree, of course, but they really could not prevent her from moving out if she decided to do so. The question was, did she dare?

"Francesca? I can see that you are concocting some scheme," Julia said sternly.

Francesca swiftly smiled. She would raise that issue at another time. "Mama, I promise to be careful but I cannot quit my investigation now. The police have asked me for their help, as I am somewhat personally involved in this latest crime."

Julia stared, her face tight. "And what crime is that and how are you personally involved?" She shuddered with dread as she spoke.

Francesca grimaced. "A woman was murdered. A woman who lives two doors from Maggie Kennedy. You know how fond of her I am. I don't like the fact that she lives so close to the crime scene. A killer is loose in her neighborhood, Mama . . ." She hesitated. "We think it is the Slasher."

Julia cried out.

Francesca took both of her hands. "I am working with Bragg again. I have the entire police force behind me. I won't get hurt. But that madman must be brought to justice before he takes another life!"

Julia erupted. "Now you are working with Rick Bragg again? And don't you care that his wife remains in the hospital? His wife, Francesca. W-I-F-E," she said, spelling out the four letters.

"This is not a romantic involvement," Francesca cried. "I am engaged to another man!"

"You were in love with Rick Bragg until a few weeks ago. I am no fool. I know very well that you accepted Hart on the rebound," she said firmly, turning away.

Francesca ran after her. "What are you going to do?"

Julia did not answer her directly. "You are late. Hart is waiting."

Francesca followed her downstairs, worried now.

"Does he know about this latest investigation of yours?" Julia asked, not glancing back, her hand on the gilded railing.

"Yes, he does," Francesca said.

"And he approves?"

"Hart has no wish to mold me into a stereotype," Francesca said as they reached the ground floor. "He will never put me in shackles and chains. You know he admires me for my courage and my intellect."

"I doubt he *approves*," Julia said.

Francesca now sighed. "I admit that it is more like he *tolerates* my penchant for sleuthing," she said. "But if it will make you feel better, I promise to let the police manage the bulk of the matter. I will limit my involvement to asking a few questions of Maggie and her neighbors." She knew she was pleading now.

Julia faced her and shook her head in exasperation. "I know you mean well, Francesca, but I also know that you will never bow out of anything that claims your interest. We will continue this discussion later, because Hart is waiting — as is that hoodlum."

Francesca did not move. "Joel doesn't pick purses anymore, Mama," she said, and then she cried, "What are you going to do?"

"I am going to put an end to this nonsense," Julia said flatly, and she walked away.

Francesca did not like the sound of that. She knew how much her marriage to Hart meant to her mother. She should have never mentioned that she was sleuthing once again with Bragg. Hurrying somewhat grimly through the marble-floored reception hall, she found Hart and Joel conversing in the gold salon. They stood before the fire that crackled below the marble mantel of the hearth. She skidded to a halt and they both turned at once.

She clung to the door, trying to catch her breath and her composure. Hart was a devastating sight in his white dinner coat and black evening trousers, a black bow tie at his throat. He was such a seductive man — his magnetism was simply inescapable. A slow smile spread across his face and his gaze slipped as slowly over her, from head to toe.

She wished she knew what plan Julia had up her sleeve.

"I am late," she gasped. "I am sorry!"

He strolled to her and pulled her close, whispering, his mouth on her ear, "I don't care how late you are as long as you are finally here with me."

She melted immediately, forgetting Joel was present, and could think of nothing but his large, strong hands on her waist, his firm lips on her ear, his musky scent and the cloak of male virility and power he had somehow enveloped her in. She drew back and their gazes touched. The expression on his face seemed oddly tender, though the gleam in his eyes was not. Her heart skipped.

"Sometimes you do say the most romantic things," she teased, but her heart beat like mad and she wished they were dining alone at his house, not at the Waldorf-Astoria. And then she thought about his ex-mistress and their conversation earlier.

Francesca stiffened. She did not want to worry about the veracity of Daisy's comments now.

"Is that what you consider romantic?" he asked with amusement, his grip on her waist tightening.

She met his gaze and could not manage a smile.

His smile vanished; his gaze became searching. "What is it?"

She wanted to blurt, Will you love me forever? But of course she did not, as love was not in the promise he had made to her. He had offered her friendship, respect, admiration and fidelity, but not love. Never love. He had made it clear that love was for

155

fools, and the one thing Hart was not was a foolish man. She swallowed hard. "Nothing," she managed to say, trying to pull away from him.

But he did not let her go. "Something is bothering you."

She bit her lip so hard that it hurt. "Mama and I had it out in the corridor upstairs. She wants to end my sleuthing once and for all, I think," she whispered, painfully aware that while she was telling him the truth, she was also lying to him. A part of her so wanted to tell him about the encounter with Daisy. But another part of her refused to do so — the proud, sensible part. Hart would not admire a jealous, insecure woman.

He stroked her cheek once as he released her. "Really?" There was vast skepticism in his tone. "And that is what is bothering you now?"

She wished he were not so astute. "No," she whispered roughly. Then she forced a smile. "I have so looked forward to this evening, Calder, please. I don't have to share my deepest darkest secrets with you, do I?"

He stared far too thoughtfully at her. It was a moment before he spoke. "Of course you don't, darling," he said, but there was something odd and clinical about his tone.

156

She shivered. He wasn't happy with her right now and she could sense it. And that was not how she wished to begin their precious evening alone.

Then his finger moved down her neck to linger about her collarbone. "I see that you rushed to dress tonight," he said flatly.

It was almost as if he was withdrawing from her. "Yes."

"And how is your latest case progressing?" he asked, clearly aware that her investigation was the cause of her tardiness.

"Well," she said with a genuine smile, "we have learned that it is the Slasher at work, Calder, and we must work frantically now to find him before he strikes again this coming Monday," she said eagerly.

He gave her a sidelong look, smiling very slightly.

And she knew that even though he said nothing, he was thinking about who "we" was. It was a moment before he tore his speculative gaze from hers. Looking reflective indeed, he put his hands in the pockets of his satin-trimmed trousers and strode slowly toward the fireplace.

Francesca felt that the evening was in a downward spiral. But before she could go over to him and make light of the fact that she was working with the police — and his arch rival — she saw Joel, standing not far from her. The boy was almost hopping from foot to foot, he was so eager to speak with her.

She had entirely forgotten that he was present. "Joel!" She rushed to him. "Joel, what have you found out?" she asked eagerly. "Did someone see a man leaving Margaret Cooper's?" How she hoped that was the case!

"Sorry," he said ruefully. "No one seems to have seen anything, Miz Cahill."

"Then why have you come uptown at this late hour?"

"It's Miz O'Neil. Bridget's mum."

Francesca started. "Has something happened? Bragg and I were with her only a few hours ago." Then she winced and glanced at Hart. But he merely smiled at her, his real feelings impossible to discern.

"I dunno. But I went to see Bridget, an' Miz O'Neil spent the entire time standin' in the kitchen, cryin' her eyes out. She's so scared!"

Francesca stared. "Did she say anything?"

He shook his head. "No. But she kept going to the window and lookin' out on the street, then runnin' back into the kitchen. Like she was lookin' fer someone outside, but was afraid to be seen herself. I dunno. I

158

have a real bad feeling, Miz Cahill. Something ain't right."

Francesca had a very identical feeling as well. Gwen had seemed jumpy when she and Bragg had last spoken to her, and she had also seemed distressed, although no more so than the day before. Had something happened that she had failed to mention earlier when Francesca and Bragg had been at her flat? Francesca was used to people hiding facts from the police and sometimes it was easier to conduct an interview without an official police presence. Of course, there were times when the strong arm of the law was exactly what was needed.

"I think you need to speak to her, Miz Cahill. I know ye got fancy plans fer tonight, but mebbe they could wait?" He was hopeful.

She touched his wool cap. "I think you're right. Hart and I can dine a bit later. And while we are at it, we can give you a ride home." She smiled at him and then turned to Hart. "Calder? We need to make one stop before we dine. Can we possibly do that?"

"Gwen O'Neil's?" he asked.

She nodded, praying he would not mind. "I have no curfew," she said earnestly, "so we can dine later."

Hart shook his head, but with tolerant af-

159

fection now, for he was smiling. "Are you certain you even wish to bother with supper, Francesca? Instead of spending our romantic evening sip ping champagne and nibbling on caviar, we can spend it sleuthing by candlelight in the slums downtown."

She heard the humor in his tone and was terribly relieved that they had weathered their brief crisis. "Thank you. Thank you for being so understanding."

He approached her and took her arm. "Empathy is not my forte, but with you, I shall try." And he seemed far too reflective again.

Which made her far too uneasy. She wet her lips. "I do hope you are not too hungry."

He laughed and guided her to the entry hall, where a doorman promptly opened the front door. "Frankly, I am famished," he said. "But I must admit, I am intrigued. Accompanying you on your investigation should prove far more interesting than our previous plans."

"Do you mean it?" she cried.

"I do," he said, amusement in his eyes. And he added, "The evening suddenly promises to be an extremely unusual one."

Chapter Seven

Wednesday, April 23, 1902 7:00 p.m.
Peter appeared almost magically in the front hall the moment Bragg stepped inside. He took Bragg's duster without a word; the huge manservant, who was a jack-of-all-trades, rarely spoke unless it was absolutely necessary. Bragg paused as Peter went to the hall closet. He strained to listen and finally, from upstairs, he heard Katie's gentle laughter.

He was too tense to smile.

He then heard Dot shriek in glee, but did not hear a sound from his wife.

"Peter."

The six-foot-four Swede paused. "Sir?"

"I take it all went well when you brought my wife home from the hospital?" he asked.

"Yes, sir."

Bragg felt more guilt. He had insisted that she come home, and so had the doctors. Perhaps to punish him for not allowing her to remain at Bellevue, Leigh Anne had requested that he send Peter to bring her home and that he not interrupt his busy schedule on her account. How polite she had been. How calm, how detached. He had agreed, knowing damn well that it wasn't his schedule motivating her. Even if she did not wish to punish him, she certainly wished to avoid him as much as possible. And maybe she was right.

He wondered now if he was right in forcing her against her will to come home. He thought it was best for her and for the children. Here she was loved, here he had newly hired staff to see to her special needs.

But maybe he was being selfish. He had his own needs. And in spite of the crushing burden of his guilt, he wanted her home, where she belonged. Although he was torn, the urge to take care of her was far stronger than the urge to flee.

Besides, he had already learned that he could not flee his own remorse.

"Mrs. Bragg was very happy to see the children," Peter said quietly. He hesitated.

Bragg was surprised. Peter clearly had something more to say. "What is it?"

"She does not know how to use the chair you ordered for her, sir. She is distressed about it. And she sent the nurse home."

Bragg started. "She dismissed Mr. Mc-Fee?"

"No, sir. She told him to return in the morning."

That was a relief. They could not manage without the male nurse. "She will become accustomed to the wheeled chair in no time," he said, more to reassure himself than Peter.

Peter inclined his head. He was blond and blue-eyed, his hair thinning, his face round. "Will you be taking supper, sir?"

"No, thank you," he declined. He had no appetite. How could he, when his heart felt as if it had sunk into his stomach? Slowly, his hand on the worn banister of the narrow Victorian staircase, he went upstairs.

Conversation drifted from the girls' small bedroom. Bragg approached with care, his nervous state increasing, glancing inside before he was even on the threshold. Leigh Anne sat in her wheeled chair, excruciatingly beautiful in a pastel green silk dress and a jade necklace. Her hair was pinned up and she was smiling, an angel in their midst. Dot was on her lap, Katie seated on the floor and snuggled up to her feet. She was reading them a children's bedtime story and in the small room, the wallpaper a beige-and-gold print, the furniture darkly stained and old, the scene was a charming and cozy one.

He smiled and his heart ached. He should be in that room, too, a welcome part of the family. Instead, he had somehow become the outsider.

But Katie saw him. She stood and hurried to him, flinging her arms about him, hugging him hard. "You're home!"

He stroked her soft, ash-brown hair. "Yes. And your mother's home," he said softly. In the past he had not allowed himself to refer to Leigh Anne as the girls' mother. The children were fostering with them, after all, and he had not intended for Leigh Anne to stay with them for too long. But that had now changed.

Katie smiled up at him, nodding. "I'm so happy," she said.

Just a few months ago, after her real mother was murdered, the eight-year-old had been withdrawn, sullen and depressed. He was thrilled at the change in her and he stroked her cheek. "It's a happy day," he said, and slowly, he glanced at his wife.

She had been looking at him; now, she flung her gaze to the open book on her lap. Dot, an angelic toddler, blue-eyed and fair, clapped her hands and beamed. "Papa!" she shouted enthusiastically.

His heart beat wildly in the cage that was his chest. Leigh Anne refused to look up. Was this her way now of avoiding him, even when they were in the same room? And as he leaned down to greet Dot, who grabbed some of his hair and tugged, he wondered if he should have let Leigh Anne stay at Belle-vue the way she had wished. He inhaled baby and woman, powder and something floral and spicy, something soft and seduc-tive.

As he kissed Dot's soft cheek, he could see Leigh Anne's hands on the book, where they trembled. He began to straighten and then dared to feather Leigh Anne's cheek with a kiss. "Hello. Welcome home."

When he was standing straight, she said, "Thank you." She did not look him in the eye. "Girls? Let's finish the story and then, Dot, it's time for bed."

He shoved his hands helplessly into his pockets, feeling unwanted. The fact that Leigh Anne did not ask him to sit down was glaring. He wanted desperately to join his family, but he lacked the courage to do so. His cheeks began to burn.

Katie jumped to sit down on the floor, careful not to touch Leigh Anne's legs, and Dot cried, "Read, Mama, read more!"

Leigh Anne cleared her throat and began

to read. " 'So the little boy felt sad. Robert started to walk away . . .' "

Bragg turned and left the room.

In their bedroom, he stripped off his tie. It fell to the floor and he realized he was angry. He shrugged off his suit jacket, unbuttoning his shirt. He had no right to be angry and he knew it. She was crippled because of him. There was simply no getting around it and she had every right to blame him, avoid him and even hate him.

But damn it, he wanted to be in the children's room, with Leigh Anne and the girls, not alone in the master suite, feeling caged up and enraged.

If only he could fix this!

Bragg flung his jacket to the floor but did not feel better. He stalked into the bathing room and paused, removing his shirt and dropping that as well. He leaned on the vanity, staring at his reflection in the mirror. He looked tired, disheveled, grim, with the eyes of a haunted man. He rubbed the stubble on his jaw, biceps bulging, and heard Dot shout with laughter. His heart hurt even more.

God, how was he going to manage this marriage now? He had thought his life a living hell before, when he had refused to accept a reconciliation with Leigh Anne, only doing so when his wife had forced his hand. He had hated her so much for denying him the divorce, for coming between him and Francesca and then for promising him that very divorce, providing he meet the conditions she laid down.

He had let her move in for the six months they had agreed upon. She had promised him that, if after six months, he still wished for a divorce, she would not contest it. And that was when she had had the accident.

Now, divorce was out of the question. Not only would he never abandon Leigh Anne in her state, he didn't want to. All he wanted was to take care of her and the children. He wanted them to become a family. But God, that seemed like an impossible dream.

He needed a drink.

Bragg went into the bedroom. A brass bar cart was against one wall by the bookcase, and he poured himself a stiff bourbon. He was sipping it repeatedly, determined to find some mental and emotional relief, when he heard Leigh Anne telling the girls that she would be back to tuck them in after Mrs. Flowers readied them for bed.

He hesitated, knowing she would refuse his help, but the gentleman in him demanded he try.

He set the glass down, shrugged on a

smoking jacket, and stepped into the hall. Leigh Anne sat in the wheeled chair in the children's room, looking grim and unhappy. He forced a smile. "Let me help," he said, approaching.

"No!"

He froze.

She smiled back at him. "I'm fine. I need to do this by myself, don't I?" Her tone was one of forced cheer.

Unable to dissuade her, he returned to the bedroom, straining to hear. But as the moments ticked by he heard only the sound of the nanny and the girls in the bedroom. There was silence in the hall. He slammed down the bourbon and walked to the door.

Leigh Anne sat in the chair, now in the center of the hall, tears on her cheeks. When she realized he was present she looked up, anger sparking in her eyes. "Don't," she warned.

He realized she was stuck. One of the chair's wheels was jammed against one wall. He ignored her, rushing over.

"I don't want help."

His hands were on the chair's handlebars and he flinched as if burned. "It is going to take some time to get used to moving about," he said more quietly. "There's no reason for you to expect to master the chair the first time you try it."

She covered her face with her hands.

"Please," he added, and he heard the anguish in his tone. Not waiting for a response, he moved the chair down the hall and into the bedroom. His wife's seductive fragrance enveloped him.

She dropped her hands, wiped her eyes. "I apologize. That was rude."

He walked around the chair so he could face her. "Don't treat me as if I were a stranger," he heard himself say.

Her gaze slipped down and he realized he had belted the smoking jacket so loosely that a good deal of his bare chest and abdomen were revealed. She flushed, looking away as he quickly pulled the lapels closed and tightened the belt, although she had seen his chest bare a dozen times since their reconciliation. And suddenly he thought about being in bed with her — about holding her gently in his arms and stroking her hair, her face, until she slept. Unfortunately, desire slammed over him, stiffening every inch of his body.

He ignored it. "It will get easier," he said to her. "I feel certain of it."

"That's easy for you to say," she said, refusing to look at him.

And he couldn't stand it any longer. "If I

could undo it all, Leigh Anne, I would. Right back to four years ago! I wish I had paid attention to you then! I wish I hadn't taken that damn job defending crooks and indigents. I wish I'd gone to that fancy law firm the way you wanted, the way we'd planned, I wish we'd bought the mansion next to my parents, I wish we'd started our own family! I wish I'd brought you back from Europe when you left instead of turning around and coming home alone! I would undo it all if I could."

She stared, her face suddenly devoid of color.

He started. "Are you all right?"

It was a moment before she managed a small, uncertain smile. "Yes." She looked away, closing her eyes and trembling.

He knelt and took her hands. "Please. I don't mean to distress you any further. But that is how I feel. I regret every choice I have made since we married," he said earnestly.

Leigh Anne suddenly turned her face aside, wiping her eyes. "It doesn't matter anyway, not now," she said. Her smile was odd.

He didn't stand. He was terribly aware of her and wanted to lay his cheek on her lap. "Yes, it does matter, because my regrets are sincere. I have treated you terribly since you arrived in the city. I'm sorry."

She bit her lip and said nothing.

He got up. "I know you blame me for this. And I don't blame you. I know the accident was my fault, just as I know that my apology changes nothing. Still, I am so sorry."

She stared, two bright spots of color appearing on her cheeks.

"I can't fix what happened. I can't undo the damage to your leg. But I am determined to take care of you," he said, and he managed a smile. "I swear it."

She looked away, closing her eyes tightly. And he had no idea of what she was thinking or feeling.

He reached for her small, cold hand. "Just let me take care of you," he whispered. "Things will be different now, I promise."

Tears slid down her cheeks, escaping her tightly closed eyes.

"Leigh Anne?"

She swallowed and looked at him. "You don't have to take care of me, Rick."

She had spoken so softly he thought he had misheard. "What?"

"The accident wasn't your fault. I don't blame you. I don't blame you for what happened at all."

He stared in disbelief. And then he felt

the relief begin to well. "Do you mean it?"

She nodded. "How could you blame yourself for an utter accident?"

But he did blame himself — and he always would. He was beyond relieved, though, that she did not. "If you don't blame me for the accident, then why didn't you want to come home? Then why are you avoiding me every moment we are together?" he heard himself ask.

She hesitated. "It's too late, Rick."

Comprehension began. "Too late?"

"You can wish on the moon, but the past is real. The misunderstanding, the lies, the lovers, that hate. It's all very real," she said. She was starkly white and she began to shake.

"What are you saying?" he cried, but he knew.

She shrugged, more tears falling. "It's simply too late for us to have a second chance. Not now. Not like this."

"Your six-in-hand is drawing undo attention," Francesca remarked, having just climbed down from the large, handsome barouche. Pedestrians passing by had paused to stare, as had several men leaving the corner saloon.

"I think it is you receiving the undo attention," Hart murmured, his hand firmly grasping her arm. His gaze met hers and then slipped over her stunning turquoise evening gown. The velvet shawl she wore, a deeper, darker shade of blue, concealed very little.

They were out of place, Francesca realized, both of them in their elegant evening clothes and having come by such a lavish coach. The men going into the saloon wore shabby wool shirts and patched trousers. Many were drunk. And she happened to be the only woman present on the sidewalk. "Joel? We'll walk you to your door before we speak with Mrs. O'Neil. It's late. Your mother must be worried."

"No one's home," Joel declared. "They were gone earlier — left me a note. Went to supper, they did, with your brother."

Francesca started in sheer surprise. Then delight began. "Maggie is with my brother?" She glanced down the block. "Maybe they have returned —"

"Light's out," Joel announced. "They're not back."

Francesca glanced at the window that she thought probably belonged to the Kennedy flat and it was black. She continued to smile. "I wonder where they went," she murmured, more to herself than Hart.

"You are insatiable," Hart said in her ear. "And it shows."

She smiled up at him, keeping her voice low so that Joel wouldn't hear her suppositions. "I can't help myself. This is beyond intriguing — my brother is far too fond of Maggie for it to be mere friendship."

"I would highly advise you not to meddle," Hart said with a sudden smile. "If you can restrain yourself."

"Of course I can," she returned, somewhat indignant.

"We shall see." He took her arm more firmly. "Lead the way, Joel," he said.

Joel was more than pleased to do so, and a moment later Gwen O'Neil was opening her door. "Miss Cahill!" She gasped in surprise. She was very pale and her red nose and swollen eyes were testimony to the fact that Joel had not exaggerated the situation. Clearly she had been crying for some time.

"Mrs. O'Neil, this is my fiancé, Calder Hart. I know it is late, but may we come in? I'd really like to help you if I can," she added.

Gwen clung to the door. She nodded. The moment they had filed past her and were inside, she slammed and bolted the door. Then she wiped her eyes with her fingertips.

"I have an allergy," she whispered. "Spring fever."

Francesca saw that the drapes were drawn at the far side of the room, indicating that Bridget was asleep behind the partition. She laid a palm on the woman's narrow shoulder. "How can I help?" she asked kindly. "Has something happened that we do not know about? That you have not told us?" She kept her voice down.

Gwen shook her head, looking ready to burst into tears.

"What is wrong? You weren't this distressed a few hours ago when I was here with the police commissioner." And as she spoke, she felt Hart's sudden interest. His gaze bored into her back. She wished she had not brought up the touchy subject of Rick Bragg.

"Before, I thought I might be imagining it," Gwen whispered.

"What did you think you were imagining? Did you think you were being followed again?"

"On the crosstown omnibus," she said hoarsely. "I could feel his stare, I swear, but I saw no one, and then I had to walk the last few blocks. It seemed fine, normal, you know, so I thought I had made it up in my mind!"

"And what has changed since this afternoon?" Francesca asked.

Gwen swallowed. "I've seen him. Out there, through the window, on the street. He's there now, in a doorway, by the saloon. I've caught him staring up at my window, Miss Cahill, I am certain of it!"

For one moment Francesca stared, trying to recall a man in the doorway near the saloon as the men exiting it had paused to gawk at her and Hart. But she had no image of any figure lurking there. Hart said, "I'll see what I can find."

"Yes, that's a good idea," Francesca said. As Hart started for the door, Joel racing to accompany him, she restrained Gwen from rushing to look out of the window. A plan occurred to her. "Calder, maybe you should drive by in the coach, slowly —"

"I think I can handle this, darling," he said with some amusement and a shake of his head. And then he and Joel were gone.

Francesca had the insane urge to watch, too. Her heart beat hard with excitement and alarm. If Gwen was right, if someone was stalking her now, there was a possibility that he was the Slasher. And that meant he was a killer. And Hart was going after him.

It crossed her mind that he was unarmed, but she had a pistol in her purse.

He could be in danger.

"Stay here," she cried, opening her bag as she raced across the flat and out the door. The stairwell was dark and empty, Joel and Hart on the street by now. On the landing below she paused, taking the pistol out of her bag and then using the velvet clutch to hide the weapon from any casual onlooker's view.

Her heart pounding, she went to the tenement's front door and saw that Hart had left it ajar. She peered outside.

Instantly, she saw that Hart and Joel had split up. Hart was across the street, clearly on his way into the saloon, undoubtedly on the pretense of wanting a drink. That was an excellent plan. She did not see Joel. Undoubtedly he was staked out somewhere, in case their quarry made a run for it.

She swallowed and fought to see into the shadows that covered the various cellar doorways surrounding the saloon. The lamp on the corner did not cast its glow very far. Beyond the saloon entrance, it was impossible to see. If a man loitered in one of the doorways, she simply could not tell.

For Gwen to have seen him, he must have stepped well out onto the sidewalk. Why was he now being so cagey? Did he suspect their presence? Or had he simply gone?

Hart clearly did not see anyone either, for he never broke stride, disappearing into the saloon.

Her palm was wet. She eased her grip on the tiny revolver, dismayed. If the stalker had been present, Hart would have seen him and pounced. The minutes ticked by. Two rowdies entered the saloon, but otherwise, the street was empty and deserted, due to the late hour of the night. Francesca stared so hard at the opposite doorways that her gaze blurred. And suddenly she saw a man emerge from the shadows into the glow of lamplight.

Gwen had been right.

Francesca glimpsed no more than the huddled shape of him and the pale skin of his face, but if she did not miss her guess, he was staring directly up at Gwen O'Neil's window.

She did not know where Hart was, damn it, but she was not going to let the man escape. She dropped her purse and started from the doorway at a run, aiming the gun in the vagrant's direction.

He saw her and froze.

"Hands up," she shouted as if she were a policeman, the entire street between them. "Halt and put your hands up!"

Ignoring her, he started to run past the saloon.

At that precise moment, Hart burst from the saloon. He tackled the man before he got to the corner of the block, knocking him down on his belly. A moment later, as Francesca ran up, Hart was astride him, pulling the man's hands behind his back. And then he was using his necktie to shackle the man's wrists.

Panting, Francesca halted beside them. Joel joined her at a run, also out of breath.

"I didn't do nothin'," the man cried. "Nothin'!"

Hart stood and turned to Francesca, his eyes wide with disbelief. "I said I would handle it!"

She bit her lip. "But you went into the saloon and I thought —" She stopped in midsentence.

"And you thought what, Francesca?" Calder demanded, taking the gun right out of her hand.

She felt wretched. "I knew you didn't have a weapon so I came downstairs to protect you if things went awry."

His gaze widened. "You thought to protect *me?*"

She nodded glumly. Now she was in trouble, indeed.

"You were not protecting me by barreling out of that tenement and demanding that this man put his hands up!"

She grimaced. "But you went into the saloon instead of apprehending him. I thought you did not see him."

"I saw him, Francesca. I went into the saloon to take off my tie so I had some means of restraining him, as I do not carry a gun like you do." He was very angry, indeed.

"I'm sorry," she whispered as meekly as possible.

"I doubt it," he said coolly.

He was right — she really wasn't sorry. He wasn't hurt and they had the stalker! But they could argue about this later. "Hart, take him up to Gwen's so we can interview him!" she cried, a satisfied smile appearing on her face as she peered down at the man who had now sat up.

Hart gave her a dark look that meant that she was not off the hook, not by any means, but he hauled the man to his feet. "Do you have a name?" he demanded.

"You're not coppers. If you're not coppers, who the hell are you?" the man demanded in a strong Irish brogue. He was very slim and rather tall, with dark brown hair and pale blue eyes. He wore the coarse cotton and wide-weave wool of a working man.

"I am Francesca Cahill and I am a sleuth," Francesca said briskly. "And I have no problem taking you up to police headquarters, if that is where you wish to go."

He scowled at her. "I done nothin' wrong."

"Of course, if you speak to me, there is no need to bring the police into this," she said, and she smiled winningly at him.

The man scowled and spat in her direction.

Hart moved. With a sudden growl, he seized the man by the back of his corduroy jacket and threw him face first into the building. "What's your name," he said calmly, holding him hard there. And he lifted him as if prepared to smash his face on the wall again.

Hart was so elegant that Francesca had forgotten how he had grown up. He had been born a bastard on the Lower East Side, not far from where they now stood. She cringed even as she gaped at him.

"Speak up," he warned threateningly, his face a dark mask of ruthless intent.

"Hanrahan!" the stalker cried. "David Hanrahan and I done nothin' wrong! It's my right to be here!"

Hart released him abruptly. "You have your answer," he said coolly to Francesca.

And realizing just how angry Hart remained with her, some of her elation died.

CHAPTER EIGHT

Wednesday, April 23, 1902 10:00 p.m.
Gwen simply stared at her husband as they led him inside her flat.

Francesca had expected a bit more of a reaction. Still, Gwen was pale and wide-eyed. But there were no hysterics and the extent of her surprise — the lack of shock — was more than odd, it was telling.

Hart shoved Hanrahan onto a kitchen chair. Then he loosened his bow tie, flipped a chair backward and sat down himself. He still seemed annoyed. Francesca hoped it was because of Hanrahan and not because of her reckless behavior earlier. Of course, her hopes were foolish, indeed.

"David?" Gwen whispered.

He nodded at her, his expression grim.

"It was you? You were outside?"

He nodded. "I got every right to be here! You're my wife!" he erupted.

Gwen covered her face with her hands,

releasing a sob.

And Bridget suddenly stepped out from behind the drapes in her flannel nightgown. Her eyes were huge with surprise. "Papa?"

Francesca quickly stepped over to her as Gwen whirled with a cry. As she put her arm around the child, Bridget said, "It was really you. I really saw you after school today!" She began to tremble. Clearly the child was stunned to see her father.

And while Francesca realized that Bridget was shocked and upset, she could not be certain that the girl was happy to see her father, either.

"It was me," David said flatly. "Hello, my little poppet."

Bridget did not move.

Gwen rushed to stand between them. "You stay away from her!" she cried.

David made a sound of disgust.

Bridget pressed closer to Francesca. She could not decipher the complicated family relationships. "Joel? Take Bridget into the hall for a moment, please."

Joel flushed as he approached Bridget, but he was kind. "C'mon. They'll be plenty of time fer you and your papa later, after Miz Cahill an' Mr. Hart finish their questions."

Bridget looked worriedly at Gwen. "Mama?"

"Go outside, baby," Gwen whispered, her mouth barely moving as she somehow formed the words. "We won't be too long."

Joel took her hand and the two children left. Francesca stepped forward. "Did you follow your wife this afternoon when she left work?" she asked Hanrahan bluntly.

He scowled. "An' if I did? It's my right!"

Hart stood. The action was highly threatening, and not simply because Hart was tall and strong. His intention was undeniable, as was his air of authority and power. He was not to be denied. "Stalking is no man's right," he warned softly.

David Hanrahan's expression became vicious. "She's my wife and that means she belongs to me. She had no right runnin' away, no right comin' to America. She's got no rights, none!" Then he became meek and added, "Sir."

Francesca winced. According to the law, most women had no rights and he was, for the most part, correct. In fact, Gwen could be forced to return to him. In this city, no one would bother to interfere. She imagined it might be very different in a small village in Ireland.

"You told me to go!" Gwen dropped her hands. She was shaking. "You told me to get out of your sight, that you never wanted to see me again!"

"I changed my mind," he spat. Now he was trembling with anger.

"How long have you been following your wife?" Francesca asked flatly.

He shrugged.

"Do you wish to go uptown to police headquarters?" Hart asked coldly.

David blanched. "I didn't follow her!"

Francesca made a sound of disgust.

"I didn't! I been outside, on the street, hopin' to talk to her. But she won't talk to me! You can surely see that? I want her back an' she refuses to talk to me!" he cried, looking from Francesca to Hart and back again, as if pleading with them.

Gwen walked over to the sink, standing with her back to everyone. She did not run the water but she toyed with a chipped plate.

How odd this was. "Gwen? You don't seem very surprised to see your husband. You don't seem very surprised that he has followed you to America and that he wants a reconciliation," Francesca said.

She walked over to Gwen. "How long have you known that he was in the country?"

Gwen was stiff. "A few weeks."

"How did he get out of jail? Was he in jail? For attempted murder?" Francesca asked.

186

"They couldn't prove anything!" David cried.

Gwen hesitated. Finally, her voice barely audible, she said, "Yes."

"He dropped the charges," David snarled. "His Lordship admitted it was a lie! He admitted I didn't try to kill him!"

Gwen choked on a sob.

Francesca faced David, doubting the veracity of his statement. He clearly hated Lord Randolph, but did he hate him enough to have attempted murder? Had Randolph dropped the charges? Or had Hanrahan somehow escaped? "How did you know where to find your wife and daughter?"

"She told a neighbor back home, Mrs. Reilly, that she could be reached through Father Culhane. Gwen left the father's address with her. The good father was only too obliging to tell me where my wife and daughter were." David stared at Gwen, not looking once at Francesca.

Gwen said, hoarse and low, "I am not going back. Not to Ireland and not to you."

"You are making a mistake," David said just as low.

That was a threat if Francesca had ever heard one. "Have the two of you already discussed a reconciliation?"

"I will not go back!" Gwen cried.

Francesca went to her. "Please, I am asking these questions for a reason. I need your honest answers."

Gwen looked at her, tearful now, and nodded. "Yes. He asked me if I would go back when he first arrived in the city, and I was clear. I said no."

Francesca felt savage satisfaction then. She looked at Hart who stared back. She assumed he understood her thoughts completely, and then he nodded slightly at her, telling her to go on. She faced David. "Where were you this past Monday between noon and 4:00 p.m., Mr. Hanrahan?" she asked.

And she smiled grimly.

They had their first real suspect.

At this late evening hour, police headquarters was oddly quiet, half of the staff dozing on the job. Hart slipped his arm around Francesca's waist as they left the reception area, David Hanrahan having been put in the lockup for the night. Francesca started in surprise as they paused before going down the building's front steps. Hart met her gaze and smiled a little at her. His arm tightened.

Their evening work was done. It was late, but they were entirely alone. Francesca was

188

frankly exhilarated from finally uncovering a suspect, but Hart's sudden gesture presented her with an entirely different feeling. Warmth mingled with the leftover excitement. "I take it you are no longer quite so angry with me?" She smiled at him.

"I am frankly appalled with you," he murmured, a soft gleam in his eyes.

"We have a suspect, Hart," she said with jubilation. And she laughed.

"You have a suspect," he agreed.

She turned and found herself in his arms. A soft breeze caressed them both. "Aren't you pleased? Hanrahan has motive and no alibi!"

"If he were the killer, I imagine he could do better than coming up with a statement that he was wandering about the streets, looking for work, on Monday. And he would surely have an alibi for the previous two Mondays, but he does not."

Some of her elation vanished, as if a balloon had been popped. "But he is not very clever."

"No, he is not." He caressed the soft hairs at her nape almost thoughtlessly. "Do not be too disappointed. He does have motive. Perhaps you have your killer after all."

"The Slasher is clever," Francesca disagreed. She intuited that with all of her being. She felt certain he was no thug.

"You do not know that."

"I sense it."

He cupped her shoulders. The gown had tiny cap sleeves, but in spite of them and the light shawl she wore, the feeling of his palms was thrilling. She tensed and looked into his eyes. "I have never seen more reckless, rash behavior," he murmured, "than I have this night."

His thighs were rock hard against her softer ones. "I wanted to help," she said quietly, gripping his broad shoulders.

"I know — and that is what scares me so," he whispered, sliding his hands down her back.

She allowed herself a soft moan of pleasure. "Don't stop," she said.

"I should like to see you in this dress without a corset," he murmured, bending over her shoulder. He moved the shawl aside and kissed the bare skin near her collarbone.

Sparks seemed to ignite, quickly flaming throughout her body. "Without a corset?" she gasped. How daring that would be! And how she loved the notion!

"Without a corset," he affirmed, kissing her throat, just once. "No corset, no chemise, no drawers, nothing but your shoes and stockings and this lovely dress."

She felt faint. Somehow she opened her eyes to find Hart staring intently. His own dark blue gaze had turned to gray smoke. "How shocking," she managed to say, hoping to sound appropriately scandalized.

He began to smile. "You're not shocked." He lowered his head and feathered her lips with a kiss.

She clung. "No . . ." She opened her mouth, praying he would invade, but he did not. His lips touched the corners, the soft full center, the dimple above. "When, Hart?"

He smiled against her mouth. His weight had shifted as she spoke and she felt the length of his arousal near her hip. The urgency intensified deep in her, making her feel faint and hollow.

"When what, darling?" His every word brought his mouth against hers. Their breath mingled. "When will I kiss you? Or when will I take you soaring to the heavens above?"

She gripped his lapels and pressed against him. His smile vanished as their gazes locked. "When can I wear the dress for you?" she breathed.

He anchored her hips so she could not move. She felt the blood coursing in his body. "Such a game should wait until after we are married, until after we have had some time to explore the more traditional aspects of lovemaking."

She felt like socking him in the nose. "Then why bring it up!"

"Because I was thinking about it, that's why, but it was rude, thoughtless and teasing, was it not? I apologize." He smiled, clearly not remorseful in the least.

She could not smile back. She stared, unable to move, barely able to breathe, wedged against him. "We need to make love, Hart."

"Yes, we do."

His response stunned her.

Hart released her. "Our courtship has become difficult for me, Francesca."

She was so surprised, she did not comment.

"I'm a man with basic needs," he said with a shrug. "And I am used to assuaging them frequently." He walked away, hands in his pockets now, still in his white dinner jacket and midnight-black evening trousers, and stared up at what was left of the other night's full moon.

Did he mean what she thought he did? She composed herself — it took a moment — and went to stand besides him. "I know how important it is to you to be noble now,

192

with me."

"It is beyond important," he said, not looking at her. He stared up at the starry night.

"Why?" She was careful not to touch him. She knew the need inside her could be ignited with a mere touch or even a single glance.

Still looking at the heavens, he shrugged.

"Even if we slept together, I will never be like the others," she pointed out. His past was filled with women, but all had been experienced — divorcées, widows or married women on the prowl for a lover. Hart had never before toyed with innocence.

He made a sound. "I know that."

"Then why? I know you are worldly enough to make certain I would not get pregnant —"

He whirled. "It's about me, not you."

She blinked. "I don't understand."

"I barely understand myself." He was grim.

She dared to pluck his sleeve. "Please, Calder, please try to explain this to me."

His jaw was rigid. "There is a man . . . a different man . . . and I can feel him . . . he actually exists."

She had not a clue as to what he meant.

He stared ahead now. "Having decided to

marry you, Calder Hart would have seduced you months ago, never mind your innocence. Calder Hart has been more than tempted, more than once. Because he wants you so much. Now that he is engaged, Hart really doesn't give a damn about your innocence. Hart has actually thought about seducing you well before the wedding and he has come quite close to accomplishing the feat."

She was wide-eyed. And why was he talking about himself as if he was a stranger?

"But someone else has appeared on the scene." He made a sound of self-derision. "Someone better, in fact. Someone who can actually see that the sun exists on a gray, rainy day. Someone who actually prefers sunshine to rain."

And she understood. Her heart swelled impossibly; tears welled. "Oh, Calder."

"He isn't as selfish. He wants to be noble." He finally glanced at her. "I'm not being very clear, am I?"

"No," she whispered. "I understand completely."

"You would," he whispered softly. "Only you would understand." He touched her face then dropped his hand.

Francesca started to cry.

He did not pull her close. He shoved his

hands back in the pockets of his trousers and stared out into the night. It was a moment before he spoke. "This other man . . . this is the man that you have made me want to be."

The milliner's shop where Kate Sullivan was employed was a block and a half north of Ehrich Brothers' Emporium on Sixth Avenue, just past the west corner of Twenty-third Street. The small shop boasted a large display window filled with modest bonnets, elegant hats and fine silk scarves, with a single counter inside and a rack of more goods. Upon Francesca's presenting herself to the proprietress that next morning, Kate Sullivan was summoned from the back room where she had been stocking goods.

The Slasher's second victim was a pretty blonde in a dark skirt and white shirtwaist. As she approached Francesca, her pallor was obvious. Francesca smiled warmly.

"Mrs. Hathorne said you are a sleuth," Kate said, eyes wide.

"Yes, I am." Francesca continued to smile, handing her a calling card. Kate did not even look at it. She seemed frightened and dismayed. "I am investigating the crimes committed by the Slasher. I have some questions for you."

Kate appeared to be near tears. "But I told the police everything." She went to one of two chairs in a corner of the shop and sat weakly down.

She looked on the verge of fainting. Francesca followed her. "Can I get you some water?"

Kate shook her head. "I am trying to forget," she whispered. Then tears filled her eyes. "But how can I? Every time I close my eyes, I see him. Every time I close my eyes, I hear him."

Francesca knelt besides her. "You saw him! That was not in the police report!"

She shook her head negatively. "I never saw him, Miss Cahill, he seized me from behind. But I can see him now, so clearly, this tall elegant man!"

She was not making any sense. Francesca stood and took the chair besides Kate Sullivan. "What do you mean, precisely?"

Kate shrugged. "I can imagine how he must look. I know he was tall, because I am rather tall for a woman — I am five foot five — and he was far taller than I."

"You said he was elegant."

She nodded. "I had just disrobed." She turned impossibly pale. A tear fell.

"Do you need some air?" Francesca asked in real compassion.

She nodded weakly.

Francesca took her arm and helped her up. A moment later they were standing on Sixth Avenue. The elevated train was roaring overhead, causing the buildings around them to shake, and leaving a cloud of black smoke in its wake. Horns were blaring on the congested avenue, and a trolley was clanging its bells. Pedestrians, both ladies and gentlemen, swarmed around them. "Do you feel better?"

Kate inhaled and nodded. "I get so sick whenever I think of him," she whispered.

"That's understandable. He must be apprehended, Miss Sullivan."

"Yes, he must." She smiled faintly. "I've read about you, Miss Cahill. I've read about the Cross Killer and the City Strangler. You solved those cases! And now I read you are engaged to the city's wealthiest bachelor, Mr. Hart." Her eyes shone with unshed tears.

"I am very determined to solve a case when I take one on," Francesca said firmly, trying not to appear pleased. But it was flattering, indeed, to be such an object of interest that the newsmen reported on her doings. "So the Slasher seized you from behind after you had disrobed?"

Kate nodded again. "I had no idea he was

197

in my flat," she said. "But I was very weary from being on my feet all day. Mrs. Hathorne had asked me to come in a few hours early to help with inventory. So it was a long day, really. I was almost asleep on my feet, I must say! One moment I was pulling on a robe, the next, he had me in his arms and he had a knife to my throat." A tear fell.

"And he was tall."

"Yes."

"Why do you say he was elegant? What would make you think that?" Francesca asked. There was nothing elegant about David Hanrahan — but Kate might be wrong. Victims frequently made mistakes when it came to identifying their assailants.

"His clothes," she said. "His jacket was very fine wool, the kind of wool that only a gentleman would wear."

"Are you sure?"

"I saw the sleeve, Miss Cahill. The sleeve was well tailored and charcoal gray. It was a fine sleeve, Miss Cahill. A fine sleeve, indeed."

Francesca's mind raced. "Are you certain? Are you certain of all of this?"

She nodded. "I also saw his hand. His other hand — the one on my stomach — not the hand he held the knife with."

Francesca almost held her breath. What wonderful clues these were! "And?"

"His hands were soft and smooth. They weren't the coarse, red hands of a working man."

Francesca stared.

"And there was a ring. I can't recall it exactly, but it was gold. There was a stone; I'm not even sure what kind or color it was." Her eyes suddenly flashed. "He was a gentleman. He was a gentleman and I have not one doubt."

It was simply unbelievable, he thought, staring at the window of the milliner's shop from where he stood across Sixth Avenue. It was unbelievable that the notorious Francesca Cahill had started an investigation into the so-called Slasher; that she dared to seek out the first two bitches and question them again, after the police had already done so; that she dared to try to reveal *him.*

He knew she was clever. He had read all about her, who hadn't? But she wasn't half as clever as he was, he felt certain of that.

He watched the two of them standing outside the shop, trembling with his hatred.

God, he hated them all. Every single faithless one of them. He could count the promises, but not the lies . . . He knew now he should have killed them, instead of warning them, instead of letting them live.

His fingers twitched and he slipped his hand into his pocket, feeling for the small penknife.

Well, his plans had changed.

This one would die.

CHAPTER NINE

Thursday, April 24, 1902 Noon

Francesca had been told that she could wait in Bragg's office, as he was in a closed meeting in the conference room. Having been left alone there, she paused by his desk and saw, among the many files and folders there, a notepad with his handwriting on the page. His scrawl was very rushed and careless, so unlike the man. She saw that he was composing a report for the mayor.

It wasn't her affair, of course. But she hoped his internal police investigation would yield the results he wanted, or ones advantageous to him and his career. Unable to help herself, she wandered over to the hearth. There was no fire lit, as May was around the corner and the morning newspapers had promised the city a day that was seventy degrees Fahrenheit. She glanced at the mantel and stared at Leigh Anne's photograph.

She knew it had been taken some time ago, and Leigh Anne looked very young and very innocent. She was smiling at the photographer, unabashedly happy, seated in a chair in a lavish salon. Francesca wondered how she was convalescing. She hoped that she was now happy to be home.

She turned her back to the photograph. Hopefully there would be an explanation for the incomplete police report on Kate Sullivan.

Francesca thought about the pretty blonde as she stared vaguely across the room and out the window behind Bragg's desk. Like Francis O'Leary, Kate had been severely traumatized and as a result, she remained very frightened. Francesca thought about the fact, again, that all the victims were young, pretty, female, unattached and Irish — or at least, in Margaret Cooper's case, of Irish descent. Still, Margaret Cooper felt somehow mismatched — perhaps because she hadn't ever been married. Francesca couldn't help thinking that Gwen O'Neil matched the pattern set by the first two victims far more precisely than Margaret.

Could Gwen have been the Slasher's intended target? Had he attacked and murdered Margaret Cooper by mistake?

Francesca reminded herself to interview

Sam Wilson. She wondered if the police were making any progress in locating Thomas O'Leary. And she would not yet put too much credence into Kate's claim that the Slasher was a gentleman.

Bragg walked into his office and she quickly turned.

He was clearly surprised to see her. "I didn't know you were waiting for me." Behind him, Francesca saw several men walking down the hall, including Inspector Newman and the tall, gray-haired chief of police, Brendan Farr. Farr was glancing her way and when she briefly met his cool gaze, she flinched.

She more than disliked Farr; she did not trust him. She smiled at Bragg. "I was told to go up and wait for you here. I hope you do not mind."

"Of course I don't mind," he said, returning her smile. He shut his door and approached. "I'm assuming this is not a social call?"

She hesitated. Once, she had actually made social calls, right there at his office. Those days were long since gone. In a way, she wished she could drop by whenever she had the urge to do so. Somehow, she missed those days.

So much had changed. Aware of his wife's

photograph behind her back, she said, "It's not a social call, but may I inquire after Leigh Anne?"

His smile vanished. "Of course." He walked to his desk and busied himself with arranging the folders there.

"Is everything all right?" she asked somewhat timidly, well aware that the question was quite out of bounds.

"Everything is fine," he said, not looking at her.

She did not think so. "I guess it might take some time for her to adjust to being at home in a different circumstance."

"Yes." He faced her, forcing a smile. "She does need some time."

Francesca hated this delicate dance. "Rick . . . would it be awkward if I called on her? I wanted to call on her at the hospital, but I was a coward, a terrible coward!" she cried, relieved that she was finally being honest with him. "I like Leigh Anne. Maybe I can be of some help."

His face collapsed. "Of course you can call on her," he said softly. "Francesca —" He stopped.

"What?"

"I am at a loss," he whispered.

She really knew very little now of his intimate affairs, but she sensed his distress and wanted to take him in her arms. She did not. "Do you want to talk about it?"

"Not really." He smiled grimly at her, recovering his composure.

"Are you certain I can call? I don't want to upset her."

"I think it would be helpful if she had callers — if she had the same social life she used to have. She was never idle, Francesca."

Francesca nodded. She had an odd and terrible image of Leigh Anne sitting in her new wheeled chair in the old Victorian house Bragg had leased, never going out, a prisoner of a lack of desire.

"So what brings you here?" he asked, gesturing at a chair.

Jerked away from that horrific image, she quickly went to him, having no wish to sit. "The police file you have on the Slasher is incorrect."

He started. "What do you mean?"

"I read it very carefully after Margaret Cooper's murder. Kate Sullivan's statement is incomplete."

"You spoke with her?"

"Yes, this morning. She said the Slasher is tall, but that was not in her statement. She also said he was a gentleman, that she saw his sleeve and his hand. The sleeve was charcoal gray and of a fine, expensive wool, his hand was unblemished and smooth and not the hand of a working man. He was also wearing a ring, which she did not see clearly, but it was gold and it had a stone. She is uncertain what kind of stone and she could not even recall the color. None of that is in the statement in that file, Bragg, and she insisted that she told all of this to the police."

He gave her a dark look and strode to the door. Opening it, he seized a passing patrolman. "Have Inspector Newman report to me immediately." He returned to Francesca. "I am assuming someone has been asleep on the job," he said. "Someone inept."

"Yes, I am sure that must be the case," Francesca said. "But Inspector Newman is not inept — he is quite thorough."

"Yes, usually he is," Bragg said grimly.

Newman poked his head past the door, which was ajar. "You called for me, C'mish?" the rotund detective asked.

"Please sit down," Bragg said.

Newman's expression changed. He glanced at Francesca and then back at his boss and took a seat. "Is something wrong?"

"Who took Kate Sullivan's statement?" Bragg asked.

Newman began to flush. "I did, sir."

"Then why is the statement inaccurate and incomplete?"

Newman's red color increased. "I'm not sure I know what you are speaking of," he said, looking away.

Francesca was in disbelief. He was lying!

"Kate Sullivan remarked on the Slasher's jacket and hand."

Newman looked distraught. "Yes, sir, she did," he mumbled.

"You recall all of this?" Bragg asked in the same disbelief that Francesca was feeling.

He nodded, appearing miserable.

"Then why was it not in the file?" he demanded tersely.

Newman stared at his knees. "I dunno, sir." His voice was barely audible.

Bragg was as incredulous as he was angry. "So you failed to make an accurate report?"

Newman nodded.

"Why?"

Newman just sat there, hanging his head. "I dunno," he finally whispered. He seemed close to tears.

"I need a reason — before I suspend you," Bragg snapped.

Newman looked up, his eyes shining. "I didn't want to lie," he begged. "Sir, I didn't."

Francesca became still. And she had a terrible inkling, Brendan Farr's chilly stare coming to mind.

"I suggest that you explain yourself."

Newman inhaled, as if seeking courage.

Francesca had to intervene. "I have an idea as to what happened." She did not look at Bragg, only at Newman, who stared at her as if she were his savior. "Someone didn't want you to make a complete report, did he?"

Newman shook his head. "No, he didn't."

Bragg jumped in. "Farr asked you to withhold the facts of this case?"

Newman nodded. "Sir, I'm loyal to you, I swear! But Farr's the chief! He can suspend me, fire me, he can hurt my —" He stopped abruptly. Numbly he said, "He's chief, C'mish. He gave me a direct order. He gives me an order, I got to obey." He was trembling.

For a moment, Bragg was still, and then he and Francesca looked at one another. Bragg faced the plump inspector. "I understand."

Newman gasped. "You do?"

"Yes. And now I am giving you an order. Anytime Farr asks you to violate the oath you are sworn to as a police officer, you come to me."

Newman nodded, ashen.

Bragg clasped his shoulder. "I do not condone what you have done, but I understand the position you have been placed in. I do not want you to breathe a word of this conversation to the chief. It never took place. Do you understand me?"

He turned beet red. "Yes, sir."

"Did Farr say why he wished to delete the facts from the file?"

"No."

"Who else knows about this?"

"No one, sir."

"Good. Continue with the investigation. But all pertinent facts are to be reported directly to me from this moment forward. If Farr wishes to withhold more information, pretend to do so and seek me out privately. Is that clear?"

Newman nodded, appearing terribly relieved. "I never wanted to betray you, sir," he said.

"I understand. Did you and Farr have a suspect that we do not know about?"

"No, sir. The only suspect we have so far is David Hanrahan. Farr thinks he might have killed Margaret Cooper by mistake — that he meant to kill his own wife, and that he assaulted the first two women out of anger."

Bragg smiled at him. "Why don't you take

your lunch break."

Newman stood. "Thank you, sir," he cried.

When he was gone Francesca faced Bragg, wide-eyed. "What is Farr up to?" she demanded. "Why hide pertinent facts?"

"I do not know — yet."

Francesca stared. "He hates women. I am sure of it. But surely he isn't the killer?"

"That is a bit of a leap to make."

"Then *why?*"

"As I said, we don't know. But we will find out, sooner or later, now, won't we?" He smiled and it was chilling.

And Francesca took his hand. "Sooner, Bragg," she vowed. "We will find out sooner, not later, because I have lost patience with your treacherous chief of police."

It didn't matter that Leigh Anne Bragg was now a cripple. Bartolla Benevente had dressed exquisitely in jewels and a fabulous couturier gown to make certain she put her friend and rival to shame. Of course, while the gown was couture, the jewels only appeared real. The false emeralds surrounding her long, pale throat matched her coat and were a bit darker than the low-cut, three-quarter-sleeved dress she wore. Bartolla had also spent hours on her long red hair that morning. She wore a new rouge on her lips and cheeks, and she knew she had never been more stunning. She was staying with the Chandlers on the dreadful west side of town, so there was no opportunity for any flattering glances to come her way until she alighted from their hansom cab at Madison Square. There, a dozen gentlemen turned to look and stare.

She smiled at them all as she swept up the brick path to the ugly, dour Victorian house Rick Bragg had let. How Leigh Anne must hate living there, she thought. She knew the other woman very well. Leigh Anne had always expected a mansion, furs and jewels when she married into the wealthy Bragg family. Somehow, her working husband had managed to provide her with everything except the mansion.

Bartolla smiled widely and knocked on the front door.

She had called on Leigh Anne four times while she was in the hospital but Leigh Anne had, amazingly, been asleep each and every time and she had not been allowed to enter the sickroom. Once she had managed to steal a glance inside and she had been truly shocked when she had glimpsed Leigh Anne. The woman had been lying there in bed, her face so devoid of color that she appeared dead. She had looked ghastly, even ugly.

God, how ironic it was! How tragic, how utterly Homeric! As much as Bartolla hated to admit it, the other woman more than rivaled her in beauty. But no more. Never again. The city's most beautiful woman was now deformed, forever maimed, a cripple, for God's sake.

She knew she should not have even the *smallest* sense of satisfaction. But, in the past, when they had been together in a room, at a fête or a ball, Bartolla had not received the majority of the longing male glances cast their way. No more. No man would ever look at Leigh Anne Bragg that way again.

It was *almost* amusing.

Bartolla was let inside by a manservant as dour as the house and told to wait while he went to see if Mrs. Bragg was receiving callers. Bartolla wandered the small, garish salon, shuddering at the dark red stripes on the walls, the dark red velvet of the tacky sofa, the worn and faded rug. Leigh Anne had returned from marital separation and an opulent life in Europe to reclaim her husband, and Bartolla could not quite understand why. Of course, she had been the one to write Leigh Anne and inform her that her estranged husband was in love with another woman. Still, Bartolla would have let Francesca Cahill have him, had she been Leigh Anne. Leigh Anne had been courted by dukes and chased by Russian princes. What a fool she had been.

She heard the wheels even before she heard Leigh Anne and she turned as her hostess said hello. Bartolla froze. Leigh Anne sat in a wheeled chair, a young male nurse pushing it, clad in a stunning lavender gown with a pearl and diamond necklace and matching earrings. For one moment, as Leigh Anne smiled at her, Bartolla started in dismay. She had expected to see a corpse. But other than the fact that Leigh Anne could not walk and sat in that odd contraption that was a chair, nothing had changed. She was utterly lovely and terribly elegant and the necklace she wore was real.

"How wonderful of you to call," Leigh Anne said. She smiled slightly at the handsome, dark-haired man who was her nurse. "I'll call you if I need you, Mr. McFee."

He smiled, blushing a little, and left.

Bartolla recovered and swept forward, beaming, but inwardly she was furious. How could Leigh Anne make being a cripple so glamorous? "How are you, darling?" she cried, clasping her hands. "I tried to call on

213

you at Bellevue, but you were asleep every time and they would not let me in."

"I know," Leigh Anne said with the same slight smile. "That was very nice of you. Do sit down. Peter is bringing us brioche and coffee."

"Ah, those were the days, when my dear husband the count was still alive — when we would meet in Paris and shop together until we were ready to expire!" Bartolla laughed, recalling those two years of her marriage very vividly. She had married the Italian count at the age of sixteen — he had been in his sixties. Then he had died, leaving her with next to nothing, the bastard. He had left his grown adult children everything, except the smallest pension that came to her, one which she had already spent. Of course, no one in the city knew her little secret — that she was living on her American family's charity and was desperately impoverished.

But when she married Evan Cahill — once he was reconciled with his family and his inheritance — that would all change.

Leigh Anne's smile never faltered, though now Bartolla realized it did not reach her amazing green eyes. "I'm afraid you did all of the shopping, my dear. I never had that kind of credit, if you recall."

Bartolla took a chair. "Bragg kept you well while you were separated."

"He was as generous as he dared to be. I quickly learned to excel at pretense," Leigh Anne said. "Some of the gems I wore were nothing but paste, the gowns hand-me-downs."

Bartolla was uncomfortable, as she wore paste and a hand-me-down gown. But of course, Leigh Anne could not know that. "I had no idea. No one did. That necklace is beautiful," she added.

Leigh Anne's expression softened. "Rick gave it to me when we were newly wed. I have always treasured it. It was so hard for him to afford this."

Bartolla was annoyed now. "Oh, please, all he had to do was ask for a check from his father. He might have chosen to work for a living like a common man, but let's be frank, one day he will inherit quite a fortune when Rathe Bragg dies."

Leigh Anne's eyes widened in shock and distress. "I am very fond of his father, and I hope that day is decades away!"

Bartolla had to glance at the appalling room. "Well, Rathe does seem rather vital for a middle-aged man. So why don't you appeal to him for a, er, different residence? You surely could use a larger ground floor," she said, implying that with Leigh Anne's handicap, she did not need to be bothered with stairs. "In fact," she said, recalling that Leigh Anne had two young girls and a nanny in the house, "you must need a larger living space."

Leigh Anne flushed. Very carefully, she said, "If Rick likes this house, which is conveniently located, as police affairs often call him out in the middle of the night, then I have no wish to relocate."

"How noble you are," Bartolla laughed, wondering if Leigh Anne really was that selfless. She doubted it. No woman would want to wheel that awkward chair about the narrow halls of this awful house.

Peter entered, setting a sterling tray with their cups of coffee and plates of pastries on the table between them. "Thank you," Leigh Anne said. Then, as she reached for a cup, she said, "I am hardly noble, Bartolla. Rick is the noble one."

Bartolla didn't respond, because she had realized that Leigh Anne was going to have some difficulty reaching the cup of coffee. Peter had placed the tray squarely in the table's center, but that had been a mistake, as Leigh Anne's unwieldy chair prevented her from sitting as close to the table as one usually would. Her fingertips barely grazed the saucer beneath the cup.

Bartolla watched, her breath suspended, suddenly reminded that this woman was not normal and she never would be again. Leigh Anne was now completely focused on seizing the saucer so she could hand her guest the refreshment. Her cheeks were red and her breathing had accelerated. Bartolla knew she should help, but for one more moment she watched, savagely satisfied. Then she said, kindly, "Oh! Do not bother yourself, darling. I can do that," and she took the cup and saucer into her hands, waiting to meet Leigh Anne's gaze.

But Leigh Anne quickly put her hands in her lap, clasping them, her lashes lowered, her full bosom heaving from the brief exertion. Her cheeks remained flushed.

She couldn't even serve a guest properly anymore, Bartolla thought. She sipped her coffee. "This is delicious, thank you."

Leigh Anne made no move to take her own cup and saucer, as she clearly would not be able to reach them. She looked up. "I am glad you think so," she said quietly.

Bartolla savored another sip then set the cup and saucer down. "So, does Rick really take care of police affairs in the middle of the night?"

"From time to time, yes, he does," Leigh

Anne said, her hands still in her lap.

"Does he still work closely with Francesca?" she asked, somehow keeping a straight face.

Leigh Anne met her gaze. "Of course. She is a sleuth — and a very good one, I might add."

"I would not want my husband running about the city in the middle of the night with another woman," Bartolla said, meaning it. "How generous you are."

"Francesca seems very happy," Leigh Anne said, more color blooming in her cheeks, "now that she is engaged to Calder Hart."

And Bartolla had to laugh. "That is a coup, is it not! Our clever bluestocking and Calder Hart! I wonder, how long will that unlikely match last?"

"I think Calder is in love, finally," Leigh Anne murmured, eyes downcast.

"Oh, please! He wants to bed her and she is clever enough to deny him — undoubtedly the only woman to ever do so. I wonder how he feels about her dashing around the city with your husband?"

Leigh Anne stared. "I doubt he is worried. Hart is one of the most secure men I have ever met."

"Hart is no fool. I imagine he will put a

leash on Francesca very shortly. Admit it, dear, it will be a relief once she is wed and out of the picture."

It was a moment before Leigh Anne spoke. "I like Francesca. I imagine that, one day, we will be friends."

For one moment, Bartolla thought she meant it, and then she realized that she was in jest. She had to be. Bartolla laughed.

"How is Evan?" Leigh Anne asked, cutting into her laughter.

Bartolla grinned. "Wonderful." She hesitated, leaning close. "He is an amazing man — if you know what I mean," she whispered, indelicately referring to his sexual prowess.

"How happy I am for you," Leigh Anne said. Then, "Yes, he seems unique. Leaving his family in order to find his own way in life, giving up that inheritance — he reminds me a little of Rick. I hear Evan's father has disowned him completely," she added.

"It is a temporary family spat, let me assure you of that."

Leigh Anne did not seem to hear. "And he is so generous, is he not? My friend Beth Tyler called earlier. She saw him last night, you know."

Bartolla stiffened. "How nice," she smiled, and then heard herself demand, "Where?" For last night Evan had sent her an odd

219

note, canceling their plans.

"She saw him at the Fifth Avenue Hotel."

She was relieved. "That is where he currently lives."

"He was with a lovely redheaded woman and three small children. Apparently they all had supper together." Leigh Anne smiled sweetly.

Bartolla froze. And the blood drummed in her ears, almost deafening her. *"I beg your pardon?"*

Leigh Anne's delicate, dark eyebrows lifted. "I'm afraid I don't know any more than that. Beth did not know the woman and Evan was so involved with her and the children that he never even saw the Tylers. I heard he was so rapt he never saw anyone or anything in the dining room — other than his company, of course."

"Maggie Kennedy," Bartolla breathed, almost seeing red.

"I beg your pardon?" Leigh Anne asked.

Bartolla did not hear her. It was impossible, unbelievable, that Evan would cancel their plans to be with that faded, unhappy seamstress. Bartolla was a countess, for God's sake!

But it wasn't impossible, not if Leigh Anne was telling the truth. In that case, he had jilted her last night for the other woman.

220

Once, briefly, she had thought she had glimpsed the spark of romance kindling between her lover and that homely harpy, but she had been certain she was wrong.

Now, she knew she had been right.

Now, she must put an end to this nonsense, once and for all.

Fortunately, the timing could not be better.

CHAPTER TEN

Thursday, April 24, 1902 3:00 p.m.

Julia had dressed with care for her appointment with Calder Hart. Not only had she donned a dark red suit and some modest diamonds, her ruby-red velvet hat trimmed in black, she had sent Hart a note well before the breakfast hour, requesting the interview. Being proper was in her nature, and with so much at stake she had no intention of jettisoning protocol.

His offices were at No. 1 Bridge Street, directly across from the wharves. The five-story, square building was handsome and stately, as she had expected, the bricks worn but washed clean, the design clearly Georgian, for most of this part of the city had been built in the eighteenth century. She suspected that he occupied the top floor and with it, had a fine view of the city's harbor and the famous monument given by the French, the Statue of Liberty. Julia entered

222

the lobby, which boasted gleaming wood floors, magnificent Persian rugs, huge crystal chandeliers and several seating areas. A clerk sat at a fine wood desk across the room not far from a sweeping staircase. Julia crossed the expanse, approaching him.

The gentleman stood, extending his hand. "Mrs. Cahill, I presume?" He smiled at her. "Mr. Hart is expecting you."

"I am a bit early," Julia said, glancing now at the artwork on the walls. Hart's passion was art and his collection was infamous, as he possessed some shocking works that he dared display in public. She had heard he had a terribly provocative life-size nude sculpture in his entry hall, but she had not yet been to his home and could not confirm the rumor. She had also heard that he had a frankly atheistic oil painting hanging there as well, but she was certain Hart was not an atheist — or she prayed he was not, as Francesca would be so intrigued by that quirk. She hoped the rumor was ill founded, as well.

The art in his lobby was, for the most part, very tasteful. There were several huge landscapes, one Romanesque war scene and some fine portraits. The periods clearly varied. Julia only recognized art that dated from the early nineteenth century, but she was pleased nevertheless that there were no scandalous nudes and no sacrilegious displays.

"Mr. Hart instructed me to bring you upstairs the moment you arrived," the clerk said. "I'm afraid we have no elevator," he apologized as they took to the stairs.

"I appreciate a good walk," Julia said, meaning it. She had found some years ago that the more she walked and the less she sat about, the easier it was to maintain her youthful figure. She had trouble sympathizing with those peers of hers who had gone to fat and never ceased moaning about the fact, while sitting on their rumps all day.

She so hoped she was doing the right thing.

Andrew remained uncommitted to the engagement. His belief that the facts of Hart's past spoke for themselves and he was simply not suitable for their daughter had actually caused Julia more than a single sleepless night. A part of her truly wished not to meddle, but to sit back passively was against her very nature.

As she had assumed, his private offices were on the uppermost floor with breathtaking views of the harbor, the Statue of Liberty and the ocean. And as he came forward, clad in a dark suit and tie, smiling,

224

she took in his elegance and the elegant surroundings and she felt herself melt for the hundredth time. She could *not* be wrong about him and this match, she thought, smiling back at him.

"Julia, good day," Hart clasped her hand firmly, looking very pleased to see her. His smile was wide and his eyes sparkled. He was an undeniably seductive man.

"Good day, Calder, thank you for making the time to see me," she said, taking the seat he offered her but refusing any refreshments.

Hart seemed curious as to the purpose of her visit, but he was in no haste as he walked behind his large desk, the top inlaid with dark leather, the borders gilded, and sat down in a handsome carved chair that was clearly Spanish. "And what brings you so far downtown? I do hope you had other errands to run and did not come so far out of your way just to speak with me." He leaned back in the chair, relaxed but not indolent, seemingly confident but not arrogant.

"Actually, you are the sole cause of my journey downtown to the waterfront," she said.

"I would have called on you tonight, Julia. You had only to ask."

She had known he would, of course, as he was a gentleman, but she'd had no wish to be interrupted by either Francesca or Andrew. "I prefer a moment of privacy."

"I confess, I am intrigued." He smiled, a slight dimple appearing in his right cheek.

Julia became somber, but she did not have to decide where to begin, as she had rehearsed this speech for some time. "I have come to discuss Francesca."

"Of course," he said, clearly not surprised.

Julia sighed. "I love my daughter so, as you know. I am terribly proud of her, too, of how clever and purposeful she is. You know, when she was a little girl, just a child of six or seven, she would stand on the street outside of our home, with the nanny, of course, and hand out cookies to every impoverished man, woman and child who passed by. When she was a bit older, the cookies became pamphlets. I'll never forget when she first became involved in politics and reform and started standing on the street, soliciting votes for the cause of reform."

Hart smiled. "Let me guess, she was ten?"

"Eleven. She used to hide under Andrew's desk when the Citizens' Union had meetings at our home, listening to every word, every debate. Soon Andrew let her sit quietly in the corner, when she became too big to sit under the desk."

Hart chuckled. "That sounds like Francesca."

Julia also smiled. "There was never any doubt that she would be an activist like Andrew, really. She campaigned heavily with the goo-goos for Mayor Low's election, just as she campaigned heavily against Van Wyck four years ago."

His eyebrow lifted. "I assume there is no relation?"

Julia was aghast. "Dear Lord, no! My mother's family has nothing to do with that scurrilous gang of hooks and crooks. We share not one drop of blood!"

Hart smiled.

Julia leaned forward. "Reform has always been the dearest cause to Francesca's heart, Calder."

"And?"

She sighed. "Until she started with this investigative nonsense."

He was somber now, as well. For a moment he did not speak. "I am aware that you do not approve of her sleuthing."

"How can I approve? What mother wishes for their daughter to engage with thugs and rowdies? Francesca has been abducted and held against her will, she has had a knife put to her throat, she has been shot at! Dear God! I am amazed I am not already gray."

He smiled. "I intend to keep her safe, Julia, you may count on that."

"How? Do you intend to put your foot down and end this nonsensical investigative inclination of hers?"

His eyes darkened. "If you are asking me if I intend to marry Francesca and put her on a leash, the answer is no."

Julia started. "So you do approve of her sleuthing?"

"Not exactly." He stared thoughtfully. "I approve of her passion and dedication. In fact, I doubt I have ever met anyone, man or woman, more passionate in nature, and that I admire beyond words. I intend to support her in any cause she feels passionate enough to pursue. Indeed, I look forward to doing so," he said with a smile, and Julia wondered at his private thoughts.

This was not going the way she had expected. Every man she knew set rules for his wife. "Then steer her back to her one true passion — the cause of government reform. It is far less life-threatening than chasing down murderers, Calder."

He seemed amused. "I would certainly sleep easier if she gave up her sleuthing. But I will not ask her to do so and I won't manipulate her in any way, either. I'm sorry. I realize most husbands would — and do — dictate to their wives. I'm afraid I am not that kind of man. Maybe it is because I never had any intention of ever marrying. I've never paid any attention to the conventions attached to the matrimonial state, except to wonder at the absurdity of most of them." He shrugged. "I am marrying an independent woman." He smiled. "The notion pleases me no end."

"And if you wind up with a dead wife? Will that please you, as well?" Julia cried in frustration.

"Of course not!" Hart leaned across the desk, his expression grim. "Fortunately, as reckless as Francesca is, she is also clever enough to avoid the worst engagements. In any case, I intend to protect her to the best of my ability. And if that means I or Raoul, my bodyguard, accompanies her on her nefarious missions, then so be it. But I won't cage her, Julia. And, as I told your husband, that is why we suit."

She knew a brick wall when confronted with it. Still, even bricks could come tumbling down, given the right push. "And what about Rick Bragg?"

Hart's expression never changed. He sat back and asked mildly, "What about him?"

"A few months ago my daughter decided that she was in love with him. She still runs about the city with him. She told me they are working together trying to find this terrible Slasher. You don't mind?" Julia watched him very carefully.

If he did mind, it was impossible to tell. "I trust Francesca," he said.

Julia felt despair. "My daughter only means well, and I know you know that. But she is impulsive, recklessly so. I really don't think it helps the cause of your engagement and your marriage for her to spend so much time in the company of a man she so admires. And she does admire Rick Bragg. Surely on that score you must agree with me."

He stood. "I won't pretend to enjoy the fact that she works so closely with my half brother, but I would rather she confront the unsavory elements of her sleuthing with him at her side than alone. For he will also do anything to keep her safe. Surely you realize that?"

Julia got to her feet. "Calder, you know how much I want this marriage. It frightens me, Francesca working with Rick Bragg! I don't like it. And never mind that his wife is back in his home, she is also terribly crippled, and how long will that last? Why can't you humor me? It is hardly leashing Francesca to ask her to behave with some decorum. It is not proper for her to sleuth with Bragg without a chaperon." She was firm. "At least send Raoul with them."

"Unfortunately, he is the police commissioner and he has vast resources at his disposal — resources she needs."

"No. This isn't about resources! This is about keeping company with another man." Julia stared, trembling and hoping she had not pushed Hart too far.

Hart stared back, the silence long, his face impassive. "So, in your opinion, knowing your daughter as you do, she sleuths with Bragg merely to spend time with him?"

"Not exactly," Julia said, somewhat shaken. Would Hart never reveal his hand? "I know my daughter. I know how stubborn she is. I know that once she gives her heart away, she can never take it completely back. Rick Bragg is the first man she ever looked at in a romantic way. It may have been a brief liaison, but nothing will ever change the fact that he was her first love." Julia took up her gloves and purse. She had exaggerated deliberately but hoped Hart would not realize it. "I would recommend that you think about what I have said."

He walked her to the door. "I appreciate

231

your concern, Julia." He smiled at her, apparently unshaken. "Please, do not worry yourself. Francesca's safety is my first and absolute priority. I will keep her safe but I won't disallow her anything. It's not my place to do so."

She could have argued that every husband had every right to disallow a wife anything he chose. "And Bragg?" Julia asked tersely.

"Francesca is marrying me," he said softly. "She chose me, not him."

She smiled grimly at him. "Then I suppose it is fortunate that Leigh Anne did not die in that carriage accident."

Hart's expression did not waver. If he understood her meaning, he gave no sign. "It would have been a terrible tragedy," he said.

"Thank you, Calder, for your time," she said, but there was no happiness in her heart. Worried no end, knowing she had failed, she left.

Hart closed the door and turned. His jaw began to flex and his temples visibly throbbed; his eyes had turned black. His heart pounded as hard as if he'd just had a mad dash around the block. Then he realized his gums actually ached and he tried to soften the jaw muscles in his face. But it was not to be done.

He cursed.

As if he did not know that he was Francesca's second choice.

As if he loved the fact that she spent hours every day — and sometimes at night — in the company of his perfect, oh so respectable brother, the man she had loved *first.*

He stared unseeingly at the breathtaking view outside his office windows.

He wanted to trust Francesca. But Julia was more than right — she had given a piece of herself to Rick and he doubted she would ever take it back. Worse, she was as reckless and impulsive as she was passionate, and who knew better than he how easily lust could be kindled? Except that for Francesca and Rick it was not lust, it was love.

He cursed again and a portrait loomed in his mind's eye, a beautifully painted wedding portrait of him and Francesca in their bridal finery, smiling and happy. As he stared closer, into the background of the portrait, into the background of their lives, he saw his brother on a dark, smoky street, on the run, chasing a fugitive. The focus changed, widening and he saw now that Rick was not alone. There was a woman running at his side, a woman chasing the fugitive, and that woman was Francesca.

He wanted to trust Francesca, but he did not know if he could.

He didn't trust his brother, and why should he? They hated one another.

But mostly, it was their love that he did not trust.

Francesca paused before the door of a clockmaker's shop, briefly confused. Francis O'Leary had given the police the home and business addresses of her fiancé, Sam Wilson. She glanced at her notepad and saw that this was the correct number. Apparently Wilson worked in a clock shop. Was he an apprentice to a clockmaker, then? It was a rare craft that required more than rudimentary training. Francesca realized it was far more likely that he was a sweeper.

She stepped inside, the doorbell tinkling. A man in his mid to late thirties with heavy graying sideburns sat behind the counter, making marks upon a finance ledger. He wore no jacket, but his waistcoat was burgundy brocade, a bit out of fashion, and he had a fine gold watch in the pocket there. He looked up as she entered.

Francesca smiled. "Are you the proprietor of this establishment, sir?" she asked.

The gentleman stood, closing the ledger. "Yes, I am. We can fix the finest clocks, miss, and the most unusual ones, too, I might add." He smiled, his somewhat weary face brightening, his gaze taking in the fact that she carried no packages and hence no clock. "We also have some fine clocks for sale, and some Swiss watches."

Francesca had already noted a dazzling display of intriguing clocks in all different sizes and with vastly different hands and faces. "I'm afraid I have no clock or watch to repair and I am not really in need of a new clock or watch," she said ruefully. "I am a sleuth, sir, and I am looking for your employee, Sam Wilson. I am afraid I must ask him a few questions, if you do not mind."

The clockmaker started. "I am Samuel Wilson," he said.

Francesca quickly recovered from her surprise. Wilson had to be fifteen years older than Francis and he was rather plain in his appearance. "You are the fiancé of Francis O'Leary?"

"Yes." Extreme concern covered his features. "Has something happened to Francis?" he cried, his dark eyes wide.

"No! She is fine. I spoke with her yesterday at the Lord and Taylor store." Francesca smiled reassuringly. But she wondered how Sam would react if he ever found out the truth about his fiancée — that legally, she remained married.

Wilson sat down, clearly relieved. He had become pale.

"I'm sorry I gave you such a fright," Francesca said. Now she carefully looked Sam Wilson over. He was on the tall side, but shy of six feet. He clearly wore a suit — she saw the jacket hanging on a wall peg and it matched his trousers. It was not gray but a brown tweed, and not of the best quality. She looked at his hands.

He wore no ring, but his hands were the hands of a craftsman or an artist. He had almost delicate hands and long, capable fingers. He clearly did not have the blemished hands of an ordinary worker. When she said goodbye and shook his hand, she would determine if he had any calluses. She doubted it. "Is something wrong?" Wilson asked.

"I must ask you some questions about that terrible assault on Francis," she said.

"I already spoke with the police. You said you are a sleuth?" He was less distressed now and mildly disbelieving.

Francesca handed him a business card. "I am working with the police on this matter," she said firmly. "How long have you known Francis?"

"We met in March." He began rubbing his chin.

Was he distressed, she wondered. "How did you both meet?"

He smiled then. "On the street. It was raining and we were running to get inside from the cold. We crashed into one another in the doorway of a small grocery store. She was so pretty . . . I apologized profusely and somehow we wound up sipping coffee in a small restaurant bar."

Francesca glanced at the shop again. A handsome rug covered the floor and two upholstered chairs, appearing new, faced one another in front of a wall mirror. He had dozens of fine clocks for sale. A man like Sam Wilson was a step up in the world for Francis. "She is very pretty," she agreed. "I heard you are now engaged."

He nodded, but he remained pale. "I never meant to marry again. I have a grown son and a granddaughter. My wife died a few years ago of a colonic cancer. But when Francis was attacked, I realized I could not lose her. I realized how much I love her." He began to tremble, clearly distraught.

"Did you see her the day of the attack?"

"I walked her home," he said, hushed. "It was two weeks ago, Monday, April 7. I left her at the front door of that awful building where she lives." Suddenly his voice rose. "The sooner we are married the better. The sooner she moves in here, with me, the safer she will be! I own the entire building," he added proudly. "The two floors above are for living and there's a garden out back. We have roses in the spring."

"So you left her on the street? You did not walk her up to her flat?" Francesca asked, beginning to take notes.

He blushed. "I didn't want to be that bold. I was trying to be a gentleman. I know Francis truly appreciates my respect."

"Did you see anyone on the street? Do you remember seeing anyone lurking about?"

"No."

"Think hard, please, Mr. Wilson. What kind of day was it?"

"It was a cool, windy day. She was cold and her coat wasn't warm enough. The sky was gray, but not the kind of gray that means rain. I wish now I had taken her upstairs!" he cried passionately.

She reached for his hand. As she had thought, it was smooth and uncallused. "You could not have known what would happen. Were there any passersby?"

"Yes, a pair of shopgirls, giggling over some gossip. They were fair and I noticed them." He looked away as if guilty of a crime.

"What were they wearing?" Francesca asked, hoping to spark his memory. Still, it was interesting he had noticed the shop-girls.

"Gray skirts, I think — no, blue, a grayish blue." He suddenly smiled at her. "One had on a tweed coat. She had red hair, I think."

Margaret Cooper had had red hair. "And you saw no one else on the street?"

He suddenly straightened, very somber. "Wait a moment, Miss Cahill." He blinked, then blinked hard, again and again. "I think . . . we bumped into someone. We were laughing after the shopgirls had passed — I asked her to supper and we bumped into someone — no, a man bumped into us — some tall gent — and he begged our pardon. He was English — no, Irish . . . I'm not sure, but he wasn't American." He suddenly shrugged. "I'm afraid that's all I can remember, two shopgirls and some gent in a bowler hat."

Francesca was chilled. Was Sam Wilson a master manipulator and clever liar? Had he just fabricated the story he had told her? Or was he a capable clockmaker in love with a pretty shopgirl almost half his age? Had Sam Wilson assaulted Francis and Kate and then killed Margaret Cooper, or had he just described the Slasher — a gent with an accent in a bowler hat?

Or was neither the case?

"Mr. Wilson? Where did you go after you left Francis?"

He blinked. "Why, I hailed a cab and went home, of course."

She studied him but he was wide of eye. "I'm afraid I do have to ask you where you were on the evening of Monday, April 14," she said.

He started. Then he cried, "What is this about, Miss Cahill? You think I am the Slasher?"

"I said no such thing," she returned calmly, surprised by his outburst. And now, tears filled his eyes.

"I don't recall where I was that night! Why should I? Most evenings I am here, in my repair shop, working on my clocks. Sometimes I have supper at my son's home. But I haven't dined there in some time — not in a good month, I think."

He was flushed and Francesca could not help but think that the Slasher would make sure he had a solid alibi. Wouldn't he?

Suddenly a clock began to strike and then another one chimed and a cuckoo sounded and another clock rang and another and the shop was resonating with a hundred clocks marking the evening hour.

It was 5:00 p.m.

Hart was going to be at Sarah's at six for the unveiling of her portrait.

Francesca straightened. "I am late!" she cried. She smiled at Sam Wilson but all she could think of now was her fiancé. "Thank you so much for your time."

He watched her flee in astonishment.

CHAPTER ELEVEN

Thursday, April 24, 1902 5:55 p.m.

"He's not here yet," Francesca cried breathlessly. As she had run from the cab to Sarah's front door, she had not seen his six-in-hand.

"No, he's not. It's not quite six, Francesca," Sarah said with a smile.

Francesca laid her purse and gloves on a small table in the huge entry hall, then began to wring her hands. "What if he *doesn't* like it?"

Sarah took her arm. "Then that only means the theme is too suggestive for a respectable wife." Her eyes danced with laughter as she spoke.

"I am hardly respectable now, and I doubt that will improve when I am married," Francesca said. Her pulse raced with worry and anxiety. "Maybe I should hide."

"Hide?" Sarah clearly had not a clue as to what she meant.

"I know this is vastly immature, but I could hide in your studio to see his reaction and —"

"That *is* immature," Sarah said, laughing. "Francesca, if he doesn't like it, that doesn't mean he isn't smitten with you. He obviously finds you beautiful. Maybe, though, you should wait here in the hall while I show him the portrait."

"Maybe you're right," Francesca whispered when the doorbell rang. Instantly her anxiety heightened. She turned nervously as the Channings' doorman let Calder Hart in.

He handed off a walking stick as he entered, hatless as usual, dressed in black, never looking at the doorman once. His gaze was on both women. "I wondered if you would be here," he said to Francesca, smiling.

She was so nervous she could not respond.

He took Sarah's hand and he seemed amused. "Good evening. You look rather pleased with yourself, indeed," he said, before glancing at Francesca, rather curious now.

"I am very pleased with the portrait, Calder. I only hope you like it as much as I do," Sarah said eagerly.

"I have little doubt," he remarked, but he

was already standing before Francesca, his gaze mild on hers. "Have you had a difficult day, darling?"

She nodded, then shook her head. "I mean, it has been a very good day, we have a small lead, Kate Sullivan swears that the Slasher is a tall gentleman and Francis O'Leary's fiancé might fit the bill," she cried, aware that she was nearly babbling.

He tucked her arm in his rather firmly. "I actually understood all of that," he said with good humor. "What's wrong? Why are you ready to jump out of your skin?"

She met his gaze and found it had become dark and intent. She shook her head again, breathlessly.

"Has something else happened?" he asked rather sharply. "Was there another attack? Have you been stalked, threatened, assaulted?"

"No, nothing else significant happened, really," she said, refusing to admit her insecurities to him now. Then she thought about Brendan Farr. She shivered. "Actually, we learned Farr ordered Inspector Newman to incompletely file a report on the case. We caught the omissions, but Farr doesn't know we are on to his game — whatever it might be. Newman will now report directly to Bragg if he is asked to compromise the investigation again." She smiled a little at him. Discussing the case felt like firm footing, indeed.

"So you and Rick are already up to your shirtsleeves in this case," he mused.

"Yes," she said, and added eagerly, "There's one more detail, a possible clue. In my interview with Francis, she told me she has been dreaming that the Slasher called her a faithless bitch. She says it is so real, she can't help but wonder if he did speak to her that way."

He was silent for a moment. "Does Kate Sullivan have any similar recollections?"

"No," Francesca admitted. "But remark this. Francis's husband abandoned her two years ago and she is engaged now to Sam Wilson. He is a well-off clockmaker, and he has not a clue as to the fact that she remains married."

He studied her for a moment. "Perhaps he has found out the truth about his fiancée. That would be motive to assault her — and other women like her."

"I don't think so. The police have been trying to locate Thomas O'Leary but it will be a miracle if they actually do so. He may have gone out West. Bragg thinks he could be dead. Not a soul has heard from him in all this time."

"What do you plan for tomorrow?" he asked after a brief pause.

"I wish to speak with Father Culhane, as I am running out of clues to pursue. I can ask him what he knows about David Hanrahan." She sighed, feeling a bit grim. "If Kate is right, and the Slasher is a gentleman, it is not David Hanrahan."

"He could never pass for a gentleman," Hart agreed. "But you are suspicious of Wilson?"

"He is a gentleman, firmly middle class, and as much as I hope he is not our killer, I simply cannot rule him out."

Hart studied her and finally he smiled, tipping up her chin. "I think you will solve this case in record time," he said softly.

His praise was merely implied, but still, she was thrilled. But she tried to hide her pleasure. "I hope so! We must prevent another attack this coming Monday," she said as briskly as possible. But she was terribly aware of him as he removed his hand, and of the portrait Sarah was about to unveil.

"Let me know how I can help," he said, and then he gestured at Sarah, who stood not far from them, wide-eyed and listening raptly to their every word. "I think our hostess awaits. I am sorry," he apologized to her.

"Francesca's investigations become addictive in no short time."

"So I can see," Sarah said, both dark eyebrows raised. Then she beamed. "Do follow me, please!"

Francesca dismissed all thoughts of the case. She stole a glance at Hart, who was darkly devastating, as always. There had been so many beautiful women in his life, in his bed . . . Did she really expect him to admire her portrait? For her, it was a highly significant moment. Posing had taken courage and commitment. Perhaps, for him it would just be another pretty nude.

"Shall we?" Hart murmured, guiding her forward.

She dared to meet his dark, probing gaze. "Of course," she said, reminding herself that if she could face killers alone, she could surely withstand some slight criticism from the man she loved.

Her heart lurched as they followed Sarah down the hall. It was becoming harder and harder to deny the feelings growing inside her, she thought. In his arms there was always passion and so much of it, but at times like these, it truly felt like love.

All the lights were on in Sarah's studio. Like the Cahill home and the most modern of the city's residences, the Chandlers had electric lighting, a telephone and hot and cold running water. Sarah paused to let them precede her inside, and then she went to the covered easel in the middle of the room and stood beside it, no longer smiling.

Francesca bit her lip and slipped free of Hart's grasp.

He didn't seem to notice. "Please," he said to Sarah.

Sarah seemed pale. She pulled the cloth from the easel, revealing the nude.

Francesca did not look at her portrait — not yet. She stared at Hart and saw his eyes widen.

He focused on the canvas, very intent, and she watched his gaze slip over her likeness, in the exact way he had so often looked at her.

Her pulse quickened.

Hart didn't move. His gaze returned to the face in the portrait — *her* face — and moved slowly from feature to feature. His regard slid down her throat and moved even more slowly over the swollen profile of her breast. Then his eyes were drawn down the length of her back, the swell of her buttocks and finally, he gazed at the rest of the portrait and the red dress.

Francesca hugged herself, a roaring in her

ears. Her cheeks were warm.

The room was hugely, heavily silent. Hart seemed to have no inclination to speak. It no longer mattered. He was looking at the portrait, but he was as acutely aware of Francesca as she was of him.

Desire, huge and hot, gathered in him, in her, between them, around them.

Her heart felt like a trapped winged bird in the cage that was her chest.

Hart finally turned to Sarah. And while he might have been looking at the artist, Francesca knew his real attention never wavered, not even once, from her as she stood there behind him.

"You have created a beautiful portrait, Sarah. I more than like it. You have captured Francesca exactly as I wished her to be portrayed."

Sarah beamed. "I am so glad you like it, Calder."

He turned to the portrait again and stared. A huge silence fell.

Francesca wondered what he was thinking, exactly.

Finally, slowly, Hart turned. Francesca did not move as he faced her. Their gazes instantly locked.

He was imagining her nude, she knew it. And he wanted to take her in his arms —

she knew that, too.

Suddenly Sarah said something, something Francesca could not decipher. Hart did not seem to hear her either, as he remained utterly still. Francesca was vaguely aware of Sarah ducking her head and hurrying out. She was vaguely aware of a door closing.

Hart continued to stare at her.

She wet her lips and tried to find her voice. It was as if her tongue had been cut out. "You really like it?" she managed to say.

A faint, faint smile. "Yes. I really like you."

The gathering heat threatened to erupt. "Do you —" She stopped.

"Do I what?" he asked very softly. "Do I want to see you in the flesh just like that? Yes, I do," he said, and somehow he was standing before her, his strong hands on her small waist, his breath feathering her ear. He was smiling, so much more seductive than any man had any right to be.

"Do you really think I look like that?" she heard herself ask, desperately wanting him to say yes.

"Oh yes," he said softly, and she saw him wet his lower lip. "Oh yes, Francesca, I do."

"Calder," she whispered, a plea.

His grip tightened. "I don't feel noble

tonight, Francesca. I don't feel noble at all," he warned quietly. And he bent and kissed the lapel of her jacket, folded back directly over the center of her breast.

She cried out, stunned, and not just physically. Did he mean what she thought he did? Was he finally ready to cast all reservation aside and make love to her? Because just then, she wanted nothing more, and her trembling body was the proof.

He smiled at her, just a little, as his palm cupped the side of her face. "Darling," he whispered, "you look ready to faint."

She was choking on the ache of need inside of her. "I am ready to do far more than faint, Calder," she said desperately. "Last night wasn't enough."

"No, it wasn't, was it?" He pulled her closer and brushed his mouth tenderly over hers.

Francesca gasped with pleasure as their lips brushed. Hart seemed in no hurry and she gripped his shoulders and strained against him, shaking like a leaf. Hart made a sound, beginning to kiss her with some urgency, his own hands tightening on her.

Suddenly he exploded. He pulled her close, crushing her so she lost the ability to breathe, his mouth opening, taking hers, fusing hungrily with hers, and she felt him shuddering with pent-up desire. And then he yanked off her jacket. Francesca glimpsed his face as he did so and saw the dark lust there and was so stunned it was a moment before she realized that she had never seen this side of him before.

He wanted her desperately and for the first time, he was not masking his emotions.

He pulled her close again, kissing her, murmuring her name, and as she opened desperately to accommodate him, as she tried to remain standing, she realized he had already unbuttoned her shirtwaist. She could barely assimilate that fact when it was tossed aside.

And he looked at her.

She saw the hunger in his eyes, the hunger, the warning and even some surprise. And she suddenly knew that tonight he would not be denied — that tonight the courtship was over.

And then she could look no more. His face hardened and he tore open her chemise. Francesca gasped as his mouth closed over her nipple, his teeth tugging and the pleasure rushed through her with deliciously painful force. She clung, moaning, stunned, and he laid her on the floor.

She began to shake, wet heat pooling dangerously now. "Hurry, Calder, hurry," she begged, stroking her hands down his hard, powerful back.

He held her face in his hands. "Do you know what you are asking?" he demanded.

"Yes."

He stared, eyes wide, mouth hard. Then, "I am dangerously close to doing as you ask." He lowered his head, tugging her into his mouth.

Francesca wept with pleasure and pain.

Hart whispered roughly, "You're too beautiful like this, Francesca. I want to rub myself all over you. Would that be too shocking?"

She could barely understand him as she whirled through the maelstrom of desire he had created. His hand was between her thighs, exploring the wet heat there, encouraging her to fly harder, faster, farther. And even as immersed in pleasure as she was, she reached for him. He leaped firmly up against her hand, through his trousers, thrilling her. He quickly kissed her. "How quickly you learn," he murmured.

She felt a rush of pleasure and she unfastened his trousers. "Tell me what to do."

He paused, watching now, carefully, and she helped his massive length spring free of the dark wool. "You do nothing, Francesca, nothing except take the pleasure I am about to give you."

Their gazes met; he kissed her again, long and slow.

And then he moved. She could not smile or even think. He was hot, hard and as smooth as velvet as he brushed between her breasts and over them. The knot of desire in the pit of her being twisted and tightened, oh so precariously. Francesca began to sob as he brushed over each painfully hard nipple and she could no longer stand this, it, him. She cried out, exploding.

He kissed her frantically as she spasmed uncontrollably into what seemed to be infinity, hearing her own wild cries as if she were someone else, the pleasure simply too much to ever bear. The orgasm seemed to last forever when suddenly she was floating and aware of Calder Hart once again.

She started, for he was lying on top of her now and her skirts were gone — her bare legs were wrapped around his wool-clad ones, his manhood pressed insistently against her naked thigh and his fingers brushed the wet, swollen mound of her sex, caress after caress. His mouth was pressed against her throat and she became aware now of his kisses there, hot and urgent, each and every one of them.

Her sex tightened deliciously, beginning

to heat and throb; dazed, she realized he had only to move very slightly and he would thrust deeply into her and sweep her away into another climax very, very quickly. She held him hard, gasping. Were they going to make love?

She gripped his shoulders, to hold him at bay. And Francesca did not know what to think. All she could see was herself as a bride and Calder as the groom, standing in the master bedroom of his house on their wedding night.

But this wasn't their wedding night and the floor of Sarah's studio was hard and cold beneath her bare shoulders, her back and legs.

Hart embraced her so tightly that she could not breathe. His manhood felt like a knife but he did not tear into her. He merely held her, his entire body trembling, and she knew he had come to his senses, too.

She held him as tightly, eyes closed, breathless and afraid and relieved.

He suddenly moved off of her, away from her. She did not move. Tears suddenly came and she squeezed her eyes tightly closed to prevent them from falling. She was a woman, not some child, and she must not cry. Besides, there was no reason to cry — no reason at all.

As she sat up, reluctantly now, she realized how she must look. She fumbled with her skirts, keeping her eyes downcast; he stilled her hand.

"Look at me," he said quietly.

If she did, he would see her tears. Francesca tried to compose herself. She was a capable, clever, professional woman and she had wanted Calder Hart's lovemaking. She still wanted his lovemaking. But not like this on the dirty floor.

"Francesca, please do not turn away from me now." There was an odd note in his tone.

She swallowed and looked up, trying to pull her torn chemise together.

Silence filled the room.

He stared at her grimly. Then he reached out and wiped the tear from her cheek with his forefinger. "Why are you crying?" he asked.

"I'm not."

His look was skeptical; she gave up. "I don't know. I've so longed for this — for what almost happened — and then I became afraid."

He cupped her cheek, his eyes dark. "That's understandable, I think. I was very rough and very demanding. I am sorry. And no apology will do. But now you know the truth. The beast is far stronger than that other man. He doesn't exist. It was a sham, Francesca, a total sham."

"No!" she cried.

Hart straightened and began to pace. "There is no excuse for my behavior," he said tersely. "We can both pretend that I am noble, but in the end, the truth will out."

She covered her breasts with her shirt. "You are noble! You have been nothing but noble with me!"

He made a disparaging sound. "I promised you a wedding night, Francesca, but tonight I actually changed my mind." His eyes darkened with more anger. "Tonight I wanted to take you on the floor."

She became uneasy knowing he had a point to make and afraid of what it might be. "We both lost control, Calder, not for the first time," she added, trying to smile and soften his mood.

"I am always in control," he said, staring down at her. "The fact is, you deserve someone far better than myself. Tonight I almost took you for all the wrong reasons. I could have hurt you in more ways than one."

She did not like the look in his eyes or the expression on his face. Her heart raced with sickening force. She slowly said, "But you didn't hurt me. And you didn't break the promise you made, either. And that is what counts."

He stared for a long moment. "Will you ever admit that I am not half the man my brother is?"

She cried out. "You are a good man, Calder Hart! A very good man! Please, don't bring Rick between us!"

"I can't decide if you really believe that or you are merely determined to pretend to believe what you wish to believe."

She strode to him, forgetting how barely clad she was. "I won't let you do this. Yes, we lost some control, and yes, we almost slept together, but we didn't. Not because you are trying to be noble, but because you *are* noble, Calder."

He softened and his gaze slipped. "Your chemise is slipping — but I don't mind."

She realized she had ceased covering herself. Pulling the garment closed and blushing, she returned his smile, praying they had finished a subject she had no wish to continue.

He turned away, raking his fingers through his short hair. She was surprised to see his hand trembling. "You had better get dressed before someone catches us in this very compromising position."

She slipped on the shirtwaist and buttoned it with clumsy fingers. "I fear that posing for that portrait has already ruined me."

He glanced at her, his gaze skipping to her cleavage as she did up the remaining buttons. "Your portrait remains our secret, Francesca. As much as I would love to display it to the world as a work of art, I never will."

Something sexual stirred within her. "Then I should certainly be the scandal in this city."

He turned and gazed oddly at her. "Yes."

Her unease escalated. His tone had lightened but his mood remained the harbinger of some terrible, deadly storm. Hart was the most complicated man she had ever met and she felt certain she would never fully understand him. "Why are you looking at me like that?" she asked in dismay.

He said grimly, "Your mother called today."

She stiffened in alarm. "I see," she said. "Julia is at the bottom of this!"

"She worries about your welfare, as she should."

"Because of you?" she gasped.

"No, because of your sleuthing. I did my best to reassure her," he added, his gaze holding hers.

"Thank you," she said warily.

"Of course, I did point out that you work closely with the police, and that guarantees quite a bit of protection."

She wished he had not returned to the topic of Rick Bragg. "Working with the police does insure some amount of protection," she agreed very carefully.

He faced her, hands on his slim hips. "Julia thinks it inappropriate for you to continue to work with my brother."

She smiled and it felt like a grimace. "So now we get to the heart of the matter."

"An interesting choice of words." His smile was brittle. "I would have said the *bottom* of the matter."

She bristled. "Calder, don't. I am marrying you, not Rick."

He stared at her.

She stared back. Then slowly, "And what do you think?"

He turned away. "You already know what I think."

She knew he wanted to marry her — although she still didn't quite comprehend why — and she knew he hated the fact that she had once been in love with his half brother. She knew he chose to view himself as selfish and self-serving. She sighed. "I am not referring to what you think about our relationship or yourself. Do you agree with my mother?"

"I actually prefer you to chase hooks and crooks and the worst sort of felons with Rick than by yourself."

Relief filled her; she smiled. "Thank you."

He faced her sternly. "From this moment on, I am giving you Raoul as your driver. He will go everywhere with you, Francesca."

She tensed. "He will be my driver or my chaperon? Or perhaps he will be a spy?" Her tone had turned to acid.

He said far too smoothly, "He will actually be your bodyguard, darling. And this is not negotiable. I promised your mother I would protect you, and if I cannot roam the streets with you, then you shall have Raoul."

She paused, well aware of how convenient it would be to have her own driver. "Do you trust me?"

"I want to. I do. It's . . . I just wish you were less impulsive, and less caring." He hesitated and added, very firmly, "I do trust you. I would trust you with my life." And he met her gaze.

There was something in his eyes so direct and so profound that she was thrilled, for in a way, he was trusting her with his life by marrying her and forsaking all others. She went to him and wrapped her arms around him. "I trust you, too, Calder, with far more than my life." She smiled warmly at him but did not explain that she was handing him her heart and trusting him not ever to break it.

He raised an eyebrow in question.

She merely said, "You are going to be a wonderful husband."

"And you are deluded if you think that," he said, but he smiled.

"A little jealousy can be endearing."

He gave her a disbelieving look as they both knew his jealousy was not minimal when it was aroused. "It's nonsensical to wait an entire year to wed. We are both more than ready. I will speak with Andrew this weekend."

She gaped. Then, delighted, she cried, "Yes! Moving up the wedding would be wonderful! When, Calder? When would you really like to have the nuptials?"

He pulled her closer. "Your enthusiasm is so adorable," he murmured, kissing the tip of her nose.

She shivered with warmth and pleasure. "Tell Papa we want a June wedding."

He laughed. "June sounds fine, Francesca."

Then she worried. "But he is so determined to test your resolve and character for an entire year. Have you ever lost a negotiation?" she asked.

"Not in years," he assured her.

CHAPTER TWELVE

Thursday, April 24, 1902 7:00 p.m.

"Darling," she murmured, her palm on his chest, her thigh crossed over his. "That was so wonderful." Bartolla Benevente kissed his shoulder.

He was drifting in the pleasant aftermath of their wild lovemaking, not quite awake and not quite asleep. Evan didn't really hear her and he really didn't want to. The woman in his arms was exquisite, soft and silken and warm, her breasts full, surprising him, her legs somehow too long. He succumbed and drifted deeper and when he realized that her hair was the most amazing shade of strawberry and terribly curly, his heart lurched with excitement. *Maggie.* He wasn't quite sure why she was in his bed but he wasn't about to question it, oh no. He ran his hand over her smooth silken skin again and again, turning to take her more fully in his arms. He was completely aroused and when Maggie kissed him on the flat, hard plane of his chest, he finally made a protest.

He moved over her, claiming her mouth, tasting her for what had to be the first time, tasting, inhaling her . . . She was so lovely, so sweet, so pure . . . like the sunshine, or an angel. . . .

"Again?" she whispered with some surprise.

He could not speak and his answer was to slide deeply into her, shaking with excitement. And as he moved, as the desire instantly crested, he was jolted awake. She was moaning in pleasure, but so was he; he smiled, murmuring her name, opening his eyes, his hand in her wild, unruly hair.

He stiffened in absolute surprise as Bartolla climaxed before his very eyes and for a terrible moment, he could only stare, utterly dismayed.

Jesus.

He had been dreaming that he was making love to Maggie Kennedy.

Stunned — and aware of an impossible disappointment — he started to pull away from his lover. She clasped his arms. "Darling, what are you doing? What's wrong?"

He smiled at her, and it felt ghastly. "Sorry," he murmured, closing his eyes and finishing what he had mistakenly begun.

And when he began to climax, the Irish-woman appeared in his mind, smiling at him, and no matter how hard he thrust or how hard he tried, she would not leave him alone.

He flung himself onto his back, panting wildly while Bartolla laughed, sitting up. "You are such a man, darling," she whispered.

He threw one arm over his eyes, beyond shaken. He did not want to think about some pretty seamstress while he was making love to his mistress!

"Evan? Are you all right?"

He got up from the bed in one fluid movement, indifferent to his nudity. He gave her a brief smile and crossed the bedroom of his hotel suite. In the salon he poured himself a drink. His hand trembled.

And then he was angry. This was utter nonsense! Imagining another woman in his bed meant nothing at all — he had done so a hundred times, for God's sake. And Maggie Kennedy was not his type of lady, oh no. She was too sweet, even meek, for God's sake, and too damn good anyway for a rake like him.

"May I join you?" Bartolla asked.

He turned, quickly hiding his frown. Bartolla smiled in appreciation at his lean, hard body. She had slipped into her peignoir. A few weeks ago, shortly after their affair had commenced, she had begun leaving her possessions in his suite. He hadn't minded then but now, suddenly, it irritated him.

He took a bottle of champagne from the ice bucket and opened it. Champagne was her choice of drink.

She accepted the flute when he handed it to her. "Shall I get you a robe? Not that I mind, but if a maid walked in, she might never recover from such a view."

"Thank you," he said, absolutely indifferent to her suggestion. When she had left the salon he walked over to the window and gazed down at Fifth Avenue, where traffic remained heavy. The city's upper crust was out on the town, on their way to this fête or that, to a supper party, a ball, a charity or the theater. The urge to walk down the block to a private club he knew suddenly overcame him. He tensed.

It wasn't the first time. Every evening the urge came, and every evening he began to sweat, thinking about entering a game, any game, poker, craps, he didn't care what it was. God, there was simply nothing that came close to the rush of excitement of being at the tables, the stakes so high now, being life or death.

He tossed down his scotch.

Maggie's image came to mind, sweet and smiling. Then she looked him right in the eye and shook her head no.

Bartolla returned, smiling, handing him his robe, navy blue velvet with his initials embroidered in black and gold on the chest pocket. He slipped it on, belting it. "What are our plans for this evening?" he asked. He wasn't going to walk down the block. If he was very lucky, one day the urge would lessen, and if there was a god, it would even disappear.

"We have theater tickets, but I'm afraid the curtain goes up in an hour. I doubt I can be ready in time."

He finally faced the fact, as he stared out of the window, that he would rather be alone that evening than be with his mistress. But he didn't trust himself to be alone. Not one single bit.

"Darling." She took his empty glass and refilled it, handing it back to him. "I must speak with you about something."

Her tone was oddly serious. He glanced at her and saw that she wasn't smiling and some alarm began. Was she going to leave him? He truly liked her and definitely appreciated her skill in bed. There had been a time when Evan had thought himself in love with the countess. Now he realized he was not in love with her at all.

"It's all right," he heard himself say, and he realized he wouldn't be dismayed at all if their affair ended. In fact, maybe it was time for it to end.

Maggie smiled at him.

He was so surprised, that he felt himself gape. Why was she haunting him now? Why?

"Are you unwell?" Bartolla asked, guiding him to a chair.

"I'm fine," he said, very grim now. "I hope you're not thinking of leaving me." He had changed his mind. "I'm enjoying being with you immensely."

Maggie's eyes turned reproachful.

"You think I want to leave you?" she cried, clearly stunned. "Evan, darling, I am in love with you!"

There was no denying his dismay.

"Darling, I do hope you will be pleased."

He just looked at her, thinking about the club and the tables there, able to hear the roulette, the die, the laughter and conversation, able to feel the excitement. All the while, he kept thinking about Maggie Kennedy, too. "What are you talking about?"

She clasped his hand. "I'm pregnant, darling. I'm pregnant with our child. Isn't that wonderful?"

Even though it was only nine o'clock, Leigh Anne lay in bed, the lights out. But she wasn't even trying to sleep. The events of that day replayed in her mind while she listened to the sounds on the street.

She had taken a walk with the girls around Madison Square. Or rather, her male nurse had wheeled her chair while the girls had strolled alongside her, with Mrs. Flowers and Peter in tow. The girls had been so happy, Katie regaling Leigh Anne with stories of her day at school and her new best friend, Dot constantly interrupting with her attempts at communication. Leigh Anne fought the tears and the depression without success.

She bit on her hand to choke down a sob. She would never stroll in any park with the girls again.

How had she taken her health — her legs — her life for granted?

She wondered, not for the first time, if she was being punished for walking out on her husband four years ago, but she had never really believed then that she *was* walking out. She had been certain he would follow her and bring her directly home and then change his life to suit her needs. How naive, selfish and stupid she had been!

But, apparently, he *had* followed her. More tears came. Apparently he had come to Europe and then never identified himself, returning home alone. If only she had known he was there, nothing would have stopped her from finding him and returning with him.

But she hadn't known and she had waited and waited, and after a year and a half she had allowed herself to be seduced. She had been desperate for affection but the affair had been bitterly sweet. It hadn't eased the heartbreak and the comprehension that had then begun — her marriage might really be over.

At some point she had heard that he'd taken a mistress, a beautiful woman a bit older than he, a widow and intellectual, a suffragette like his mother. She had been terribly hurt but had pretended to herself that it didn't matter. There had been days when she still expected to see him enter a room, arriving to bring her home.

But he never came, not after that first time, and finally she had returned home to nurse her ailing father, trying to ignore the fact that only miles of railroad track now separated them and not an entire ocean.

But when Bartolla had written her inform-
ing her that Rick was falling in love with
another woman, she had rushed to New
York City on the next departing train.

And he had despised her from the moment he had set his eyes on her.

Now he said he wanted to take care of her.
She looked up at the ceiling and laughed
while she wept. *Never.*

She wiped her eyes. Did he really think to
attend political functions with his wife in a
wheeled chair? Did he think to wheel her
about himself, or would her nurse be in at-
tendance? And did he think she could hostess their parties when she could not even go
to the toilet by herself? The tears fell. And
what about making love? The one thing she
remained certain of was her husband's
amazing virility. Would he be celibate now?
She laughed rudely at the ceiling. Or was
she to look the other way as he took a
mistress? Pain stabbed her heart. He certainly wasn't going to touch her now!

She clapped her hand to her mouth to still
a sob. She hated herself for her self-pity, but
she was no martyr and no heroine. Francesca Cahill was brave and courageous. She
would somehow navigate life as a cripple if
this had been her fate. Leigh Anne knew
she should have never come back. God, he

deserved Francesca, he did.

The front door slammed.

Her tears stopped. She froze in alarm and strained to hear, and in sinking dismay she recognized his voice in the entry just downstairs. Quickly she exhaled, wiping the tears away with the sheet and then closing her eyes, pretending to be asleep.

Some minutes passed and he did not start up the stairs. Relief began. If only she could really fall asleep before he came up! But sleep eluded her now, when she spent so much time in a chair or in her bed, when all she wanted to do was sleep, sleep, sleep. And then she heard him.

She stiffened, reminded herself to breathe, and listened to his every footstep. The stairs were old, like the house, and each plank creaked. The footfall changed on the landing, where a thin runner was in the hall. She heard him pause in the doorway of their room, where Mr. McFee had left the door ajar.

She tried to breathe naturally, no easy task when her body was rigid with fear.

He approached the bed.

She prayed he would think she was asleep.

She felt him hesitate and then lean closer. His hand drifted over her shoulder and she shivered, tensing even more. As he moved

273

some hair from her face and adjusted the covers, she bemoaned the fact that his most innocent touch remained a sexual invitation. It had always been that way for her with him.

"Leigh Anne?" he whispered, and she knew that he knew she was awake.

She hesitated, wanting him to believe he was mistaken, that she was asleep, wanting him to leave.

"Do you need anything?" he asked softly, clearly not fooled by her pretense. And he touched her again, this time on the side of her cheek.

Her jaw ground down. She wanted to scream at him not to touch her. "I'm fine," she managed to say.

He hesitated, still leaning over her, not moving.

She became very alarmed and her eyes flew open and she met his intense, unwavering golden stare. "What are you doing?"

His temples throbbed visibly. "It's been a long day. I am getting ready for bed."

He never slept this early! She wanted to be alone! If only the house was larger, if only she had her own room, her own bed! "It's nine o'clock," she heard herself say, and she sounded terrified.

He just stared at her.

"Don't do this," she begged.

He hesitated for one more moment, then went around to his side of the bed, still completely dressed, even in his shoes, and he got in to lie down.

"What are you doing?!" she cried.

He moved close and pulled her into his arms. "Just let me hold you," he said.

She tried to say no. She tried to protest. But she couldn't speak; she wept instead.

It was so late and so dark — if only Bridget were safe!

Gwen left the omnibus and began walking as fast as she could. Her supervisor had made her stay late with two other workers to fill a large order for a major department store, an order that was overdue. There had been no choice; he had ignored her protestations, her fears. Hans Schmidt simply did not care that a cold-blooded killer was on the loose and that her daughter was home alone.

The night was black and still, starless and cool. A whispering breeze caressed her cheek, chilling her to the bone. Gwen could not breathe, choking on her fear for her daughter. There was very little traffic on the street as she paused on the sidewalk at the corner, waiting for a lone carriage to pass.

She saw no one. It didn't matter. A killer stalked the young women of the city and Margaret Cooper was proof of that. Even now, he could be in her flat, attacking Bridget . . .

But maybe David was there. She knew that he hated her now, with all of his heart. His demand that they reconcile was vicious, for he only wanted her back so he could spend the rest of his life flinging the fact of her single love affair in her face, every chance that he got. That, and to poison Bridget against her own mother. But she didn't think he hated his daughter, his flesh and blood. Still, she could not be sure. He was a weak, mean, cowardly man.

God knew he wouldn't help Bridget if she was in danger, but his presence might be enough to forestall the Slasher.

The carriage, pulled by a single bay, passed. A pebble flew out from its wheels and skittered her way. Casting one more glance behind her, she rushed across the cobbled street, thinking about how late it was, how dark. She was ready to weep.

Damn David. He had always been good for nothing and while she could not wish that she'd never met him — he was Bridget's father — she could wish that she'd never married him and had borne her child alone.

She reminded herself that the Slasher struck on Mondays, and today was Thursday. He also assaulted women, not children. But Bridget looked fifteen, not eleven, and she was so terribly beautiful. Men older than Gwen turned to ogle her all the time. And last month that awful man, Timothy Murphy, had abducted her to add her to his ring of beautiful child prostitutes. God, hadn't they suffered enough?

Gwen knew she only had two more blocks to go but it felt like two miles. She tried to continue to run, but she was exhausted and her legs were failing her now. She faltered, panting terribly and holding on to a street lamp for support. And then she felt the eyes, boring into her . . .

And she felt him there behind her . . .

As she realized he was there, he seized her arm.

Incapable of screaming, filled with terror, somehow knowing the Slasher had found her this time, Gwen whirled.

Slowly, he smiled.

"This is very wicked," Francesca said with a sigh. She smiled at Calder as she sat on a sofa in one of the many salons in his home, her jacket unbuttoned, her kidskin shoes on the floor, her feet tucked up beneath her.

She took another sip of the very old scotch and positively sighed. "Sooo wicked."

He sat in a facing chair, watching her with a smile, making no effort to taste his own drink. "I'm very glad you appreciate a finely blended and very old scotch whiskey."

She gave him a sidelong look. "Accepting your invitation to dine with you here, alone, could be even more wicked." How she hoped so.

His smile widened and he stretched out his long legs. "Our supper will be ready at any moment."

"Are you avoiding me?"

He chuckled. "Most definitely, darling. My full house is empty tonight. Rathe and Grace are out to supper. My cousin, D'Archand, is out on the prowl, I think, and Lucy went home last week. Other than the staff, we are very much alone."

The crisis they had just weathered felt very far distant, but the interlude of being in his arms did not. Francesca smiled at him, thinking about how nice it would be to be in his arms right now, enjoying a few kisses before their meal. She set her glass down.

"I should like to meet your second possible suspect, Francis O'Leary's fiancé."

Francesca had just stood up; she started. "You would?"

278

He sipped his scotch and eyed her over its rim. "I am a very good judge of character," he murmured.

She stared, debating his motives, hands on her hips. "You wish to distract me," she declared.

"I do." He grinned.

She approached, feeling very seductive, indeed. "Alfred will knock. No one is home. A kiss between fiancés is hardly unusual."

"A kiss," he said, smiling as he watched her very carefully now.

She came up to his side, her heart racing with excitement, enjoying being the predator, oh yes. She stood behind his chair. "A simple, little, tiny kiss," she breathed, leaning over him. Her bosom flattened against his upper back.

He turned his head to meet her gaze and he seemed somewhat amused. But his eyes held a familiar gleam and she knew he was hardly immune to this new game. "Do you really think to seduce me?"

She grinned. "Yes. And if that is a challenge, I accept," she said, delighted to be goaded.

"A challenge," he repeated, shaking his head. "It is not a challenge, Francesca."

"A warning, then . . . darling?" She laid her hands on his shoulders, caressing the strong muscles there. And his body tensed.

"A warning you will not heed," he murmured, his head tilting back.

She stroked the hair at his nape. "You know how I hate being told what to do." She bent lower and whispered, her mouth on his ear, "Let's wager, then. Can you resist me — or not?"

He shifted and met her gaze. His smile was lazy, but it did not reach his eyes. "And what do you wish to wager, darling?"

Their gazes locked. His eyes smoked and she thought with surprise and a rush of delight that he was as aroused and enthralled as she was. Somehow, he never did act very jaded around her. She leaned over him, brushing her mouth against his, his cheek now pressed solidly into her breast. Desire stabbed through her with unyielding, consuming force. She paused, briefly stunned at how playful passion could so quickly change into something so powerful, and she said, her tone odd and husky, "I want a few more hours in your bed, exactly like the last time."

He looked at her, unsmiling, and she knew he was remembering every moment of that wild interlude.

He reached for her and pulled her down and their mouths fused.

The door slammed open. "I heard Francesca was —" Rourke stopped.

Francesca leaped away from Hart, cheeks burning, heart rushing, feeling as if Rourke Bragg had just caught them in bed — with her in the dominant position. She smiled brightly at him. "Hello," she cried, tucking too many tendrils of stray hair to count behind her ears. Then she remembered she was shoeless, and she tried to hide her feet beneath her skirts.

His cheeks blotched pink. "I'm sorry."

Hart slowly stood. "The door was closed," he drawled.

Still blushing, Rourke said, "It was. I'll come back at another time."

"Don't leave. Francesca needs a chaperon," Hart said, laughter in his tone. "Scotch?"

Rourke, who took after the Bragg men with his dark, golden-brown hair, amber eyes and sun-kissed complexion, nodded and glanced at Francesca. "I seem to have left my good manners in Philadelphia."

"It's all right," Francesca said, meaning it now that she'd had a moment to recover her composure. She was terribly fond of Rourke and not because he looked like Rick Bragg's younger but nearly twin brother. He was a compassionate, considerate gentleman and he'd been rather heroic on several occasions, as well as helpful on more than one investigation. "I heard you have applied to Bellevue Medical College?" she asked with a wide smile.

"I had an interview yesterday and I believe it went very well," he said, returning her smile and accepting the scotch Hart handed him. "My final examinations end in mid-May and I will relocate then."

"I will be more than glad to lease you a room," Hart said with a straight face.

Francesca laughed but Rourke said, very seriously, "I doubt I could afford to lease a room from you. My tuition is very expensive and my personal budget doesn't leave much for rent."

Francesca was very surprised, as his family was extremely wealthy.

As if reading her mind, he said, "I'm not comfortable being lackadaisical with my family's money. Rathe and Grace have wanted to buy me a house, but I refused. I'm single and I can get on well enough in a room. It's really enough that they are paying my tuition and all my living expenses. I try to be frugal."

"Well, I cannot say I am surprised," Francesca said.

"Rourke, I was in jest," Hart said. "You'll

stay here. I have dozens of empty bedrooms. Take as many as you want."

"I'll think about it," Rourke said. "Thank you."

"You'll save yourself the cost of renting a flat," Hart pointed out.

Francesca tugged on Rourke's sleeve. "He needs the company — and the moral guidance you can offer him, as well."

Rourke laughed.

Francesca smiled at Hart, who smiled back, but she was actually serious about the former issue. When she had first met Hart, he'd been living completely alone in this huge house of his. But since Rathe and Grace had returned to New York with young Nicholas D'Archand, Rathe's nephew, they had been staying with him. Rourke's visits had also become frequent, and he also had been residing at Hart's when in the city. Francesca felt certain that the Calder Hart she had met at the end of January had been a lonely man, although he would deny it to his dying day. She was as certain that he enjoyed having so much family around him now.

Hart went to Rourke and clapped him on the shoulder. "She's right. Now that I am to give up my rakish ways, I need some severe moral support."

"He is being transformed before my very eyes," Rourke said to Francesca. He was smiling, but he seemed very earnest.

Francesca looked directly at Hart. "Actually, he is not." Her smile vanished. "Nothing's changed except that a prickly outer layer, meant to conceal, is finally being peeled away to expose what is really there."

Hart stared at her, and his cheekbones seemed to have a flush.

Rourke murmured, "It must be love."

And Francesca thought, you are noble and good, Calder, and I have not one doubt.

"She has a heart of gold. One must be a cold-blooded killer for Francesca to think ill of him." Hart turned away, fiddling with his drink.

"As I said, it must be love," Rourke said, glancing at his half brother and clearly meaning now that Hart was the one stricken by Cupid's arrow.

Hart shrugged.

Alfred appeared but no servants and no supper cart were with him. "Sir? There is an urgent telephone call."

Hart started for the door.

"Sir? It is for Miss Cahill," the balding butler said.

Hart turned to her as Francesca came forward, puzzled. "But I sent Mama a note telling her I was dining here. Who else would call?" And even as she spoke, she knew.

It was the case; something had happened; it was Bragg.

"It's Police Commissioner Bragg, sir."

Francesca bit her lip and looked at Hart. If he was dismayed — or anything else — she could not tell. For one more moment, she made no move to go to the telephone, awaiting his real reaction.

"Alfred, please show Francesca to the telephone. And I do believe supper has been postponed," Hart said.

Francesca started eagerly forward when Hart took her arm and said, "Darling, your shoes."

CHAPTER THIRTEEN

Thursday, April 24, 1902 9:00 p.m.

The door to the flat was wide open and inside, Francesca saw Bragg and Newman in discussion, standing in the center of the single room. A roundsman in his blue serge uniform and leather helmet stood in the hall. Francesca nodded at him as she entered, Hart at her side.

Bragg looked up. His gaze widened when he saw his half brother, but only for an instant.

Francesca stared beyond him at the bed, where Kate Sullivan lay, very much dead.

She hugged herself, hard.

Hart touched her elbow as if to steady her.

"She was so afraid when I last saw her. That was only this morning!" she said in dismay. And Francesca was shaken. Today was Thursday. They had been wrong, incredibly wrong, to believe the killer would wait until Monday to strike yet again.

Bragg walked up to them. He appeared disheveled and grim, his tie askew, some golden hair falling across his forehead. Looking at Francesca, he said, "I'm sorry to interrupt your evening."

She shook her head, briefly incapable of speech, her gaze on the young blond woman who lay fully dressed on the bed, arms flung wide, head turned so grotesquely to the side that her neck must have been broken. Her hair was down, cascading about her shoulders, her chest, her neck. It was tangled and crusted with blood.

Hart responded in her stead. "We don't mind." He stared at his half brother.

Bragg stared back. "Are you on this case now, as well?" There was tension in his tone.

Francesca tore her gaze from Kate, wishing she could have somehow prevented this terrible murder. She glanced at Bragg and then at Hart and almost stepped between them. As usual, a battle line had somehow been drawn. Hart's smile was clearly mocking. "He offered me a lift," she lied quickly, before Hart could speak.

Bragg shrugged as if he did not care.

Francesca turned back to Kate. She didn't have to walk over to the bed to see that the body did not lie in a pool of blood. Instead, some splotches of blood were on the side of the bed and then a bloody trail led to the center of the room. Clearly she had been dragged from that spot, just beyond where they now stood, to the bed.

"He cut her here," Hart murmured, noting what she had just deciphered. "But was she still alive when he deposited her in the bed? Is her neck broken?"

"It appears so," Bragg said. "I am guessing she did not die from the knife wound but from the broken neck."

Francesca shivered and was ill. "You think he broke her neck and cut her *afterward,* and then dragged her onto the bed," she said, low.

Both men looked at her.

"We cannot know," she said.

"You're right," Bragg agreed. "We can't know. We can only know for certain that she was first cut while she stood in the center of the room and that he then dragged or carried her to the bed, where he laid her down. We also know that it is Thursday, not Monday. Most serial killers do not deviate from the pattern they set."

"You think we have a copycat on our hands?" Francesca asked, referring to slang recently coined by the press to denote a murderer who imitates the crimes of a previous killer.

"It's too soon to say. The coroner needs to examine the body."

"Even though it is Thursday, even though her neck is broken, the culprit could still be the Slasher," Hart commented. "I imagine that the victim fought the killer this time. That would explain her broken neck."

Bragg eyed him coolly. Then he said, "Francesca, tomorrow we have a meeting with Dr. Lillington at Bellevue. He has the police reports up until the events of this evening and he has agreed to advise us on the case."

Francesca had walked over to the bed, to Kate. She wanted to retch. She reached down for her hand; it was warm. She blinked back a tear. "She was killed very recently, in the last hour or two, I think."

"Yes," Bragg said, coming to stand beside her.

Francesca reached for the woman's bloody hair and moved it from her neck. The wound was raw and gaping and she briefly closed her eyes. Then, turning away from Kate's body, she said, "They could have struggled there in the center of the flat. He cut her — fatally. But as he dragged her to the bed she did not give up. She continued to fight even as her life was seeping away. He then snapped her neck. Accidentally."

"You are determined to believe this is the Slasher."

She looked at Bragg. "I know it is the Slasher. I can feel it."

They stared grimly at one another, gazes locked.

He smiled finally, slightly, at her. "You have the best instincts of anyone I know."

"Thank you." She smiled as slightly back.

"He is upping the ante," Hart said, interrupting them. "He dragged her to the bed, cut or not, neck broken or not, and took her hair down."

Francesca blinked at him. Her mind raced. "He certainly did not have to drag her to the bed," she said slowly. "Had everything happened over there in the center of the room, he could have left her there, on the floor. Margaret Cooper was found in her bed, and she was clearly killed there. But Kate was killed while she stood over there. Why drag her to the bed? And why do you think he is the one who took her hair down?"

"Darling, she is fully dressed. What woman do you know takes her hair down before undressing? The hair is the last to go."

Francesca thought about it and had to agree. Every woman she knew left her hair intact for as long as possible. "Why?"

Hart shrugged. "I fear his intent has changed."

She inhaled, glancing at Bragg. "Yes, murder is clearly the name of the game now. Margaret Cooper began a new pattern, I think."

"There is more." Bragg glanced at them both. "The door was left wide open."

Francesca gasped. "He must have wanted someone to find the body right away!"

"I agree."

"He wanted the police to find the body right away," Hart said sharply. "He is toying with you both."

Francesca stared at him, as did Bragg. "So now you are an investigator?" Bragg said.

She seized his hand. "I agree with Hart. This man is clever and capable and efficient. He would only leave the door wide open to alert us as quickly as possible to his foul deed. I truly sense a new game here."

"I don't like it," Hart said quietly, walking over to her. And his words were meant for her and her alone.

She met his gaze and understood. If the killer felt superior now — to the police, to her, even — then what would happen next? "Will he strike again on Monday?"

"He could strike again tomorrow," Bragg said.

She glanced his way. "But why go back and kill Kate now? When he let her live last week?" Francesca asked. "What changed to make the killer return and finish what he began?"

"The killer is a madman. God only knows what he is thinking and why," Bragg said.

That, of course, was true. "What has changed is that you and I have become very active on this case," she said thoughtfully. "Hart is right — he must be toying with us now."

Hart murmured, "Do I not recall you mentioning that she was separated?"

He had an amazing memory, she thought. She nodded. "She left her husband some time ago. I believe it was over a year and a half ago." But she understood where Hart was leading. She turned to Bragg. "Can we locate her husband?"

"I've already put Newman on it. His name is John Sullivan and you are right, Kate left him a year and a half ago. When she was interviewed after the first assault, she said he was a drunk and that she hadn't seen him in a good year. She did not know where he was living. Hopefully he remains in the city and we can locate him before too long."

Francesca rubbed her temples. Instantly Hart took her elbow. "Are you tired, darling?" he asked quietly.

She smiled a little at him. "I am worried," she returned.

"You cannot save the world."

"I can try," she said, meaning it.

His gaze searched hers. She looked at him sadly. "Poor Kate."

He released her and turned to Rick. "Will you give Francis O'Leary police protection?"

"Obviously," Bragg said.

"What about Sam Wilson?" Francesca asked, worried now about Francis. "Do we know where he has been these past few hours?"

"I already sent two officers to pick up Wilson and bring him to headquarters for questioning." He stared at the bed and the body for a moment and then said, "I inspected the lock. I saw no sign of forced entry. I am beginning to believe that the killer has somehow followed the victim inside."

"Who found the body?" Hart asked.

Bragg turned and looked directly at Francesca. "Maggie."

Francesca cried out.

■ ■ ■ ■

When she and Hart stepped out onto the street, she saw that a crowd had gathered. She faltered and Hart took her arm. Perhaps two dozen men and women stood in front of Kate's building, the men huddled in their ill-fitting jackets, some in flannel shirts, the women wrapped in scarves and shawls. Francesca saw nothing but worry and fear in the expressions facing her, and she also saw hopelessness.

"That's Miz Cahill," Joel Kennedy cried with pride. "She's a famous sleuth!" He appeared in the front of the crowd, grinning at her.

But before she could smile back, a very worn and faded woman stepped forward, her dark eyes filled with fear. "Who did it, Miz Cahill? Who is murdering these good women? *Who?*"

Francesca bit her lip. "We don't know," she began.

An angry murmur rippled through the crowd.

Hart's grip on her arm tightened. "Let's pass," he said very quietly.

But Francesca balked, refusing to move. "I will find the killer," she told the woman.

294

"There will be justice, I promise you."

Tears filled the woman's eyes. "Justice? For Kate and Margaret? For all of us? There is no such thing for an honest, hardworking woman."

"Let's go," Hart said firmly as someone male agreed too emphatically with the woman's statement.

Francesca stiffened, not allowing Hart to drag her past the woman. "What is your name?" she asked kindly. "Were you friends with Kate and Margaret?"

"Francesca," Hart said grimly, a harsh whisper in her ear. "This is not the time."

Before the woman could respond and before she could jab Hart with her elbow telling him to have some patience, a heavy-set man in a plaid shirt and corduroy jacket pushed his way to stand before her. "You're gonna find the Slasher? A rich fancy *lady?*" He sneered. "Like you care about us! What's in it for you?" he demanded, his eyes burning with anger and hatred.

"Damn it," Hart said with no inflection. He stepped in front of Francesca before she could insist that she wanted nothing but the truth and justice. "Move aside and let the lady pass."

"Fancy snobbish highbrows," the man shouted.

Some men in the crowd agreed, cheering and booing at once. "Tell 'em to go home! Back where they come from!" a young man shouted.

"Yeah, send 'em home. It's their kind that's killin' us, not the Slasher!" a woman screamed.

Francesca realized a riot was in the making. Just as she had that terrible comprehension, Joel darted to stand beside Hart, his face red, shouting, "Miz Cahill will solve this crime! She knows her stuff, she does, an' I can prove it!"

But no one heard him because Hart very calmly put his fist in the nose of the man in corduroy. "That is for not stepping aside when politely directed to do so," he said.

The man held his bleeding nose, looking ready to assault Hart but clearly debating the merits of doing so.

And just as a few men stepped forward, looking ready to commit murder, a short, brawny man with curly black hair appeared at Hart's side. He was wearing a dark suit and he held a big black revolver that he aimed at the crowd. He did not speak.

"Thank you, Raoul," Hart said. He turned and seized Francesca. "Now may we go?"

"Yes, that is a good idea," she said somewhat meekly. And with Raoul covering them from behind and Joel in tow, they dashed down the block and around the corner to the building where the Kennedys lived.

Gwen put the teakettle to boil with shaking hands. She was so upset she could not breathe, much less think. But she was acutely aware of the gentleman who sat at her kitchen table.

"Gwen," Harry de Warenne said tersely. He cleared his throat and said, "Mrs. O'Neil. Please." He stood up.

She didn't turn, fighting tears, remaining stunned. He was here, here in America, in the city, in her flat. But why?

"Gwen." His tone was rough now. "I mean, Mrs. O'Neil. I'm sorry. I didn't mean to frighten you. I suppose I should have sent you a note."

She must compose herself, she thought wildly. He must never know how deeply she had fallen in love with him — how intensely and how foolishly. She inhaled hard and slowly turned to face him. Bridget stood near the sink, her eyes huge in her utterly white face.

Harry — no, Lord Randolph — was staring at her with the blue eyes his family was famous for, a very grim expression on his masculine face.

"There is a killer lurking in the neighborhood," Gwen managed to say. "My neighbor was murdered on Monday. You frightened me very much."

"I know," he said. "I read about it in the papers." He hesitated and added, "How can you live here?"

She straightened her shoulders and lifted her chin with all the pride she had left. "This is our home now."

He never looked away from her face. No, that was not right, he never looked away from her eyes, and she was drowning in his, drowning in a pool of blue nobility. "Do you like it here . . . in America?"

"Yes," she lied, her smile brittle. She hadn't seen him in five months, but he had changed so much. Oh, his face was the same, impossibly handsome, all high cheekbones, strong jaw and equally strong nose, but she remembered warm glances, soft, seductive smiles and more kindness than anybody had a right to bear. But all men were kind, she thought bitterly, when what they wanted was a woman's body.

He hesitated and said, "I'm happy for you, then."

She wrapped her arms around herself as the kettle began to boil, singing. Why had he come? How had it come down to this?

He hadn't smiled once. There had been no gesture of kindness or concern — not that she expected concern or warmth or anything, of course she didn't, but once, there had been affection and laughter. Now, the room was so dreadfully cold.

He started toward her, his expression far more grim than before.

Gwen froze.

But he did not touch her. He lifted the kettle from the fire and set it aside.

She turned away, trembling. For one moment, she had been waiting for him to take her into his arms. She remained the most foolish of women — worse, she had shamelessly yearned for him to do so.

"We don't want you here!" Bridget suddenly cried. "Why did you come? You heard Mama, we're happy here. We like it here, we do!"

He looked at the child. "I'm sorry, Bridget, I am sorry if I am intruding, but I had business in the city and I merely wished to inquire after you and your mother."

So he had come on business, she thought, staring at his classic profile. The mouth she remembered had been so mobile; this one never moved, remaining compressed in a firm, tight line, impossibly, even when he spoke.

He turned to her and she felt trapped, her backside against the counter, a sink just inches to her right, the stove to her left. "I feel responsible for all that has transpired," he said, with no emotional inflection whatsoever. He removed his wallet and from that, a cheque. "Please take this, Gw— Mrs. O'Neil," he said, and he coughed. "I am sure it is the least I can do, but it will find you better accommodations, far from this neighborhood, and it will help you feed your daughter."

The anger began. "I don't want that," she heard herself say.

His smile was odd, all twisted and half-formed. "Please. Please accept this small gesture on my behalf. I know it hardly makes up for what I have done and —"

"You have done nothing," she cried, clenching her hands so tightly into fists that she knew her nails were drawing her own blood.

He started, eyes wide, and for the first time she saw a man she recognized, revealed by the disbelief in his eyes. "I have destroyed your marriage — your life, actually," he said.

"I had no marriage with David," she said, holding her chin high. "You destroyed nothing. It was time for me and my girl to move on." She forced a smile.

"Maybe so. Still, for my part in what happened, please accept my offer."

"I don't want anything from you," she cried.

He stared at her for an interminable time.

And behind them both, Bridget breathed hard.

He nodded and walked to the table, two steps from where he stood, and laid the bank cheque there. Then he walked to the door, where he paused, shoulders rigid, and he glanced at her.

She realized she was crying but she could not look away.

His mouth tightened. "I am sorry, Gwen," he said. He touched the brim of his felt hat and he left.

"Come in," Maggie breathed, her eyes wide, her complexion ashen. She opened the door wider to let Francesca, Hart, Raoul and Joel inside.

"Are you all right?" Francesca asked the moment she had bolted the door behind them.

Maggie looked at her, nodding, her eyes shining with tears.

"Oh dear," Francesca whispered, and she embraced the other woman who, briefly, clung in return.

Then Maggie stepped back, managing a smile. "I am sorry I am being so foolish. But I decided to call on Kate, as she lives just around the block from me. And now she is dead! The Slasher has struck again," she cried, keeping her voice down. Clearly, her three younger children were all asleep in the flat's single bedroom.

Francesca put her arm around her as they walked toward the small sofa that defined the room's parlor. "It may or may not be the Slasher. We will not know until a clinical examination of the body has occurred."

Maggie confronted her. "What do you mean, it may not be the Slasher? If he didn't kill Kate, then who did?"

"We simply don't know yet," Francesca said.

Maggie clasped her hands together. "I have forgotten my manners," she whispered. "Francesca, Mr. Hart, do sit down, please," she said.

"We are fine," Hart said firmly. He had walked over to her window to look down on Tenth Avenue. "Kate's apartment is but a minute's walk from here," he remarked.

That was very true. One had to walk only to the corner of Tenth and Avenue A, turn right, and go up Tenth Street a few doors to her building. Guessing his unspoken question, Francesca said, "Francis is on Eleventh Street and Avenue B."

Hart turned to her very seriously. "Do not tell me that every victim lived on this square block?"

"No! She is on the northwest side of Eleventh and Avenue B. Still," she said, their gazes locked, "the proximity is amazing."

"Maybe we had better go to my brother-in-law's," Maggie said softly.

Francesca faced her. "I would feel much better if you did move temporarily, just until the killer is caught. Maggie, my mother has no objection if you wish to stay with us."

Maggie smiled weakly. "I can't think clearly right now, not with poor Kate dead. But I have to do what is best for the children."

"Yes, you do, and that means you must move out of this flat until the killer is caught."

"My brother-in-law only has a one-bedroom flat. He has two children of his own. It would be so cramped." Maggie shook her head. "I am hysterical, I apologize. How could Kate be dead?"

Francesca had a sudden idea. She grasped Maggie's shoulder, smiling at her. "I have a perfect solution, one that does not involve your staying with us again."

Maggie gazed at her hopefully. "You do?"

She glanced at Hart briefly and faced Maggie. "Calder has more room than anyone. Come and stay with us — I mean, him!"

Maggie faltered, darting her eyes at Hart. "I couldn't!"

"Of course you can. Calder doesn't mind, do you?" Francesca said eagerly.

"I have dozens of empty bedrooms, even with my family in residence. And no, I don't mind," he said, looking now at Francesca with a wry smile.

"Maggie, this is the perfect solution!" Francesca cried. "I know you thought that staying with my family again would be an imposition. Well, it is no imposition with Calder, as he is my fiancé."

Maggie seemed to waver.

"And we shall soon rename my home l'Hôtel des Étrangers," Hart said with a shrug, "if Francesca has her way." He walked over to the flat's single window.

"That means the hotel of strangers," Francesca said, sitting down beside Maggie and taking her hands in hers. "Calder is joking. I'll send a driver for you first thing tomorrow."

Maggie bit her lip. "Six in the evening,

then. I have to work," she reminded Francesca.

Francesca was pleased, but it was time to move on to business. Briskly, she said, "Why did you decide to go visit Kate?"

"I had the strongest urge to see her." Maggie shrugged. "I saw her at church last Sunday, of course, and I so wanted to ask her how she was, but we really did not speak. She seemed upset, distraught, and I did not want to intrude. Last night, I decided I would call on her. I wanted to ask her how she was and if I could do anything for her." Tears filled her eyes. "If only I had gone earlier, maybe the killer would have seen us together and gone away."

Francesca clasped her shoulder. What if Maggie has seen something? What if she had glimpsed the killer? "What time did you go over to visit?"

"It was half past seven, maybe eight," she said. "I fed the children and tucked Lizzie and Paddy into bed. Then I walked over, leaving Joel here to watch the children."

"It would be best if you didn't wander the streets after dark," Francesca said.

Maggie nodded. "Kate's door was wide open. Completely open, so much so that the moment I paused on the threshold, I saw her in the bed. The second thing I saw was the blood. I screamed." She had blanched again.

Francesca patted her hand. "I assume you left?"

Maggie nodded. "I ran out faster than I have ever run before. I ran out screaming for help, for the police. There wasn't a roundsman in sight!" She was angry then. "But Joel found one on Avenue B a few blocks up."

"So you went from Kate's back to your own flat to ask Joel to find a police officer," Francesca said. Maggie nodded and she took her hand, continuing, "Did you see anyone? Anyone at all? Either on your way to her flat or on your way home?"

Maggie just looked at her.

Francesca could not decipher the look. "Maggie?"

"The streets were absolutely deserted, both times, not a soul in sight . . . except for one man."

Francesca straightened.

"As I was going over to visit Kate, I bumped right into a man when I turned the corner."

"The corner of Avenue A and Tenth Street?" Francesca tried to restrain herself now, but she had tensed with anticipation.

Maggie nodded. "I bumped into him so

306

hard he grabbed me and steadied me. He was a perfect gentleman — it was my fault but he apologized."

She had bumped into a man on her way to visit Kate — a man who was a perfect gentleman. *What if he had been the killer?* "Was he really a gentleman?" she pressed. "Did you get a look at him? Did he speak? Did you?"

Maggie inhaled and said, "He was a gentleman, a fine gentleman, with the most brilliant, remarkable eyes. Even at night, I could see how blue they were."

"Did he wear a ring?" she cried, on her feet. "Was he tall?"

"I don't know if he had jewelry on, but he was quite tall, as tall as Mr. Hart. Francesca, there's more. He was Irish."

"Are you certain?"

"He spoke briefly, and it was but a murmur, but yes, I recognized his accent."

Francesca trembled with excitement. If this man was the Slasher, they had just learned that he was an Irishman.

Hart came over. "We don't know that this gentleman is the killer," he warned.

She ignored him. Her every sense told her that Maggie had bumped into the killer as he was leaving Kate's flat after perpetrating the deadly deed. "Maggie, if you saw him again, would you recognize him?"

"Yes," Maggie said, very firm now. "Oh yes, I couldn't possibly forget a man like that."

CHAPTER FOURTEEN

Friday, April 25, 1902 8:00 a.m.

Francesca paused on the threshold of the breakfast room, a cheerful salon papered in a bright, sunny gold with windows overlooking the Cahill back lawns. They were verdantly green and freshly cut and the imported Belgium tulips were already blooming. Francesca barely noticed any of that.

Andrew Cahill sat at the head of the table, a copy of the *New York Times* in his hands, the *Sun* and the *Tribune* set aside, just beyond his plate. He laid down the *Times* and looked up. "Good morning, Francesca. Do not tell me that you are joining me for breakfast today?" he said with bemusement.

Francesca adored her father. He was a rotund man of medium height with an equally round face and a perpetually benign complexion. He had an even and pleasant disposition, which both her sister Connie and Evan had inherited. Rare was the day that he lost his temper. He was as passionately dedicated to reform as she was, and she had learned everything she knew about reform, politics and the world from him. She smiled as she entered the room. "We always share breakfast, Papa."

"Yesterday you fled this house before I even sat down," he said, his tone not quite as fond as usual.

She almost cringed as she went to the head of the table to hug him. "Yes, I did depart rather early."

His expression was partly stern and partly resigned. "Your mother is in despair! She tells me you are chasing another killer, this one the Slasher, dear God."

Francesca did not know what to say. She pulled out a chair and sat down. "Papa, you know how important justice is to me. Two women have been cruelly murdered, and we are very afraid more murders will follow."

"I do know how important justice is to you, Francesca, no one knows it better than I — and no one is prouder of you than I am. I also realize that you have found your true passion in this life. Unlike your mother, I know better than to try to insist you cease sleuthing. But, like your mother, I worry terribly about the jeopardy you put yourself in during these investigations."

She hugged him, hard. "Thank you, Papa! I knew I could count on you."

"I am not exactly approving of this new pursuit of yours. But as you have thus far saved half a dozen lives and brought as many criminals to justice, I am not disapproving, either."

She beamed at him and then smiled at the servant who filled her cup with coffee. "Thank you," she said. "Do you want to hear about the case?"

He studied her. "Yes, I think that I do. But first, is it truc that you are working with Rick Bragg again?" he asked quietly.

She hesitated. Then, "He is your friend. And you admire him as much as I do. You believe in him the way that I do. Surely you cannot be opposed to our working together?"

He was grim. "I am not opposed to your working with him, if that is what it is. But you are engaged to another man. Need I remind you of that?"

She grinned. "I am happily engaged to another man. Does this mean you are coming round to the fact of my marriage to Calder?"

"I have made myself clear. Hart needs to prove himself worthy of you. My opinion is hardly set. He doesn't object to your working with Rick?"

Francesca hesitated. "He has his jealous moments. But, Papa, those feelings I had for Rick, they are in the past. I really want to marry Calder," she said, unable to help adding, "and a year is far too long to wait!"

He merely raised an eyebrow. "I think your life is much more complicated than you realize," he said. "Will we see you tonight at your sister's? You do recall she is having a lavish affair."

Francesca winced. She had entirely forgotten the buffet supper party her sister was holding for some hundred guests. It was a charity event. The supper was costing a hundred dollars a plate and the funds were going to an organization that supported the city's homeless children. "Yes, of course," she said.

The Cahill butler appeared at the breakfast-room door. "Miss Cahill? Mr. Hart is here. He wishes to speak with you."

Francesca leaped to her feet in surprise, wondering what Hart was doing at her home at this unsocial hour. Not that she minded! She was fully dressed for a busy day ahead of her. And she remembered with lightning clarity the events of last night.

They had left Maggie's and gone the few

blocks uptown to Mulberry Street to meet Bragg, hoping to be present during the questioning of Sam Wilson. But the police had not brought Wilson in, because he had been nowhere to be found. By the time Hart had finally dropped her at home, it had been well past midnight. This morning she had awoken recalling being in his arms and his lingering good-night kiss.

"Papa, I will be right back," she said, and before Andrew could react, she was dashing from the room.

Hart was waiting in the hall, clad in a nearly black suit, looking well rested and impossibly attractive. His eyes brightened when he saw her and he smiled warmly.

She went right into his arms. "What is this?" she queried.

"I've rearranged my morning schedule. In fact, I postponed two clients," he said, sliding his arms around her and giving her a brief kiss. Then he stepped back. "I think we should call on Wilson."

Delight began to grow. "Wait a moment. You have canceled your business affairs so you can sleuth with me?" She was absolutely thrilled.

He grinned and the cleft in his chin deepened, his slight left dimple winked. "I am *postponing* two clients, importers who need me far more than I need them. I have an extremely urgent meeting this afternoon with the ambassador to Hong Kong that I must attend. It is in regard to my shipping interests," he said.

Suddenly she had an inkling. "Is this sudden interest in sleuthing about the danger that Wilson might pose, or my working this case with Bragg?"

"I plead guilty," he drawled, "to all of the above. I think we should hurry," he added. "Unless Wilson has fled the city, he will be at home, getting ready to open up his shop."

She agreed. "If we arrive early enough, we can interview him before the police do."

He lifted one eyebrow. "I know you are not thinking to undercut my brother."

"Never. But I want to speak to Wilson alone, without any police officers present. I feel certain, Calder, that sugar will get far more than vinegar this time."

He smiled at her and gestured for her to precede him out.

As they paused at the door of Wilson's shop, Francesca suddenly recalled Gwen O'Neil's plight. She faced Hart quickly. "I forgot to mention something to you," she said quickly.

His dark eyebrows lifted. "I will not even

try to guess."

"Would you mind giving Gwen O'Neil employment? She worked as a ladies' maid in Ireland. She has no references, though, as her employer there — one Lord Randolph — happened to seduce her and cause her no end of trouble."

He seemed mildly amused. "I have no idea if we need another maid."

"Hart!" she protested, exasperated.

He smiled at her. "Darling, if you adopt a stray for every case you investigate, we really will need to turn my home into a hotel."

"Just agree, please," she said.

"Of course I agree." He was reflective. "I know an Irishman named Randolph. He comes from a very old, well-established family and he shares a shipping venture with an English cousin. We met in Istanbul and renewed our acquaintance in London. Of course, even though he is heir to an Irish earldom, I doubt he was Gwen O'Neil's employer."

"That would be an amazing coincidence," Francesca said as she rang the doorbell. "Was his home near Limerick?"

"I really don't know. I know he had a manor somewhere in Ireland, but as I said, he also kept a home in London and that is where we met the second time." He added,

"He was actually a handsome fellow, but his reputation was rather dour."

Before Francesca could ask him what he meant, the door was opened and Sam Wilson stood there. He started at the sight of them.

"Hello," Francesca said brightly. "May we come in?"

"Yes, of course, although it is *very* early," Wilson said, stepping aside with a smile. He seemed bewildered by their presence.

"It's well past nine," Hart said as they followed him into the shop. "What time do you open?"

"If a customer knocks — I thought you were customers — I will accommodate him or her. But otherwise, we open our doors at noon." He paused by the display counter. "I use the morning to work on repairs in the back."

Francesca studied him closely. He could be considered tall by someone as small as Kate, but he wasn't particularly so. He certainly wasn't Irish, but then, they did not know that the man Maggie had met on the street was the killer — she might have bumped into an innocent passerby. She looked at his hands and was surprised that today he wore a ring on his left hand.

If the killer were right-handed, he had

316

worn the ring on his left hand, too.

She stared. The ring was gold but there was no stone. The center had a flat smooth surface with some engraving upon it.

Witnesses and victims often mistook, and sometimes wildly, the details of the crime. Francesca wondered if his ring, at night, in a shadowy flat, might look as if it had a stone in it.

She wondered how she could get into his closet and look at his clothes.

"We actually stopped by last night," Hart said, giving her an odd look. Clearly he had expected her to do the questioning. They had decided not to tell Wilson that the police had tried to round him up. They would proceed very quietly, without putting him on the defensive.

She tried to signal her discovery to him by glancing pointedly at Wilson's hand and more specifically at his ring. But Hart appeared exasperated — he did not understand.

"Last night? You stopped by my shop last night?" Wilson seemed very surprised. And he did not comment on the fact that he had not been at home.

Francesca stepped forward. "I recalled some questions I wished to ask you," she said. She hadn't decided whether to reveal

Kate's murder or not.

"Oh," was his response.

She became impatient. "Actually, we tried your door for some time — but you were not at home."

He blinked. His expression did not change. "Of course I was at home," he said after an odd pause.

"I beg to differ. We rang the doorbell repeatedly — we even banged on the door," Hart said, repeating the account given by the police officers who had failed to locate Wilson at his home last night.

"I was working in my shop," he said, turning pale. "I was engrossed — I undoubtedly did not hear you at the front door."

That was a lie if Francesca had ever heard one. "May we see your repair shop? Perhaps you could show us what you were working on."

He stiffened. "What is this about? Why are you asking me questions about last night? I simply did not hear the door."

"Please humor my fiancée," Hart said with a very serious expression.

Wilson clearly thought about throwing them out. Then, as clearly, he decided not to go against Hart. "Come with me," he said.

As they followed him through a back door,

Francesca slowed her steps, pulling Hart back with her. "In his shop, occupy him. I want to search his bedroom," she whispered.

"Absolutely not!"

"Just keep him occupied," she said, and then she realized that Wilson held another door open. A stairwell on his right clearly led to the living quarters above the shop.

"Right in here," he said.

Francesca walked into a good-size room. There were two tables in it, both the size of dining tables, each covered with clocks and watches in all stages of repair. The oddest assortment of tools and gadgets, all miniature in size, were located on a tray on the closest table.

"This clock is seventeenth-century Italian," Wilson said with reverence. He showed them a large clock in bronze with a gilded face and pearl hands. "The owner brought it in very recently. She was a lovely girl, recently widowed, and the clock belonged to her husband's family. I simply must get it running for her, as it has so much sentimental value now."

As Hart commented upon how elegant the clock was, Francesca glanced around. The back windows opened out onto the gardens Wilson had spoken of. A swing was beneath the single oak tree, some of his roses were

319

in bloom, and there was a small cast-iron table, two chairs and a badminton net. When Francis married Wilson, she would have a wonderful home. "Excuse me, is there a rest room I could use?"

"Of course," Wilson said, startled. "Just up those stairs, first door on your left."

Francesca gave Hart a warning look and hurried out.

Once upstairs, she ignored the bathroom, a simple affair with a walnut vanity, porcelain sink and water closet. The parlor was cheerful and cozy, the striped sofa facing a brick hearth. She pushed open a door and found, to her surprise, a small salon with a large piano. Did Wilson play? She quickly went to the remaining door and stepped into his bedroom.

He had opened the pale muslin draperies and sunlight streamed into a pleasant room of medium size, the walls covered in a green-and-white striped paper. The bed was dark oak, almost black, with four posters and a heavily engraved headboard. The bedspread was a green print, covering the pillows, with one decorative emerald neck roll atop that. The bed was so precisely made that she had to wonder if he had even slept there last night.

She went to the walnut bureau and studied

the single photograph. It was of his wife, she assumed, a plain woman with a pretty smile and sweet, kind brown eyes. Then she moved to his closet.

There were three suits hanging there, but not one was charcoal gray.

Of course, Kate could have been wrong. The suit could have been brown or black — and he had two very dark brown suits hanging in his closet.

Francesca thought she heard a noise on the stairs and she jumped. She quickly pushed closed the closet door and ran across the bedroom to the door, then peeked out.

Wilson was not standing there in the salon, staring accusingly at her.

She took a breath and exhaled. She had found nothing of value, she thought grimly. Then she corrected herself. Wilson did wear a gold ring.

And where had he been last night?

An idea struck her with stunning force.

Very quietly, making sure each step was soundless, Francesca went downstairs. As she did so, their voices became louder. Hart remained in the repair shop with Wilson, encouraging him to explain the intricacies of clockwork to him. *Good man,* Francesca thought, and she fled down the hall and into the front shop.

There, she did not pause. She went outside, closed the door and rang the doorbell just once.

A moment passed and Wilson opened it. His pleasant smile vanished the moment he saw her.

But Francesca smiled at him.

He could hear the doorbell from his shop, oh yes, he could.

Wilson had lied.

Hart had left her at headquarters after gaining a promise from her that she would not leave Mulberry Street until Raoul had returned to take her wherever she chose. His appointment with the ambassador was at half-past twelve, and with midday traffic, it could take him an hour to get to Bridge Street. Francesca had wished him a successful interview and had proceeded upstairs to Bragg's office.

Unfortunately, she found him with the chief of police, Brendan Farr.

She hesitated in the open doorway, the strangest feeling of dread instantly forming in her chest. Both men were seated, and Bragg was the first to see her. He stood with a smile. "Come in."

Farr turned and also stood, his smile

barely discernible and not reaching his cold gray eyes.

"I did not mean to interrupt," Francesca said.

"You are not interrupting," Bragg said firmly, leading her in. "Farr had Maggie look at the mug book this morning. She did not recognize anyone."

Francesca stared at Farr and imagined him knocking at Maggie's door with some of his bullies at an ungodly hour and forcing her to go to headquarters. "Was she late for work?" There was no way she could have been on time, as Maggie's shift started at eight in the morning.

Farr smiled at her. "We have a murder to solve, Miz Cahill. Two murders, actually."

"I hope her supervisor was understanding." Francesca heard how cool her own tone was.

Farr's smile never moved. "Mrs. Kennedy seems smart enough. I imagine she's taken care of herself all these years, with no man to look after her and not even you, and she can do so now."

Francesca decided to ignore him, making a mental note to make certain that Maggie had not been dismissed for her tardiness. "When you have a moment, I'd like to speak to you."

"We're almost through. Why don't you wait outside." Bragg's gaze met hers and it was calm, rock steady and oddly reassuring.

And Francesca was relieved. Whatever game Farr was playing, Bragg would figure it out and do what he had to do to take care of matters. Farr wasn't half as intelligent as Rick, but she knew better than to underestimate him.

"I understand that Miz Cahill is working on the case," Farr said flatly. "Do you have some information that would be useful to us?"

"I'm afraid I know nothing more than you." She hesitated. "What are you going to do about Sam Wilson?"

Farr smiled. "He should be here at any moment. I sent two men to his shop to bring him downtown. Meanwhile, we are trying very hard to locate John Sullivan. He seems to have disappeared after not paying the rent at his last known address."

"Well, you are the city's finest. I am sure you will find him," Francesca said.

Farr saluted her. "Anything else, C'mish?"

Bragg told him no, and a moment later they were alone.

He closed the door and faced her. "What have you learned?"

"Wilson gave me a false alibi. We saw him

this morning, an hour ago, really, and he claimed to have been in his repair shop last night." Francesca then proceeded to tell him what had happened.

"That was clever," Bragg said. "What do you think?"

"In spite of Kate's belief that the Slasher is a gentleman and a foreign one, he could be our man." She frowned. "It's just that there is something off about him."

He accepted that. Then, "It was the Slasher last night. Same knife, same dull blade, a right-handed assault."

"Does the coroner have any idea if she was cut after she died or not?"

"No. He shed no clues on the sequence of the assault. But he found some dark gray thread under Kate's nails."

"Kate insisted the Slasher wore a dark gray suit. Charcoal, to be exact."

Bragg nodded. "I know."

Francesca suddenly sat down. "Poor Kate — and poor Francis, if Wilson is our man!"

"We need to locate John Sullivan, even if he is only a carpenter and not a gentleman."

"Yes, we do. Have you spoken with David Hanrahan?"

"Yes. He has a rather solid alibi — he was drinking with two pals at a waterfront bar last night. Both men have corroborated his story. However, they are highly disreputable types, and I personally believe he could have conned or bribed them into saying anything he wished."

"What you are saying is that David remains a suspect," Francesca said.

"Wouldn't you agree?"

"Yes, but I can't shake the feeling, Bragg, that the Slasher is a gentleman, in a hat and a dark gray suit with an elegant gold ring."

"Wilson isn't elegant."

"No, he isn't, but he is hiding something, I would bet a small fortune on it."

"Hart's?" He actually joked.

"Hmm. He might not appreciate that. Besides, apparently his fortune is rather large. How are you, anyway?"

He hesitated. "Would you call on Leigh Anne?"

"Yes, of course. I said I would and I should love to do so." She stood. "Is she having a difficult time?"

"Yes, an extremely difficult time. And I feel helpless. I can't reassure her — I don't know how."

"Just tell her that you love her, that you always have and always will," Francesca said softly.

He made a sound of disgust. "That is easy for you to say!"

"But if it is how you feel —"

"I don't know how I feel anymore and I am tired of trying to decide what, exactly, I am feeling," he cried.

She started in real surprise.

"I'm sorry," he apologized instantly. "That was uncalled for."

"I'll visit tomorrow," Francesca said, touching him lightly.

He smiled at her. "Thank you."

Francesca smiled back. She took his hand and squeezed it.

A police officer that she did not recognize poked his head in. "C'mish, sir! Newman sent me — we got a lead." His eyes were huge and he was flushed with excitement.

Francesca dropped her hand. Bragg said, "What is it?"

"We found Sullivan. But there's a problem." He took a breath. "He's dead."

CHAPTER FIFTEEN

Friday, April 25, 1902 1:00 p.m.

Hart was going over the representation he intended to make to support his growing monopoly of the trade in gold bullion from Hong Kong when his personal clerk stepped in. "Sir?" Edwards was flushing a deep shade of crimson.

Hart could not gather why. He sat back casually in his chair. "Send Sir Lawrence in."

Edwards, a young, fair man, turned an even brighter shade of red. "The ambassador is not here yet. There is a woman — a lady — to see you."

As Edwards and his entire staff knew to admit Francesca with no formalities, he was mildly bemused. "Does she have a name?"

"Yes, sir." Edwards fought to breathe. "Miss Jones."

He was very surprised — and he was not an easy man to surprise. Only Francesca

had the ability to consistently do that. But then, she was entirely unpredictable and it was one of the reasons he found her so intriguing. He now paused. Daisy had never before come to his office. Nor should she — it was out of the question to have his mistress or ex-mistress anywhere near his place of business. It was not about morality or convention, although for another man it might be. Hart had no time for any dalliance when he was immersed in his business affairs.

He hadn't seen her in almost a month. He sent her the allowance he had promised her and paid her bills. He had not a clue as to the cause of her sudden appearance at Bridge Street. "Send her in," he finally said.

Daisy walked into his office, every bit as gorgeous as he remembered, in the most ethereal way. She seemed to float as she moved, as if she could defy gravity with her slim, sensual body. He studied her clinically; his manner had always been objective toward every woman he met. There was only one woman who had so swiftly and easily swept aside that particular barrier, and that was Francesca. He could never look at her and feel even remotely detached about her presence, her appearance or her behavior and affairs.

Daisy *was* beautiful and if he were not on the verge of wedlock, he would still be enjoying her favors. There would be no reason not to. But he was engaged, and so thoroughly distracted and preoccupied by his future bride that he could not find the remotest desire for the other woman. Then again, in the past few years his desire had become clinical, too: a matter of function, a means to pass the time, a means of escape from the gray that was his life.

He stood and approached her, taking her hand and politely kissing it, his lips never making contact with her skin. "Good afternoon. I must admit, you have succeeded in surprising me by your call."

Daisy had dressed very well for the occasion in an expensive pale blue gown that was modest, fashionable and elegant. Still, any man would know with a single glance that Daisy was not a lady. She smiled softly at him. "I do hope it is a welcome surprise. After all, we remain friends."

He had but one friend, his fiancée, but he did not dispute her. "Frankly, I never mix business with pleasure. But I assume there is some urgency to your cause, otherwise I know you would not have ventured so far afield, much less to my place of business."

"I'm afraid I have disturbed you," Daisy

said, downcast. "I apologize, Calder, but I did not think it appropriate to call on you at home."

He folded his arms across his chest, sensing a new game in the making. But why would Daisy think to play with him when he continued to be so generous with her? She remained in the house he had bought for her, and would do so for another three months until their agreement was over.

"If you had sent me a note, I would have made an appointment and called on you." He grew impatient. "I have a significant meeting, Daisy, so I suggest you tell me why you have called."

"May we shut the door?" she asked, appearing somewhat hurt.

He wasn't moved. "I see no reason to cause gossip," he said. He hardly feared being alone with her — in fact, his lack of desire was amazing, considering he had once slept with every beautiful woman who was not of good character who dared cross his path — but he did not want Francesca hurt by gossip.

"First, I wanted to tell you how truly happy I am for you. You have been nothing but kind and generous with me and you deserve a wonderful woman like Francesca," she said so earnestly another man would have believed her.

But he did not. She was standing in his place of business for a reason, and he wanted to get to it now. "Thank you."

She went to him and took his hands in hers. "But I miss you, Calder, I really miss all the time we have shared," she said so softly that anyone passing in the corridor beyond his open door wouldn't hear.

He moved away from her. "If you have come to seduce me, I would rethink my position. I promised Francesca that I would be loyal to her, and I have no intention of breaking that vow."

She stepped back, her thin shoulders squaring, her chin jerking high. Was that anger he saw in her eyes? She had no reason to be angry with him. She was a whore, very beautiful and somehow elegant, but a whore nonetheless. He knew her background was genteel, although he had never asked her story, but she had chosen to sell her body and could expect nothing except for gifts, cash and favors in return.

It was a moment before she spoke. "I saw Francesca the other day."

He stilled. He sensed an attack on Francesca and that would be a very dangerous mistake. "Really?"

Daisy smiled a little. "In the Lord and

Taylor store. That is a stunning ring you gave her. You must be smitten."

"Is there a point?"

Daisy shrugged a little, but she said, "She seemed so radiant, so in love with you, Calder."

In spite of his resolve to remain in control of himself, his heart leaped. If Francesca did love him, after all, he realized suddenly how thrilled he would be.

Daisy looked at him almost slyly. "Rose and I have been so concerned for her, because she is so naive. We really thought she would never be able to manage you, but clearly we were wrong."

"That's right," he said. "As I have no intention of being the kind of man that Francesca must *manage*."

She smiled and laughed. "You need not worry. She appeared radiant, but that must have been due to another cause. Francesca made it clear that she is not really in love. She is only marrying you because she cannot marry Bragg. But you already know that, don't you?"

He tensed. He knew damn well he should not continue this conversation. "Is that what she said?" And there was dread, but also anger.

"Very directly, I might add." Daisy came

up to him and laid her small hands on his shoulders, pressing her slim, trembling body against his. "How ironic this is! We both know you are the last man in the world to be faithful to any woman, yet you have promised fidelity to Francesca. But she is in love with someone else." She shook her head, her expression at once dismayed — as if she cared — and disbelieving.

He set her away, refusing to be shaken. "Do you really think to seduce me back to your bed with these antics? Francesca and I are basing our marriage on friendship and respect, not love."

"Yes, that is exactly what she said. And I won't pretend I don't miss you in my bed, Calder. How could I not?" She stared, no longer smiling. "You are the first man to awaken me. You are the first man to genuinely give me pleasure." Her voice had dropped, turning husky.

It was hard to pay attention to Daisy now. All he could think about was whether or not Francesca had really said that she was marrying him for friendship and respect — and only because she could not have his damn half brother. Even though he knew he was being conned by his ex-mistress, he could not stop thinking about it. He knew damn well that this was what Daisy wanted

— to interfere in his relationship with Francesca, although he could not consider why in that moment.

Could Francesca have really shared such a confidence with his ex-mistress?

Such an ingenuous utterance sounded exactly like his impulsive fiancée.

"I'm afraid those days are over." He was abrupt. "I gave my word to Francesca and I intend to keep it." He heard himself speak as if he were an outsider viewing the scene. Did she still really love Rick? After all the times she had been in Hart's arms? Was it at all possible? And he closed his eyes, trying to thwart the anger, but his heart pumped with it. *Damn it.* He had to admit that he had started to think that finally she was falling in love with him. *He wanted her to love him, not Rick Bragg.*

And he was so stunned by his comprehension that briefly he could not even breathe.

Daisy said, her tone harsh, "Darling, do you really think to reform for a woman who doesn't even love you?"

And she cut into his brooding the way a whip cuts into naked flesh. He met her gaze but it was too late. He had realized what he wanted, what he needed, and it was going to be his Achilles heel. And before he could comment, she said, half smiling in a twisted way, "I know who you are. No one knows who you are better than I do. Because we are *exactly* the same."

"That is hardly true," he said, shaken to the core of his being. He didn't need to be loved — he didn't want love, not from anyone!

"No?" Now she smiled widely. "We both know you are going to become bored with your virgin bride. It's only a matter of time. Come, Calder. You're the man who has spent a dozen nights in my bed — with Rose there as well. We both know you hate the mundane, the ordinary."

He started and memories he did not want flooded him then. He had shared Daisy's bed several times with her lover, Rose. There had been other times in his life, in Europe, when he had sexually indulged himself with more than one woman. But he hadn't given a thought to such decadence in a long time — not since he had met Francesca. The boredom, the ennui, the growing disinterest in sex — all of which had led him to such occasions — had miraculously vanished. Now, he felt paralyzed. Daisy had just verbalized his worst fears — fears he had not dared admit even to himself. He had once had a dark sexual side and he was afraid he had merely repressed it; that it would never die.

He was horrified.

Daisy laughed softly, touching his arm. "You are the most darkly sensual and sexual man I know. That dark side will never disappear because it is who you are! So why bother? Why bother to give a woman *who doesn't even love you* such an absurd promise? It's a promise you cannot keep."

And the fury came, so huge it shocked him. *"Get out."* His heart was racing with terrible force as he seized her arm, dragging her to the door. "You have gone too far," he said, very low. "You may pack your things, Daisy, and vacate the premises of my house immediately."

She stiffened in shock, impossibly pale. "But you know I am right! You know Francesca will soon bore you! And then what will you do? You will come back to me, or Rose, or someone else, won't you?"

"Edwards!" he said furiously, shaking. "Show Miss Jones out."

Edwards appeared, flushing. "Miss Jones?"

Daisy's expression hardened. "Perhaps I am wrong. Perhaps you will merely corrupt Francesca to satisfy your appetites. She is a very curious woman, isn't she? Who knows? Maybe you will show her that she has her own dark side!"

He stalked into his office, slamming the door closed behind him. And only then did he tear loose his tie and breathe. But the room had become airless, claustrophobic. He stormed to a window and shoved it wide. The fresh air, tinged with sweet salt, did not help. He gripped the sill, panting.

She was right.

He was a bastard in every sense of the word, a sexually depraved man with no morality whatsoever, a man with a huge and ugly past, and she had just proven it, hadn't she? Because no matter how hard he tried, images he did not want were haunting him now.

He covered his face with his hands. He was such a fool, thinking he could change, wanting to change — wanting to become someone else, someone better, finer, someone noble for a woman who did not even love him.

For a woman who loved his own brother.

Well, it was over now.

A leopard simply could not change his spots.

But now he was afraid. The last thing he wished to do was drag Francesca down into the gutter with him.

They went across town en masse, with

Inspector Newman and Chief Farr. Two roundsmen and a junior detective were at the scene when the foursome arrived there. John Sullivan's flat was just off of Eighth Avenue in a particularly squalid ward. Francesca glimpsed a single room with two bunk beds, a stove, sink and rickety table with four chairs. She instantly saw Sullivan and she halted in her tracks. Bragg crashed into her and his arm went around her. "Christ," he said.

The body which had belonged to Kate's husband lay on the floor near the table, half of his head resembling the smashed pulp of a watermelon. "Oh God," she cried, seriously ill, turning away and into Bragg's arms.

Bragg held her for another moment. "You don't have to come in," he said quietly. "Let the police handle this."

Francesca fought to recover her composure and not to retch. She held his eyes as he released her. "What happened?"

"Shot in the head," Farr intoned.

Francesca turned but made no move to enter the tiny, sordid room. She avoided gazing at the body but Farr knelt over him, Newman standing behind him. "Yeah, he was shot point-blank," Farr remarked. "In the side of the head, from the look of it, at

339

real close range."

She wondered if Chief Farr had any feelings. Francesca had to look — peripherally. "Is he holding a gun?" she asked, glimpsing the dead man's right hand and the gleaming black weapon there.

"He sure is," Farr said cheerfully. He stood. "It's been fired, too, from the smell of it, and I'll bet that bullet is the one lodged somewhere in his head."

"What?" Francesca gasped.

"It might be a suicide. It sure looks like one. You agree, C'mish?"

"Suicide!" Francesca said, stunned.

"I think we should examine the weapon he is holding and the bullet in Sullivan's head before leaping to any conclusions. Newman, make a sweep. Perhaps that is not the murder weapon. If it is not a suicide, I want to find the gun that killed this man."

"Yes, sir," Newman said, rapidly leaving the flat.

As he did so, he almost collided with a very thin man with dirty-blond hair, not much older than Francesca. He gripped the door as if to keep standing upright, crying out, "What the hell happened?"

Bragg walked over to the interloper as one of the roundsmen in the hall moved to block his path, making no effort to be discreet.

"Are you a neighbor?" Bragg asked.

The man turned away, as white as a sheet.

Francesca went to a window and yanked it wide open. She breathed in deeply, her mind racing in disbelief. Had Sullivan killed himself? And if so, why? Was his murder related to that of his wife's? She heard the man finally say, shaken, "No. I live here. What happened to Sullivan?"

"I'm afraid he's dead," Bragg said. "And you are?"

"Ron Ames."

"Let's step outside. We need to ask you a few questions."

Francesca turned as Bragg and Ames stepped into the hall. Farr was rummaging through some drawers and Francesca wondered what he was looking for. He finally produced a framed photograph that had been hidden amongst some other items. It was a photo of Kate. She was smiling and holding the hand of a young man in a dark suit. He seemed a bit older than herself. "Who's the gentleman?" she asked.

"Don't know," Farr said in inordinately good spirits.

Seized with avid dislike, Francesca stepped outside. Ames was saying, "About a year. Yeah, we been rooming together about a year, and a few months ago Josh Bennett leased a bed with us. The fourth bunk is empty."

"Do you know any reason why Sullivan would commit suicide?" Bragg asked.

Ames shrugged. He had recovered his composure remarkably, and his pallor had eased. "Why wouldn't he? He's been out of work for months, he's behind on the rent he owes me, fcr crissakes, he got no woman, he got nothing but the booze."

Francesca stepped forward. "Did he ever refer to his wife?"

"Kate?"

Francesca was surprised Ames knew her name. "Yes, Kate."

"Yeah, he spoke about her every time he got drunk — that is, just about every night." Ames grinned. "Do the police have women on the force now?"

Francesca glanced at Bragg, not bothering to answer. Here was something, then. "How long were they separated?"

"Since before he met me. Over a year, I guess. You a police *woman?*"

"I am a sleuth, Mr. Ames. But yes, I am working with the police. Did he still love her?" Francesca asked briskly.

And Ames thought that was amusing, because he laughed, hard. "Love her? I don't think so, miss. He hated her, he did.

He hated her with a vengeance, in fact, for being such a slut, for walking out on him. All he ever talked about was how he couldn't wait for the day that she got hers."

They sat in the Daimler in front of police headquarters, making no move to get out. Francesca's mind was racing and she knew that Bragg was immersed in his own thoughts, too. She finally twisted to face him. "Do you think it's a suicide?"

"It certainly appears that way, but we will know within a few hours for certain." His gaze locked with hers.

"He hated her with a vengeance, Bragg."

"I know. I heard — I was there."

"Could Sullivan have been the Slasher?"

Bragg smiled a little at her. "What brings you to that conclusion?"

"He hated Kate with a vengeance."

"So you are thinking that John Sullivan is the Slasher?"

"We need to go back to his flat and see if he has a suit in the closet."

"There was no closet, and I did not see a suit on the wall pegs, but just about every working man has a Sunday suit."

"Of course you're right." She stared grimly at the police wagon parked in front of them.

He touched her hand. "Why assault her and let her live? Why assault Francis first? Why kill Margaret Cooper? And why go back to finish off his wife if she was the one he hated enough to murder all along?"

"Bragg, those are my questions exactly. But consider this scenario. Maybe the assaults began as acts of anger, without the intention of murder. But then his rage escalated and he killed Margaret Cooper — and it felt good in his sick mind. So he went back to finish off the real target of his twisted rage — his wife."

"That is a credible theory," Bragg said. "And now he killed himself in belated grief?"

"Or belated guilt," she said very seriously. Then she recognized the carriage parked at the end of the street. It was a very handsome black affair drawn by six black horses. She started. "Oh dear! I promised Hart I would wait for Raoul to return before I went anywhere! In the heat of the moment, I simply forgot."

"So Raoul is now your driver?"

She glanced at him to gauge his reaction to that fact, but his expression was impossible to read. "I think Hart intends for him to be more of a bodyguard than anything else," she said.

"I heartily hope so," Bragg said. "Raoul was one of the Rough Riders in the war for Cuba's independence. In fact, he was a part of a secret operations unit and he is a very skillful man."

Francesca could only stare. "Hart never mentioned it."

Bragg shrugged and got out of the motorcar. As he came around for her door, he said, "You should take advantage of the situation. Raoul could certainly be useful to you in your various adventures."

Francesca smiled her thanks as she got out of the roadster. "Will I see you tonight at my sister's?"

He didn't hesitate. "No."

"I understand," she said softly. "I'm sure in some time Leigh Anne will want to get out and about again."

He shrugged. Before they could move toward the entrance of the building, a woman came running down the front steps, crying out. It was Francis O'Leary. "Miss Cahill! Miss Cahill! Please wait!"

Francesca hurried toward her, wondering at her state of hysteria. "Is everything all right?" she asked in concern.

Francis had been crying. Tears streaked her cheeks and her eyes and nose were red. "Is everything all right? How can anything be all right when my fiancé is in jail and the police refuse to release him?" she cried, trembling. "How could they suspect him of anything? How could they suspect him of being the Slasher?" She began to weep. "Please, help me get him home! He is innocent!"

Francesca took her hands. "Francis, try to calm yourself. They aren't charging him with any crime. I think they merely wish to question him." She glanced at Bragg. He nodded at her, urging her to ask the question now on both of their minds.

"He is a good, kind man, not some monster!" Francis said. "He would not hurt anyone, much less stalk and murder them!"

"He seems like a very good man," Francesca agreed, putting her arm around the woman. "Francis, do you have any idea where Sam was last night?"

"When Kate Sullivan was killed?" she asked sharply, eyes huge and wide.

"Yes," Francesca said. She smiled encouragingly. "Sam claims to have been in his repair shop, but frankly, it was clear that he was not telling us the truth. Unfortunately, we have caught him in a lie. But if he is innocent, why would he lie?"

Francis stared speechlessly.

"Francis?" Francesca felt terribly for her now.

She swallowed hard and began to turn red. "He was with me," she whispered, her voice so low it was almost inaudible.

Francesca doubted that. "Francis, please do not perjure yourself."

"He was with me," she said again. She glanced wildly from Francesca to Bragg and back again, highly flushed. More tears welled in her eyes.

Francesca stroked her back, but she was trembling and too agitated to be calmed. "Well, if that is the case —"

"No, he was with *me*." She was crimson. "All night . . . the first time . . . it was our first time and you see, he couldn't have killed Kate Sullivan." Tears rolled down her cheeks. "He didn't tell you the truth because he was trying to protect me."

Francesca realized what she meant. Thoroughly startled, she searched her gaze as Bragg said, "I will see to his release. But I am afraid we will need your sworn statement, in writing."

Francis nodded, but she stared back at Francesca, continuing to shake.

"Well, clearly Sam has an alibi," Francesca said after a pause. The problem was, she knew it was a lie. She could see it in Francis O'Leary's eyes.

CHAPTER SIXTEEN

Friday, April 25, 1902 7:30 p.m.
Francesca paused breathlessly in the reception hall of her sister's home, a mansion just around the block from the Cahill home on Madison Avenue. She was late, but other guests were still arriving, too. As she handed off her wrap, she searched the crowd that was mingling in the room and overflowing into a large salon not far from the stairs. In that salon, the furniture had been removed and the buffet that would serve a hundred guests was against one entire wall. Huge floral arrangements of white lilies were set on pedestals throughout the room, towering above the guests. Dozens of tables, each seating eight and covered in linen, crystal and gilded dinnerware, surrounded a dance floor. A pianist, accompanied by a violinist, was already playing a waltz.

Francesca was looking forward to the evening, her first social engagement on

Hart's arm. At the few previous affairs they had attended, they had been secretly engaged and had arrived separately. Smiling, she espied her sister at the far end of the reception room.

Connie was her best friend. As always, she was stunningly beautiful and terribly elegant in a lavender chiffon evening gown. She was smiling as she conversed effortlessly with several guests. But then, her sister was always the perfectly gracious hostess. Once, not so long ago, her life had seemed perfect, too.

Francesca did not want to recall the terrible way in which the new year had begun for Connie and her husband, Neil. For one more moment Francesca stared, noting that her sister seemed her usual self again — genuinely happy and truly at ease. Francesca was relieved.

Francesca had yet to see anyone else that she knew, other than her handsome brother-in-law, who stood close to the front door, greeting the guests as they came in. Where was Hart? Was he late as well?

"Hello," a warm, familiar voice said.

Francesca smiled, turning to face Rourke. "Hello! I am so pleased you are here," she said, meaning it. "I don't know a soul, do you?"

He smiled at her. "Rathe and Grace are in the salon and your fiancé is somewhere about."

Her heart fluttered. She was wearing the very daring and provocative dark red gown that Sarah had portrayed in her portrait, just for him. "He must be hiding, otherwise I should have seen him instantly."

He took her arm. "Come. Let's wander into the other room and see who we can find."

They made their way through the crowd, pausing before Connie. "Francesca," Connie cried in delight, embracing her warmly. "I haven't seen you all week — I was beginning to worry." Like Francesca, Connie was blond and blue-eyed, although every aspect of her features was simply paler. Her hair was almost platinum, her eyes baby blue, her skin ivory. She was considered to be a great beauty and Francesca agreed heartily with that acclaim.

"I am on a case," Francesca said with a grin. She lowered her voice. "We are after the Slasher, Con. And I am afraid that last night he murdered another young woman."

Connie glanced at Rourke. They exchanged greetings and then she said, "Fran, Mama told me that you and Bragg are

351

working together again. Do you think that wise?"

"We are partners, nothing more," Francesca said, flushing because Rourke, who was Rick's half brother, stood there at her elbow, listening to their conversation. "And we do make a very fine investigative team."

Connie frowned just a bit — a real scowl would be far too unladylike for her. She lifted a pale eyebrow and nodded at the salon where the ensemble would dine. "I know how enthusiastic you are about this new hobby of yours," she said. "But you are engaged now. Maybe you should start planning the wedding. In any case, Hart is inside."

Francesca followed her gaze and saw Hart in his tuxedo, impossibly virile, impossibly male, leaning against one of the eight columns in the room. His posture was undeniably indolent, an irreverent habit that he had. A flute of champagne was in his hand. She was about to smile and wave in an attempt to catch his eye when she realized that he was chatting with a very stunning brunette she had met once before. She stiffened instantly, all eyes now.

"Isn't that Darlene?" Rourke murmured.

Francesca stared, some dismay beginning. Darlene was clearly flirting with Hart, and it was not the first time. She reminded herself that she was now Hart's fiancée and it was official. Darlene had to know about the engagement, as it was all the talk, indeed. But then why did she keep touching Hart's arm as she spoke? And was she mistaken, or did he not seem to mind her attention? Francesca reminded herself that she had no reason to be jealous. Still, she knew a flirtation when she saw one. "You work with her father, do you not? He's a doctor at the hospital in Philadelphia where you are in your residency."

"Yes, Paul Fischer is a fine internist. Shall we?" he asked, holding out his arm.

Francesca had not stopped staring and she could feel her cheeks heating now. She was jealous, never mind the fact of their engagement. She wanted Hart to look her way, see her in her daring red dress and smile reassuringly at her. "Yes, we should go over and make our presence known," she heard herself say.

"Darlene is terribly coy," Rourke whispered, patting her hand. He smiled at Connie when Francesca made no response, continuing to stare instead. "Your home is lovely," he added to his hostess.

Connie thanked him and leaned close. "Fran, do behave. At all costs!" she whispered in her ear.

And every single word Daisy had uttered suddenly seared Francesca's mind. But it was too soon for him to wander from her side.

Rourke guided her into the salon. "Francesca, you seem upset."

"Is Hart flirting with that witch?" she heard herself ask before she could stop the words.

Rourke stumbled. "I don't think so. Hart is used to the admiration of females. He is very eager to marry you. I am sure he is merely being polite."

Hart suddenly saw her, and her breathing became suspended. He stared. She waited for him to smile at her in that seductive way he had. Instead, he leaned more comfortably against the column, his glance moving over the dark red dress she wore.

She smiled uneasily at him.

He smiled back, waiting for her to approach. But his smile was very reserved — it was, in fact, distinctly odd.

Darlene was speaking to him but Hart's gaze remained on Francesca. And in that instant, in spite of the distance separating them, Francesca knew that something was very wrong.

"Are you all right?" Rourke asked quietly.

Unable to look away from Hart, she said, "Something is wrong."

"I beg your pardon?"

She finally glanced at him, unsmiling. "Something is wrong with Hart. He is upset."

Rourke's expression was bemused. "And you can tell all of that with half of a ballroom between you and him?"

"Yes, I can," Francesca said. Suddenly Darlene tugged on Hart's hand, and as she forced him to return his gaze to her, she stood on tiptoe and whispered in his ear. Francesca felt her fists clench. Perhaps a single inch separated the brunette's bosom from Hart's chest.

"Be calm," Rourke advised. "Calder has never been anything but respectful of you. I have actually been impressed by the gentleman he has become. Come, Francesca, we both know that Darlene isn't the first woman to chase him, and she won't be the last. Unfortunately, engaged or not, there will always be women out there who do not care what his status is." He smiled gently at her. "You may have to get used to it."

She inhaled hard, because she really felt like starting a catfight. But Rourke was right and she knew it. "Would you dance with me? I am in the mood to pull the hair off of someone's head and I need a moment to compose myself."

"Don't do that!" Rourke laughed, taking her hand and leading her to the dance floor. He said, "You have his undivided attention now."

Francesca wanted to look back over her shoulder, but she refused to do so. Still, she badly wanted to give Darlene a piece of her mind. And as she slipped into Rourke's arms and began to follow him about the dance floor, she wondered what she would do should she ever find Hart with a woman in a far more compromising position. If she was so disturbed by his allowing some eighteen-year-old beauty to flirt, then how would she feel if he genuinely strayed — the way Daisy had promised he would soon do?

She would never survive, she thought grimly. "What are they doing?" Rourke was an excellent dancer and she had only to remain light on her feet as he turned her about the dance floor.

"Hart is watching you like a hawk. I wouldn't worry too much, Francesca. I imagine he will be on his way over here in an instant."

She moved closer to Rourke, looking up at him and smiling. "I hadn't realized I could be so jealous or so possessive."

Rourke hesitated. "Passion makes for some strange bedfellows. I would ignore women like Darlene if I were you, Francesca. I have never seen Hart behave with any other woman the way he does with you. I have never seen Hart smile as often as he does since he has met you, Francesca. But do not misunderstand me. You have chosen to marry a very complicated man, and I would be surprised if your marriage was not, at times, a difficult one."

"There have been times when I have wondered what I am doing," she said frankly. "Rourke, I care so much for him, but it's his past that worries me so. Sometimes I wonder . . ." She hesitated before blurting out her concern. "I wonder if I can really hold his interest."

He laughed a little. "I have a strong feeling that you can and you will. I actually think he will try to be a good husband, Francesca. I think he cares deeply for you."

She was somewhat reassured. "Is he still watching us?"

"He is watching you. Do you want me to hold you a bit more closely?" Rourke asked with a devilish grin.

"Yes." And as Rourke pulled her too close for propriety, she had to peek over his shoulder at the subject of their conversation.

Hart was coming toward them. He looked very annoyed. All indolence was gone.

"Well, I think you have won — he is coming this way," Rourke said, low.

Hart tapped on Rourke's shoulder as they abruptly stopped dancing. "I think I will cut in," he said to Rourke. "If you do not mind?"

"Of course not." Rourke smiled. He gave Francesca an encouraging look and stepped aside.

Hart took her in his arms. Briefly, their gazes met. Francesca's moment of satisfaction vanished and she tensed, watching him now as he whirled her across the dance floor. His expression was dark. Something was wrong, oh yes.

"I take it you have had a busy day?" he asked politely, his smile distant.

Francesca gripped him more tightly, aware of the guarded look in his eyes, in his tone. His body rippled with a tension she could not identify.

If she were a woman like her sister, she would greet him warmly and not pry into the cause of his dark mood. But she was not her sister. As her mind raced, she said, "Yes. We found Kate Sullivan's husband.

He's dead."

He swept her around the dance floor, as effortlessly as Rourke had, but his hands were not Rourke's, oh no. They were large and strong and warm, one on her waist and the other holding her hand. "It was a recent demise, I assume?"

She nodded. "It might be a suicide. He might even have been the Slasher." And she ceased dancing but she did not let him go.

He halted in midstep as well.

"What is it?" she heard herself ask. "I can see that something is wrong."

He stared at her. It was a moment before he spoke. "Nothing is wrong. I have had a difficult day." He hesitated. "I apologize. I am sorry if I have given you the wrong impression." His smile was forced. "You are beautiful tonight. You are always beautiful, but you know how much I like that dress on you."

She hesitated. Hart was one of the most charming men she knew, but now it was as if he spoke prepared lines of dialogue that he did not feel. Now there was no charm. "Are you angry with me because I did not wait for Raoul?"

He seemed indifferent to the notion. "I hadn't realized. Raoul did not mention it — he is not my spy."

It wasn't Raoul, she thought, and she was terribly worried now. "What is wrong, Calder? You seem very disturbed. Has something happened? Please, you must tell me." She smiled a little at him. "We are engaged. You can share all of your deep dark secrets with me."

He flinched, looking taken aback, and then he took her arm and guided her away from the center of the dance floor. "We are being remarked upon. People might think we are at odds."

"It feels as if we are at odds," Francesca said quietly. "Are we? You have always enjoyed sharing your thoughts with me."

His jaw flexed. "No. I am not angry with you, Francesca, how could I be?" And this time he attempted a smile and utterly failed.

And even though his words rang with sincerity, his distress was obvious. She was shaken now. "Was it the meeting with the ambassador? Did it not go as you planned?"

He made a dismissive sound. "Even if it had been a miserable affair, I would hardly care. I am only expanding those ventures because it seems to be the thing to do. I do not need the extra wealth."

If he wasn't angry with her and if nothing untoward had recently happened then she could only draw one conclusion. "Have you seen Rick today?"

"No, I have not." His gaze darkened. "Leave well enough alone, Francesca. Would you like a drink?" And finally he smiled a little at her.

She seized his arm to prevent him from finding a waiter. A tiny voice in her head told her to let him be and try to discover the cause of his dark humor another time. But she said, "One day we will be married. Or at least, that is what we plan. But our marriage will never work if you shut me out. I can see very clearly that you are disturbed, even unhappy. Please, Calder, tell me what this is about."

And he was angry now. "Again, I have had a difficult day, and I am sorry if I have upset you." His tone was harsh and abrupt, final. "I have no intention of boring you with the details, either. *Leave well enough alone.*"

She recoiled. How would they get along for an entire lifetime if he intended to behave like this when something went afoul?

He seemed to read her mind. "You knew my reputation when you accepted my proposal. No one forced you to accept. If you wish to change your mind, I will not object."

She was so stunned that she gaped. Then she cried, "What are you saying? You . . . are you saying that you wish to end our engagement?" She was too shocked to feel anything but monumental surprise.

He stared, his expression so brittle it appeared in danger of cracking apart. It was a moment before he spoke. "We need to stop pretending," he said. "I am not a noble man. That is a script I wrote for you because you wanted me to write it. But it is only a goddamn script, Francesca. The facts of my life speak for themselves. I am a selfish, self-serving man and I am not Rick Bragg. You may take it or leave it, my dear."

She cried out, horrified, wanting to protest his description of himself, but she could not get a single word out.

"I'm sorry," he said flatly, his face now devoid of emotion. "I'm sorry I am not who you want me to be." He bowed. "I'll go get us champagne."

"Your sister is one of the finest hostesses in the city," Bartolla said, beaming with pleasure as she held on to Evan's arm. They had arrived at the Montrose residence and she had just handed off her velvet wrap. Now, glances were turning her way, both male and female. The male glances were startled and longing, the female glances were green with envy. Triumph filled her.

She smoothed down the dark burgundy

velvet gown she wore, having next to nothing underneath. Small straps encrusted with diamantés held the plunging bodice up; burgundy velvet gloves, the buttons diamanté, covered her arms well past the elbows. As she walked, the gown clung to her hips and thighs. She knew that because she had admired herself in a full-length mirror for some time before leaving the Chandler household.

"Connie is a fabulous hostess," Evan said, seeming distracted.

She pressed her bosom against his arm. "You are such a dear to bring me here, when we are immersed in our own personal crisis."

His jaw flexed and he glanced at her. His voice very low, he said, for the hundredth time, "Are you sure, Bartolla?"

And for the hundredth time, she nodded, looking dismayed, whispering, "Please, Evan, please. You don't have to do this. I can return to Europe to have our child and no one will ever know."

His jaw looked ready to crack apart. "You will do no such thing," he said flatly.

She turned away, hiding her smile. He had insisted that they would elope immediately. "There's your sister, and Lord Montrose. Come," she said, leading him over.

"Connie, my lord, how wonderful to see you both. And how lovely the decor is!" she cried.

Connie smiled, kissing her cheek, while Neil Montrose, a very tall, handsome man, kissed her hand. Bartolla strutted a bit before him, smiling warmly at him, as well. But his regard merely skimmed her low-cut bodice once, a reflex most men had. She realized he had his arm around his wife and his body pressed closely to hers. "I'm glad you made it," he said to his brother-in-law.

Evan smiled grimly. "How could I refuse an invitation from you and Con?"

Bartolla pushed out her chest, wishing she could poke Evan in the ribs, for his expression was so morose. Connie noticed her action; amazingly, her husband did not.

"That is a stunning dress," Connie said. "You wear it so well, Bartolla." She spoke without malice. In fact, she seemed incredibly content.

Bartolla suspected they had recently made love. "Thank you." Bartolla smiled and decided not to waste her time on Neil Montrose.

Neil said to Evan, "Julia and Andrew are here. I hope the evening will not become uncomfortable for you."

Evan clasped his hand. "Neil, thank you

for your concern. But I have other matters on my mind now, matters that do not involve my father."

Neil released his wife and put his hand on Evan's shoulder, briefly stepping aside. Bartolla strained to listen to them. He said, "I had lunch with Andrew the other day. He is upset, Evan, and rightly so. Can you not think about some kind of compromise? You are his only son."

"Neil," Evan warned, "I appreciate your concern, I really do, but I am afraid that the issues between my father and me are not your affair."

Montrose hesitated, his very turquoise eyes unwavering on his brother-in-law. "I am afraid I cannot be indifferent to your plight. Connie and I are both, frankly, worried."

"I am happy," Evan said, looking anything but. "So you need not worry about me."

Bartolla knew she must take her lover aside and chastise him for his lack of social graces. She sighed and suddenly noticed Calder Hart, standing in the other room with several women, all of them stunning and all vying for his attention. Hart's expression was hard to read. Bartolla could not decide if he was indifferent, bored or interested. She glanced around, but saw no sign of Francesca. "Where is your sister?" she asked Connie, and found that Connie's gaze had also veered to Calder Hart. Her expression was openly concerned.

"She went outside onto the terrace," Connie murmured, tearing her gaze from Hart with obvious reluctance.

"He is certainly a magnet, is he not?" Bartolla laughed but wondered why Hart was not fawning over his future bride.

Connie looked at her oddly. "I think he is in love with my sister." And she turned to glance at Hart again.

All kinds of interest flared. Were Hart and Francesca arguing? A very young and very pretty brunette, whom Bartolla did not know, was clinging to him now. Her gaze narrowed. Hart could take care of himself. He must be enjoying that young lady's attentions or he would have disengaged himself. "I doubt Hart has ever been in love," Bartolla said. Then she quickly smiled and added, "Until now."

Connie turned her back on the scene in the salon, clearly displeased with her future brother-in-law.

Evan and Neil stepped back to them. Evan said, "Is Francesca here?"

"She is on the terrace, I think," Connie said.

"I need to speak with her." He glanced at Bartolla, and then said to his sister, "She is on another case."

"I know. Apparently the Slasher struck again last night."

Evan turned white. "God, I didn't read it in the *World*!"

"It was in the *Tribune*," Neil remarked.

Bartolla did not like Evan's reaction.

"Who was it? I mean, surely it wasn't Maggie — Mrs. Kennedy — Francesca would have told me immediately!" He was aghast.

Bartolla slipped her arm in his, furious and hiding it. Did Evan have some kind of affection for that horrid little homely seamstress? She was certainly beginning to think so!

Connie touched his arm. "Of course it wasn't Mrs. Kennedy. She has moved into Hart's home with her children. The woman's name was Sullivan, I think."

Evan made a huge sound, clearly of relief. "Mag— Mrs. Kennedy has moved into Hart's home?"

"Yes."

"Good," he said firmly. "She will be safe there."

Bartolla pressed close. "Darling, don't you think your concern for your sister's seamstress is a bit . . . out of place?"

He seemed startled. "She is a friend of the family, Bartolla, and you know I am very fond of her children."

Connie and Neil exchanged a glance, which Bartolla did not miss. Her cheeks started to burn with humiliation. Would he display his absurd and misplaced affections to the entire world?

"How kind you can be," she said, smiling. "I am so proud of you." She kissed his cheek.

He did not seem to notice. "Can I get anyone a drink?" he asked.

"We're fine," Neil said. Then he turned to his wife, smiling into her eyes. "All of our guests have arrived and we should separate and mingle. Will you promise me the first dance after we dine?"

Connie beamed. "You know I will."

He leaned down and kissed her far too intimately for a husband and wife in a public room.

"Can you get me a glass of champagne?" Bartolla asked Evan.

"Certainly," Evan said.

Feeling vicious now, her glance strayed to Hart. "I'll be outside, with Francesca," she said.

CHAPTER SEVENTEEN

Friday, April 25, 1902 9:00 p.m.

Francesca was far too upset to be cold. She leaned on the plastered terrace railing, shaking terribly as she gazed down at Madison Avenue and the coaches and carriages below. She had been standing outside for the longest time, and Hart hadn't come looking for her.

Did he really want to end their engagement?

Francesca was so upset that she could not think straight. She was certain of one thing. Something was wrong with Hart. He was cold and distant, and it seemed as if he wished to push her away. Was this merely a black mood that would pass? Or had he changed his mind about them?

The thought of losing him now hurt unbearably.

She wiped moisture from her face. This morning he had been himself and everything had been fine. Somehow, within a few hours, everything had changed. *What had happened?*

She began to think clearly now. Surely something had happened! One did not walk away happily from one's fiancée and a few hours later try to break things off. But did it even matter? Her heart was breaking at the very idea of losing him. She was such a fool. She should have heeded her father's advice, Daisy's warnings, and even Hart's own claims about himself. Instead, she had chosen to believe he was someone fine and noble, a sheep in wolf's clothing. But it was too late now. She was in love — and she had never been more vulnerable.

But the real problem was that a part of her continued to believe that he was good and noble — not selfish and depraved. A part of her would simply never give up believing in him.

She wiped her eyes roughly. She was going to have to fight, somehow, for his heart. She simply could not cave in and give up. Too much was at stake — she loved him too much.

The thought of chasing Calder Hart was beyond terrifying. So many women had done just that and they had all failed.

"Francesca? Is that you?" a man's voice said.

She didn't recognize the intruder, although the voice was familiar. Francesca quickly wiped her eyes again with the back of her hand and turned, smiling widely at the stranger.

A lanky man came forward, smiling. "It's I, Richard Wiley," he said. "What are you doing out here by yourself?"

"Mr. Wiley, hello," she said, relieved it was someone she could easily manage. Once, Julia had tried to get her to accept Richard's courtship. That seemed a lifetime ago. "I am on another investigation, and I am trying to sort out some clues," she lied.

"You have been so busy since we first met," he exclaimed, smiling down at her. He had brownish hair and an oval face that was pleasant enough, if unexciting. "I have read so much about you these past few months."

She smiled in a more genuine manner. "I seem to have found my calling," she said. "I enjoy investigative work."

"And you do it so well. May I congratulate you on your recent engagement to Mr. Hart?"

Somehow Francesca continued to smile. "Thank you." Another guest stepped outside and when she saw that it was the countess Benevente, she was dismayed. She did not

371

want Bartolla to even suspect that anything was amiss with her and Hart.

"Can I escort you inside?" Wiley asked. "You must be cool standing out here in that gown."

Bartolla was approaching and she clearly wished to speak. Francesca knew the countess would not be dissuaded and in the dark it was less likely that she would surmise anything. The terrace had only two widely spaced gaslights. "I am so enjoying the fine April evening." Francesca smiled at him.

Wiley left after nodding at Bartolla. Shivering, the countess cried, "Francesca, why are you out here alone? Where is that dastardly man you call a fiancé? You will catch your death!"

Francesca plastered a smile on her face, inhaled hugely and said, "I am on a new case and I am trying to piece together some clues. I am afraid I am not in the mood for a fête."

Bartolla put her arm around her. "Darling, no matter what your mood, do you think it wise to leave Hart unattended?" And she smiled, laughing.

Francesca briefly closed her eyes. Somehow, she knew this woman was going to take a knife and twist it in her heart. Then she opened them and faced Bartolla. "Why would you say such a thing?"

Bartolla stared at her, her smile slowly fading. Then she touched Francesca's hand. "You are very upset," she said.

Francesca tried to appear disdainful. "A very good woman was murdered yesterday, Bartolla. I am preoccupied with her death — and with preventing another murder, if I can."

Bartolla studied her for an interminable time. "You know, Francesca, you are the bravest woman I have ever met, and probably the most sincere."

"I doubt that," Francesca said warily, taken aback.

Bartolla rubbed her arms, a reaction to the cool April breeze. "You have always been honest with me. You have always been kind. You are hiding out here, aren't you?" she said quietly.

Francesca started. "No, I'm not!" she cried far too quickly.

Bartolla studied her in the darkness. A pause ensued, making Francesca uneasy. But when Bartolla spoke, her tone was different, subdued. "Did you really think that being attached to Hart in any way would be easy?"

Francesca bit her lip. She knew she must not discuss her private life with Bartolla, whom she did not trust. But she so desperately needed someone to talk to and Bartolla knew Hart as well as anyone.

"Only a very foolish woman would have ever thought such a thing," she said with an attempt at a smile.

Bartolla smiled back. "A wiser woman would have told him to go to hell, wouldn't she?"

Francesca had to agree. Nodding, she said, "He is very difficult to resist. He is persuasive when he chooses to be."

"And tonight, he is enjoying a flirtation with someone else. Are the two of you arguing?"

Francesca stiffened instantly. So Bartolla had noticed. Had the entire world seen his lack of attention to his future bride and the attention he was directing elsewhere? She said, "I hardly mind his flirting. It does not affect me — or us — at all."

"I came here tonight feeling rather catty," Bartolla said thoughtfully now. "I thought to make myself feel better at your expense. I was going to join you on the terrace and pour salt in your wounds. But I do like you, Francesca. And instead, I think I should give you some advice."

Francesca froze. What ploy was this?

"Go back inside, darling, and fight for

what you want," Bartolla said. "But do not stand out here alone, sulking in childish tears."

Francesca gaped. But Bartolla was terribly right. She was hiding and sulking and, in general, feeling sorry for herself. She wanted to fight for Hart, but she was afraid to compete with Darlene Fischer and her like. "I don't know if I can," she whispered. "I am half as beautiful as all the women he has always preferred in his bed."

Bartolla pulled her close. "Nonsense! You could improve your daytime fashion, of course, and get rid of those ugly blue suits. But you are every bit as alluring as the rest."

"I don't know how to do what you are suggesting," Francesca said, wide-eyed.

"Of course you do. You *are* wearing that dress, aren't you?" Bartolla smiled in a conspiratorial manner. "It is all a game, Francesca, even if you dare to really fall in love. It is the right dress, the right sway of the hip, the right glance, the right moment."

"But I am hardly a seductress," she whispered.

"Any woman is a seductress. You just must be better at it than the others, and as you are far more clever than us all, it should not really be a problem, now, should it?"

She had been very seductive in that oil

painting, she thought. And more times than she could count, Hart had responded to her as if she was a femme fatale. "But something is wrong. Something has set him off." She hesitated. "And I feel certain it is not desire for Miss Fischer."

"He's a man. A very virile one. Men like him wander. So even if tonight he is pre-occupied with some other matter, one day he will genuinely stray. I know you know that! But you can pull him right back." She smiled then. "I've seen him watching you. It's so much more than lust. If it were mere lust, I'd tell you to break the engagement and have some simple fun. He admires you immensely and I've seen it in his eyes. There is hope, darling — if you are strong enough to weather the ups and downs of a relation-ship that will undoubtedly be very stormy."

Francesca hated the fact that Bartolla, like Daisy, believed in Hart's eventual disloyalty. But she wondered if she had the strength to do as Bartolla had described. And suddenly, in that moment, she was determined to take up just such a battle. It felt as if her entire life was at stake, and perhaps it was. She couldn't imagine living without Calder present in her every waking moment, her every thought.

"Thank you," she finally said. "Thank you

for being sincere."

Bartolla winked. "Don't tell anyone! I shall be ruined."

Francesca smiled, about to reply, but then she could not speak.

Hart stepped onto the terrace, and even shadowed as he was, she knew his form and felt his presence instantly. He came forward, his strides filled with purpose.

Francesca watched him emerge into the moonlight. His expression was hard and determined. He glanced at Bartolla just once, dismissively. He disliked her and did not offer even a polite greeting.

Bartolla clearly didn't care. She gave Francesca an encouraging look and hurried inside.

Francesca felt paralyzed.

He took off his jacket and wrapped it around her shoulders. "Will you stand outside all night?" he asked quietly.

"I have been considering doing just that," she said, impossibly aware of his hands as they slipped off the jacket and her shoulders. She searched his eyes. Had she heard a normal resonance in his tone?

"I have behaved in the most reprehensible manner," he said. "Francesca, I am sorry. There is simply no excuse for my harsh words earlier this evening."

Relief flooded her, making her knees useless — she found herself clutching his lapels as he gripped her waist, offering her his strength and support. "Why? What has happened? What is wrong?"

He shook his head, but his hands pulled her close. "I don't know," he murmured, and his eyes closed. He kissed her cheek several times, her jaw, her throat.

She shivered, desire an instantaneous flood, no matter how upset she was. She realized he was shaking as his mouth moved over the swell of her breasts. She held on to him as if he were a ghost that might vanish at any time. "Can't you talk to me? Calder, how will our marriage ever succeed if you shut me out this way?"

He flinched, meeting her gaze, now holding her face in his hands. "I don't want to talk, not now, not about anything," he said. And his mouth claimed hers.

It would have been so easy to cave into his desire — as there was no mistaking his raw need — and be swept away to a very safe place. Instead, her mind raced as he kissed her, again and again, hungry and insistent. They could not solve their problems this way. She pushed him away. "No."

He was out of breath. His eyes widened.

"No?" And suddenly she saw a gleam in his eyes.

She knew him well enough to know that he thought her refusal a challenge. She braced her hands against his chest. "You have given me a terrible fright," she said slowly. "And I think I have every right to know why."

He stepped away from her now, raking one hand through his hair. "You do have every right," he said finally. "But I also have the right not to share every single aspect of my life, every single thought, with you." He became wry. "You really do not want to know."

She was very still, in some disbelief. "Actually, I do. But you are right — there is no law, no rule that says I must be privy to your private thoughts."

He smiled at her, just slightly, but it was genuine enough.

At least their crisis was over, she thought. "Why did you tell me that I could end our engagement?"

He hesitated. "I was in a very black mood. I regret my words. And I am more than sorry. If you let me —" and he smiled far too seductively "— I will show you just how sorry I am."

"Is that it?" she asked incredulously. "You

indicate that you wish to end our engagement — that you wish for me to back out, sparing you the cruelty of doing so — and you will offer me no explanation?"

"No," he said flatly. His smile was gone. "Do not push me now."

The warning was clear. His good mood and the Calder Hart she had come to know and love was clearly in jeopardy. But she could not help herself. *If he was having doubts about their future, she simply had to know.*

She went to stand before him, laying her hand on his chest, over his heart. "Do you want to end our engagement?" she asked.

He did not react with surprise; he did not protest or deny it. His jaw flexed, hard, his eyes turned black and he stared.

Oh my God. He wanted to end it.

Her hand fell from his chest. She stepped back, away from him.

"Let's go inside," he said roughly. He smiled a little at her. "I promised you that champagne."

"No," she whispered, refusing to move. "We have been honest with one another from the start. We agreed there would never be any lies between us. If you have doubts about us — about me — you owe me the honesty we agreed upon."

380

He wet his lips. "I never want to hurt you. It still remains the last thing I ever want to do." He added, "Please, Francesca, leave this alone." And it was a plea, the first he had ever made to her or anyone that she knew.

But she could not hear him now. *He had doubts, grave doubts.* "You wish to end our engagement," she heard herself say. It wasn't a question. Her world began to blacken and spin.

"Don't push me," he said harshly. "Not now, not tonight."

She somehow managed to remain upright. She became aware of Hart holding her arm. "Let's go home, Francesca. I think we could both use a good scotch." As if he hadn't just warned her with real anger to let the past hours alone, he brushed his mouth over her cheek. There was urgency there.

She thought she nodded. She needed to think, never mind that she felt dangerously shocked and incapable of any thought at all.

Hart was guiding her inside and across the reception hall. It was oddly empty except for staff, and she was vaguely aware that most of the guests in the salon had taken their seats with their suppers. Somehow, Hart had his arm around her waist.

She briefly closed her eyes, leaning against him. Even now, when her every instinct told her that he was the one she should run from, she found comfort in the strength of his powerful body, in the strength of him.

His step faltered.

She felt his tension and knew it had nothing to do with their recent conversation. She looked up at him. "What is it?"

He met her gaze, his expression lightened. "Are you at all inclined to sleuth tonight?"

She followed his gaze, surprised. A very handsome gentleman had just entered the house and he was handing off his walking stick and gloves. "Why? Who is that?"

"That, my dear, is Lord Randolph."

Francesca instantly forgot the previous moments and stared. Randolph was a few years her senior, perhaps twenty-seven or -eight. He had dark hair, fair skin and even from the distance separating them, she realized his eyes were a brilliant, remarkable shade of blue. "Yes, I do want to sleuth — how could I even consider missing this opportunity?" she asked, never removing her gaze from her quarry. He was a striking man, the kind of rake even a good woman like Gwen might fall victim to.

How interesting it would be if he were Gwen's former lover and employer and now in the city, while the Slasher was on the loose.

And hadn't Maggie said the gentleman she had met on the street corner the night of Kate's murder had remarkable blue eyes?

Francesca bristled inwardly. How she hoped that Randolph was their Slasher!

Hart smiled at her. "I can see the gauntlet being thrown. Let me introduce you, then."

"Wait!" She met his gaze. "You made some comment about his reputation."

"Ah, yes. He has the unenviable reputation of being absolutely dour."

"Dour?" she asked.

"Apparently he lost his wife and children in a fire, Francesca," Hart said somberly. "Although that was quite a few years ago, he rarely smiles and is known to be dour, grim and reclusive. He avoids society, female company of all kinds, and seems to have no intention of ever remarrying. That, I suppose, is what has really set the gossips off. He is a wealthy catch and the ruling matriarchs are terribly annoyed with him."

"Perhaps he cannot be blamed, having suffered such a tragedy," Francesca said. She began to think that he could not be the rake who had seduced Gwen. "Quickly, Hart, before he goes in to dine."

Hart hurried forward, Francesca following. It was a relief to be investigating again. "Randolph, good evening," Hart said very pleasantly.

Randolph started as he recognized Hart. "Hart, good God, is that you?" He smiled slightly as the two men shook hands. "What an amazing coincidence," he said.

"May I introduce my fiancée, Miss Francesca Cahill?"

Randolph was clearly surprised by that. "You are engaged?" He then flushed. "Miss Cahill, Harry de Warenne at your service, and may I add my congratulations?" He bowed.

"Thank you. Do you know my sister or brother-in-law? They are your hosts tonight." He wore several rings, Francesca noticed, but only one on his left hand. The stone was black onyx, an unusual choice, and some carving was upon it. It was also gold.

"Yes, I know Montrose rather well. He has a house in London not far from mine," Randolph said.

"Oh, so you are from England," Francesca smiled. "I had thought your accent Irish."

Randolph glanced at Hart. "Your fiancée is very clever. I am from Ireland, in fact, although the majority of my family is English. We are the black sheep, actually, us

Irish de Warennes."

"I am sure you are hardly a black sheep," Francesca said lightly. "So you prefer to reside in London? I am partial to the green Irish countryside myself." Actually, she loved London, having been there numerous times, and she had never been to Ireland.

Hart said smoothly, "I am surprised to see you here. Usually you send your lieutenants to manage your business affairs."

Randolph shrugged. "This time there were matters that required my personal attention."

Francesca became thoughtful. "I am friends with a very beautiful woman and I believe she is from the vicinity of Limerick. Perhaps I should invite her to our supper party. You might know her. She resides here in the city now."

"Perhaps, although I would doubt it. Who is she?" Harry de Warenne asked.

"Her name is Mrs. Hanrahan, Mrs. David Hanrahan, although we are so close, I call her Gwen," Francesca said, her smile never slipping, her gaze unwavering upon his face.

And his polite expression did not change, not in the slightest. "I am afraid I do not know the woman in question," he said.

CHAPTER EIGHTEEN

Saturday, April 26, 1902 10:00 a.m.

"Hello." Francesca greeted her sister. Anxiety filled her but she managed to smile.

Connie looked radiant as she came forward, wearing a lovely pink and ivory striped gown, but her eyes reflected some surprise. "Fran! Is everything all right?" she asked as she quickly embraced her.

Once, before sleuthing had come to take up so much of her time, Francesca had been a frequent, if not daily, visitor at her sister's home. She adored not only her sister, but her two nieces as well. Recently, her visits had become twice weekly, much to Francesca's chagrin. There simply did not seem to be enough time in the day to accomplish all that she wished to.

Francesca looked directly at her sister. She had tossed and turned half the night, trying to decipher every word and gesture Hart had made. In the end, when she had fallen asleep, not a single conclusion had been reached. "I don't think so," she said. "But frankly, I am not sure."

Instantly, Connie turned and closed both salon doors, insuring the utmost privacy for them. Then she returned to Francesca, taking both her hands and guiding her to a pair of burgundy chairs. As they sat, she said softly, "I take it this is about Calder?"

Francesca nodded, stabbed with a dreadful combination of dread and fear. "How did this happen?" she whispered. "How did I fall in love with such a man? My entire life I believed that my husband would be someone exactly like our father. Instead, I am head over heels for the most notorious womanizer to ever grace the city's halls."

Connie inhaled, her blue eyes wide. "Do you think he is pursuing other women?"

"No." But Francesca bit her lip. "I mean, I know you saw him last night. He hardly spent a moment at my side and he allowed that Darlene Fischer to flirt with him quite endlessly. But no, I do not think he wishes to stray yet. But something is bothering him and he won't tell me what it is."

"Then maybe you had better let him be, until he wishes to confide in you." When Francesca started to object, Connie raised her hand. "I know that will be incredibly difficult for you! I cannot imagine any feat harder than restraining yourself when it comes to Calder Hart. But trust me, Fran. There is a time to press, and there is a time to stand down."

Francesca comprehended her sister's words and meaning, she really did. But how could she let this go? "When I finally accepted his proposal, I instinctively knew that he had the power to completely destroy me. What should I do? I cannot decide what action to take," she cried.

Connie paused thoughtfully for a moment. "You know I will always be honest with you. Giving your heart to a man like Calder is a dangerous proposition, indeed. I, too, always thought you would find true love with someone like our father — someone like Rick Bragg."

Francesca sighed. "He would have been so safe."

"Yes, he would. Why don't you tell me what really happened last night?" Connie asked.

Francesca met her gaze. Her heart slammed with her entire recollection of the prior evening. "Yesterday morning everything was as it always was. Hart was completely attentive and extremely affectionate and charming. The moment I arrived here last night, though, I sensed that something was amiss. I could almost see this dark cloud hanging over his head."

"Did you ask him what was wrong?"

"Yes. He refused to discuss the matter. I pressed and he became very angry with me." She tensed. "Con, he told me I knew his reputation when I agreed to become his wife, and he would not object if I changed my mind!"

Connie gasped. "He wants *you* to break off the engagement?"

"Later he denied it. But isn't that the only conclusion to be had? He has doubts about us and I believe he would not mind if I pushed him away!"

Connie took her hand. "Fran, I am not going to even attempt to comprehend a man like Calder Hart. I mean, I thought my life with Neil was perfect, and look at what happened."

Francesca studied her sister closely. They had both learned during one of Francesca's cases that Neil had been having an affair with another woman. To this day, Francesca could not understand why he had done such a thing when he truly loved her sister. He, of course, had refused to explain, and it was not her business, anyway. Her sister's marriage had barely survived, but now they seemed back on track, if not happier than ever.

"But clearly Calder Hart is having second thoughts about such a monumental decision as a lifelong commitment," Connie said.

"I cannot agree more," Francesca said grimly.

Connie squeezed her hand. "Would that really be so odd? He is twenty-six years old and he has never courted any woman before you. He has been a shameless and dissolute rake. Now, apparently, he wishes to reform. Perhaps it would be strange if he *didn't* have some doubts?"

"Is that supposed to make me feel better?" Francesca asked. "And what should I do? In the end, he apologized for his behavior, but he still refused to explain himself. And it hurt me, Con, to see another woman flirting so liberally with him! I was actually green with jealousy watching him with Darlene Fischer."

Connie sighed. "I don't know how to make you feel better, but I do have some advice — advice I feel very strongly about."

Francesca leaned forward, eager to hear her sister's words. After all, she was an experienced woman. "Please!"

"First, answer this. Do you have any

doubts about him?"

Francesca did not hesitate, even as she thought about Rick Bragg. "No. At first I was uncertain — at first I still loved Rick, but now we are truly friends. And that has allowed me to realize how much I love Calder." She hesitated and added, "I do not doubt my feelings. I doubt his ability to keep his promise not to ever be unfaithful."

"Fran, you must take a life with someone else one step at a time. Don't even think ahead to some faraway future day when he might break his word to you." She flushed a little and Francesca knew she was thinking about Neil. "Even the best marriage with the noblest man will have some difficult moments."

"I guess I can agree with that. So you advise me to fight for him — to fight for his heart?" she asked, thinking about Bartolla's words.

"No," Connie cried in dismay.

Francesca was surprised. "No?"

Connie shook her head. "Do *not* chase after Hart! That is the worst thing you could do. If he ever sensed you were in pursuit, I feel certain he would lose interest."

Francesca stiffened with confusion and dread. "So what should I do? Walk away?" She was in some disbelief.

"No. Stand firm in your heart and be yourself." She smiled then. "You are so eccentric, Fran, and that is the woman who has turned Calder's head. Not some coy debutante like Darlene, but a beautiful, brave and clever sleuth, a woman committed to justice and reform, a woman absolutely selfless. You are unique — remain that way. Do not even *think* to compete with women like Darlene. Because then you would be like the others!"

Francesca was wide-eyed. "So I should do nothing?"

"No, you should bring all your efforts and all your interest to your current investigation. Do you not have a murderer on the loose?"

Francesca started to relax. "A killer who must be found, and quickly!" she said with some genuine relief.

"Find the Slasher, Francesca. Be yourself. If Hart wants to flirt, let him. Because if this is meant to be — if this will ever work — he will get over his doubts and the marriage will proceed. But he must be the one chasing you. It must *never* be the other way around."

Francesca hugged her sister. "You are right! I feel certain. As worried as I am, I must be brave and try to prevent another

murder. Either Calder will remain committed to our engagement, or not. In any case, I know that competing with the likes of Darlene is not my strong suit."

"Your strong suit is who you truly are," Connie said with vast affection.

Francesca smiled, knowing that Connie was being kind. Her sister recognized that Francesca should not — and could not — compete with the city's most beautiful and seductive women. Hart was clearly having doubts but he still was extremely fond of her, and she would not dwell on what she could not control. Francesca stood. "You have been so helpful," she exclaimed.

Connie grinned. "That is what sisters are for. And where are you off to now?"

"I do have a killer to catch," Francesca said, returning her smile. "But before I interview John Sullivan's other roommate, I promised Rick I would call on Leigh Anne."

Connie's pale eyebrows lifted. "How is she?"

Francesca's smile faded. "I don't think she is doing very well."

It was so odd and so pleasant, Maggie thought, her heart fuzzy with warmth, as she watched two of her sons as they sat on the sofa together. Mathew was trying to

teach Paddy the alphabet and he was being very serious about it. Paddy was attempting to be as serious, but he could not grasp the concept of the letter A at all. Both boys were freshly scrubbed and clothed in their Sunday best, and they were dwarfed by the gold velvet sofa they sat on. Behind them was a huge red wall, an incredible painting of two women and a child from some bygone era, the high, high ceiling above painted red with a gold and cream starburst in its center. Her sons looked like two little princes.

Almost.

Her heart lurched with sadness then. They would never be princes; the best they could be were honest, hardworking, godly men. Once, that had been enough. Recently, it did not seem enough at all.

She glanced around at the huge and opulent room, which, in fact, wasn't large at all compared to the other rooms in the house. Calder Hart had been kind enough to tell her she could use the house as freely as if it were her own home. Of course, she would never do such a thing — she had warned her children not to touch anything, afraid they might break some priceless treasure. His butler, Alfred, had shown her to an entire wing that was exclusively for her and the children. He had even wanted

to give each child his own room! Those instructions had been given by Mr. Hart, who clearly did not know much about children. Last night all of the children, except for Joel, had crawled into her huge, canopied bed, frightened by the vast spaces, the dark, the house.

If only, she thought, she could give her children an education. Not the few years of learning that Joel had had, but an education that might enable them to find the kind of employment that would allow them to live as gentlemen. Maggie thought of Evan Cahill now. Her sons were never going to be a gentleman like him.

"Mama!" Lizzie cried, running into the room, Joel following at a leisurely pace.

Lizzie had a red smear on her face. Maggie hurried to her, dismayed by the untidiness. "Joel! What has she been eating? Why didn't you clean her face? What if someone saw her looking like some farmer's brat?" She scooped her little daughter up, using a kerchief she kept in her bodice to clean what was jam from the corners of Lizzie's mouth and chin.

"I got to go, I gotta meet Miz Cahill. Cook gave her these special cookies," Joel explained with a grin. "Ma, I never had such good food in my life! Not even at Miz

Cahill's!"

"Don't get used to it," Maggie said too sharply as she set Lizzie down. The child ran, toddling, over to her brothers, and then tried to climb onto the sofa but failed.

Joel had ambled over behind her and set her on it, next to Paddy. He glanced at Maggie, folding his thin arms over his chest. "I know where we live," he said, understanding her fears exactly. But then, he was just like his father, and not only in looks. He was clever and so perceptive that, at times, it dismayed her.

She almost smiled and told him that. Instead, she said, "I know that you do. But look at your brothers. In a few days, they won't even remember our home. They'll think this is their home. And then what will happen when we do go back?"

Joel shrugged. "It won't take 'em long to be themselves again."

Maggie sank down in a chair. This wasn't right. Her children were in for a terrible letdown and they were her life. Even she, herself, as hardworking and God-loving as she was, could get used to this kind of home. And Evan Cahill's image came so strongly to mind that her heart ached.

Don't be a fool, Maggie girl.

Maggie froze, because she had just heard

her husband's voice as clearly as if he were still alive.

Tears came to her eyes. Once, she had conversed with him as freely and frequently as if he were still alive. He had been her best friend, a childhood sweetheart, and she had thought, when he died, that she would miss him forever. He had been gone for a few years, but it was only recently, in the past few months, that their conversations had eased and then ceased. Hearing his warning so clearly now, as if he stood there in the room, handsome and smiling, made her heart flutter wildly.

If only he were here. How she needed his advice.

Maggie girl, I am here, I will always be here. And I know you know it, deep in your heart.

Evan Cahill's dark, dashing, blue-eyed image was now engraved on her mind. Her heart fluttered again, but differently, almost madly, and she closed her eyes in despair. She had been thinking of him so often, and not just because of the other day. For several months now, he had been a constant source of her dreams, an unwanted shadow in her days.

How can you let your heart go there? Maggie, I told you this before. He is not for you!

"I know," Maggie whispered aloud, miserably.

"Ma? Don't be sad," Joel said urgently. "It's only fer a few days and when we get home, I'll make sure the boys eat as good as they do here."

Maggie jerked and met Joel's anxious eyes. She clasped his shoulders. He had far too much responsibility for one so young. "What would I do without you?" she whispered. "And have I ever told you that you are just like your father?"

He smiled, but with worry. "Only a hundred times."

Maggie caressed his thick black hair and then realized that someone had come to stand in the doorway. She started and met her host's dark gaze. "Mr. Hart, sir," she cried, smiling. Did he think he was interrupting them? "Do come in," she said, and then she flushed. "I mean, it is your home."

Hart smiled a little as he accepted her invitation, strolling inside. He clasped Joel's back, who beamed. "I did not want to interrupt," he said, glancing at the three children on his sofa.

Maggie prayed no one had jam or anything else on their hands. "Children, get down! We will go to our rooms," she said, wringing her hands.

"Mrs. Kennedy, please, do not send them out on my account," Hart said.

Maggie flinched and met his gaze. He seemed very grim, she thought, and very tired. There was no smile on his face, not even a trace, or anything at all in his eyes. "Alfred said we could use a room. I thought this room appropriate, as it isn't as large as the others in the house. But —"

"Please, Mrs. Kennedy, use any salon you desire. I am on my way out and I merely wished to inquire if all of your needs are being met."

She nodded, barely able to believe how kind he was — how kind everyone was. There were other guests in the house, Grace and Rathe Bragg, a brother, a nephew. Everyone was pleasant and friendly, as if she was a real guest and a real lady, herself.

Maggie! Don't go foolin' yourself. You're not gently bred and you never will be!

"We are fine. Thank you so much for your hospitality. I must thank Francesca again," she said breathlessly.

His expression hardened and he faced Joel. "Do you know where Miss Cahill is today?" he asked. "I have sent a note, but she is already out for the day."

Joel smiled eagerly at him. "Yes, sir! We got plans, we do. She had personal matters with her sister, Mr. Hart, and then we got to call on Mrs. Bragg, as she promised to do so. After that, she got to interview Sullivan's flatmate, the one she didn't speak to. An' if there's still some time, she said she wants to visit some lord who's stayin' at the Holland House."

Hart's eyebrows rose. He seemed reluctantly amused. "And she thinks to do all that in one day, does she?"

"Yes, sir, she does. Miz Cahill is determined, ain't she?" He grinned proudly.

Hart tousled his hair. "Can you give her a message from me?"

Joel nodded eagerly.

"Tell her I would enjoy taking her to supper tonight."

"Yes, sir!" Joel replied.

Alfred paused in the doorway. "Mrs. Kennedy? You have a caller," he said.

Maggie was startled. How could she have a caller? And then Evan Cahill walked into the room.

Her heart raced wildly and she felt herself flush. Evan bowed. Impeccably attired in a fine dark suit, he looked disheveled, nonetheless. "Mrs. Kennedy, good day."

She mumbled a greeting in reply, unable to take her eyes away. He was the most dashing gentleman she had ever laid her

400

eyes upon, and she knew for a fact he was also the kindest.

"I think I will excuse myself," Hart said, some humor in his tone. He and Evan exchanged friendly words and he strode out.

Maggie knew her cheeks were red. How had it gotten so warm in the room? She tugged at the collar of her shirtwaist.

Evan did not see as he knelt now, embracing the two younger boys and Lizzie, who insisted on being hauled up in his arms. Mathew started to tell him that he was teaching Paddy his letters, while Paddy tried to tell him that he had eaten eggs *and* sausages *and* flapjacks for breakfast, all at once, with real sugar syrup, and milk! "Is that all?" Evan teased, still holding Lizzie in his arms. She was pulling on the curls of his dark hair, but he did not seem to mind. "And does your belly ache?"

"No." Paddy grinned. He rubbed his stomach, sticking it out. "It feels good!"

"Cookie," Lizzie beamed. "Cookie!"

Evan looked her in the eye. "I'm afraid I came empty-handed today — almost." He finally looked directly at Maggie and her heart sped. "Joel," he said, not looking away. "There's a shopping bag in the front hall. I think there are some items in the bag that might be of interest to the children." Still

401

staring at Maggie, not smiling at all, he slowly set Lizzie down.

And suddenly all the children were gone, Joel taking Lizzie out by the hand. Silence filled the room.

Maggie could not find a single breath of air. She so wanted to fan herself, but would not dare. Why was he staring? Why did he look so grim? "Mr. Cahill?" she whispered nervously.

"Evan. I thought we agreed at supper the other night that it is Evan . . . Maggie."

She bit her lip. *Maggie girl, don't!* "Yes," she somehow managed to say.

He suddenly sighed, the sound reluctant and painful, and he turned to the window that was behind him, staring at it.

Oh dear, something was wrong. Somehow she had come to stand behind him; somehow, she was touching his hand.

He started, whirling, and they stood facing one another, just inches apart.

She knew she must leap back and away, but her feet refused to obey. Instead, her heart pounded desperately with the insane desire to move forward into his arms, just this once. She whispered, "What is it? Why do you look . . . so sad?"

Suddenly he lifted his hand.

Disbelief filled her and something incredulous — hope.

He cupped her cheek. "You are so sweet," he said roughly.

His simple touch affected her as no caress had in years. She wanted to throw her body against his, press her mouth to his, and cling hard, for all eternity. *But something was terribly wrong.* He had helped her so many times — he had been a godsend for her children — she had to help him now. She pulled away. "Something is wrong," she said quietly. "How can I help?"

His face collapsed. He turned away, looking defeated.

Maggie was filled with alarm. "Evan? What has happened?"

He did not face her, so she went around him, standing in front of him, taking his hand. "Is someone ill? Has someone died?" she asked in fear.

"No." His mouth barely moved as he spoke. Then, flushing, he continued. "The countess is pregnant."

Maggie gasped. And when his words penetrated through her shock, a knife pierced through her heart. "Oh."

"Yes, oh," he said grimly.

Now she felt her cheeks heat. She dropped his hand. *I told you, Maggie girl, I told you he is not for you! But you didn't listen, did you?*

No, she hadn't listened, not to her own conscience, her own common sense. "But you love her," she heard herself say. "I mean, the child is yours." It was a question and she knew her cheeks flamed.

He looked into her eyes. "The child is mine."

She realized she wanted to weep. "This is wonderful, then, this is cause to celebrate —"

"I don't love her."

She froze.

He stared at her in agony, and then he turned and walked across the room.

She was breathing hard. The beautiful countess, who was so perfect for him, was having his child. And he did not love her . . . not that it mattered. Suddenly she chased after him. "Surely you have feelings for her! Surely you must — she is so beautiful, so elegant, such a lady!" He turned to her, appearing disbelieving. She couldn't stop. "You are so kind and good with my children. I see how much you care. Why, you will make a wonderful father. This is joyous news, it is!"

"I don't love her," he said intensely.

She could only stare. She felt tears forming in her eyes. *He isn't saying that he loves you, Maggie. Don't be a fool! You are an Irish farmer's daughter and he is a gentleman.*

And she found every single ounce of strength she had. "The child is yours. You are going to bring a beautiful life into this world — a life you are responsible for."

"Yes, of course, I know that," he said. But he was staring now so directly, so boldly, that her knees became weak. Why was he looking at her that way?

Somehow she said, "One day, you will think this is the best thing that ever happened to you."

He grimaced. "Yes, I know. One day. One day, that is what I will think." His gaze remained unwavering upon her.

She wanted to hold him, comfort him, stroke his forehead, his hair. But now reality fell, brutally, crushing her soul. He would marry the countess, they would have a child. How could it hurt her so? *Because you let yourself fall in love with him, Maggie girl.*

The tears rose. She swiped them aside. He must not see how affected she was. "How can I help?" she asked quietly.

His nostrils flared; their gazes locked. "I don't know." He hesitated, and suddenly he reached out and cupped her cheek again. "I have told no one except you."

He would have to marry the countess. They both knew that. But as her body came alive the way it hadn't in so long, she closed her eyes. And for one moment, she allowed herself to rejoice in the feel of his strong hand on her face. *Oh, God, if only . . .*

And suddenly she felt him leaning toward her.

Maggie opened her eyes, stunned.

His eyes were open, his brilliant blue eyes, and their gazes met, his wildly searching.

She knew he was going to kiss her, the way she had known he would someday, sometime, because she had known it forever, and she did not move as he murmured her name. "Maggie." And finally his lips touched hers.

Her heart expanded impossibly as his mouth brushed hers and she loved him the way she had never thought it possible to ever love again — and suddenly he stopped.

She felt sanity return, too.

Her gaze flew open and she met his dark, surprised, unhappy eyes, his mouth still perilously close. Slowly, a flush appearing on his high cheekbones, he released her shoulders.

As he stepped away, she fought for air. "You will marry her," she somehow said.

"Yes," he returned, his shoulders square. "Immediately. We will elope."

CHAPTER NINETEEN

Saturday, April 26, 1902 Noon

He knew Francesca was not at home, but as he handed off his gloves, he glanced toward the stairs, almost expecting her to come down them at any moment. Not amused by his own unbridled interest, Calder Hart mocked himself.

But it would always be this way and he was astute enough to know that. Somehow, Francesca had become a vital ingredient in his life. Somehow, he had come to eagerly anticipate her presence, as if he never saw her at all. He had meant it when he had told her that she had become the sunshine in his life. He was not pleased.

He had spent his entire life relying on no one but himself. He had learned the day his mother had died that he was absolutely alone in the world, never mind his older half brother, Rick. Francesca might have become vitally important to him, but he must not ever lose his independence. He was resolved not to.

He had recovered from the disaster of the previous night. Briefly, Daisy had so upset him with her insights into his character and her predictions of the future that he had wanted to push Francesca away. He remained distinctly displeased with himself, because the one truth he lived and breathed was his desire to protect Francesca from the worst that life had to offer. But last night he had done exactly the opposite. Last night he had hurt her, selfish bastard that he was.

Now it was another day and his mental acuity seemed to have returned. He should have foreseen this. Daisy had been unhappy with his engagement and the demise of their relatively new relationship. He did not think he was being excessively arrogant, but he thought she harbored real feelings for him. It would not be the first time a woman, either lady or whore, had fallen in love with him. In any case, the moment she had walked into his Bridge Street office, he should have prepared for battle — no, for war. She had wanted to upset him, and she had managed to do just that.

How ironic it was. He thought to battle his ex-mistress, but the real enemy was the truth she had so aptly revealed — the truth that was himself.

Today it did not matter. Today he had a grip on his unholy, decadent past. Today he was that nearly noble man, the man who made Francesca's eyes shine in such a way that it gave him the greatest pleasure. Daisy was right. He was a hedonist at heart. His past was proof of that. But he could keep that side at bay. He would have to, because Francesca must never look at him in horror, utterly comprehending the truth. He had become far too fond of his new life and the woman now so predominantly at the heart of it.

He would take care of Daisy once and for all.

"Mr. Cahill is in his study, sir," the butler said, politely leading the way through the spacious marble-floored foyer.

Francesca's father had sent him a note that morning, requesting that he present himself at his earliest convenience. Had Francesca spoken to him about moving up their wedding date? After his rotten behavior last night, he doubted it.

Cahill had been at the Montrose affair last night; Hart assumed he was being summoned for an interrogation and a set-down. As he hoped to have a good relationship with Francesca's father, he would have to accept any chastisement, a burden he was unaccustomed to bearing. Hart hoped he could be as humble as the moment required.

Andrew was seated behind his desk, his hands clasped together, looking very solemn indeed. Hart stiffened as he entered, now wary, as Andrew rose to his feet. He nodded at the butler, who closed the mahogany doors behind him, leaving the two men alone. Even though it was April, a small fire crackled in the hearth.

"Good morning," Andrew said, moving from behind his desk. The two men shook hands. "Do have a seat."

Hart had no intention of sitting in front of Andrew's desk while the other man took the large chair behind it, as the position he would be in was psychologically inferior. He walked over to the sofa and sat, stretching out his long legs, refusing to show any tension, although extreme caution filled him. He recognized a battlefield when invited to tread upon one. Andrew Cahill was distinctly displeased — as he should be.

He smiled as Andrew came forward, forced to sit down in a chair facing Hart, giving Hart the position of power after all. "We have much to discuss," Cahill said flatly.

"Please, do not delay." Hart smiled at him. "The subject is, of course, Francesca."

This Hart already knew, as they otherwise had no affairs in common. He did not bat an eye. "Of course." He would not give an inch — not yet.

"I think I will strike directly to the point," Cahill said, his shoulders rigid now, his expression foreboding. "I have always held that you are not worthy of my daughter and that you will only cause her undue grief and pain."

"I doubt any man is worthy of Francesca," Hart murmured.

"Francesca was clearly unhappy last night. Have you already begun to pursue other women when the two of you are not even married yet?" Cahill had become flushed.

He stared coolly. It was very hard to believe that Cahill would attack him so openly. But he was determined to remain pleasant and obsequious. "I was not pursuing anyone. There is only one woman I am interested in, my fiancée."

"Really?" Andrew was in disbelief. "Several guests remarked on the tension between you and Francesca. Several guests noted your dalliance with Miss Fischer. I did not care for your behavior last night, Hart. The two of you are supposed to be in love!"

His heart lurched uncomfortably. "I have never claimed to love your daughter, sir. I have vowed to cherish her, protect her, admire and respect her, while providing her with a life she will thrive upon."

"You hardly cherished her last evening!"

"I allowed Miss Fischer a mild flirtation, which, of course, is not a crime." He sighed, his expression appropriately humble, he thought. "You are, of course, right. Last night I did not cherish your daughter as I said I would."

Cahill was clearly surprised. "I beg your pardon?"

"I never thought the day would ever come when I wished to wed anyone, Andrew. Yesterday I started to think about the commitment I am making." He smiled with a shake of his head as Cahill's eyes widened. "You know very well that I was a confirmed bachelor before I met Francesca, a confirmed bachelor and an unrepentant rake. I never expected the day should come when I would freely wish to marry anyone. But then, no lady is like your daughter, sir."

Cahill grunted.

He seemed to be giving way. Hart continued earnestly, "While I have vowed to give up my ways — freely, I might add — my reprehensible behavior at the Montrose supper was a result of the anxiety I have just expressed. Anxiety, I might add, that any previously confirmed bachelor in my position might expect upon making that monumental commitment to wedlock and, hopefully, wedded bliss."

Andrew stared at him.

Hart wondered if he had overdone it.

And Andrew shook his head, flushing. "You are too smooth for your own good. Do you really think I believe a word you have just said? Clearly you have some feelings for Francesca, but you will never change your ways. A man like you simply cannot change who he is."

Hart stiffened, for instantly he could hear Daisy as clearly as if she stood before him. *Do you really think to reform? You cannot change, Calder, not for her, not for any woman, and not for very long.*

Briefly, he hesitated. Whom was he fooling? Was he only fooling himself?

And the doubts came rushing back. He should let Francesca go.

Then he heard Cahill cough and instantly he came to his senses. He was in the midst of a battle now, one he must not lose, because he had made up his mind and he was never going back to that place of gray despair, that place in which he had lived his

413

entire life until so recently, that dark, dank place in which there was no Francesca. "Will you fault me now for my honesty?" He smiled self-deprecatingly. "Or for feelings that any man in my particular position would have? If I could undo my behavior of the night before, I would. It will not happen again. Andrew . . . I am determined to change. You have my word on that."

"I do not trust your word. Nor do I trust that you are indeed being honest with me. So save your silken words for someone far more naive than I. I only wish I really knew your game."

"There is no game," Hart said coldly now. "And my word is always good."

"Somehow I doubt that. Or will you now claim integrity of character?" Cahill leaped to his feet, his eyes ablaze.

Hart slowly stood and eyed his adversary. What was this? There was far more here, he mused, than anger over his brief lapse last evening. And even as he awaited the blow, he began to categorize Cahill's business affairs and think of how he might gain leverage over his most precarious interests. "I do not claim integrity of character," he said. "But I do claim integrity for my word," he said.

Cahill made a mocking sound. "You may

make any claims you wish and I will continue to stand firm in my opinions, sir. And I can fault you otherwise, and that I intend to do."

He cast aside all pretense now. Cahill wanted this war, and so be it. "Really? Do I detect a gauntlet being thrown?"

"I do not bother! It has come to my attention that you continue to keep a mistress while engaged to my daughter. How dare you, Hart! I am appalled — beyond appalled. You should know that your engagement is off." Hands on his hips, appearing dangerously apoplectic, he stared.

Hart never justified his actions, not to anyone, except of course, recently, to Francesca. He stared, the urge to crush his foe overwhelming. But Francesca's beautiful face swam in his mind, her gaze pleading. He knew he should explain the situation now, but every fiber of his being went against the very notion. He had been more than loyal to Francesca, and in fact, he hadn't even looked at another woman with desire. His interest had become centered on one woman and one woman only. "You do not want to go up against me, Andrew," he warned very softly. "And I advise you here and now to cease and desist."

"Do you deny that you are keeping a

mistress, for God's sake?" Andrew demanded, clearly not understanding the magnitude of the mistake he was making.

Hart felt his lips firm in an icy smile. Cahill had several outstanding loans at the Bank of New York. Hart knew one director there very well — the man had a penchant for male whores, never mind his wife and children. He also knew the president of the board. Several years ago when the man had been on the verge of bankruptcy, Hart had done him the vast favor of shipping his goods at cost, with no payment expected until those goods had sold. No, Cahill did not want to go up against him, no indeed. Loans could be called in prematurely, and that would only be the beginning, should he wish to bring Andrew Cahill to heel.

But how clearly he could see Francesca, her blue eyes wide and filled with a desperate plea. She adored her father. He sighed, realizing he should make one final attempt to bring a truce about before he really went after Francesca's father.

"Sir." Hart was brisk. "The day I became engaged to your daughter was the day I ceased my affair with Miss Jones. She continued to reside in my house because I promised to take care of her for six months. Although three months remain on our verbal contract, I have actually told her to leave. Francesca knows all of this. That is the truth and I resent the conclusions you have so erroneously drawn."

Andrew Cahill's eyebrows lifted. "Do I appear a fool to you? What nonsensical explanation is this!" Then he smiled coldly, showing the ruthless side that had helped him rise from his birth as a farmer's son to an American millionaire. "Even if you have just told me the truth, I don't care. I have never been in favor of this match and it is off, Hart. I will tell Francesca tonight."

Hart stared. A terrible tension arose as he faced his newest enemy.

It would not be hard to hack away at the wealth and power Andrew Cahill had made for himself, oh no. It would not be hard to force him to give him what he wanted. Cahill was simply no match for him, he was certain of it.

But he would be going to war against Francesca's father.

Francesca would be the one made to suffer, caught between father and lover.

Hart was stricken senseless then. It was an extraordinary moment.

He was damned if he did and damned if he didn't.

Cahill raised an eyebrow. "I see you do

not really object."

Hart said coldly, "You are making a mistake." He then nodded politely. "I shall see myself out."

Madison Square was busy on a Saturday afternoon. As Francesca alighted from Hart's coach with Joel, she saw a dozen ladies in the small park, with many children skipping about, and a few gentlemen strolling as well. Every park bench was occupied, but then, it was a perfect spring day, a harbinger for May. Since speaking so frankly with her sister, her spirits were high and she smiled to herself. Connie was undoubtedly right — and hadn't she just received Hart's invitation to dine from Joel? They had barely put her plan in action and already there was a good result.

"Raoul, I may be an hour," Francesca said to the driver. He merely saluted her with one finger; although he wore a very exquisitely made suit, like his employer, he never wore a hat. She touched Joel's shoulder as they started toward Bragg's house. "Come, Joel."

"Can't I wait here?" he asked with a frown.

"No, you cannot. It's about time you became friendly with Rick's girls." She

418

rapped smartly on the door knocker and Peter answered at once.

She smiled at him. "Is Mrs. Bragg at home?" she asked formally, and then she looked past his big body and saw Leigh Anne in her wheeled chair in the hall. But that was not all. Leigh Anne wore a coat, as did both Katie and Dot, and Mrs. Flowers was entering from the kitchens, wearing a cape and carrying a wicker basket.

"I see I have called at an inopportune time," she said. Leigh Anne looked her way and their gazes met.

And for one moment, Francesca saw not the other woman's beauty, which had always disturbed her, but the cloak of sadness she was enveloped in. As she gazed at Leigh Anne, she saw that her beauty had somehow dimmed, as if a blazing inner light had gone out. She was so stunned that she could only stare and it was Leigh Anne who smiled first.

"Francesca, please, come in. How nice of you to call. We were on our way to Central Park for a picnic, but we can delay. Or rather —" she glanced at the girls "— Mrs. Flowers can go on ahead. Peter, after you settle them, can you return for me?"

Before Peter could respond, Francesca hurried forward. "Do not delay on my account," she said. "I do not want to upset your plans, as it is a stunning day." She had to lean down to take Leigh Anne's hands and kiss her cheek. It was very awkward.

"It is so kind of you to call," Leigh Anne said, a slight flush now adding to her flawless complexion. But once, her skin had glowed like mother-of-pearl. Now it was merely a woman's pale, unblemished skin.

"Frack!" Dot shouted, clapping her hands together in glee.

As Francesca scooped the impudent toddler up, kissing her cheek, she said, "I must confess that I went to Bellevue several times to visit you, but I lost my courage every time." She smiled at Leigh Anne as she hugged Dot one more time and replaced her to her feet.

"I doubt you have ever lacked courage for anything," Leigh Anne said, "and even if you did not come to my room in the end, thank you for thinking of me."

Francesca did not hesitate. "How could I not?" she asked simply.

Leigh Anne lowered her voice and her eyes. "And this is why my husband has fallen in love with you."

Francesca started, about to protest. Surely Leigh Anne referred to the past, to that brief moment in time when they had almost fallen in love. Surely she did not still think a flame burned! Francesca knelt beside Leigh Anne's chair and finally her knees touched the floor. "Your husband loves you," she said low and urgently. "And I . . ." She hesitated, about to blurt out the extent of her feelings for Hart. "I am very happily engaged to another man, a man I intend to wed."

Leigh Anne smiled at her. It was soft and sad. "We both know why I came to New York. Bartolla wrote me and claimed that Rick was in love with you. I realized I could not lose him to someone else . . . now, how I regret my decision."

Francesca was aghast.

And Leigh Anne flushed. "What I mean is that you two belong together. He does not belong with me." Suddenly she looked very upset and she turned her head, but not before Francesca saw tears shining in her eyes. "Katie, darling," she called, extending her hand.

Katie ran to Leigh Anne and instantly hugged her. Leigh Anne buried her face in the child's soft brown hair. Francesca wanted to cry. She could feel the other woman's pain and misery and she could also feel how much she loved the girls. She

421

would swear Leigh Anne also loved her husband.

Leigh Anne looked up, smiling now, but her eyes remained moist. "But if I hadn't returned I would not have my girls, now, would I?"

Francesca remained kneeling in order to be on a level with her and she took her free hand. "There is a saying, and for good reason, not to cry over spilt milk."

"I am not thinking about my accident. Rick deserves happiness and I cannot give it to him."

"Why not?" Francesca exclaimed. "He loves you!" She almost added that he had told her so, but she also recalled his despair of late and his evident confusion, and she knew she must not meddle. It was so hard not to do so.

Leigh Anne became pink. "Francesca, dear, please, get off the floor. By now, your knees must ache."

They did, and Francesca stood, trying to sort matters out. Dot grasped her hand, beaming up at her and Francesca smiled back at the beautiful blond child. Dot demanded, "Park! Park! Go park!"

"Mrs. Flowers will take you, Dot, and I will join you soon," Leigh Anne said gently but with firm authority.

Dot pouted but did not have a tantrum. Francesca was impressed.

Katie tugged on Leigh Anne's hand. "Mama, can Francesca come to the park with us?"

Leigh Anne was briefly surprised and then she glanced questioningly at Francesca. "Would you care to join us for a bit? You are more than welcome and I know the girls would love the company — and Joel may come, as well."

Francesca thought of the interview she wished to have with John Sullivan's second flatmate. But that could wait. This woman was far more important. "I would love to," she said. "And Hart's coach is large enough to accommodate us all."

Dot shrieked happily, as she never missed a word, and Joel groaned.

"Hey," Joel said, hands shoved deep in his pockets. "Want to fish?"

Katie blinked at him in surprise. Francesca sat beside Leigh Anne on a red plaid blanket, nibbling ham sandwiches, while Dot played industriously with a small doll. As it was such a beautiful day, the park was filled with families and couples, some picnicking, others merely taking a stroll or a carriage ride. "I don't know how to fish," Katie said, glancing at Leigh Anne.

"It's real easy," Joel said. "We can make a hook out of a hairpin and dig up a worm. All we need is some string, and the napkins were tied with that."

Katie smiled shyly, glancing again at Leigh Anne. Leigh Anne smiled at her. "Why don't you try it, darling? It sounds like fun."

As the two children ran off to the lake, just a short distance from where they were having their picnic, Leigh Anne called, "But be careful, Katie, not to fall in!" Then she turned to Francesca. "Joel is such a clever boy."

"He is, isn't he? He has been invaluable to my investigations, and he feels very much like another younger brother." Francesca glanced at the children. Joel was tying a hairpin shaped as a hook onto a line. "I am very fond of him — and his entire family, as well."

"How is your brother?" Leigh Anne asked pleasantly enough. But the words were hardly out of her mouth when she turned starkly white, appearing terribly dismayed.

Francesca followed the direction of her gaze. Rick Bragg was approaching at a walk, his hands in the pockets of his jacket. Warmth filled her, and just as she thought about what a pleasant surprise his appearance was, she realized that her reaction was distinctly different from Leigh Anne's. Francesca looked at the other woman, and found her nervously patting her skirts, her hands trembling, her face stiff with what could only be tension. What was this?

Bragg paused before them, his expression carefully neutral. "Hello," he said, and he bent on one knee to kiss his wife's cheek as Francesca hopped to her feet.

Leigh Anne did not look up as he touched Dot lightly on the head in greeting and straightened, facing Francesca. She smiled at him as he kissed her cheek. "How wonderful that you can join us," she cried, glancing again at Leigh Anne.

"It is certainly the perfect day for a picnic," he remarked, gazing at Leigh Anne and then past her. "Ah, Katie is fishing with Joel."

Francesca did not speak. She was utterly stunned by the tension she was witnessing and she simply could not understand it. Of course, she must make an exit, and quickly. Or would leaving them alone be worse?

Finally Leigh Anne looked up. How miserable she seemed. "You're not at headquarters?" she asked, her tone strained.

His answering smile was even more miserable. "I thought to work this afternoon at

425

home," he said. "When Peter told me you had gone for a picnic, I decided to play hooky."

"You never work at home, except when it is midnight," she breathed, her lashes lowered, making it impossible to read her gaze.

"I think it is time to change that," Rick said, clearly forcing lightness into his tone. "Is there a sandwich to spare?"

Francesca could not bear it. She saw his hurt and his pain and Leigh Anne's answering anguish, and she wanted to hold him, comfort her, and then maybe bang their heads together. What was this mess? And how to straighten it out? "There are plenty of sandwiches left," she said quickly. "And I must go, actually, as I have yet to interview Sullivan's second flatmate."

"We questioned Josh Bennett thoroughly this morning," Bragg said. "He has shed no light on the situation, as his statement was almost identical to that of Ron Ames. He said Kate left her husband about a year and a half ago. John Sullivan was a drunk and an angry one. Not a night went by that he did not proclaim his hatred of his wife." He nodded at her. "But if you wish to interview him, feel free. I suspect it will be a waste of your time."

Francesca now thought so, too. She found Leigh Anne watching them and quickly smiled. "I think I will try my hand with Bennett anyway. And what of that photograph Farr found in the flat? Have you identified the gentleman in it?"

"Newman is working on it."

Francesca nodded. "Very well." She turned to Leigh Anne to thank her for her hospitality, but was not given the chance to do so.

"No, don't go!" Leigh Anne said vehemently.

Francesca started. Before she could respond, Leigh Anne said, flushing, "Rick, I do not feel well. I have a terrible migraine. I am going home to bed. Please help me up."

As Rick rushed to help her into her chair, Francesca wrung her hands. She felt certain that this was a ploy to escape.

"But you should stay here and have a pleasant picnic with the girls," Leigh Anne said, now seated in her wheeled chair. "I mean, you have taken half the day off, and it would be a shame now that you are here not to take advantage of it. Peter can see me home. Francesca, there is no need to rush off! Joel is having a good time with Katie, and you and Rick can discuss your investigation while he eats his lunch." Leigh

Anne smiled but it was terribly forced.

Francesca was dismayed, wondering if Leigh Anne thought to push her and Rick together, and she looked at Rick and saw that he was resigned. No, it was worse than that — she saw defeat in his eyes. He touched Leigh Anne's hair. "I'll take you home," he said.

"No! You enjoy yourself. We all know you deserve it. Peter! Please wheel me to the carriage." Her face was taut with determination and her eyes shone with unshed tears.

Francesca felt her own tears forming. She did not move.

Bragg dropped his hand as Peter hurried forward. Rick nodded and the big Swede began pushing Leigh Anne toward the carriage path where a buggy waited. Leigh Anne turned to look at Francesca, smiling so brightly it had to be painful. "Thank you for such a lovely afternoon," she said.

For once, words escaped Francesca completely. As Leigh Anne was wheeled away, she could only think that she should be the one leaving.

"Mama?" Dot said, but not with any distress.

Bragg knelt. "Mama is tired and she is going home." He stroked her hair. "We will finish our picnic and then go home and join her."

Dot grinned and held up her blond doll. "Dolly Frack!" she said.

Bragg cupped her cheek and then straightened, facing Francesca. "I believe she has named Dolly after you."

Francesca could not stand it. He was miserable, and so was Leigh Anne. "How can I help?" she cried. "Surely there is something I can do!"

He shrugged helplessly, turning away. Francesca ran to him. "What is happening?" she demanded, grasping him by the arms.

He met her gaze, his haunted with sadness. "I don't know."

Francesca pulled him into her arms. He laid his cheek against her shoulder and his arms went lightly around her. She held him close, aching for him. "Rick, I am so sorry," she whispered.

"I don't know what to do," he said, choked.

Francesca held him hard. "Neither do I," she answered, and laid her cheek against his.

He knew just how clever and bold Francesca Cahill was, for he had read all about her exploits in the newspapers. He had admired her terribly for her courage and daring, for helping the police bring killers to their just deserts. But now he stared in absolute shock. She was in Rick Bragg's arms and engaged to another. She was a faithless bitch just like all the rest.

His fingers itched.

His heart raced.

He fondled the knife, barely aware of it.

How could this be? How? How could she be a whore like the others?

He did not know what to do. He had made his plans. He knew the bitches he must punish. Now he began to consider the question burning in him. Just what should he do about her?

And when she laid her cheek on Bragg's, he knew.

CHAPTER TWENTY

Saturday, April 26, 1902 6:00 p.m.

"Mr. Hart, sir?" a very cautious female voice said.

Hart was in his library, at his desk, his jacket gone, his shirtsleeves rolled up to the elbows. He was recalculating the expenses he would incur from his upcoming Hong Kong venture and he was so engrossed it was a moment before he realized that Maggie Kennedy stood in the doorway. He looked up, startled.

She was blushing. "I can see I am interrupting," she said. "I'll come back at another time."

Hart leaped to his feet. "No, please!" He smiled, quickly rolling down his sleeves and reaching for the gold and ruby cuff links on his desk. "How may I help you, Mrs. Kennedy? Is everything to your satisfaction?"

She became somewhat wide of eye. "Yes, sir, Mr. Hart, your hospitality has been wonderful — if not somewhat overwhelming." She continued to stand in the doorway and he saw that she toyed with her skirts with one hand anxiously.

"Please, come in," he said, having managed to insert one cuff link in his sleeve.

She took two steps forward. "How may I repay you for your generosity, sir?" she asked, avoiding looking at what he was doing.

For a moment, surprised, he did not respond. Then, as he began to protest, Joel came skidding into the room, grinning and flushed. "Hey, Mr. Hart," he said. "Ma, I'm home."

Maggie laid a restraining hand on her son's shoulder. "This is hardly your home," she chided softly. "Where have you been all afternoon?"

Hart had been about to ask that very question, as he knew that Joel had been with Francesca, sleuthing about the city. He stepped out from behind his desk, giving up on the left cuff of his shirtsleeve, although his arm was now covered. "Did you and Miss Cahill just get in?" he asked, knowing very well that as it was already six and he had to pick her up at seven, she would be late. It was her only flaw and he did not mind, not at all, as the cause was her pursuit of justice and not the vain primping other women indulged in before their mirrors.

"Yes, sir." Joel grinned. He turned to his mother. And just as Hart was going to ask if the afternoon had been a productive one from the point of view of Francesca's investigation, Joel said, "We spent the afternoon in the park, having a picnic. I taught Katie how to fish!" Then he sobered. "But we didn't catch nuthin'."

Hart felt himself still. In fact, the entire room became motionless, terribly so, and he felt a burn begin deep inside of him. He hardly had to be a genius to know that Katie was Bragg's fostering child. He reminded himself not to overreact; no one worked more diligently than his half brother and undoubtedly Bragg had spent the afternoon at headquarters. Out of kindness, Francesca had somehow gone to picnic with his wife, he told himself. No one was kinder than his fiancée. "You and Miss Cahill enjoyed a picnic with Mrs. Bragg and the children?" he asked casually. But he did not feel casual at all.

"Yes, sir," Joel said eagerly. Then, "I mean, Mrs. Bragg didn't stay for very long. Mr. Bragg came an' joined us an' she went home. I ain't never had a picnic like this before! He tried to help me and Katie catch a fish and he taught Miz Cahill how to fish, too." He grinned. "Miz Cahill caught a fish — her very first!"

Calder was in disbelief. He could only stare.

Francesca actually ran into the front hall of the house, breathless and dismayed. It was just past six and Hart was taking her to supper at 7:00 p.m. After their crisis of the night before, she wanted to look her very best. She intended to wear a new gown, a pale green silk he had yet to see, with jewelry she had borrowed from Connie. She knew she barely had time to tong her hair. "I need Bette," she cried, asking for the maid as she spotted her mother entering the hall at the far end.

Julia came forward and did not reply.

And even as Francesca raced forward, she was haunted by the terrible afternoon she had spent. In the end, she had not been able to leave Bragg alone with the girls in the park. Far too acutely aware of his anguish, she had stayed as he had eaten a sandwich, changing the subject to that of their investigation. They had spent several hours rehashing every clue and analyzing every suspect. They had not come to any new conclusions, but the light in Bragg's eyes had changed by the time they had begun to pack up their picnic basket. Before she had left with Raoul, he had taken her hand and squeezed it. "Thank you."

Francesca had smiled as brightly as possible, not wanting to send him back into the dark tunnel of his marriage. "You have nothing to thank me for," she had said.

Now, Francesca reached her mother, vaguely noting that Julia looked distinctly somber. She simply could not bear any more bad news. "Mama! I need Bette! I have to bathe and do my hair and dress, all in an hour! I refuse to keep Hart waiting tonight."

"Your father wishes to see you in his study, Francesca," Julia said quietly.

Francesca had been about to hike her skirts and run up the stairs. She faltered and looked directly at her mother. And suddenly she recalled the fact that Hart had intended to visit her father to request an earlier June wedding. But would he have done so after the fiasco of last night? She felt certain he would not, but then, Hart was so unpredictable that she simply could not know. "Mama? You look worried," she said with the utmost wariness.

Julia suddenly hugged her. "You know how much I love you and how much I want you to be happy," she cried.

Francesca jerked away, knowing that such an expression and statement on the part of her mother could only bode ill, indeed. "What is it?" she asked sharply. "What has happened? I feel certain that no one has died."

"Your father is waiting," Julia said abruptly.

"Mama!" Francesca protested in real alarm.

"Very well. Andrew has called off the wedding."

Francesca gasped, shocked, barely able to comprehend what her mother was saying.

"We were both so upset to see the two of you at odds last night," Julia said. "I tried to calm Andrew down, but then Roberta Hind told us about his mistress. Dear God, Francesca, even I cannot support your engagement if he is carrying on openly with such a woman."

Francesca cried out in horror as the words sank in. She managed to say, "But he isn't. This isn't what you think." *Her father had called off their engagement.* She remained dazed, and tried to summon up a coherent thought.

"The whole of society knows he keeps that Jones woman in the house he just bought for her!" Julia cried. "How could he do this to you? How? I had truly believed that he cared."

Francesca stared, aghast, knowing Julia would never believe her if she explained the matter. But Papa could not do this — not without her consent, not without her opinion, not without her feelings being considered. And then she lifted her skirts and ran down the hall and into her father's study.

She did not knock, but the doors were wide open. Andrew was reclining on the sofa in a smoking jacket and slippers, reading the *Sun.* A fire blazed in the hearth and a glass of red wine was on the occasional table. He looked up over his newspaper as she halted before him.

"You cannot have possibly broken my engagement without speaking to me first," she said, beginning to shake. This could not be happening — she would not allow it to happen.

Calmly, Andrew set the paper aside. "Come sit with me, Francesca," he said, patting the sofa beside him as he sat upright.

She refused. "I love him. I am going to marry him. And it is not what you think — he isn't with Daisy Jones!"

"I am thinking as I always have," her father said, standing. "He is a self-serving cad. He is currently somewhat fascinated by you — and it is nothing more. Last night he was far more interested in another woman than he was in you, his fiancée. Last night you were hurt by his behavior — I saw it on your face, so do not deny it. The two of you have barely begun a life together and already he is showing his true colors. Is this the kind of life you want to have? By God, Francesca, I will not allow it. This man isn't good enough to sweep the floors you walk on."

She was trembling almost convulsively and shamelessly close to tears. "Papa, don't do this. Hart is good, I know him as no one else does, and you are wrong about last night."

"I have broken off the engagement," Andrew said firmly. "I know that right now you are smitten, but in time, you will recover. In time, you will find someone else."

"No," Francesca cried. "Papa, please —"

He cut her off. "My word is final. And Francesca, consider this — when I told him the engagement was off, he did not object."

Still shaken, Francesca rang Hart's bell several times. She knew she should *not* be at his door in such a state of fear and panic, strands of hair behind her ears. Her hat was crooked and she attempted to right it, but she dropped the two hairpins. *As if she cared about her hat.* She smoothed down her jacket hem and nodded at Alfred.

He opened the double door. "Mr. Hart, sir? Miss Cahill is here to see you."

Francesca began to tremble. She glanced into the drawing room and saw Hart seated with a scotch, grimly staring at his drink. Clearly, his humor was black. That was a good sign, was it not? For surely it indicated that he was as upset with what Andrew had done as she was. And he slowly looked up.

For one moment, she stared back, aware of an incredible tension in him. And then he rose, setting his drink aside. Francesca became vaguely aware of the others in the room. Grace and Rathe Bragg sat on the sofa near his chair. Rourke was in another chair and Maggie was on a love seat with Joel, an open book between them. Although she knew Maggie continued to stay at Hart's house, she had not expected to see her just then.

All eyes were trained on her now. Clearly, everyone was remarking her unkempt appearance — or was it her nearly-hysterical state?

But Hart's eyes were the worst. They

for her sister's words advising her never to pursue him were somewhere in the shadowy background of her mind. But she *had* to know what was happening. *He had not objected to the breaking of their engagement.* She did not believe it.

Surely he had protested. Surely they had recovered from the awful tension of the night before. Surely Hart would greet her warmly and hold her and kiss her and, in his usual arrogant manner, remind her that nothing would come between them, as his mind was made up.

Alfred opened the door and when he saw her, his calm demeanor vanished. He almost gaped.

Francesca tried to smile as she gazed past him, but no one was in the spacious foyer. "I must see Hart," she said tersely. "Good evening, Alfred."

"Miss Cahill, please, come in," Alfred said, his eyes remaining wide as he let her inside. "Can I get you some tea, perhaps, while I tell Mr. Hart that you are here? He is not expecting you," he added, and while she had often called impulsively in the past, the butler's statement seemed to be a reprimand.

He had noted her dishabille. But Francesca did not really care that her hair was coming loose or that her jacket was askew, that she wore no rouge and was undoubtedly as white as a ghost. She faced him, folding her arms across her chest. "Alfred, you do not have to be formal with me. Yes, I am distraught. Yes, I should go home and compose myself. However, I have just learned that Hart and my father have had a terrible falling-out and that my father has broken our engagement!" Alfred started. Francesca continued in a rush, "And surely Hart has not accepted the sudden demise of our engagement! I am not going home, Alfred, oh no. I must see Hart."

"Oh dear," Alfred said, his tone hushed. "Mr. Hart is in a drawing room with some of his family. Miss Cahill, please, why don't you sit down in the gold room. I shall bring you some tea and sweets — it will calm you, I think — and then I shall tell Mr. Hart that you are here."

"Nothing will calm me and especially not chocolate and tea," she said, looking him right in the eye. "Alfred, I must see Hart now. What is his mood? How is he? Has he indicated anything to you?"

"He seemed fine when he came in a bit earlier, Miss Cahill," Alfred said reluctantly. "Miss Cahill, I respect you so. Would you mind very much if I dared to be terribly bold with you?" he asked, leading her across the huge entry hall.

Francesca and Alfred had reached a silent and mutually agreeable understanding some time ago. Alfred wholeheartedly wished for her to marry his employer and he had made it clear he thought that nothing could be better for Hart. "Of course," she said.

"I feel certain that Mr. Hart will not appreciate a scene," Alfred said, glancing at her with real worry. "I have seen him tolerate unhappy ladies in the past. One scene and they were never to be seen or heard from again." A bead of sweat had appeared on his forehead.

Francesca touched his arm. "Thank you, Alfred, for your concern, and I shall keep that in mind," she said. Even as panicked as she was, she was sane enough to know that Alfred was right. Hart would despise a scene, and if he had the same doubts he had last night, she might even put the final nails in the coffin of their union by carrying on recklessly. Still, their future was at stake and she had to know what he intended to do about it. "But let me remind you, he was not engaged to any of these other ladies."

Alfred inclined his head slightly. "That is true."

Francesca swallowed, tucking some loose

seemed cold and very black and somehow menacing, indeed.

Francesca forgot everyone else, staring at Hart, thoroughly taken aback.

Hart approached, his expression impossible to read. Suddenly overcome with anxiety, she said, "I would like a word with you, please."

His jaw flexed. "We will step into the library," he said without formality and he watched her so closely that she shivered.

Something was not right.

Just like last night.

He turned to his family and Maggie. "Excuse us."

No one said a word.

Francesca could not look at anyone, even knowing that later she would have to apologize to everyone, and she quickly turned and rushed ahead of him down the hall. He followed her and she could hear his strides, long, hard and controlled. The library was a spacious affair with pale green walls, dark wood and gilded furniture, not to mention many stacks of bookcases. She whirled, facing him.

He closed both doors behind him and turned to her. "Whyever are you so distraught?"

She was silenced, but only for a moment.

"Are you going to tell me what happened today?"

"I was wondering exactly that, myself," he said, walking past her to a bar cart.

She did not hesitate. She raced after him and seized his wrist, preventing him from lifting the decanter of scotch. "I have no clue what you mean. Papa ended our engagement and he said you made not a single objection!"

Hart faced her, his jaw hard, and the storm clouds were there in his eyes. "Yes, he did."

She made a disbelieving sound. "And you did not object?"

His expression tightened. "I did not." He hesitated and added, "But not for the reason you are thinking."

"For what reason, then?" she cried.

"Timing," he said flatly.

"Timing?" She could not believe her ears.

"Timing, my dear, is everything in this life, but that, apparently, is a lesson you have not learned." He was cold, almost cruel, and he turned away from her, pouring a scotch.

One, not two, she saw miserably. "Does this mean the day will come when you will object?"

He did not answer, his back to her, lifting

444

the glass to his lips.

As he drank, she saw how rigid his shoulders were. He was angry, and it felt as if he wanted to be mean and nasty, too. She was sick. Why was he angry with her? What had she done? And would he now seize Andrew's behavior as the excuse he needed to end their engagement? "So we are over, then?"

He set the glass down so hard that the bar cart jumped. He turned. "We will never be over, Francesca," he said harshly.

It was perhaps the most romantic thing anyone could say to her, and it was certainly the most romantic thing he had ever said. But the meaning was ruined by his black glare and his angry tone. Her spirits fell with sickening force. "I do not understand you, not at all," she somehow whispered, consumed with dread.

He gave her a mocking look. "Why not be realistic, Francesca? Your father has not changed his low opinion of me — and if I were him, I would think the same way."

"You want him to break this off, don't you?" she asked in despair.

His jaw flexed, a muscle rippling there. "Actually, I did not. Actually, I do not like explaining myself and justifying my behavior to *anyone*," he said with vast warning.

If he wanted to use this as an excuse to

end their engagement, it was truly over then. "I am aware of that," she said miserably. "And if it is over, if *we* are over, then I am the fool Bragg has said I was." She swallowed down a lump of tears.

He made a mocking sound and it was ugly. "I heard you had a picnic today."

She froze. What was this? He knew she had been in the park? And suddenly everything became clear. She thought about how she had been alone with Bragg in the park after Leigh Anne had left, how she had comforted him — and how it must have looked to any passerby.

Hart confronted her. "What? Can you not admit to such a pleasant afternoon?"

"Yes," she breathed, her heart lurching with dread. "But it is not what you are thinking."

"Ah, and you do know what I am thinking?" he mocked.

She swallowed hard. "Their marriage is in trouble, Calder. They are both in so much misery and I only wanted to help."

"By spending the afternoon with Rick."

"You said Raoul was my driver, my bodyguard. Clearly he is your spy!" she cried, tears finally blurring her vision. How much had Raoul told him? She prayed he had not said that she had been in Rick's embrace, because Hart would never believe it had been an act of comfort and friendship and nothing more.

"Raoul said nothing. Joel is the one who raved about his afternoon." Hart's black gaze bored into hers. "Of course, I then summoned Raoul and interviewed him at length."

He knew. He knew she had held Bragg in her arms. "I was comforting him," she said, trembling. "I have done nothing wrong."

"Yes, of course, for that is what you do best — comfort my half brother. Do you still love him?"

She cried out.

Hart seemed to shake. "Now is the time for real honesty, Francesca. I need to know. I demand it!"

She knew she must choose her words with care. "This is not what you are thinking."

"Do you love him?" he ground out.

"Yes — but not the way that you mean," she cried.

Hart turned away, his hands shaking.

"I love him as a friend," she said firmly — desperately. "And that is my right."

He downed some of the scotch with a harsh, guttural laugh. "Yes, the friend you spent an entire night on that train with — the friend whose bed you warmed before you ever were in mine."

"That's not fair."

He stared.

She was, amazingly, afraid of him now. But she touched his arm and he flinched. "You are the man I have chosen. You are the man I want to wed."

A moment passed. *"Do you still love him?"*

She recoiled. Her mind raced and she felt tears come. "No," she whispered. *Yes,* she wanted to say. But as a friend, damn it, as if I were his sister, not as a lover, not as a wife.

He suddenly flung the scotch glass with all of his strength, across the entire room, no easy feat. It fell short of the far wall and miraculously did not shatter when it hit the floor. Francesca flinched. "You were in his arms," Hart shouted. "Yes, I interviewed Raoul, at length. *You were in his arms.* I went to your father to *fight* for our engagement and you were in his *arms.*"

"I was comforting him," she tried, the tears falling freely now.

"I know all about his marital problems," he said savagely. "It is the talk of this family. So now what? Your father disapproves of us, but he loves Rick! Will you wait for Rick to divorce his wife? Will you marry him on the grave of a divorce made to his invalid wife? Shall his broken marriage be the altar upon which you make your eternal pledges of love?"

She tried to say no, but could not speak. Instead, she shook her head, more tears falling.

He turned his back on her, starting from the room.

"It wasn't romantic," she gasped.

He did not pause.

"It wasn't romantic and it wasn't passionate! But you would not understand, as you do not understand friendship or loyalty!"

He whirled so rapidly that she flinched, even with half of the room separating them. And then he was striding back. "You were my friend," he said. "And I have been nothing but loyal to you. I have not looked, even once, at another woman sexually since I asked you to marry me! When Daisy came to my office the other day, I was more than loyal to you!"

He was towering over her now. She tried to take his hand but he flung it away. "I am still your friend," she said, and realized how pathetic the declaration sounded. She wanted to tell him that she loved him and always would, but she was afraid that he would not care, not now, not anymore. "You don't have to compete with Rick," she begged. "There is no reason to compete with him!"

He laughed disparagingly. "I have been competing with him my entire life."

"Then stop! And trust me. My feelings haven't changed. You're the man I want to marry, Calder. *Not him.*"

His expression remained black, but she could see he had a grip on his anger and that it was under control. But she could also see something even worse — disbelief.

"You don't believe me?" she managed to say, aghast.

"I know this much." His smile was brief, mirthless and twisted. "If he were free, we would not be together."

"That's not true," she cried, seizing him.

He shook her off, turning away. And as he started from the library, she raced after him. "You said we would never be over."

He made a mocking sound.

"Are we over?" she demanded.

"You tell me," he said darkly.

She couldn't speak. They were standing on the edge of a terrible precipice and one false step would finish them, she was sure of it. Somehow, between her father and Rick Bragg, the odds had been stacked against them.

"I see you are simply speechless," Hart said cruelly.

"No," she whispered. "I am not speech-less, I am merely terrified."

He walked out.

CHAPTER TWENTY-ONE

Saturday, April 26, 1902 7:00 p.m.
Francesca stood in the doorway, staring after Hart as he strode away. She was in shock.

She continued to tremble and felt as if she had to sit down. She could no longer breathe and a huge knot had formed in her heart, causing so much pain. She turned and went back into the library, sitting on the closest suitable piece of furniture, an ottoman. She tried not to cry.

We will never be over, he had said.

She wiped her eyes. He had been in a jealous rage — he had gone to her father to *fight* for their engagement. He had used that very word. That had only been earlier today. Surely, in a few more hours, he would be filled with regret.

How could she live this way?

Francesca was so afraid of the question that she refused to entertain it.

"Are you all right?" Rourke asked.

She looked up, knowing she must appear as ill as she felt. Rourke stood in the doorway, compassion written all over his face. Francesca tried to force a smile and gave up. She stood. "No."

He hesitated. "If it is any consolation, he looks even worse than you do. Perhaps tomorrow the two of you will manage to sort things out."

She stared, wishing that were true and thinking of a lifetime spent with a man prone to such jealous rage. "He is furious because I spent the afternoon with Rick, not investigating, but having a picnic in the park."

Rourke was mildly surprised. "Francesca, has it ever occurred to you that maybe you need to be less of a friend to Rick if you are to succeed with Calder? I might even be jealous if I were in Calder's shoes."

Rourke was so levelheaded and so objective that she highly doubted that. "Rick will always be a dear friend, and he needs all of his friends and family now," she said emphatically.

"Yes, he does. But you may have to make a clear choice between them. Calder and Rick have been at odds as long as I can remember. I don't think the rivalry they

453

share is ever going to change." He then smiled kindly at her. "I am going out to supper. Would you like to join me?"

"No, thank you," she said, knowing she could never make such a terrible choice, especially not now, when Rick needed her so desperately as a friend.

He waited for her and she left the library with him. As she was approaching the front hall, she tried not to wonder where Calder was, but she was painfully aware that he was somewhere in the house — unless, of course, he had gone out. Why couldn't he trust her? she wondered miserably. But the answer was obvious. He had been her friend, holding her hand, when she had first fallen in love with Rick Bragg. Apparently he was never going to recover from that bygone era; apparently he was never going to believe that he had somehow secured her heart.

He had accused her of such disloyalty, she thought in anguish. It wasn't fair. She hadn't been disloyal to him, not once since she had realized that he was the one she truly loved.

Suddenly she faltered. Rourke reached out to steady her but she wasn't even aware of him. What had Calder said? That he had been loyal to her even when Daisy had come to his office?

When had Daisy gone to his office? No mistress, or ex-mistress, would ever dare to go to her lover's place of business! What did this mean?

"Francesca, you look as if you have just seen a ghost."

She blinked and saw Rourke gazing at her with concern. Behind him, she saw Maggie and Joel, both as riveted by her demeanor.

Her mind raced. She must speak with Daisy and find out why she had called on Hart at his office. However, while she and Hart were most definitely in a crisis, a killer was on the loose. Her personal life must not interfere with her investigation. And apparently she no longer had plans for the evening. "Maggie!" She smiled firmly now.

Maggie came forward hesitantly. "Hello, Francesca." Her gaze was searching. "How are you? Are you all right?"

She shoved all thoughts of Hart far aside. "I am fine. I am so glad to run into you this way. Maggie, I need your help, and I think there is no time like the present, as it is rather early yet."

Maggie raised her eyebrows. "Of course I will help. But what can I do?"

"Can Joel stay here with the children? You and I must go downtown. It is time we paid a friendly call on Lord Randolph, my dear," she said, and she smiled broadly.

Maggie was bewildered. "Lord Randolph? I am afraid I don't know any gentleman of that name."

"Ah, but you may have met him once — on the street, outside of Kate Sullivan's building the evening of her murder, within an hour of her demise."

Maggie was wide-eyed.

Francesca felt much better. There was nothing like sinking her teeth into an investigation to get her mind off the terrible ache in her heart. She turned to Rourke with a smile. "Would you like to join us for an evening of investigative work?" she asked. "If you are not too hungry, that is."

Francesca and Maggie climbed into the back of Hart's handsome black coach and Francesca rapped smartly on the ceiling, indicating that Raoul could drive off. Rourke had declined her invitation, so when her door suddenly opened and he stepped up into the cab, she was very surprised. A moment later, as he took a seat facing them, the light of the interior lantern fell across him and she stiffened in shock. It was not Rourke, but Hart.

He settled himself on the rearward-facing

seat, dominating the interior of the coach and making it seem far too small and airless. "Raoul, proceed," he said, knocking once on the roof. And the six-in-hand rolled off.

"What are you doing?" Francesca managed to say.

"I am joining you," he said, unsmiling.

She stared at him and he stared back. From his terse expression, she could surmise that little had changed in the past quarter hour. "Why?"

"I suspect the evening will become a very late one. My feelings have not changed. I do not like you traipsing about the city in the midnight hours of the night, chasing the worst sort of criminals."

Her heart raced with some trepidation and some small elation. How easy it would be to refute him. It was only seven o'clock and Lord Randolph was hardly a thug — although he might turn out to be the Slasher. And Raoul was her bodyguard. There was no reason for Hart to be present, other than the reason that he still cared, rather excessively, for her. She dared to smile just a little at him.

He said, unsmiling, "I believe you are on a fool's errand." He turned and faced out the window, not saying another word.

And from the hard-set look on his features, she thought that any attempt to draw him into a civil conversation would certainly fail. Nonetheless, her heart pounding now, she said, "We have a very tenuous list of suspects. David Hanrahan, Lord Randolph, Sam Wilson and John Sullivan. Hanrahan has no alibis, Randolph we have yet to question, Wilson has an alibi for last Thursday, but I am not quite sure whether to believe Francis or not, and Sullivan apparently went out drinking every night — including the night of his wife's murder. We still do not know if he committed suicide. If he did, he could very well be the Slasher." She forced another smile, but Hart continued to stare out of his window and did not see. She tried, "So what do you think?"

He gave her a brief, dark look. "I have yet to leap to any conclusions, solid or otherwise," he said flatly, and he faced his window again.

Francesca felt crushed; she gave up. She turned to look out of Maggie's window, as she did not want to be confronted with Hart. How perilously fragile her emotions were. Maggie gently patted her hand. Francesca smiled a little at her and no one said another word for the next half hour as Raoul proceeded downtown. The tension in

the coach was thick enough to cut with a knife.

The Holland House Hotel came into sight. It took up half of the block between Twenty-ninth and Thirtieth Streets and was on the west side of Fifth Avenue. It was a handsome, square building of granite built several decades ago. Francesca forgot about Hart, staring at the canopied entrance where two liveried doormen stood. Their carriage slowed and her mind raced. She turned to Hart. "There is no need for subterfuge, I think. You can enquire after Randolph at the front desk. We will go inside with you, claiming to be a dinner party. If he is somewhere in the hotel, we can have you send a note to him to meet you in the lobby." She looked at him. "Would you mind, Calder?"

His gaze flickered over her face rather studiously, and slowly he nodded. "Of course I do not mind."

Raoul had alighted from the top seat where he drove and he opened the door for them. Francesca followed Maggie out onto the sidewalk, excitement rising within her, Hart behind her. He said in her ear, "And if he is out for the evening?"

"So much the better," she said cheerfully. "There is only one public entrance to the hotel and we will sit in the lobby until he returns. He is not sociable," she reminded him, "so I doubt he will be out until the wee hours."

Hart's expression appeared to be in danger of thawing. He shook his head, and took her arm. "As I said, the evening threatens to be a late one." He smiled at Maggie. "Shall we?"

As they entered the hotel it was briefly as if nothing was wrong. Francesca remained beside Hart, on his arm. They approached the front desk, a long gleaming teakwood counter where two clerks in dark suits stood, and Francesca eagerly scanned the lobby.

The room was large but not half as spacious as that of the city's higher-end hotels. There were only three seating areas, all occupied by gentlemen and ladies. Francesca instantly surmised that Randolph was not present. She did not recognize anyone, in fact.

"How may I help you, sir?" a young clerk was asking.

"I believe a friend of mine is staying at your hotel," Hart said. "Lord Randolph. I should like to get a word to him. Do you know if he is in this evening?"

Francesca fidgeted as the clerk said that

he believed Lord Randolph was in his rooms. It was the supper hour, but if he were as dour as Hart claimed, perhaps he was dining alone in his suite. She glanced past the crowd in the lobby, trying to peek into the dining room on the hall's other side. But from this distance, it was simply impossible to distinguish any of the guests inside. The elevator bell chimed.

Francesca glanced impatiently at the gilded arrow, indicating the elevator was arriving on the first floor. Hart was scribbling a note, which a bellman would deliver to Randolph's room. She leaned close and said, "Invite him for a drink in the lobby."

"That is already done," he said, signing his name without any flourish. He eyed her closely. "Are you a bit warm, Francesca?"

She was delighted because his tone seemed very normal, as did the light in his eyes. In fact, she knew he had caught a whiff of her excitement and was mildly amused. She was about to grin and ask him if she was forgiven, when the brass door of the elevator opened. Three people walked out and the gentleman in the rear was Harry de Warenne.

Francesca was so excited she poked Hart hard in the ribs, hard enough to make him utter a breath.

"Sir." The clerk had just espied Randolph as well. "There is Lord Randolph."

As Hart made some kind of reply, Francesca grabbed Maggie and dragged her away from Hart, toward a large wooden column. "That is Lord Randolph, the handsome gentleman with the ivory-headed cane. The one Hart is walking toward."

And indeed, Hart was leisurely approaching their quarry. Randolph saw him and stopped and the two men shook hands.

Francesca turned to Maggie. "Well?" she demanded.

Maggie was pale.

"Do you need a closer look?"

Maggie shook her head. "No. That's him, Francesca, that's the gentleman I bumped into outside of Kate's building."

They were standing fifty feet away. Francesca was thrilled; still, she took Maggie's hand. "Are you certain?" Hart was glancing at them. She knew he was about to signal them to come over and join them.

"I am positive," Maggie breathed, flushed now. She gazed at Francesca. "What does this mean? Is he the killer?"

Francesca shook her head at Hart and he gave her his back instantly. She pulled Maggie back around the column, ducking her head so she would not be remarked. "It doesn't quite mean anything yet."

Maggie seemed nervous, glancing toward the center of the lobby. "They are walking toward the front doors. I guess Randolph is on his way out. Hart seems to be joining him," she said rapidly.

Francesca looked their way as the two men disappeared onto the street. "Come on," she said, hurrying after them. She paused briefly before leaving the hotel, just in time to see Randolph getting into a cab and Hart nodding goodbye. As the horse-drawn hansom pulled away from the curb, she darted out onto the avenue and over to Hart. "It's him," she cried, pausing beside him and staring after the cab. She was out of breath. "Maggie has no doubt. We have to follow him, Hart!"

Hart raised his hand. Raoul was standing beside Hart's brougham farther down the block and he instantly climbed onto the driver's seat, releasing the brake. And finally, Hart smiled at her. "After you, darling," he said.

Gwen O'Neil smiled warmly as she pulled the covers up to her daughter's chin. "G'night, darlin'," she murmured, but Bridget was already soundly asleep. For one moment she stared at her beautiful daughter, filled with the warmth of love, but then her smile faded as she recalled her husband. Bridget had gone to work with her on Saturday and David had been waiting for them at the day's end outside the candle factory. He had begged her to take him back and had threatened them both if she refused.

She didn't believe for a moment that he was the Slasher, but she did believe that he would hurt her and her daughter terribly if he was not sent back to jail. He was a petty-minded and vengeful man and his new purpose in life was to make her miserable, she thought.

And it was working.

If only Harry had not dropped those charges against him.

And as a painful image of Harry de Warenne came abruptly to mind, she leaped to her feet, more than disconcerted. A lump of anguish remained raw in her chest. It had been shocking to find him in New York, and his presence in the city had rekindled memories she had hoped to leave far behind in Ireland, where they belonged.

He must have found her the same way David had, she thought as she vigorously cleaned the counter by the sink. Now she regretted leaving Father Culhane's name with her neighbor in case anyone had to contact her. She wondered if Harry remained in the city or if he had left.

It was shocking that he had even bothered to look her up. Or was it?

Gwen paused, the rag in her hand, swept back in time to a perfect spring day, the lawns the color of emeralds, the sky brilliantly blue, as she slipped out of the manor house with no small amount of guilt. But no one was home and the day simply beckoned. Before she knew it, she was running barefoot down the hill in a moment of sheer joy and real freedom. As she ran, her life with David did not exist. There was only the wet grass beneath her feet, the sun shining mildly upon her face, the faint chill of the air, the overwhelming scent of hyacinth. Then she fell.

She tripped on a stone. Briefly, she rolled over, once, twice. And then, like a child, she rolled over again and again, all the way to the bottom of the hill, and laughing out loud, she stopped on her back and stared up at the passing white clouds. She floated there in the grass, so wonderfully relaxed. Then, her laughter gone, she sobered and came back to reality. She had a job to return to and her black dress was wet and stained with dirt. Worse, her white apron was now blotched green. Gwen sat up, thinking to rebraid her hair.

And the lord of the manor sat on his bay horse, his eyebrows raised, staring at her.

She jumped to her feet in dread and dismay, her hands falling to her sides. "My lord, sir!" She bowed her head, her heart racing wildly. "I beg your pardon, sir, I . . . I," she faltered, for she did not know what to say and he was dismounting — he was approaching!

She dared to look up, unable to breathe.

Randolph walked closer, an impossibly handsome man, a man she had never seen smile, not even once. "You don't have to apologize for enjoying our first good day of spring, Mrs. Hanrahan." He bowed.

She met his gaze and felt herself drowning in his remarkable blue eyes and in wave after wave of her own surprise. She knew her cheeks were hot. But it was impossible not to be aware of Harry de Warenne as a most attractive man, even if he was a nobleman and her employer. Fortunately, she rarely glimpsed him more than once or twice a day.

Unfortunately, she dreamed about those glimpses in the wee hours of the night.

Now a dozen questions filled her mind. Why had he bowed? How terrible did she look? For how long had he been watching her? "How do you know my name?" she whispered.

He did not smile. She knew all the rumors. He had lost his wife and children in a fire some time ago and continued to grieve for them, and she felt terribly sad for him. He was too young to spend the rest of his life in mourning. "You are in my employ," he said with a shrug. "I asked the steward."

Alarm began. He must have asked about her because he intended to reprimand her — or worse. But before she could get a word out, he said, "Your foot is bleeding."

She somehow tore her gaze from his face and looked down. He was right. She must have cut it on a stone. "I'm fine," she managed to say. She realized she must, somehow, escape back to the house and the duties awaiting her there.

But he knelt, swiftly producing a crisp linen kerchief.

Gwen gaped.

"The wound is not deep, I think," he said, and she had to bite down not to cry out as he put the unfolded linen on her foot, tying it in place. His hands were stunningly gentle.

What was he doing?

Swiftly, he stood. And his cheeks were red

as he said, "I don't think you should walk. You may ride Storm back to the house."

She had become incoherent, wanting to protest, for surely this could not be. She was no lady, to be treated this way. But then, as the crimson stain on his cheeks darkened, he swept her into his arms before she could utter her protest.

He set her in the saddle. She was staring at him, remaining more shocked than she had ever been in her life, and his gaze met hers. "I'll walk," he said. "Just hold on to the saddle."

And he led the horse with her on its back up the hill and to the house.

Now, Gwen had to sit down at her kitchen table. The tears began, tears she had thought finished a long time ago. That had been the first time she had ever been in Harry's arms. The first time they had ever exchanged words. After that, once or twice a day, he would pass her in the hall or study and inquire politely after her or her daughter. Eventually she and Bridget had run into him on the street of the village and he had bought Bridget a sweet. He began to appear outside their church on Sunday — David did not go to church and Lord Randolph was, of course, Protestant — and he would give them a ride home in his handsome carriage.

Christmas came. His gift to the family was a huge basket filled with exotic coffees and teas, biscuits and chocolates. Buried in the midst of the gourmet refreshments was a vial of the most delicate, sweet and floral French perfume.

She was wildly, hopelessly in love. She did not know what their strange relationship meant to him. She lived for the brief moments each day that they came face-to-face and those warm, sunny Sunday afternoons when he would drive her and Bridget home from church. She knew his reputation — and he did not dally with women of any class, so he could not be flirting with her. And she had heard that he had vowed never to remarry. But they did have some kind of relationship, a very tense and formal one. Yet oddly, it was also a friendship. It had been a year since she had first glimpsed him, the day her employment had begun.

And then she and David had another huge fight. He'd been missing for two days but Gwen knew that meant he was on a drunk. It was not the first time he'd disappeared and she knew it would not be the last. A part of her prayed he would never come back. When he did come home, he chose to pick a fight — accusing her of being less than a wife, a good-for-nothing lack wit — and his alcoholic rage had escalated until he began to beat her with his fist. Her face was badly bruised and Gwen knew she could not go up to the big house the next day. She sent a note to the housekeeper at Adare that she was ill and she would not be in for several days.

The next day Randolph came.

In a panic, she refused to answer the door, but he let himself in. And when he saw her face, she saw how much he cared. Before she even knew it she was in his arms — in his embrace — and he held her close and demanded she tell him who had done this so he might beat the man to a bloody pulp.

She begged him to leave it alone.

And he kissed her, telling her he could not leave it alone, and it was like the cork exploding from a fine bottle of champagne — one kiss and passion claimed them both.

Gwen wiped the tears from her face. She hated the memories, just as she cherished them, and she wished Randolph was not in the city, just as she wished he would come back, one more time. And when the knock sounded on her door, her wish was answered, because she somehow knew it was him.

Gwen stood slowly, stunned.

He knocked again.

Her heart filled her breast. Gwen hurried forward, unbolting the door, and not even inquiring as to who might be in her hall, she opened it.

Harry de Warenne stood there, staring intensely at her.

She felt as if she were back in Ireland, back in the little cottage she called home, as if time had gone backward, somehow retracing its steps, and she was a maid in his employ — a maid and his lover.

He reached out.

Gwen rushed into his arms.

"Oh God!" Francesca cried, seizing Hart's arm. They had followed Randolph's hansom across town and to Avenue A and then to Tenth Street. She watched as Randolph paid the cabdriver and turned to face the building where Gwen lived and where Margaret Cooper had died. And then she watched him as he went inside.

"Hart!" She faced him in horror. "He is going after Gwen. We must go up — we must stop him!"

Hart did not look very pleased. He faced Maggie. "Mrs. Kennedy, I think we are going to pay a call on Mrs. O'Neil. Please wait here."

Maggie blanched. She nodded, whispering, "Be careful."

Francesca could hardly believe that her instincts had been right. But there were only a few choices now. Either Harry de Warenne was the Slasher, or he was Gwen O'Neil's ex-lover and ex-employer, or both. She thought the former possibility far more likely, as she could not see Randolph pursuing any woman across an entire ocean, especially not a woman who had been a housemaid in his employ. "Hurry," she cried, fear for Gwen choking her. She fumbled with her purse while Hart stepped from the coach.

She leaped out behind him, her gun in hand. Hart caught her around the waist. "If that is loaded, you could shoot someone — including me."

"Of course it is loaded," she said in a hush. She gave him a look. "A fool's errand?"

He pushed the barrel of the small revolver down. "Do you have to carry that?" he asked.

Francesca hurried past him, leading the way to the building's entrance. "If your friend Randolph is up there murdering

Gwen, we shall both be very happy that I am armed," she said in a low tone.

He stepped around her to push open the front door. "I agree, his behavior is suspicious, but that does not mean he is a murderer."

Francesca did not answer, racing up the stairs. She paused before Gwen's door and unable to help herself, pressed her ear to the rough, splintering wood. She could not detect a thing.

Hart said, clearly amused, "Shall we knock?"

"Hush!" She strained to hear but there was nothing. Her alarm grew as she straightened. "Hart, break the door down," she ordered, her heart pounding.

He gave her a mildly incredulous look.

"Hurry!" she cried, terribly afraid for Gwen's welfare.

Hart tested the knob and the door was unlocked, for it opened instantly.

Francesca stood on tiptoe to see past him and started.

Randolph held Gwen tightly in his arms, kissing her deeply. The woman clung.

Engrossed, the lovers did not hear them.

Francesca lowered her gun.

Police headquarters was stunningly busy

that night. The holding cell was filled with drunks and hoodlums. Several officers stood at the front desk, processing two more rowdies, and a pair of civilian gentlemen looked ready to come to blows, barely being kept apart by a couple of weary policemen. Only one typewriter could be heard, though, when usually dozens were industriously at work. That night, there was no pinging of the telegraph and only the occasional ring of the telephones.

Gwen was ashen. "You can't be doing this! He has nothing to do with that awful Slasher, Miss Cahill!" she cried, one arm around her daughter.

They had asked Randolph to come with them to headquarters and he had agreed, his expression impassive and impossible to read. Francesca had explained that he might be useful in solving the case she was working on. Gwen had been determined to join them and had roused her daughter to do so, in spite of Randolph insisting that she remain at her flat. Now Gwen clasped her daughter to her side.

"We merely wish to ask him a few questions," Francesca said with a reassuring smile. "You should really go home, Gwen," she added, wondering why the woman had leaped to the conclusion that Randolph was a suspect.

Hart said, "My driver has taken Maggie home, but I can find you a cab."

Gwen had a terribly stubborn look on her face, one that was answer enough.

"Miz Cahill?"

Francesca turned at the sound of Inspector Newman's voice. "Did you reach Bragg?" she asked quickly.

"He is on his way," Newman said. "Randolph is in the conference room. C'mish said you could go up and start questioning him if you want to."

"That would be wonderful," Francesca said. She reached for Gwen's hand. "It is so late. You really should go home."

"I am staying," Gwen said hoarsely. "I am staying until you release him!"

As they moved toward the stairs, Hart murmured, "Should we advise the inspector to go down to the Holland House and search Randolph's room?"

She was pleased. Hart would make a good sleuth, if he ever wished to. "That is an excellent suggestion, and I agree that his hotel room should be searched for any clues. However, I think Bragg will have to send someone over when he gets here." She started up the stairs, Hart at her side. "I thought you were certain Randolph is innocent."

"Most murders seem to be committed by family members, or spouses, or lovers," he said.

"But Gwen hasn't been murdered," she remarked, playing the devil's advocate.

"If they were lovers in Ireland, he has come a very long way to rekindle the romance," Hart remarked.

"Meaning that the affair is hardly an ordinary one." Francesca smiled at him.

"Meaning that there are at least a dozen questions I wouldn't mind asking him, myself. Remember, this man does not womanize, Francesca. Not with whores and not with ladies. So what does an affair with a housemaid mean? I cannot understand why he is really here in the city."

"I don't know, but even I am not romantic enough to think it anything but extremely suspicious." She pushed open the conference room door.

Randolph sat at the long table, alone, apparently brooding. An armed officer stood by the door, leaning against the wall. He nodded at her.

Francesca recognized him. "Good evening, O'Reilly. The commissioner has said we could question Lord Randolph." She went to the table and sat down across from Randolph. He stared at her, his expression tight, but did not utter a word.

Hart paused, standing behind her. Randolph looked up at him. Hart said, "Randolph, you have not once asked why we wish to speak with you here at Police Headquarters."

He folded his arms across his chest. "Miss Cahill said I might be able to help her investigation into the Slasher. That seems reason enough."

Hart raised a brow. "That does not surprise you?"

"Of course it surprises me. But if I can help, I will."

Francesca leaned forward. "Why did you lie about your acquaintance with Mrs. Hanrahan?"

"I had no idea the lady you referred to was the Mrs. Hanrahan I had once employed."

"You mean the Mrs. Hanrahan who was your mistress."

His jaw flexed. "I prefer not to discuss Gwen."

"Unfortunately, she is the reason you are here. You see, she might be the Slasher's next victim — in fact, Margaret Cooper might have been killed erroneously, in her stead."

Randolph shot to his feet. "But what about the others? How would they be connected to her? And there is only one person endangering Gwen's life — David Hanrahan," he ground out.

"How long were you involved with Mrs. Hanrahan?" Hart interposed calmly.

He was red with anger. "I fail to see how this is anyone's business but my own."

Bragg had stepped briskly into the room. If he was surprised to see Hart there, he gave no sign. "Lord Randolph, I am Commissioner Bragg. Unfortunately, with a killer on the loose, you have no choice but to answer our questions."

Still crimson, Randolph said, "Six months."

"You knew her for six months or you had an affair with her for six months?" Francesca asked.

"I knew her for a year and a half," he said tersely.

"So you were lovers for six months," Francesca said.

"I fail to see the point of this line of inquiry," he cried.

Francesca thought about the fact that he had known Gwen for an entire year before he had seduced her.

"Where were you last Thursday evening,

Lord Randolph?" Bragg asked, cutting to the chase.

Randolph started and then glanced at Francesca and Hart. "They know where I was. I was at the Montrose affair. I beg your pardon, but why are you asking me this?"

"You arrived late," Francesca pointed out. "You arrived sometime after 9:00 p.m., perhaps even at half past nine. The affair started at seven. Where were you before you arrived at my sister's house?"

His gaze widened. "I was in my rooms at the hotel," he said.

Francesca stiffened, glancing at Hart and then Bragg. "Alone?"

"Yes, alone. I was planning to dine in my rooms — as I usually do — and then I decided to go to your sister's affair." He glanced from Francesca to Bragg and then to Hart. "What difference does it make?"

Francesca stood up, thinking about the fact that he had no alibi for the time of Kate Sullivan's murder.

Bragg stepped forward and leaned on the table. "Did you know Kate Sullivan, Lord Randolph?"

His eyes widened. "No. Who is Kate Sullivan?"

Francesca turned. "Kate Sullivan was murdered by the Slasher Thursday night, between 6:00 and 9:00 p.m."

He paled and then he was on his feet. "You think I am the Slasher?" he cried.

"No one is accusing you of anything," Bragg said.

"Why have you come to New York? Hart told me you usually have your assistants handle your overseas affairs," Francesca said.

He stared at her, his brilliant blue eyes wide. "Certain matters needed my personal attention," he said after a pause.

"What matters?" she shot back. "Gwen?"

He flushed.

"Are you in love with her?" Francesca asked. "Who ended the affair? Did you approve of her coming to America?"

He remained sheet-white. He finally said, "Her husband found out. There was no choice but to end the liaison." He hesitated and added, "I had no idea she would leave Ireland. It all happened so quickly."

"Is Gwen Hanrahan the reason you came to New York City?" Francesca pressed.

He briefly closed his eyes. Then he opened them. "Yes."

She inhaled, hard. "And what day did you arrive here, precisely?"

His blue gaze never wavered. "I arrived here March 31," he said.

Francesca felt the air leave her lungs in a rush. *He had arrived in the city the week before the Slasher had begun his deadly work. And he had come to the city because of Gwen.*

"Where were you Monday evening, April 7?" she heard Bragg ask, referring to the night Francis O'Leary had been attacked.

"I'd have to check my calendar," he said flatly. "But I would imagine I was dining alone in my hotel room."

Francesca paced restlessly in Bragg's office. Her mind raced and her temples throbbed. It was very possible, she thought, that they had the Slasher in custody. She turned to face Hart.

He stood at the window, looking down on Mulberry Street, which was extremely busy even at this late hour, most of the pedestrians drunk and many on the arms of prostitutes. Sensing her gaze, he glanced at her.

"He followed Gwen here. An Irish nobleman, a recluse with a reputation for being dour, followed his lover across an entire ocean — his lover, who fits the profile of the Slasher's victims perfectly," she said.

Bragg walked inside before she had finished her thoughts.

"Well?" she cried. "He doesn't seem to

481

have a single alibi for any of the nights in question."

"No, he doesn't. And I find it odd that a man like Randolph would not be clever enough to have some very solid alibis," Bragg said. "But frankly, if he has an obsession for her, I cannot comprehend it."

Hart murmured, "An obsession is not rational."

"Neither is stalking and slashing and murdering a certain type of woman," Francesca said tersely. "That is psychotic."

Bragg faced Francesca. "I am releasing him."

"What?" She was shocked. Randolph was clearly obsessed and he could very well be their killer. But did he wish to harm Gwen, or just other women who were like her?

"I am releasing him with a tail. He has also agreed to hand over his calendar and I have sent an officer back to his hotel with him to retrieve it."

Francesca ran to Bragg. "It is Saturday! It's almost midnight. In a little more than twenty-four hours it will be Monday! Is that what you are thinking? That even though the Slasher chose to kill Kate Sullivan on Thursday, he could strike again on Monday as he has on the three previous weeks? And we will catch him in the act?"

"The Slasher will strike again, but frankly, I cannot hazard any guess as to when that will be. Except I fear it will be soon," Bragg said, his gaze riveted to her face. "If Randolph is our man, he will be caught redhanded. I have put a tail on David Hanrahan as well."

She seized his arm. "If Randolph is our man, he might be planning to go after Gwen this time. I cannot decide if she is his real target or he wishes to hurt any other woman he deems is like her! Bragg, can you give her police protection?"

"Of course," he said. "And Francis O'Leary as well."

She was vastly relieved.

"Sir?" Newman knocked as he poked his head into the office. "I just got the report from Heinreich," he said. "An' Chief Farr isn't in, so he hasn't seen it yet."

Bragg waved him in and took the pages from the rotund detective. He glanced at them and then looked up. He was scowling.

"What is it?" Francesca asked in alarm.

"Sullivan wasn't a suicide," Bragg said.

Chapter Twenty-Two

Sunday, April 27, 1902 After midnight

"What do you think?" Francesca asked.

They were alone in Hart's coach, sharing the back seat, as it raced uptown through mostly empty streets. He faced her, his posture relaxed. His expression, although shadowed in the dimly lit interior, was pensive. "I think Randolph might be our man."

"I am inclined to agree," she whispered, feeling terrible for Gwen and her daughter. "And Sullivan?"

"The Slasher wanted to mislead us," Hart said. "He murdered Sullivan to make us think Sullivan committed suicide after killing his wife."

Francesca thought so, too. "It is so extreme for a man like Randolph, a man reputed to be reclusive and to have never recovered from the death of his family, to have an affair with his housemaid and then

484

follow her to America." Impulsively, she reached for his hand.

His gaze flew to hers.

She suddenly recalled their terrible argument of just a few hours ago and she released his palm. But she did not look away.

He met her stare.

With real trepidation, she said, "Are you still angry?"

His jaw was tight. "I am not all that happy."

She nodded and bit her lip, looking away.

He took her hand and held it.

"How did we come to be in this dark place, Calder?"

"I don't know." But he pulled her closer and kissed her forehead. Then their gazes met. "I'll take you to Kate's funeral tomorrow," he said.

She nodded, that terribly familiar knot of dread congealed now in her chest.

The entire ward, it seemed, had turned out for Kate Sullivan's funeral, along with most of the press.

The church was two centuries old, small, square and hewn out of rough stone. As Hart's coach paused alongside a more modest carriage, just in front of the two wide gray steps, Francesca glanced in real surprise at the crowd outside. The funeral guests were mostly Kate's friends and peers and were clad in their Sunday best. Francesca watched various couples hurrying inside, some with children in hand. Her gaze veered. She instantly recognized a group of newsmen who had congregated near the church's front steps but had yet to go up. These men wore shabby suits and derbies or felt caps, and carried pads in their hands. In their midst was Chief Farr. Apparently he was giving an interview.

"Shall we?" Hart asked in her ear.

She could barely take her eyes from Farr, wishing she could hear what he had to say. And she did not see Bragg anywhere yet. She nodded at Hart.

Maggie was with them, somberly clad in dark gray, and he helped her down to the street first. As Francesca stepped out, Farr looked in her direction and from a relatively short distance, their gazes met. He smiled at her, but no warmth reached his cold gray eyes.

She quickly turned away; Hart steadied her. She looked up at him. "What do you think he is up to?"

"I think he might merely wish to steal the limelight," Hart said in a low voice.

"I think he wants to discredit Rick, in the

hope of toppling him," Francesca said harshly. As she spoke, she saw the Daimler cruising slowly up the block, toward them. She was relieved that he was present. She did not like Farr's usurpation of authority. And now Farr left the group of newsman, as if he did not wish to be caught speaking with them by his boss.

"Miss Cahill!" one of them cried.

She espied David Hanrahan coming up the block, alone, and seized Hart's sleeve. Hanrahan was wearing a dark suit, but the jacket was a size too large on his lean frame and the trousers were too short. "He is wearing a dark suit," she murmured, "but no one would ever mistake him for a gentleman."

"Darling, everyone is wearing a dark suit — we are at a funeral."

She continued to stare. "Hanrahan has a very strong motive to hate Gwen and other women like her, just like Lord Randolph. And he has not a single alibi for any of the murders in question — Hart, I am taking him off my list of suspects!"

Hart gazed at her with some amusement. "Is that wise, darling?"

"I feel very strongly that he is not our man," she said. "I am operating by instinct alone."

"I happen to have some of that feeling, too," he returned.

"Miss Cahill! How are you?" It was Isaacson, from the *Tribune* peering eagerly at her. "Rumor has it that the Slasher is a gentleman. Is that true? And last night the police took one Harry de Warenne, Lord Randolph, in for questioning!"

Francesca heard Isaacson, but she did not reply. Down the block, Francis O'Leary and Sam Wilson were approaching, arm in arm, and also in their finest clothes. From this distance, Wilson had the appearance of a fine gentleman, as well, and no one would ever suspect he was a clockmaker. She gave Hart a pointed look and quickly answered Isaacson. "We have some reason to believe that the Slasher is a gentleman, but until he is caught, I am afraid we are not one hundred percent certain."

"Is Lord Randolph a suspect?" Arthur Kurland asked, stepping out from behind several of his colleagues. "I understand that he comes from quite a fine family in both Britain and Ireland."

She felt her smile vanish. Hart squeezed her hand in warning. "No, Mr. Kurland," she said. "I am afraid that was a dead end."

Kurland smiled at her. "Speak of the devil," he said. "I guess I'll just go talk to him myself."

Francesca whirled as Randolph alighted from a hansom, his ivory-tipped walking stick in hand. "What is he doing here?" she cried.

"Paying his respects, I would assume," Hart said, his voice low.

"He doesn't know Kate Sullivan — or that is what he said." Francesca whispered back, unable to tear her gaze from him.

"Perhaps he has other motives," Hart said with a nod, indicating that she should glance across the street.

There, on the east side of the avenue, Gwen O'Neil and Bridget were hurrying down that block, hand in hand, clearly in a rush. "Are we missing anyone?" Francesca asked. The turnout was an incredible one.

"I don't think so," Hart began as another hansom pulled up. And then he stiffened, sheer disbelief crossing his face.

Instantly she became uneasy. From where she stood, a dozen feet from the curb, Francesca glanced warily into the hansom. She froze.

Daisy Jones was seated there.

Francesca stared, real dread unfurling. Her heart skipped hard and then raced wildly. Someone was with her. It was her lover, Rose, a tall, dark, exotic woman of

European descent who was now calmly paying the driver.

Francesca took Hart's arm and pulled him away, toward the front steps of the church. From the corner of her eye, she watched both women alight, her mind racing at lightning speed. What were they doing here? Somehow, she knew this was about her and Calder and not the woman being buried that day.

Then instinct made her glance in the opposite direction, for she knew more trouble was in the making, and sure enough, she saw Kurland conversing with Randolph. And then she thought she saw something else of high significance and she whirled around. Yes, she was correct. David Hanrahan stood on the top step of the church, staring at Randolph with utter hatred. She gripped Hart hard. "I have a very bad feeling about this day," she said breathlessly.

"I will make certain that she leaves," Hart said tightly, his gaze on Daisy.

Francesca finally focused on him and saw that he was very angry. "No." She tried to smile at him, but she wanted to know why the sight of Daisy had sent him into a temper. His eyes were black, his face a dark mask. He wasn't looking at the woman who had briefly been his mistress now, but she could feel his tension.

Her mind raced. Why had Daisy gone to his office the other day? Had she thought to seduce him away from his fiancée, or back into an illicit liaison in spite of his engagement and his vows? She smiled more brightly at him. "Daisy is undeniably kind. If she wishes to attend Kate's funeral, it is her right." She did not believe a word she said.

He looked at her in disbelief. "She is not kind unless it suits her to be so. The press are here, Francesca."

She had an awful inkling. She slowly glanced at Kurland, who was smiling widely at her and Hart. "Does he know? Does he know she was your mistress?"

"Can you think of another reason for him to be smirking? Fortunately he does not write a social column," Hart said grimly.

Francesca did not want him to chase Daisy away. She wanted to confront her and find out exactly what the woman wanted from Hart. "Calder, please don't make a scene. She's here and Kurland has seen her. *Everyone* has seen her. Besides, we both know the truth — that she isn't your mistress anymore." She tried to smile at him. But it was hard not to feel humiliated. She could imagine what everyone was thinking, and that was exactly what her own father chose to think, too.

"You have one good point — a scene will only make things worse. I suggest we go inside, as it seems almost everyone has arrived." The sidewalk had become far less populated, with most of the funeral guests going in to take their seats.

Francesca held on to Hart's arm, her stomach rather ill, watching as Daisy and Rose walked past them and up the front steps of the church. Both women were striking in contrasting ways. Daisy was so slender and pale, clad in a dark rose and gray dress, a half veil on her hat, while Rose was tall, lush, olive-skinned and black-haired. She was as finely dressed in a dark navy blue ensemble and small, jaunty hat. She had not a doubt that they both knew they were the center of attention wherever they chose to go. Heads held high, they floated as they walked, as if unwaveringly proud of who they were and how they chose to live, as if acutely aware of the fact that most eyes were now trained upon them. Daisy held Rose's arm as if she were her beau.

Francesca told herself that she must not hate Daisy Jones. Once, they had been friends. But as Daisy smiled at her in passing, she did hate her. And worse, she was afraid of her, too.

Hart looked as if he was about to commit murder himself.

Bragg walked up to them, having finally double-parked so as to not congest the street. "It is an interesting turnout," he said. "Are you all right?" he asked Francesca as if Hart were not present.

"I'm fine," she lied. "Come sit with us," she added. And his presence provided her with no small amount of comfort.

Father Culhane was very slim and very fair, with pale brownish hair. As he leaned on the podium, his expression suitably somber, Francesca decided he was in his late twenties but no more. He had a large, hookish nose and his temples were graying. Francesca had meant to interview him after Margaret Cooper's murder, but had never gotten to it. Now, she made a mental note to find out what he knew about the Slasher's victims. After all, two of the women had been in his parish.

"Kate Sullivan was a blessing to everyone who knew her, even in passing," he began, apparently giving the eulogy himself. "The woman I knew worked hard and honestly every single day of her life, giving to others when others were in need. She led an exemplary life, a godly life, a good life. She first came to me six years ago, a young newlywed. I'll never forget the day we met, when she had just moved into this ward. She was so full of life, so full of happiness, and so genuinely hopeful." He smiled at everyone, pausing.

Francesca was barely listening, as she was much more interested in the crowd that had come to pay Kate their last respects than in the sermon. Gwen sat several pews ahead and she was clearly trying not to cry, her arm around her daughter. Her husband sat across the aisle and he kept staring at her. She did not seem to notice, or perhaps she did not care.

Randolph sat two rows ahead of Francesca and just to her right. He had been staring at Gwen from the moment he had taken his seat. His gaze was frighteningly intense and terribly morose.

He remained high on her list of suspects.

"Her passing was a terrible tragedy, and I am sure that many of you are thinking, as I am thinking, why? Why such a good, honest, godly woman? Where is the justice in that?" Culhane was saying, his tone filled with passion.

Francesca spotted Francis and Sam Wilson, seated behind her. Francis was ashen, her nose red, clearly unable to control her tears. Wilson had his arm around her. He seemed saddened, too.

His gaze met hers.

Francesca quickly faced forward. Had she seen a cool light in his eyes? An expression absolutely uncharacteristic for the man she thus far knew?

She shifted to look directly to her right, across Hart, and met Farr's cold gray gaze. This time he did not smile at her, he merely stared, and a chill went down her spine. He was up to something, she thought. And hiding evidence on this case was just the tip of that iceberg.

As she turned away, she saw Daisy whispering to Rose and then Daisy got up and made her way out of the pew and down the aisle, clearly leaving the church.

Her heart slammed as she faced forward, for this was her chance, indeed.

"How can I answer you?" Culhane was asking sadly. "We all know God works in mysterious ways."

Francesca whispered in Hart's ear. "I will be right back." And before he could respond, she leaped to her feet and slipped past him. Once in the aisle, she hurried out of the church.

Daisy stood on the top step, waiting for

her. Francesca was breathless as she closed the church doors behind her. "Did you know Kate Sullivan?"

"No," Daisy said with a small shrug. "How would I know her? We hardly walked in the same salons," she said with some superiority.

Francesca took a deep breath. There was no small amount of dread as she faced the other woman now. "Then why are you here?"

"To pay my respects." Her expression was truly remarkable — absolutely impassive, with no hint of what she might be feeling, but there was a glint in her eyes, and it was, perhaps, smug.

Francesca knew that there was no reason for Daisy to be present at Kate's funeral. Then she corrected herself. There was a reason: Hart. But would she have guessed that Hart was attending?

Maybe Daisy was present because she, Francesca, was there. "Why are you really here?"

Daisy shrugged. "It's terrible, the Slasher murdering such good, honest, godly women, as Father Culhane said."

She did not care. Francesca wondered why she had ever, even briefly, liked this woman. "Why did you go to Hart's office?"

Daisy smiled at her and said softly, "He's my benefactor. We had matters to discuss."

They were enemies, Francesca thought, deadly enemies. She didn't see it in the other woman's expression, but she somehow knew it in her heart. She knew it the way she knew that she loved Calder Hart with all of her heart and that she would not let this woman come between them. Francesca stared and said slowly, "Why don't you tell me what you want? Clearly, you came outside to speak with me. Clearly, you came to this funeral to see *me*."

"No," Daisy said softly. "It is Calder I came to see. It is Calder I want."

The gauntlet had been thrown. "Did you go to his office to beg him to take you back?" Francesca demanded.

"I have never begged any man for anything," Daisy said with vast superiority. "I have never had to beg any man for anything. I always get what I want, Francesca."

She was as rigid as a board, uncomfortably so. "And you want Hart back?"

Daisy smiled at her. "When he tires of you, I expect him back," she said simply.

Francesca wet her lips. "So you failed to seduce him. You *did* try to seduce him in his office, didn't you?"

"I am hardly that naive," she laughed.

"Then what happened?" Francesca cried, shaking.

Daisy's eyes turned ugly. "Hart is no different from me, Francesca. He thinks to reform. He is smitten with you, for some reason, and he thinks to become a gentleman like all the others. Well, he can't! This man has an appetite for very unusual fare. Feed him a constant diet of beef and chicken and he will die for lack of variety! Your bed will soon bore him, Francesca. How much clearer do I need to be?"

Francesca hugged herself. "Maybe he was once that way. But he is tired of that life." She heard how hesitant and uncertain she sounded, because in truth, she believed Daisy. It was not that she thought that Hart was depraved, but that he would soon come to find her boring. With such a man, it simply seemed inevitable.

"I don't think so. A leopard cannot change his spots," Daisy said, and she was far too sure of herself. And then she laughed, shaking her head. "You are so innocent! Hart is jaded, terribly jaded, and he cannot reform, not for you, not for anyone. Give him time and you shall see the real Hart return. You have created a mere impostor and you clearly know it as much as I do."

Her heart beat with sickening force and

she turned away. She could not find her voice to insist that the Hart she knew was good, even kind and noble. In fact, she could not think of a single reply.

Daisy laughed. "Enjoy him while you can, my dear. Enjoy his bed while you can, as he *is* so magnificent. And continue to lie to yourself. I am sure you will do so for a long time."

She almost clapped her hands over her ears. "You're wrong," she managed to say knowing how pitiful her response was. "I know you are wrong." But even her tone seemed weak.

Daisy seized her wrist. "That night will come that he does not return home when you expect him. And he will have a perfect excuse. And you will accept it, of course you will, but deep in your heart you will know he was with someone else." And she smiled tightly at her.

Francesca jerked away. "How can you be so cruel? Once, we were friends!" She reached for the door of the church, only too late realizing that the last place she wished to go was inside. She did not want Hart to even guess at the conversation that had just taken place.

Daisy pressed on the door before she could pull it open. And she leaned so close

Francesca felt her arm against her and her breath on her ear. "You are so upset," she whispered maliciously. "So distraught! Why? Because your little fairy tale is over? Because you must now hold on to Hart with your fingertips as he slips slowly but surely away?"

"What do you want?" Francesca cried furiously, twisting to face her. But now they were face-to-face and far too close for comfort.

Daisy never stopped smiling. "I told you."

"No, I don't believe it. If you really wanted Calder, you would simply wait this out." She sucked down air. She was shaking. "This is about revenge, isn't it?"

Daisy stared, no longer smiling. Then she leaned close, her lips almost on her cheek. *"You haven't seen anything yet."*

Daisy had left and Francesca stood alone on the church steps, shaken to the core. She finally gave up and sat down, as her knees and legs seemed useless.

Daisy was dangerous, oh yes. That morning at the Lord and Taylor store, she had made Francesca doubt her own value and her relationship with Hart. Today, it was even worse. No matter how she might try to convince herself otherwise, Francesca knew that Daisy was right and that Hart was going to quickly tire of her.

And in the future, either near or far, that night would come — a night of lies she would choose to believe, a night spent in the arms of another woman.

She closed her eyes, desperately wishing she could find some faith in her fiancé. And a part of her stubbornly refused to cave in. A part of her shouted back that Hart was fine and good and misunderstood, and he was as noble as any other gentleman.

She inhaled hard, opening her eyes and seeing a cheerful blue sky with cotton-candy clouds. And she began to think and analyze, which was what she did best. Hart had been fine on Friday morning. He had not been fine that evening, at her sister's charity affair. They had been at odds ever since. And he had seen Daisy on Friday afternoon in his offices.

Clearly he had refused to be seduced. But had he been tempted? Francesca did not know what to think. But somehow Daisy had upset him, too. He had been having grave doubts about their future ever since that time, but was this all Daisy's doing? Just what, exactly, was he thinking — and why?

Behind her, the church doors suddenly

opened and a dozen people began coming out. Francesca quickly stepped to the side to let them pass. Randolph was one of the first gentlemen to leave the church and he paused on the sidewalk, hands in his trouser pockets, watching the funeral guests as they left. Francesca assumed he was waiting for Gwen.

Hart walked out. He came directly to her, his regard searching. "What happened?"

She forced a smile. "I needed some air."

"You were with Daisy," he exclaimed. "I am hardly a fool. What happened?"

She opened her mouth but no words came out, as she had not a clue what to do or say.

He took her arm. "You are very distressed," he said harshly. "Francesca, that woman is not to be believed or trusted."

"I know," she whispered, and impulsively she hugged him, burying her face against the rock-solid wall of his chest.

He held her loosely, one large hand cradling the back of her head beneath her hat. "I am going to take care of Daisy," he said.

She looked up and smiled at him. He wiped what must have been a stray tear from her cheek and they stepped apart. As she turned, she saw Bridget and Gwen walking past them, David Hanrahan directly behind them. If Gwen knew her husband was there, she gave no sign. She had eyes only for Randolph. She smiled at him, her pace increasing as she went down the steps.

Randolph stared at her.

Someone shouted — it was David Hanrahan. He rushed past Gwen and seized Randolph, throwing him backward against a parked carriage. "Fucking bastard!" he cried, his hands on Randolph's throat.

Randolph tried to break his grip.

"David!" Gwen screamed. "Stop! Stop, please, stop!"

Hart rushed down the steps, Francesca reacting a moment afterward and following him. As Hart reached Hanrahan, Bragg raced past her, and together they pulled him off Randolph. Hart stepped back as Bragg threw Hanrahan down on the street.

Two officers in uniform appeared, standing ominously over him. Hanrahan sat up, panting. "You stay away from her!" he shouted past Bragg and the policemen at Randolph.

Randolph gave him a disdainful look and turned to Gwen. "I'm all right," he said very quietly.

Gwen's face was a mask of anguish, her feelings terribly clear. She was obviously in love.

Francesca had reached Hart's side, but

she strained to hear. Randolph said, low, "Can I give you a lift home?"

Gwen nodded, smiling, the stars shining in her eyes.

Francesca was very dismayed for Gwen. Now she prayed Randolph was not their man. "Are you all right?" she asked Hart.

"I'm fine," he said, also glancing at the unlikely couple. Randolph was greeting Bridget with a smile. The girl did not seem to know what to do. Her gaze kept wavering between the handsome Irish nobleman and her father, who was now standing and in handcuffs.

Francesca hurried over to Bragg. "Take him downtown," he said in disgust to the officer holding Hanrahan.

"I done nothing wrong!" Hanrahan was incredulous. "That fancy bastard is after my wife and daughter."

Bragg ignored him, facing Francesca. "I'm going to lock him up for the night and let him ponder his poor temper," he said.

She nodded. It seemed like a good idea, especially considering Gwen might very well be in Randolph's bed before the hour was out. "Where is Randolph's tail?"

"He's here, but in civvies. Francesca, don't worry," he said quietly. "We won't lose him."

CHAPTER TWENTY-THREE

Sunday, April 27, 1902 2:00 p.m.

Francesca blinked in disbelief. "Kate was your *sister?*"

Hart had joined her and Bragg. The gentleman shrugged. "I'm afraid so."

Now, Francesca could only stare. How had working-class Kate come from the same family as this gentleman?

Bragg stepped into the fray. "I'm Rick Bragg, commissioner of police," he said. "I'm sorry about your sister."

"Thank you," the man said. "I'm Frank Pierson."

"Would you mind explaining how Kate wound up a shopgirl and the wife of John Sullivan?"

Pierson's jaw tightened. "I'd rather not. This is a dismal day, sir."

Bragg reached out to restrain him before he could turn and leave. "Sir," he said very softly, "I am afraid I was not clear. I am not giving you an option. Please explain why a woman from such a genteel background married a man like Sullivan and lived in the financial circumstances that she did."

Pierson smiled. "I'm sorry. I am distraught. You see, I haven't seen Kate in years, not until now."

"How many years?" Bragg asked.

"She ran off with a scoundrel, sir, five years ago. He was from a good family, but disowned for his absolutely immoral ways. The day she left was the day my family disowned *her*," he said with some vehemence. "She broke our hearts," he added.

"What happened to this scoundrel?" Francesca asked. "Surely it wasn't Sullivan?"

"Of course not," Pierson said quickly, smiling a little. "His name was Bradley Hunter. He left her shortly after. I believe he resides in Paris. She, of course, was ruined, and I imagine that she had no choice but to marry Sullivan."

"You imagine?" Francesca's own heart began to break for Kate. "Did you not speak to her when Hunter left her? Surely you went after her and tried to bring her home."

"I did no such thing," he said coldly. His eyes had turned to ice. "She may be buried today, Miss Cahill, but the fact is my family buried her five years ago, on February 14, the day she chose to run off with Hunter. That morning at breakfast was the last time I saw her and the last time I spoke to her." His face was rigid. He nodded at Bragg. "Have I sufficiently answered your questions, sir?"

"In a moment," Bragg said. "Where were you last Thursday night, Mr. Pierson?"

Bragg led the way into his office, but paused at the door. Francesca followed him inside, barely aware of her surroundings, her mind racing. She was analyzing every moment spent with Frank Pierson. When Hart walked in, Bragg shut the door behind him.

Francesca faced both men thoughtfully. "His alibi is ironclad."

"Yes, it is ironclad," Bragg said.

"And convenient," Hart murmured. "Having supper at home with his dear elderly mother while his sister was murdered."

"There was a house filled with staff," Francesca said. "The cook, the housekeeper, the butler and a valet."

"And two housemaids." Hart was wry.

"He has an alibi for every night the Slasher attacked," Francesca cried. "On Mondays, he always attends the Lions Club."

Bragg went to his desk but did not sit

down. "Newman is verifying every alibi, but I feel certain no one will admit that Pierson was not where he said he was when he said he was there."

Francesca raced over to him. "This is too sweet! Here is our first suspect with solid alibis — which is exactly why I suspect him."

Bragg smiled a little at her. "I agree," he said softly.

She smiled back, her every instinct telling her now that they had their man. Kate Sullivan had been conned by a scoundrel and had foolishly run away from home. Apparently, her brother had never forgiven her. It was unbelievable that she had not been allowed back home when Bradley Hunter had abandoned her as swiftly as he had seduced her. According to Pierson, their father had died six months later of a broken heart, apparently losing his will to live. He had suffered a stroke a few months before Kate's lapse from propriety, but had been recuperating until then. And to this day, Mrs. Pierson, Kate's mother, suffered from grave melancholia. And it was all Kate's fault — according to her brother.

"I concur," Hart said, moving to stand beside Francesca and interrupting her thoughts. "He probably put in an appearance at his gentleman's club, but I doubt anyone would know precisely when he arrived or when he left. His staff undoubtedly fear dismissal should they go against his word. His alibis are utterly pat."

Francesca smiled at him, too. Then she turned to Bragg, "How will we proceed?"

"I will have a plainclothes officer keep an eye on him as well. I have only one problem," he said.

"What's that?"

"Why the hell would he come to Kate's funeral and reveal his hand?"

They stared at one another for a moment. Bragg's telephone began to ring. He went to get it. Francesca looked at Hart. "He has made a mistake. They all do, eventually — or at least, the ones who get caught."

Real warmth filled his eyes and she smiled, reaching for his hand. "I want to talk to you," he said softly, so Bragg could not hear. "When we get home."

Her eyes widened and her heart lurched. Her grip on his palm tightened. "Should I be afraid?"

"I don't want you to ever be afraid of me," he said, "but I cannot answer that." He hesitated while her mind scrambled and raced. "I want to discuss Daisy," he said.

She nodded. "Yes, that's a very good idea."

He smiled a little at her then turned his

gaze to Bragg. His smile faded. "What is it?" he asked sharply.

Bragg had walked over to them, his expression rather serious. "That was Sarah Channing," he said.

Francesca gasped. "Is she all right?" There was no reason under the sun for Sarah to call Bragg, and especially at police headquarters.

"She is somewhat hysterical," he said, his gaze dark and on her now. "It seems that your portrait is missing."

"Missing?" she echoed in disbelief.

"Stolen," he said.

Sarah was waiting for them. She was wringing her hands, appearing ashen, as they were ushered inside. Bragg hurried to her.

Francesca did not follow. She remained shocked and disbelieving. They had left the police station as if it were on fire and she could hardly recall the ride to Sarah's. "Calder. This is impossible," she whispered hoarsely.

His jaw was so tight his face appeared in danger of cracking. He was as distressed as she was, and that was not reassuring. "Apparently not."

"Calder, someone other than you, me or Sarah has seen that portrait." Dread consumed her now. How vain and foolish she had been to pose nude with such abandon for that portrait. She knew her cheeks were on fire. Who was staring at her portrait even now? Who had stolen it? *And why?*

"Francesca, it is far worse than that," Hart said.

"What in God's name do you mean?" she cried.

"I mean, that portrait may very well wind up on public display. Art is usually stolen in order to be fenced."

The sound that escaped her was high-pitched and choked. She clung to him and he steadied her. "We won't let that happen," he said firmly.

Her horror knew no bounds. She was mortified. It was one thing to pose for Hart nude, but another to have half the world gaze upon her in such a state. And society would hear all about it — no secret like this, once let loose, could ever be kept. Oh, God! She thought about her family. Julia would be horrified, Andrew ashamed. . . . They would all be ruined, she thought. They would be ruined by association. But it was embarrassment that consumed her now. If that portrait surfaced, how would she ever appear in public again?

Bragg and Sarah had approached. Bragg

looked from Francesca to Hart and back again. Sarah suddenly blurted, "I am so sorry! I should have kept my studio locked! Francesca, please, forgive me!"

Francesca managed to nod. She could hardly form any words. She licked her lips. "It's not your fault."

Sarah started to cry.

"All right," Bragg cut in. "I see I am missing something. We seem to have a crisis at hand — one a stolen portrait hardly merits. What exactly is going on? Why do the ladies look as if someone has died, and why do you look ready to murder someone?" he asked, directing this last bit to Hart.

Francesca turned away, somehow moving into Hart's arms. He said, holding her close, "The portrait is a highly suggestive one."

Francesca closed her eyes, hard.

"Highly suggestive?" Bragg echoed.

Sarah tugged on his sleeve. "It's a wonderful portrait, really. Francesca is lovely and the likeness is unmistakable . . ." She faltered and broke off miserably.

"It's a nude," Hart said.

There was a moment of silence.

Francesca decided to be very brave and turned to face Bragg.

He gaped at her in shock.

She stared back. There was absolutely

nothing to say.

"I see," he finally said, color now flooding his cheeks. And then he directed his attention to Hart, and he was furious. "You taint everything you touch."

Hart stiffened. "I take all blame," he ground out. "The idea was mine, of course."

Francesca whirled. "This is hardly your fault!"

Hart made a mocking sound.

"Like hell it isn't! He has never given a damn about anyone but himself. Even now, engaged to you, he only thinks about his own hideous appetites. What in hell were you thinking to expose Francesca this way?" Bragg demanded. His fists were clenched.

Hart made no attempt to defend himself.

"That's not fair." Francesca stood between the two men, facing Bragg. "I didn't have to be persuaded. I wanted to pose . . . that way. Hart planned to hang the portrait in his private rooms . . . after our marriage," she added lamely.

Bragg stared at her in disbelief. "Even if the painting hadn't been stolen, did it not cross your mind that even a whisper of such a portrait would compromise your reputation?"

She shook her head. How foolish she had been. "No."

"You leave her alone." Hart seized Bragg, who shook him off. "I suggest you focus your efforts on doing what you are paid to do. This theft is a crime and it needs to be solved before any damage is done."

"I doubt there is any way to prevent the damage that will arise. It is hardly possible to conduct a secret investigation!" Bragg flared.

"Untrue. In fact, I think the police should not be involved at all," Hart said slowly but very firmly. "I'm hiring my own detectives. I will get that painting back."

Francesca turned to him. Maybe Hart was right. If they assembled a small, independent team, they could find the portrait before any word leaked out of its existence — much less before it was ever displayed. She turned to Bragg and bit her lip. "He's right. We should keep the police out of this."

His expression tightened. "You don't want my help?"

She touched him. "Of course I want your help. But unofficially," she said. "The fewer who know, the better."

His jaw was hard, but he nodded. Then he glanced at Hart with sheer disgust. "I pray for the day when she comes to her senses," he said. "You will never be good enough for her."

■ ■ ■ ■

Bragg paused as he stepped into the front hall of his house, the weight of dread settling upon his shoulders like a terribly heavy yoke. Instantly he heard the girls upstairs, Katie's tones soft and quiet, Dot alternately giggling and shrieking. His heart warmed, in spite of the fact that his wife was somewhere in the house and that he was afraid to see her. It was impossible to guess what kind of mood she would be in. The only thing he could be sure of was that every day was worse than the one before. Every day she grew more distant and sadder.

Bragg closed the door and started up the narrow stairs. Leigh Anne was waiting for him. She sat in her wheeled chair in their bedroom, appearing sad and pensive. Clearly, there was some matter she wished to discuss. Just down the hall, he saw that Mrs. Flowers was watching the girls, their bedroom door open.

"I'm sorry," he apologized. "I thought I would be able to come home directly after the funeral, but there was a new lead, a major one, into the case of the Slasher," he said, pulling off his tie.

She tried to smile at him and failed. "I

517

know your work comes first. You don't have to apologize," she said.

His heart lurched. She remained the most beautiful woman he had ever laid eyes upon, even now in that wheeled chair, the light gone from her emerald eyes, and he wished that four years ago she had been as understanding. He turned away and hurried into the dressing room, the ache in his chest expanding. But when they had first been married she hadn't been understanding at all. She had refused to accept the importance of his work and his priorities — just as he had refused to recognize her needs, just as he had taken his bride completely for granted. Not for the first time, he had the most absurd yearning to go back in time and do everything correctly this time.

He dropped his suit jacket on a chair, his necktie with it, and stared at his reflection in the mirror as he began to remove his cuff links. There was no going back; there was only the present and the future. A month ago, he had wanted a divorce. Now, he hardly knew what he wanted. His emotions had never been more tumultuous. He certainly wanted the two little girls to be happy and in his life forever, and he also knew he wanted to spare Leigh Anne any more anguish and pain. If only he could comfort her. But he had only to look at her to see how unhappy she was. How in hell could he make her happy when she would not even give him a single opportunity to try?

If he could, he decided, he would fix everything, including their marriage. But he simply did not know where to begin.

Images flooded his mind then — Leigh Anne radiant and glowing in a ball gown, dancing in his arms; Leigh Anne in the girls' bed, reading them a fairy tale, each child snuggled against her; Leigh Anne in his bed, moaning in pleasure, desperately accepting every inch of him.

He tossed his shirt aside, unfortunately aroused. Nothing had changed for him since her tragic accident. She seemed to have lost interest in the physical act that had until recently been their single bond. He gripped the edge of the vanity, wondering if he dared even try to make love to her. He knew he could bring her so much pleasure and it felt as if that might be the only way to reach her now.

But he was a coward, afraid to make any seductive move.

"Rick, I know you've had a difficult day but — oh, excuse me," Leigh Anne said, her cheeks coloring. She had wheeled herself into the boudoir and now glanced at her lap.

He turned his back to the mirror, facing her. He did not understand her reaction to his bare chest, not at all. "What is it?"

Not looking up, she shook her head as if she could not speak, then began to try to wheel herself and turn around, clearly wanting to leave the small dressing room. "It's nothing," she said just before she crashed the chair into the wall.

He seized the handles of the chair. "Let me help," he said, staring down at her.

She kept her face turned down, but he could see that her eyes were closed, her lashes thick and black and wet on her still-pink cheeks.

He touched her shoulder without thinking and she jerked, as if burned. "Just let me help," he repeated, acutely aware of the fact that somehow, his partial nudity disturbed her. Worse, the small room made him aware of every inch of her. He wheeled her back into their bedroom, grim.

"Thank you," she said, her tone barely audible.

He walked around to face her, taking a deep breath in the hope of recovering some composure. "Is there something you wish to discuss?" he asked quietly, sitting on the

edge of the bed.

She looked up and kept her eyes on his face. "Could you get dressed?"

He was very surprised. "You've seen my bare chest a hundred times."

She looked past his shoulder. "Everything has changed," she whispered.

He stared, making no move to retrieve a shirt. Her cheeks remained high in color and if he was not mistaken, her breathing was somewhat rapid. So many carnal images chased one another through his mind then, and the fist of desire that slammed into him made it impossible for him to breathe. The one thing he had always been able to count on was their insatiable desire for one another. Maybe, just maybe, her apparent lack of interest was a pretense, a façade, a lie.

What if he could reach her this way?

She looked up and for an instant, their gazes met. And she must have sensed his purpose. "What are you doing?" she asked warily.

And he slipped off the bed, kneeling beside her, his intent making it almost impossible for him to breathe. "What I have wanted to do since you first came home from Bellevue." And he tilted up her chin.

Alarm widened her eyes. "No, Rick," she

521

began, but he cut her off, covering her mouth with his lips.

At first he held her face with one hand, his other hand on her arm, and as he touched her mouth again, he felt like a dying man being given a new lease on life. His heart slammed wildly against his chest and he knew an insane giddiness, wondered why he hadn't kissed her sooner, because her taste was all he would ever need, and then he felt her lips soften and yield. He pressed harder, opening her, tasting all of her that he could, and the elation turned into pure, mindless excitement. His entire body shook, desire raging, so much so he had the urge to throw her onto the bed and take every inch of her then and there. But somehow, he knew he must be very gentle and very tender now. Instead, he lifted her carefully into his arms, smiling at her.

Her hands pushed against his shoulders, her eyes wide and aghast. "No! Stop!"

He could barely comprehend the words as he laid her down on the bed. "Let me make love to you," he whispered, their gazes meeting, and he felt triumph when he recognized the haze of passion in her eyes. He smiled and kissed her throat, just once, and then the hard peak of one breast.

"I said no!" she cried, two fists slamming

into him.

He jerked back.

She began to cry and he somehow knew that if she could, she would be crawling away from him, but of course her leg was useless and she could not move. "What could you possibly be thinking?" she accused.

He straightened, his chest heaving, the air burning his lungs. No, it wasn't the air, it was his heart causing him so much pain. He rubbed his chest. "I want to make love to you."

She was clearly disbelieving. *"Like this? Why? Is this an act of pity?"*

He swallowed. His heart continued to pound with maddening, lustful force. "No. There is no pity involved, just . . ." He hesitated. He was consumed with lust, but it was so much more. He was afraid, though, to name it. "I still desire you, Leigh Anne."

"Desire someone else!" she shouted at him. Tears fell now in a stream. "I want you to take a mistress. Because of the girls, we can't divorce. I mean, you have every right to divorce me now, of course you do, but I know you love the girls the way I do!" she sobbed, covering her face with her hands.

He felt certain he had not understood her correctly. "What?" He could feel all the color draining from his face. It also seemed to be draining from his life.

She looked up at him through the sheen of tears, shaking wildly. "Or do you want a divorce? I won't deny you now, Rick. If you still want the divorce, of course I will give it to you, but we must somehow take care of the girls."

What was she talking about? "I don't want a divorce," he heard himself say, as shocked as if a stick of dynamite had blown up right beside him.

"I know this isn't fair to you," she began, more tears falling, and his mind came to life.

He cut her off. "I'll decide what is fair for me and what is not," he said in absolute disbelief. Could this really be happening? "Do *you* want a divorce?"

Their gazes locked. A long moment passed before she spoke. "I want the girls," she whispered hoarsely, her mouth quivering. "I love them so much. I know you love them, too. We have given them a good home, the kind of home they deserve. I can't bear to send them away. They already love us — dear God, they would not understand!"

And he began to understand. If it weren't for Katie and Dot, she would disappear from his life forever. He folded his arms across his bare chest, when what he wanted to do was kneel beside her and hold her hands. He was sick, so sick, inside. "I don't want a divorce," he said thickly. He hesitated and added, "And I'm not taking a mistress, either." Now he began to shake, the horror of it all finally sinking in.

She was wiping her eyes with a handkerchief, and finally she looked up. "I cannot take care of your needs," she whispered. "I will look the other way . . . please."

How clear she was. He smiled coldly at her. "Don't worry, Leigh Anne. You have been very clear and I won't bother you again." Suddenly furious, he started from the room.

She watched him go.

CHAPTER TWENTY-FOUR

Sunday, April 27, 1902 5:00 p.m.
Francesca followed Hart into his library, still consumed with dread. He closed both doors behind her. "I am sorry," he said gravely.

"This is not your fault!" she cried.

He went to her and took her into his arms. "Isn't it? And isn't Rick right? If this portrait finds its way into a public gallery, I will be the reason you can never hold your head up again. I will be the reason you are scorned. I will be the reason you are hurt."

She gripped his lapels. "I agreed to pose nude. I agreed freely. There was no gun pointed at my head."

He cupped her face in his hands. "I had thought, until now, that I would begin a new life, and even acquire a new reputation with you. Suddenly the opposite seems to be the case. Rick is right. Eventually I taint every-thing I touch."

"That is not true! Do not abandon me now!" she said fiercely.

Their gazes met. "I would never abandon you. I don't want to ever be without you. In fact, I miss you terribly."

She started. "What do you mean?"

"I hate being at odds," he said vehemently. "These past few days, my life has felt so utterly cold and devoid of all meaning. The way it was once, before I met you, before you became my loyal and true friend."

She leaned close, laying her cheek against his chest, her heart pounding now. "Calder, I miss you, too. I miss you terribly! I have come to count on my days being filled with you."

"Really?" he asked softly, tilting up her chin so that their eyes met.

And the look there was so warm that it stole her breath away. Desperately, she wanted to tell him that she loved him. She wet her lips. "I cannot imagine life the way it was before we became engaged to one another. I cannot imagine life without you," she said quietly.

He started, his gaze flying wide. "Do you mean it?" he demanded, as if stunned, his hands on her shoulders. "Did I just hear you say that you could not live without me?"

Had she said that? But it was the truth —

she could not live without him. Without Calder Hart, her life would never be the same. She bit her lip even as she somehow smiled. "Yes, Calder, I mean it. I mean it with all of my heart. I cannot live without you."

He stared at her with sheer incredulity.

She swallowed. "You are an enigma — a very difficult enigma — but you are the enigma I want to be with," she said roughly.

He pulled her into his arms, his mouth finding hers, the urgency stunning. Thrilled by his fierce response, Francesca felt the urgency not just in his lips, but in every muscle and tendon of his body and she was desperately relieved. Nothing had changed, dear God, had it? And then she recalled the fact that her father was now dead-set against them. "Calder?"

He lifted his head, his eyes ash-gray with desire. "I want to make love to you," he said.

She froze.

And every single time he had declared that he did not believe in love filled her mind. But there was more. He had said he had never made love to a woman, not once in his entire life. She pressed against his shoulders. *What did you just say?*

Staring intensely at her, he repeated, "I want to make love to you."

It was impossible to breathe, nearly impossible to think. "You told me once that you have never made love to a woman."

"I haven't."

What did this mean? Was he telling her that he loved her? "Calder?"

"I want to show you how I feel," he said roughly, stroking his thumb over her jaw. "I want to make you feel the same way."

She was ready to swoon. Every inch of her body had turned to fire. She was ready; she had never been more ready. "Please," she whispered, a plea.

He smiled a little at her. "Your wish is my command," he murmured, and with dexterous fingers he unbuttoned her jacket, sliding it from her shoulders and tossing it to the floor. As he unbuttoned her shirtwaist, her heart had never beat more swiftly. She had difficulty continuing to stand.

He watched her, dropping the shirt and reaching behind her to unfasten her corset. "Don't faint now, darling," he said, pressing his thigh between hers. "We have hardly begun."

She gasped, holding tightly on to him for support as her undergarments hit the floor as well. "I am so excited," she managed to say, "and you haven't even touched me."

He smiled. "I can rectify that," he said

softly, and he touched his forefinger to her hard, distended nipple, then began to rub it. She cried out, waves of pleasure engulfing her, making her dizzy. He bent and laid his tongue over the hot, hard tip. Somehow, her skirts and petticoat dropped to the floor, pooling at her feet.

He sucked on her, hard.

Francesca moaned shamelessly, filled now with desire.

Hart lifted his head, his tone thick but surprised. "Darling, are you peaking?"

"Hurry," she gasped, barely able to open her eyes and meet his smoking gaze.

Before she knew it, he had laid her on the rug, their mouths instantly fusing, his hand now between her thighs, inside her drawers. The moment he touched her sex, she screamed, racked by a violent climax.

When she was floating somewhere in time, she felt him kissing her throat and her breasts, his hands stroking over belly, her thighs, her sex. Her drawers were, miraculously, gone.

She struggled to open her eyes and look at him.

"I want to give you so much pleasure," he said, his eyes hot. He bent over her and laid his tongue between the thick folds of her sex. Instantly, Francesca collapsed back on the floor, moaning.

He spread her wide and continued to caress her with his tongue. She spiraled out of control so quickly that there was no time to protest and disrobe him. Reaching down, clinging to his shoulders, she wept in pleasure and pain and more pleasure again.

He moved beside her when she was done and she drifted back into his arms. Toying with her breast, he whispered, "Perhaps we should argue more often."

She was still floating; she managed to look at him. Still breathless, she took his hand. "I hate arguing with you, but for some reason, your every look, word, touch is making me insane with more desire." She moved his hand down her belly and lower still.

He smiled, smug and pleased. He found her mouth and kissed her slowly, deeply, for a long, long time. This time his dangerous hand moved down her buttocks, playing there in a terribly sensual, suggestive manner.

From behind, he prodded and caressed, toyed and searched.

She tore her mouth from his, gasping in violent need. "You said you wanted to make love to me," she cried, reaching for his trousers. "I think this moment is highly appropriate."

He smiled at her. "I am making love to you, darling. I am making love to every inch of you that I can." His smile faded and he turned her onto her stomach. Her hair had long since come down and he moved it aside, kissing her nape and then slowly working his way down her spine. He had straddled her, and when he moved over her buttocks, she finally felt him and her heart dropped to the pit of her stomach. Beyond weak, beyond hollow, she arched upward, seeking to feel him again.

"Yes, darling, I know what you want and what you need," he whispered hoarsely in her ear. And she felt every inch of his manhood, hard as steel, encased in fine wool, pressing against her buttocks. She cried out.

Holding her tightly now, his breathing harsh, he moved against her, thrusting long and slow. "One day," he said, "you will know what this really feels like."

She was sobbing but soundlessly now. "One day?" she wept. "You said you are making love to me tonight!"

It suddenly crossed her mind that they had a serious miscommunication. She tensed, torn between fury and despair, and she felt his mouth on the corner of her lips. "I never said I was intending to break the vow I made to wait until our wedding night," he murmured.

"You are a complete bastard," she cried.

"So much passion in one tiny woman," he murmured, kissing her shoulder, and then she felt the naked length of him as he unfastened his trousers and sprang firmly against her buttocks. He surged deep and low, between her thighs, directly against her sex.

She rode him as he thrust, her swollen wet sex on his hard determined length, and the explosion was cataclysmic, throwing her far away into a black star-spangled universe. She wept and wept as he thrust with increasing urgency, and at some point, lost in time and space, she was vaguely aware of his climax joining her own.

And then she was in the circle of his arms.

He was panting hard, kissing her cheek, her jaw, her ear. "That was too soon," he whispered. "I want to give you so much pleasure tonight."

She found his hand and held it tightly, her composure slowly returning. Being with this man was like nothing she had ever dreamed of. She had never imagined that so much passion and desire could exist, that it could be so raw, so urgent, so consuming. Dazed, she spooned into him and he kissed the swell of her breast. Amazingly, her body was eager to respond to his again. And bemused, she realized that once again she was completely naked in his arms, and he was fully clothed. She could not form any coherent words just yet.

He raised her hand and kissed it. "We need to be in my bed," he murmured. "Because I am hardly through with you, darling."

She twisted to look up at him, smiling, while hot need shafted inside her.

He smiled with real amusement at her. "Cat got your tongue, darling?"

She had never felt more relaxed or more languid. Yet her sex had begun to ache in the most insistent manner. She closed her eyes and kissed his shirt and as she sighed, she guided his hand where it belonged. "Yes," she finally murmured.

He laughed, sounding a bit too pleased with himself. "You are such a strumpet! You are so easy to set off!"

She felt slightly annoyed and she lifted her lashes to look at his impossibly attractive face. His eyes danced now. "And that is a problem?"

The laughter died. He became thoughtful and his skilled fingers slipped low, stroking there. "It is an interesting dilemma," he said. "I wonder if I might have a certain effect on you — say, from across a crowded ballroom or a supper table?"

She understood and gaped.

And his expression became self-deprecating. He sat up. "Yes, I am depraved to the very end, it seems." His good humor was gone.

She seized his hand. "Then I am depraved, too — and happily so. Because if you meant what I thought you did, I should very much like to experiment and see what we can achieve."

He looked at her.

She stared back, aware of a blush on her cheeks. "Your very look has a certain power over me," she said softly. She cupped his cheek. "Am I being too naughty?"

"No," he said, inhaling. He pulled her close, his eyes closing, and kissed her deeply. Then he shifted and stared at her. "I sensed this in you the moment we met."

She was surprised. "Calder, I myself had no idea I was capable of so much passion."

He stroked her face, her shoulder. "I knew. I knew it right away. I knew the bluestocking and the sleuth were but the outermost layer." He hesitated. "As much as I want to take you upstairs, I can't risk us getting caught."

She understood. "What are we going to

do about Papa?" she asked.

He met her gaze, then slowly stood, adjusting his clothing. Francesca watched, making no move to get up. He smiled a little. "Have I created a monster?" he asked softly and with a tender smile.

"I think so," she said, knowing that they had to talk but also wanting to be back in his arms in a wild frenzy of passion.

He handed over her drawers and chemise. "Please."

As she put on the two garments, she thought about the way Calder had touched her and kissed her and held her. She had felt far more than passion and lust in his touch. What exactly had he meant when he said he wanted to make love to her? She thrilled just recalling his words. "Calder? You said you would not break your vow to wait for our wedding night."

He met her gaze, his expression utterly serious. "Your father has now refused us. Rick has pointed out the trouble I am causing you with the portrait stolen. And then there is Daisy."

Her heart lurched with fear. She bent and stepped into her petticoat. Then she faced him. "If you're asking me if I still want to marry you, the answer is yes."

His jaw flexed. "What did Daisy and you

speak about earlier today?"

She trembled. "She told me why she went to your office. She told me what she said. And she told me that she wants revenge."

"Revenge? For what?" he exclaimed.

"I think she is always the one to walk away, Calder, I do not think any man has ever been the one to walk away from *her.*"

He absorbed that. "Did she tell you *exactly* what she said at my office?"

Francesca tensed with dread. Her ears began to ring and her cheeks to burn. "Yes."

He stared at her. A bead of sweat had formed on his forehead.

She desperately wanted to know what he was thinking. "Daisy approached me in the Lord and Taylor store," she said slowly. "Earlier in the week. Somehow, she knew exactly what to say to me to disturb me no end. I was incredibly distressed by her, enough to begin endlessly worrying about our engagement, our future and even your loyalty."

"What did she say?" he asked abruptly, his gaze dark and intense.

She stiffened. She did not want to be that honest with him, oh no.

"Darling, if you intend for me to be honest with you on this matter, then you will have to do the same."

She walked away and sat down on an ottoman. Not looking at him, she said, "She told me what I already believe. That you will soon find me boring and stray to someone else." She dared not look up.

He knelt before her. "Look at me," he exclaimed.

She somehow managed to do so, shaking now. She hated Calder having even the briefest glimpse of her very real insecurity.

He touched her face. "The one thing I am sure of is that I will never find you boring! And how many times must I reiterate that if I wanted to pursue other women, I would not shackle myself in marriage? I am sick of that life!"

She met his steady gaze. "How sick of it are you, really?"

His smile was derisive. He stood. "Sex has bored me for some time, Francesca. It has become rather like a drug, I think, addictive, but with each dose, less intense. As a result, the addict must constantly find ways to make each act more exciting. That is why I strayed to women like Daisy and Rose, among other less usual fare."

She was wide-eyed. "You find sex boring?" But it began to make some sense now.

He smiled a little. "I have for a number of years, yes. But recently, that has changed."

She continued to stare. Her eyebrows felt as if they had risen to join her hairline.

"There is nothing boring about you," he said, kneeling again. "And I have never felt as excited as when I am with you." He smiled a little, but she thought he was blushing, for the top of his cheekbones had become tinged with pink. He hesitated and added, "I think it's the fact that I genuinely care about you. It seems to have changed everything."

"Oh," she managed to say. She was stunned.

He stood, looking very pensive now and not quite pleased. "So you do not need to listen to anything Daisy has to say. What a troublemaker! The least of our problems will be my wandering the town in pursuit of other women."

Francesca stood, continuing to reel from Calder's confession. "So why did she upset you so much? She is the reason you almost broke off our engagement Friday night, isn't she?"

He turned to face her. "Yes."

"Why? You forced me to be utterly honest with you. You can at least do the same with me," Francesca said.

"She knows me too well," he said flatly.

"I don't understand," she began, and

539

there was more dread, again.

"Daisy's entirely accurate point was I am by nature a cad, and I will never be able to change that, not for you, not for any woman. And she is right. I can never reform," he said harshly. "I am sexually depraved. Inside, I am black and hollow, and we can both pretend I am noble and good, but the truth is, I am not that man."

"No! Stop!" She took his hand very firmly. "The one thing I do know is that you are a good man, Calder Hart."

"That is what you are determined to believe, and that is why I —" He stopped. And he flushed from ear to ear. "That is why you are so sweet," he said hoarsely.

She could only stare, amazed. Every instinct told her that he had been about to tell her that was why he loved her. "I will not lie now, Calder. I am afraid you will wander one day, but I know that there is nothing black inside of you. I know it."

He took her in his arms. "Don't you see? Daisy, your father and Rick are right. I am simply not worthy of you. I do not want to taint you. I do not want my depravity to rub off on you, not in any way."

"What are you saying?" she cried, trembling.

"This is the time for us to say goodbye —

if that is what you want. Your father is against us and he is right. That portrait is missing and it is my fault. I suggested you pose nude, because of who I am. You deserve someone far better than I, Francesca. Admit it."

She clasped his face in her hands. "There is no one better. I will admit nothing of the kind. Yes, you have a dark sexual side. But you also have a good side, and don't you dare deny it. I have seen as much nobility in you as I have in your half brother."

"I will never believe that," he said softly, "but oddly, I think that you really do."

He had seemed almost sad as he spoke. She knew that she would never convince him that he was good enough for her. "That sexual side Daisy tried to seduce? Frankly, it is as alluring to me as your nobility, your intellect, and all the power you have amassed when you were born in a ghetto." His eyes widened. "Of course I know about your dark side. When I met you, your alibi for your father's murder involved sleeping with two women at once. I have known all about you from the very moment we met. I was investigating you. I had heard every rumor and every fact before I ever fell in love with you."

His eyes went even wider. His coloring

vanished. "What? What did you just say?"

She released him, backing up. "I, er . . . I . . ." She stammered.

He seized her. "Like hell! You just said you love me! Do you love me? But how can you? You love Rick! You gave your heart to him first, and you told me yourself, when we first met, that you were a woman to give her heart away once and only one time."

She swallowed, trembling. "I thought I loved him," she whispered, "but now I have true love and I can feel the difference. I respected him, I admired him, I cared for him — and it was an infatuation. Calder, it was nothing like this. I have never felt this way about anyone, ever, in my life." She felt tears rolling down her cheeks.

She had not wanted to tell him the real extent of her feelings. She knew this confession would give him so much power, but as afraid as she was, she was also relieved. "I am in love with you," she whispered. "Head over heels in love with you."

"Oh God," was all he said, as white as a ghost. He held her face and kissed her, hard and deep. And abruptly he released her, stepping back.

"You can't stay," he said, pointing at her. His hand trembled. He saw, and slipped it into his pocket. "I have a very serious loss of control," he added more calmly.

She could only gape.

His eyes were black. "Francesca, if you don't turn around and walk out that door, I am going to more than make love to you, and I know I will regret ruining our wedding night for the rest of my life."

He was shaking. She had never seen him at such a loss. She nodded, biting her lip. "Then you had better go while I get dressed," she said.

He raked his hair with his hand. "Yes. Yes, that is a good idea." But he did not move. He stared. "Did you mean it? How could you mean it?" he demanded.

She began to glimpse the small, abandoned boy who had never grown up, a boy who was frightened and vulnerable and who lived still inside the powerful, arrogant man. "I meant it." And suddenly she realized that she had not just handed Calder the keys to their kingdom. *He needed her as much as she needed him. And he needed not just her genuine love, but her genuine faith.* "I mean it."

He inhaled harshly and suddenly whirled and walked out of the room.

She stared at the closed doors. And then she began to smile, sitting down, clasping her corset and shirt to her chest. Life with

Calder Hart would never be easy, she thought, but it would always be interesting. Her smile grew.

And clearly, the wedding was on.

She was the most faithless bitch of them all. He stood at the window, staring into Calder Hart's library, watching Francesca Cahill smiling like the whore she was as she dressed. His fingers gripped the hilt of the small penknife so hard that they ached.

And the little bitch dared to call herself a sleuth, dared to think she could outwit him.

She would have to go, he thought. But not yet. Eventually, but not yet.

Clearly, she wanted to play games.

He smiled, unhinged the three-inch blade and touched it with his thumb.

Blood spurted. He had honed the blade last night, and it was no longer dull.

Let the games begin, he thought with real relish. For he knew who to strike next, oh yes, and his next victim would make Miss Cahill weep.

He could barely wait.

CHAPTER TWENTY-FIVE

Monday, April 28, 1902 11:00 a.m.

Evan stood at the window of his hotel suite, staring down at Fifth Avenue. From where he stood he could glimpse most of Madison Square. It was the beginning of the week, and even though it was midmorning, pedestrian traffic was heavy. Gentlemen in their business attire were hurrying down the street, attending to urgent affairs.

The street was also congested with vehicular traffic. Numerous drays were heading downtown, loaded with wares, causing hansoms and coaches to fight for the right to pass and move on more swiftly. His temples drummed painfully as he watched. How had his life come to this — estranged from his family, lacking sufficient funds and on the verge of wedlock to a woman he did not really care for? And then he saw a woman with pale reddish-blond hair alighting from a hansom. His heart skipped erratically.

Evan leaned on the sill, thinking it was Maggie Kennedy, his pulse now racing swiftly with excitement. He quickly realized that the woman was a very elegant lady and he straightened, the tension in his body instantly vanishing. Watching her disappear into the hotel, he was disappointed.

He closed his eyes.

Bartolla was having his child and they had agreed to elope at the end of the week.

He could hear the roll of the die, the spinning of the roulette wheel, the shuffle of cards, the hushed, intense conversation, the tinkle of fine glassware.

Sweat trickled from his forehead.

He desperately needed to go down the block and to the club, but he still owed his creditors well over fifty thousand dollars. On the other hand, the entire world knew Hart had paid off almost half of his debt, so maybe his credit was good. It would be good, he decided stubbornly, if he made the right case for himself with the proprietor of the establishment.

His blood heated and rushed.

He only needed one game, he thought, one more game and then he would quit, this time forever.

But he knew it was a lie.

If he went back to the tables, he would play until he was incarcerated by his creditors.

Bartolla would then bear his child alone.

Maggie smiled at him, but her blue eyes were so sad. *"Of course you have to marry her. She is having your child. One day, you will look back and realize this was the best thing that ever happened to you."*

How in hell had this happened? he thought, at once furious and despairing. He had used protection, goddamn it, but that had failed, and now he was going to have to marry Bartolla. He had tried to convince himself that it was a good match — she was a wealthy widow, after all, and he would never go crawling back to his father — but he had long since given up. He dreaded the day they would tie the knot. He did not want to marry her and while he knew he would love their child, he wished desperately that another woman carried it.

"Damn it," he cursed, livid with himself. He couldn't take it anymore, and if he wanted to gamble his life away, he had every right. He whirled and stormed across the suite, shrugging on his jacket. He found his hat and cane and was on his way out when Bartolla Benevente walked in.

"Darling!" She smiled widely at him,

dressed in some ruby-red ensemble that was hardly appropriate for day, as it left no doubt as to the extent of her charms. But he was immune now to her lush, exposed bosom, her narrow waist, her extraordinary eyes and lips. "Are you on your way out? Have you forgotten? You promised to buy me a ring!" She laid her gloved hands on his shoulders, her rouged lips seeking his.

He stiffened, pulling away. Damn it, he had to get her a ring.

She stiffened, too, her eyes wide and wary. "Evan? What is wrong?"

"Nothing." He was rude and abrupt but could not help himself. "I have to go out."

"But . . . but we have a noon appointment at Harry Winston."

"I'm afraid you will have to reschedule," he said coldly. He knew he was being a boor, but he could not prevent himself. He bowed. "I am sorry, but I have a pressing matter that I must attend." He turned and strode out.

She ran after him. "What pressing matter?"

He did not answer, sweating now. The roll of the die, the shuffle of cards, the spinning wheel were a symphony in his mind. One game, he told himself, it would be just one game and he would escape the misery of his life.

But Maggie's blue eyes filled his mind, not accusing, merely sad.

"Francesca! You are on your way out? I heard the news and I was hoping to talk to you," Connie cried.

Francesca was in the front hall, about to pull on her gloves. Joel had walked in a moment ahead of her sister, as he was to accompany her downtown. She beamed at her sister, who was lovely in a rose hued skirt and jacket. "Good morning!" Her hearty greeting was followed by a bearlike embrace that left Connie blinking.

Connie shrugged off her lightweight mauve coat. "My! You are in quite a good mood. Either you and Calder have made up, or Papa has changed his mind about the wedding." She smiled at Joel. "Hello there."

He blushed wildly. "Miz Montrose," he murmured, looking away.

Francesca smiled at Joel's vivid reaction to her very beautiful sister. Even her father's disapproval could not shake her current state of happiness. "I have yet to sit down with Papa and explain to him that I am marrying Calder Hart no matter what," she said. Then she gripped Connie's arm, lowering her voice, even though Joel could certainly hear. "I think he loves me!"

Connie began to smile, amusement in her eyes. "Francesca, a man is usually in love when he asks a woman he barely knows to marry him, and on the spur of the moment at that."

"Calder asked me to marry him because I am his best and only friend," Francesca said. "But that has changed, I think."

Connie slipped her arm around her. "Fran, did you really believe that lame excuse? No man marries a woman for *friendship*."

Francesca suddenly realized that her sister was right. "But he has insisted all along that we are simply well suited, that he is tired of his womanizing life and merely wishes to settle down with me."

Connie raised an eyebrow. "I doubt Hart could ever get down on one knee and profess to having fallen in love like the rest of us mere mortals."

Francesca had to stare. "You think he has been in love with me from the moment he proposed?"

"Of course I do. I just assume he refuses to admit it — to you, to anyone and especially to himself."

"He almost admitted it last night," Francesca said with a blush. Could her sister possibly be right? "In a way he did admit it, but of course, indirectly."

"And what will you do about Papa?" Connie asked bluntly.

Francesca sighed, glancing at Joel, who was, of course, all ears, while pretending with poor results, not to hear. "I need your help. In fact, the entire family must form a united front and convince him to change his mind," Francesca said firmly.

"I will gladly help," Connie said. "Where are you off to? Are you sleuthing today?"

Francesca nodded. "I must speak with one of the suspects again — Sam Wilson. It turns out the alibi his fiancée gave was a lie. I also want to speak somewhat further with Kate Sullivan's brother and other family members." She grew thoughtful. "How odd it is to suddenly learn that Kate came from a wealthy background. And her brother hardly seems to be grieving."

"You suspect her brother?" Connie wondered.

"I have three suspects, but yes, that includes Mr. Pierson, although he has some rather convincing alibis. Con, the killer has struck on subsequent Mondays and I am very afraid he will strike again today or tonight."

Connie appeared uneasy. "I am not comfortable with you running around today, not if the killer is out and about looking for another target, Fran."

Francesca smiled at her. "Don't worry. I not only have Joel, but Hart gave me Raoul as a bodyguard. And Bragg is joining me. In fact, I am running late — I am supposed to meet him at headquarters at noon."

"Then I won't keep you," Connie said. She smiled. "I am so glad you and Hart have made up."

Francesca drew on her gloves. "So am I," she murmured, and she blushed, thinking about last night.

"Miss Cahill?" Goodwin, the doorman, spoke. "An envelope was dropped off for you after you finished your breakfast. Do you want it before you leave or shall I send it up to your rooms?"

"I'll take it now, thank you." Francesca came forward, hardly surprised by the missive. She received notes every day, mostly from Sarah, who disliked using the telephone. In that moment, she realized that she had not told Connie that her portrait had been stolen. But the moment she saw her name scripted on the envelope's creamy vellum, she knew the note was not from Sarah and she decided she did not want to

be from the Slasher himself?" Hart said tersely.

She ignored him. "Hart, I mustn't be late — call Bragg, I am heading downtown. Just make sure he is discreet when he arrives. Thank you!"

"Francesca!" he began furiously, but she hung up.

She realized Connie was pale and wide-eyed. She handed her sister the note. "Keep that safe. Now, don't worry, I will be fine." She pecked her sister's cheek. "I am going to the Sherry Netherland."

"Francesca, you can't," Connie protested, ashen.

But Francesca was on her way out. "Don't worry, I have Joel, Raoul — and I have a gun."

Connie cried, "Now I am really worried!"

She paced, feeling terribly alone.

It was a pleasant spring day, the sun warm and bright, the sky blue, the overhead clouds puffy and white. If Bragg had come, she could not tell, as there was no sign of him or any detectives anywhere in sight. Joel was a bit farther down the block, begging for coins and in general, appearing absolutely unremarkable. Hart had arrived by a cab, and he had disappeared into the hotel, looking madder than hell, but he had, somehow, refrained from even looking at her once. Francesca wished his temper was not so easily ignited but she would worry about mending that fence later.

Traffic was heavy in front of the hotel, with many hansoms and coaches pausing before the gold-and-cream-colored canvas canopy to discharge the various gentlemen arriving for lunch, as well as pairs of handsomely attired ladies, mostly middle-aged matrons. Francesca loitered by the lamppost, just a few steps from the hotel's entrance, watching every passerby and every hotel guest. No one bothered to look her way, other than the occasional single gentleman who hoped for some sign of interest from her. Of course, she gave none.

She paced, dismayed. Today was Monday and even though the Slasher had broken the pattern by murdering Kate Sullivan Thursday — and probably murdering her husband as well — Francesca felt certain that he would strike again that day. Every victim thus far had been female, poor and pretty. All had been Irish except for Margaret Cooper, but she had been Irish by descent on her mother's side. Everyone except for Margaret Cooper had attended Father Culhane's church — Margaret had been Baptist. Francesca could not help but go back to her original theory that Margaret had been a mistake — the killer had intended to strike at Gwen, but had mixed up his victims.

If that were the case, would he strike at Gwen again? But Gwen had police protection — and that would keep her safe.

Francesca tensed, an alarm going off inside of her mind, one warning her now that she had just missed an important clue. She felt strongly that Margaret had been mistaken for Gwen, but Gwen was now safe. So what was she missing?

In frustration, she paced. Francesca did not feel like going over the list of suspects in her head, but she did. She knew she should not dismiss David Hanrahan as a suspect. He hated his wife, who had betrayed and left him, and he had the motive to start killing women like her. And he had not one alibi for any of the murders or attacks. Not only did he not have a single alibi, he had been in the country — in the city — when the Slasher had first struck. How easily he could be the killer. Francesca simply felt certain he was not their man. Their man was a real gentleman — and he was clever, oh yes. She would bet her life that Hanrahan was not their man.

Which led her right to Harry de Warenne. Lord Randolph she could not dismiss — like her husband, he had followed Gwen, his lover, to America and that was more than extreme. He was an Irish Protestant landlord, she was a housemaid and she had jilted him. Surely he felt betrayed. But was he insane? Insane enough to act out his grief, rage and frustration on a series of women who reminded him of Gwen? And if he was their man, would he eventually go after Gwen?

Yet how could he? Gwen was being guarded night and day by the police.

Francesca knew she was missing something — and it screamed at her now.

Francesca paused besides the tall iron lamppost once again, this time hardly seeing the group of chattering ladies entering the hotel. She rubbed her temples, turning her thoughts away from Gwen. It was indeed striking that Kate had come from a genteel background, that her family had disowned her, that her brother had come to her funeral, but not to grieve, and that he was a gentleman with a rock-solid alibi for every attack and every murder in question. Frank Pierson could certainly be the killer, she thought. He remained at odds with his sister for what she had done, and even now, with Kate dead and buried, he was not forgiving her, oh no.

Finally, there was Sam Wilson. He had no motive that Francesca could discern, but he also had no alibi for any of the nights in question — and he had let Francis lie for him to create an alibi for last Thursday, too.

Francesca rubbed her temples. The killer had to be one of the three gentlemen. But which one? And who had sent her that note? And what, dear God, was she missing?

She glanced around, a very strong image of Kate's funeral coming to mind. It did not seem that the person who had sent the note was coming after all — surely she had been waiting for a full half an hour. Hart had said it was a trap, but he had been wrong. It was a diversion.

She tensed. Her mind was seared with images of the funeral now. Everyone had been there. She and Hart, Bragg and Farr, Francis and Sam, Gwen and her daughter, both David Hanrahan and Lord Randolph, Kate's brother and Maggie. The images and faces tumbled through her mind until they were spinning and blurred. Father Culhane stood at the pulpit, giving his emotional eulogy, his blue eyes brilliant with passion and righteous anger.

Everyone had been at Kate's funeral.

Every victim, except for Margaret, had attended Culhane's church. They had all been in his parish.

If her theory were correct, Margaret was a mistake.

Francesca shook her head hard as if to clear it.

But she could not.

Father Culhane knew each and every victim.

He knew each and every victim well.

Her heart began to race. She tried to tell herself to slow down, but now, she thought about how tall he was, that he came from a fine old Irish family, and he had remarkable blue eyes — eyes that blazed, eyes that were brilliant, remarkable blue eyes — eyes a woman would not forget, not even if she bumped into him a single time by chance on the street.

Her mind raced. Everyone had police protection now — so the killer could not go after Gwen.

Everyone except for Maggie.

Maggie, who also belonged to Culhane's parish.

And she reeled. If the Slasher was Culhane, if he thought to strike again, today, Maggie was the perfect victim, never mind that she was at Hart's.

Praying she was wrong, Francesca rushed into the street, waving wildly at Raoul, who was atop the driver's seat of Hart's coach, farther down the block. He saw her and released the brakes, lifting the reins, driving the team of black Andalusians forward.

Hart stepped out of the hotel lobby and Bragg appeared at a side entrance. As they rushed to her, she cried, "I think it's Culhane, I think Father Culhane is the killer and I am afraid he will go after Maggie next!"

"But I'm tired," Mathew complained, yawning comically.

Maggie bent over him, shaking her head. "Just pretend that this is the schoolroom. You need to finish spelling out the rest of the words I gave you. As soon as you are done, we will go to the kitchen and have lunch."

Mathew scowled but picked up his pencil and began laboriously writing.

Maggie walked over to Paddy, who was reading a picture book on the floor, Lizzie beside him, drawing with colored crayons. She bent and smiled. "What a pretty picture, Lizzie," she said, but she was distinctly aware that her smile was forced. It was terribly heavy and brittle, and it almost hurt to form the expression. But then, her chest was aching so. Maybe she was confusing her feelings; maybe it wasn't the smile that hurt her so, but her heart.

She refused to think about Evan Cahill now. The beautiful countess was having his child and they would soon be married and she wished them a lifetime of joy and happiness. It was a wonderful match. She felt ill.

She straightened, closing her eyes. How could she have been so foolish as to fall in love with a man so far above her station in life, a man she could never have and only dream about?

She touched her lips, unable to forget the feel of his mouth, his hands and his body when he had kissed her that one single time.

"Mrs. Kennedy? You have a caller," Alfred said, standing in the doorway of the salon.

Maggie started, wiping a stray tear from her cheek, and for one incredibly foolish moment, hope soared. *Evan had returned.*

She smiled at her children, aware of her heart racing. "I will be right back," she said. "Mathew, keep an eye on Paddy and Lizzie, please."

She followed Alfred into the hall, her low heels clicking on Hart's white-and-gold marble floors, and down the corridor, passing numerous oil paintings, watercolors, sculptures and busts. The front hall was the size of a ballroom and it wasn't until she was halfway across the expanse that she realized whom her caller was. She faltered, surprised and then disappointed. "Father?"

Father Culhane turned. "Hello, Mrs. Kennedy."

She smiled at him, bewildered. "What a pleasant surprise."

"You seemed very upset yesterday at Kate's funeral," he said softly. His gaze held hers. "I had heard you had moved in with Mr. Hart and I wanted to inquire after you."

That was very kind of him, she thought. "How could I not be upset? Poor Kate," she whispered.

He held out his arm. "Shall we stroll in the gardens?" he asked, smiling.

She nodded and took his arm.

He stood on the threshold of Hart's huge mansion, tugging nervously at his collar. There was no reason for him to be there, none, except for the most disturbing pair of blue eyes he had ever seen and could not forget. In the end, it was those eyes — Maggie's eyes — that had stopped him from walking into Jack's.

Hart's door suddenly opened.

Evan yanked down on his jacket.

"Mr. Cahill," Alfred intoned. "Good day, sir," he said, stepping aside so Evan could enter.

He did, finding it hard to breathe. He realized he was as nervous as a schoolboy thinking about how to steal his very first kiss. He closed his eyes, trembling. He should have never kissed Maggie Kennedy — it had been a terrible mistake. Ever since that foolish act, he had done nothing but think about it — about her.

And he damn well knew he should not be calling now.

"Mr. Cahill, sir?"

Alfred cut into his indecision and he smiled grimly at the butler. "Is Mrs. Kennedy in?"

"She is walking in the gardens with Father Culhane," Alfred said.

It was such a pleasant day. Maggie tucked her hands beneath her arms, a shawl about her shoulders, trying to enjoy the blooming gardens. Father Culhane walked with her, respecting her need for silence.

She paused and summoned up a smile. "I appreciate your concern, Father, but I am fine, really."

"You look terribly sad," he said seriously.

His gaze searched hers. "You haven't been to confession in months, Mrs. Kennedy. I am very surprised." He was reproving.

She flushed. "I'll come soon," she whispered, but she didn't mean it. She didn't want anyone, not even a priest, to know that she had lost her heart to some society rake. Except Evan wasn't the rake he was made out to be; he was the kindest, most sincere and gentle man she had ever met.

"I hope so, Maggie," the priest said.

She looked up at him, startled by his use of her given name.

He smiled at her — oddly.

And she became alarmed. "Is something wrong?" she asked hesitantly.

"Why don't you tell me?"

She was suddenly nervous and wanted to end the encounter. "I am distraught over the murders," she said unsteadily. Then, shivering, she continued, "It's cold. I think we should go back inside." She turned.

He seized her before she could go. "Why don't you tell me about him?"

She gaped. "What?"

"The gentleman you allow into your flat. The one I keep seeing you with." And his eyes blazed.

And she felt him smile, his mouth against her cheek.

CHAPTER TWENTY-SIX

Monday, April 28, 1902 1:00 p.m.
They leaped from Hart's coach and ran up the front steps to his home. They did not knock, but barged in, much to Alfred's shock. "Where is Mrs. Kennedy?" Francesca cried, standing behind Hart and Bragg, Joel at her side.

Blinking, he said, "She is in the gardens, Miss Cahill, with Father Culhane and —"

Francesca cried out, following both men as they ran through the house and out the back doors. The moment they reached the terrace, she saw Maggie crumpled in the grass. Seized with fear, Francesca looked again and saw two men struggling on the lawn. With shock, she realized her brother was in the midst of a deadly struggle with Father Culhane. Dear God, she had been right!

Joel took off, racing to his mother and dropping down beside her.

Francesca ran to them, praying desperately that Maggie was all right. She dropped to her knees. Joel was weeping. Instantly she noted that Maggie was as white as a corpse. She then saw a thin red line on her throat — it was a scratch, nothing more. Francesca reached for her wrist to take her pulse as Joel cradled her face, tears falling down his cheeks.

Francesca found her pulse. It was strong and steady and relief overwhelmed her then. Just as she was about to tell Joel that his mother was fine, Maggie's eyes opened.

"Shh," Francesca said. "Don't sit up quickly."

But Maggie cried out, struggling to rise, her gaze on the deathly fight behind her. Francesca turned to see Evan landing a solid blow to Culhane's face. The priest's nose was shattered already, blood pouring from it, and now he staggered backward, crashing into the gazebo. Bragg leaped between the two men, grabbing Culhane and shoving him face first to the ground. He straddled him, cuffing him almost simultaneously. "You are under arrest," he said flatly.

Hart had put his arm around Evan, as if to hold him up. "Are you all right?" he asked.

Evan did not answer. He shoved free, rushing over to where Francesca sat with Maggie and Joel. He knelt, almost pushing Francesca aside in his haste. "Are you hurt?" he cried. Blood trickled from his mouth, where his lower lip was split. He gripped Maggie's shoulders. "Are you hurt?" he repeated anxiously.

"I'm fine," Maggie whispered, tears clouding her eyes. "But you're not . . . you're hurt." She touched his mouth.

Francesca knew when she was an intruder and she slowly got to her feet, taking Joel's hand. There was no doubt now in her mind as to which way this wind was blowing. Then she gave in to her curiosity. She looked once more and saw Evan pull Maggie against his chest. He held her hard, his eyes closed, his expression one of anguish. For one moment, she could only stare. Joel was also staring — but with a smile.

Hart pulled Francesca to him and took her hand. They exchanged a long glance and then he said, "Will you ever heed my advice?"

She began to breathe more normally now. They had their killer and the case was almost closed. She smiled at him. "Your advice, yes. Your orders? I don't think so."

He sighed, appearing equally annoyed and

relieved, no easy task, indeed. Then he slid his arm around her. "This solves it, then," he said. "We are marrying immediately, because I am not letting you run around this city by yourself, chasing killers like Culhane. When I look in the mirror tonight, I will undoubtedly be gray."

Francesca tried not to appear pleased. Keeping a straight face, she said, "There are only a few new white hairs at the temples, Calder, and it is really most attractive."

Hart shook his head.

He was so afraid.

Harry de Warenne paused in the dark, unlit corridor outside Gwen's door, acutely aware of his feelings and worse, his own vulnerability. But then, he had followed his lover across an entire ocean, unable to forget her. From the moment he had realized that he could not let Gwen go, he had begun to live in real, raw fear. He hesitated, filled with dread.

For he understood the complications and he knew the odds.

Justice did not walk hand in hand with fate.

And that terrified him.

He did not have to knock. The door swung

open and Gwen stood there, her hair haphazardly pinned up, her eyes wide, her skin impossibly pale. "Harry?" she whispered.

He inhaled hard and tried to smile and knew he failed. "I hope I am not calling at an inopportune time," he said.

"Of course not." She was the one who managed a frail smile. "Come in, please."

He walked inside, his heart beating hard, wondering how to say what he had crossed an entire ocean to say, afraid of her response. He turned. "Come home with me." And he winced. That was not what he had come to say, or at least, not that way.

"Wh-what?" she gasped.

He briefly closed his eyes. Then he opened them and found himself staring into Gwen's, vaguely aware of Bridget having come to stand behind her mother. "When Miranda and the boys died, I knew my life was over." He could not form a smile. "But I was wrong, because as much as I longed to die with them, I didn't. I continued to breathe, I continued to wake up day after day after day. I continued to eat, to sleep. But my world had changed. It was dark and gray."

She reached for his hand, tears in her eyes. "I know. I know how much you love her, how much you miss them."

"No, you don't know," he cried. "One day, years later, I walked into my study at Adare and you were there, the most beautiful woman I had ever seen. My heart, which had stopped beating the day I lost my family, began to beat again. I was so afraid, Gwen, I was so afraid of you," he said desperately, gripping her hands tightly now, afraid she would pull away.

She stared in shock. "You were afraid of *me?*"

He somehow nodded. His heart drummed. "I was afraid of betraying my wife, my children, with the feelings that began to grow inside me that very day. I was afraid of loving someone again as much as I had loved Miranda — I was afraid of losing that love again one day. I can't manage to lose that love another time, Gwen," he said hoarsely. And he wondered if she understood.

"What are you saying?" she cried, tugging her hand free of his.

"I have come to America to ask you to be my wife," he said simply.

She stared, her eyes as huge as saucers.

And he was sweating now. "I have done something rather unconscionable. I have bribed your husband into signing a statement claiming he is your close cousin, releasing you from your marriage. A part of that bribe required that he go to California, which he has done." He nervously awaited her reaction; he could not seem to breathe.

But she was too stunned to speak.

"I have friends in high places," he said urgently. "I can have your marriage annulled."

She wet her lips. A tear fell. "Did you . . . did I . . . did I just hear you say you came here to ask me to be your wife?" she asked numbly.

"Yes," he said solemnly, but his heart wasn't solemn at all. He felt as if it would pound its way right out of his chest. "I love you, Gwen. I never thought I could love again, but I do. I want to take care of you and Bridget, I want to take you both home, with me, where you belong."

She went into his arms, weeping. "I love you, too, Harry."

Francesca sat in one of the two chairs facing Bragg's desk, impossibly relaxed and really quite cheerful. Even though Father Culhane had not confessed, there was no doubt now as to his guilt. They were simply waiting for Heinreich to confirm that the pocketknife he had assaulted Maggie with was indeed the murder weapon. Bragg sat before her, speaking quietly on the telephone. Then he placed the receiver on the hook and smiled at her, light reaching his eyes. "Have I told you yet what an ingenious sleuth you are?"

She smiled in return. "Please do." Then she said sincerely, "We make a fine team, Rick. I hope that never changes."

His expression faded. He toyed with a pen, then looked up. "Hart has been very helpful, hasn't he?"

She tensed very slightly. "Yes, he has."

"You seem very happy today," he said quietly.

"I am very pleased to have caught Culhane. I confess, though, that I suspected Frank Pierson from the moment he showed up at his sister's funeral. I was wrong." She met his steady, searching gaze. "I am happy," she said quietly. "I know that so much has changed, but I am very happy with Calder. I want you to be happy, too."

He looked away just as there was a knock on his door, which was ajar. Newman stood there, smiling. Bragg gestured him in with his hand.

Newman beamed. "Sir! The pocketknife is the same one. Heinreich is certain. There is an unusual and slight indentation on one side of the blade. It is the same indentation we found on Kate's corpse."

"Good." Bragg stood and Francesca also rose. "Shall we get a confession and save the taxpayer the cost of a lengthy trial?"

"Let's," she said, unable now to stop worrying about him in a personal manner. As they walked down the hall, she said, "Will you confront Farr about his devious behavior during this case?"

Bragg shook his head. "I am keeping a very close eye on him. Whatever he is up to, I want to find out. I don't want him to know that I am aware of his treachery, at least not yet."

Francesca touched him and they paused outside the conference room. "I am worried. He is a viper in our midst and I am afraid of what he might do in the future to hurt you."

He smiled. "He can only hurt me politically, so don't worry, Francesca, although I appreciate your concern."

She had to accept that. Eventually, they would find out what Farr was really after. They walked inside.

Culhane sat in manacles in the conference room, under guard. He looked up at them and he was almost the picture of innocence. But he did not speak. He hadn't said a word since Bragg had told him he was under arrest.

"We have confirmed, Father, that the knife you assaulted Mrs. Kennedy with is the murder weapon used by the Slasher. Any reasonable jury will find you guilty of her attempted murder and I have little doubt that you will be convicted of murder in the first degree as well."

He stared coldly at them.

"You murdered two fine young ladies," Francesca cried. *"Why?"*

Culhane looked at her and she was chilled by his regard. "Ladies? I don't think so. Each and every one deserved to die for their faithless behavior. The world is a better place, Miss Cahill, without them." He never took his brilliant eyes from her.

She knew she was safe in the conference room but she had the uncanny feeling that he wished to murder *her,* as well. And he was not confessing to his crimes. "Why? Why were they faithless?"

"Kate Sullivan was a whore. She deserted her husband, just as Gwen O'Neil did. Francis O'Leary was no less a whore for carrying on with Wilson. They received their just deserts, I think." His eyes blazed.

"But what about Margaret Cooper?" Francesca asked, shivering.

He looked away.

Francesca stared at Bragg. He stepped forward and Culhane cried, "She was the mistake!" He covered his face with his hands and began to cry.

Francesca had known it, but she was not jubilant. "You wanted to kill Gwen, didn't you? But you attacked the wrong woman."

"God forgive me," he whispered, sobbing. "She did not belong to my flock, I did not know her. I never meant to hurt her, she was not a blight on my parish!"

"And Maggie Kennedy?" Bragg asked quietly. "Did she also deserve to die?"

He nodded, looking up, his face covered with tears. "She has been whoring for your brother, Miss Cahill." Then he stared at her, his eyes glittering with hatred. "I saw you," he whispered. "I saw you yesterday in Calder Hart's library." And his gaze was burning with accusation.

She jumped backward, her cheeks heating, understanding his meaning and horrified by it. "You spied on us?" she cried.

He stood and pointed at her with both shackled hands. "You are next," he cried. "You, the most faithless one of all!"

Bragg seized him and thrust him at the police officer, who had his billy stick in hand. "Get him out of here," he said in disgust.

"Yes, sir," the young rookie said. He jerked Culhane from the room, but not before the priest looked back at Francesca, crying, "Oh yes, weep in fear, because the faithless shall die!"

"Shut your trap," the officer said, pushing him out of the room.

"The faithless shall die," Culhane shouted as he was marched down the corridor. His footsteps sounded, his words almost echoed, and then there was only silence in the hall.

Francesca was trembling. She looked up as Bragg took her by the shoulders. "Oh dear," she whispered. "I wonder if I was next."

"It doesn't matter," he said fiercely. "Culhane is in custody and he will be going to the electric chair. Thank God he did not get his chance to go after you."

She exhaled, still trembling, feeling quite certain that Culhane had watched her and Hart making love. She shuddered at the notion.

"It's all right," Bragg said softly.

She met his steady regard. Then she touched his cheek. "I know. I simply am horrified to think of his spying on me . . ." She trailed off for a moment, not wanting to explain.

But he knew, for he released her, turning away. He wandered over to the window behind his desk, staring down at Mulberry Street.

She followed. "I know I've said this before. How can I help?"

He turned, smiling a little. "Your friendship is a help, Francesca."

"Should I call on Leigh Anne again? She is so melancholy, Rick. Maybe a good friend would help her out of this morass of despair."

"That would be nice," he said, not smiling.

She did not know what to do, for she felt certain she saw pain reflected in his eyes. So she took his hand and squeezed it.

He felt as if he had been sitting in the salon for hours. He was alone, a stiff drink at hand, his second or third. He couldn't seem to stop recalling the sight of Maggie in that monster's arms, his knife at her throat. He was more than shaken — he was sick to his stomach. And there was simply no denying it.

The salon doors were wide open. He heard footsteps and leaped to his feet, vaguely aware of being utterly disheveled.

His jacket had been tossed aside a long time ago, his necktie was askew, his shirtsleeves rolled up to the elbows. Rourke paused on the threshold of the salon. His gaze widened. "Have you been working yourself up? She is fine, Evan. That is a mere scratch on her throat. I am sure the trauma of the attack was far worse."

"Is Dr. Finney with her still?" Evan asked urgently.

"He just left," Rourke said, clasping his shoulder while giving him a sidelong look. "He gave her some laudanum. He has prescribed an evening of rest."

"I want to see her," Evan said, not waiting for a reply. He hurried from the salon and then stood in the hall helplessly, having no idea where to go.

Rourke pointed to the left. "Calder gave her the north wing of the house."

"Remind me to thank him," Evan said over his shoulder, hurrying down the corridor.

Rourke called after him, "The suite is on the second floor!"

Evan took the stairs two at a time, breathlessly. That horrific image of Maggie in Culhane's crazed embrace remained, her face stark with fear. The door to the sitting room of her suite was open and a fire danced in the hearth. Maggie's bedroom was to the right and instantly he saw her, lying in the canopied bed, asleep.

Joel sat with her, at her feet; the other children were nowhere to be seen. Evan vaguely recalled the housekeeper had taken them to the kitchen for ice cream some time ago.

His heart raced.

Joel saw him and jumped up. Before Evan could cross the threshold, he had launched himself off the bed and into his arms.

Evan held him, hard. "It's all right," he said softly, kissing Joel's head. "Your mother is fine. She has had a bad scare, nothing more."

For one more moment, Joel clung, and then he stepped back. His eyes were shining with unshed tears but he was trying to be manly. "You saved her, you did. Thank you, Mr. Cahill, thank you very much." He held out his hand.

Evan suddenly realized that Maggie was not asleep at all. She lay very still, but her eyes were open and fixed on them. He somehow took Joel's hand, his heart beating like a drum. Somehow, he tore his gaze free from hers and looked at the small boy. "You're welcome," he said.

Then he looked back at the woman in the

bed. "May I?" he asked as politely as possible. Being formal was no easy task.

"Please," she whispered, understanding perfectly well his request to enter the room.

He came slowly forward, wishing he'd brought flowers. There was a linen bandage on her throat. "Thank God you are all right!" he heard himself exclaim.

She lifted her hand.

He took it, holding it tightly, his heart racing now with impossible speed.

She wet her lips. "You saved me. Thank you, Evan."

He wanted to sit on the bed beside her, but that would be a terrible lapse of manners, so he did not. He simply clung to her small, slender, callused hand. There was so much he wished to say. But what could he say?

Was he in love?

He was stunned. If so, he was beginning to understand that he had never been in love before — not this way.

And he whispered, "I have never been so afraid, Maggie. I saw you with that killer . . ." He could not continue then.

Tears filled her eyes. "I was afraid, too. I thought about my children, what they would do without me, but then I knew you would look after them. Wouldn't you?"

And finally he sat down on the bed by her hip, as it was the most natural of acts, still holding her hand. "Yes, of course I would take them in, you know that. But you are fine! You have had a terrible fright, but it is over now, and you are safe."

She suddenly tugged her hand free and he was dismayed. He wanted to hold her hand for hours and hours, he thought, but then she stunned him by cupping his jaw. He went still. "I owe you so much more than I can ever repay," she said unsteadily.

His mind went blank and his heart surged with frightening force. He knew he should not kiss her, he knew it. It was his only coherent thought. And he leaned over her.

Her hand dropped away, her eyes widened.

He closed his own eyes, continuing to see her blue eyes wide with surprise, and he pressed his mouth to hers.

She gasped.

And he claimed her lips, firmly and insistently, again and again, holding her shoulders now, trying to savor her taste so he would never, ever forget it. She kissed him back, at first hesitantly, and then with growing urgency.

They kissed and kissed.

At some point, many moments later, he

felt her mouth tire, he felt her body soften, and with surprise, he felt her become still. He ceased, drawing back. And then he realized that the laudanum had taken effect.

Maggie Kennedy was soundly asleep.

He sat there, staring at her, incapable of drawing a normal breath. Time, which had ceased, began to move again. Reality, which had been suspended, returned. And his heart was flooded with anguish.

He got to his feet.

She was so pretty, lying there asleep.

How it hurt, looking at her.

In a few more days he would marry Bartolla.

He prayed Maggie would have no recollection of their kiss.

He was rigid with tension as he entered the front hall of his Madison Square flat, a bouquet of red hothouse roses in his hand. The flowers were for Leigh Anne. He felt certain that they would be rejected — that *he* would be rejected. Dread accompanied the tension, and with it, heartache.

He quietly closed the front door. He warmed, smiling, as he heard Leigh Anne explaining subtraction to Katie. He gathered that they were in the salon at the end of the short corridor. He walked swiftly past the dining room and, even as certain as he was that she did not want his flowers or him, even though he continued to feel like an intruder whenever he and his wife were in the same room, he could not help but be eager to glimpse them.

He hoped it would not always be this way, to be so hopeful and so hurt, so eager and so filled with dread.

He paused on the room's threshold. Leigh Anne wore a silvery-gray dress with a pearl and diamond necklace, her hair curled and swept back and up. She sat in her wheeled chair beside Katie, who was on an ottoman, a practice book on her lap. He thought about how much they appeared to be mother and daughter. Then he realized that in the past few months they *had* become mother and daughter.

"I still don't understand," Katie said in frustration.

Leigh Anne sighed, reaching for her hand. "I will go to school tomorrow and speak with your teacher, dear."

Bragg knew the moment she became aware of his presence. He tried to smile.

She turned and looked at him. Her eyes met his and then landed on the bouquet he held, widening.

"Hello," he said cheerfully, although it was

forced. He strode in, kissed her cheek, and then kissed Katie as well. "Perhaps I can help with that problem," he said to Katie.

"I don't like math," she said softly. "And I can't get the right answer!" Katie stood and rushed from the room.

He faced Leigh Anne, who was staring at him. He realized he was crushing the stems in the bouquet, and he eased his grip. He forced another smile. "We have the Slasher in custody," he said. "He was caught in the act, with the murder weapon, and he has confessed."

Leigh Anne looked at the flowers again as if she had never before seen roses. Then she tore her glance away, lifting it to his. "Thank God," she said.

He extended the bouquet. "These are for you."

She stared at him in obvious dismay. Finally she took the bouquet, looking away, and murmured, "Thank you."

He bent so their faces were level; surprised, she turned her face toward him. Their gazes met.

"I know how hard this is for you," he said quietly. "I know it cannot be easy to have lost the use of your leg, to be confined to a wheelchair, to be reliant now on the strong arms of your nurse, Peter, and myself to perform activities that were once taken for granted. I know how distressing this is and how difficult it is for you to accept another kind of life."

"No," she said. "You have no idea what this is like."

"I do," he said, clasping her shoulder. She flinched. "I see how unhappy you are every time I look at you."

She turned away.

"Don't," he said, taking her chin and making her face him. "I want to help."

"You can't help," she said, her eyes shining. "I don't want you to help!" A tear fell. "Why can't you understand *that?*"

"I am helping whether you want me to or not. I am going to be here with you through this dark period in your life. It won't always be this way, Leigh Anne," he said, determined to believe it.

"Why are you doing this?" she cried. "Why won't you accept the fact that everything has changed?"

"Nothing has changed," he argued, anguished. "You are still my wife, and you are still the most beautiful woman I have ever laid my eyes upon."

She stared in surprised dismay.

"I am not giving up," he said flatly. And he rose to his full height.

She was still holding the bouquet he had given her. She did not look up. "Then you are a fool," she said.

Francesca took the liberty of pouring two glasses of scotch, adding a single cube of ice to each one and carrying them to the low occasional table in front of the sofa in Hart's library. A servant had stoked a small fire in the hearth and she sat down, taking a sip of her scotch. She smiled to herself.

Culhane had confessed and the case was closed. There would be no more tragic murders. Apparently, Lord Randolph was head over heels in love with Gwen, and if she was any judge of human nature, both Evan and Maggie were following in their footsteps. Her smile increased. But they were well into a very pleasant spring, so love was in the air, was it not? And she was waiting for her fiancé to come home — the city's most attractive, charismatic and dangerously seductive bachelor. He had said he wanted to marry her *immediately.* She intended to hold him to his words, yes she did. How lucky could one woman be?

"Feeling pleased with yourself, darling?" Hart asked, stepping into the room.

Francesca stood, smiling. "I must admit, I

do rather feel like the cat who had *all* the cream."

Hart was smiling as he took her into the circle of his arms. "That was a case well solved, darling."

She flushed, aware that she loved receiving his praise. "I had the best help an amateur sleuth could have," she said archly.

His long, lean fingers toyed with the hair at her nape and his hazel eyes held hers, his gaze searching.

Her smile faltered. "What is it? I was referring to you, Calder. You were very helpful on this case."

"I know." He released her and handed her a scotch, taking one glass for himself.

She sensed the devil in him now. "Please don't brood," she said, meaning it.

"How can I brood when I am with you?" he swiftly returned.

But he *was* brooding now. "What dark thoughts are afflicting you now?" She put her drink down, taking his hand.

He drank and then set his own glass aside. "I meant what I said earlier. I want to marry immediately."

She bit her lip so she would not smile, absolutely thrilled. "That is fine with me," she managed to say.

He smiled. "Darling, I can tell you want

to shout in glee, so please, feel free."

Francesca grinned. "When?" she asked eagerly. "I mean, should we actually elope? I know we had decided against it — and Mama would never forgive me. Or we could have a very small ceremony, just with family. What do you think?"

He tipped up her chin. "I hate coming between you and your father, Francesca," he said quietly. "I know you adore Andrew. I hate forcing you to make a choice between him and myself."

Her smile vanished. "Calder, it's too late. I have already made that choice — I have already chosen you — and I am not retracting it."

He pulled her close. "If I were selfless and noble, I would back off, find patience and somehow persuade your father to our cause. But I am not selfless or noble and I am savagely glad that you have chosen a life with me. I only hope you will never have any regrets."

She stood on tiptoe and kissed him. "Calder, I intend to bring the brunt of the entire family to bear on Papa. I will be very surprised if he does not cave in. He is no match for me, Mama and Connie, not when we unite against him."

"No man could be a match for the three

of you," he said wryly. "He loves you. And he also respects your intellect. Perhaps he will come around before the fact, and not after it."

"He will," she said with genuine confidence. "I am sure of it. I will begin planning the wedding tomorrow, if that is all right with you. I will speak with Mama and Connie and we will decide on a date. I still prefer June."

He nodded with a smile. "That is fine."

She knew he had something else on his mind. "Calder?"

"There's something I want to say," he said, very seriously now.

She froze, and then her heart leaped with excitement. She nodded, filled with anticipation. Would he finally tell her that he loved her? She crossed her fingers behind her back. "Please."

He clasped her shoulders, smiling a little. His eyes had become impossibly tender. "The moment I first met you, I knew you were the most unique woman I had ever encountered."

She began to smile and opened her mouth to comment.

He touched a finger to her lips. "Let me speak."

She nodded, biting down hard to restrain herself.

His navy eyes, flecked with gold, wandered over her face. "I knew that the bluestocking had an amazing intellect, the sleuth more courage and determination than any one individual had a right to bear, and the romantic more hope and faith than any one man could possibly deserve. I knew you were as eccentric as myself, if not more so. And I knew that all of these aliases shielded a woman of extreme passion. I knew all of this, Francesca, immediately, and shortly after, I knew you were the right woman for me." He smiled a little at her. "I knew, somehow, thoroughly and completely, that we would suit beyond all expectation."

She was finding it difficult to breathe. Was Hart really admitting all of this?

"But there was one thing I did not know," he said softly, cupping her face in his hands. His eyes were shining with emotion — with tears.

"What?" she managed to say, her heart beating madly. Her own emotion seemed to be choking her.

"I didn't know that I was falling in love with you," he said, his gaze holding hers.

She couldn't speak. Tears welled in her eyes, as well, and with them, there was more love than any woman could possibly feel.

He made a harsh sound. His eyes continuing to shine from the depth of his emotion he pulled her against his chest. "Francesca, I am smitten," he whispered.

She held him hard, closing her eyes, overcome with so much love and so much joy. "So am I," she said.

The employees of Thorndike Press hope you have enjoyed this Large Print book. All our Thorndike, Wheeler, and Kennebec Large Print titles are designed for easy reading, and all our books are made to last. Other Thorndike Press Large Print books are available at your library, through selected bookstores, or directly from us.

For information about titles, please call:
  (800) 223-1244

or visit our Web site at:
  http://gale.cengage.com/thorndike

To share your comments, please write:
  Publisher
  Thorndike Press
  295 Kennedy Memorial Drive
  Waterville, ME 04901